HIGH PRAISE FOR EDWARD LEE!

"The living legend of literary mayhem. Read him if you dare!"
—Richard Laymon, author of *Endless Night*

"Edward Lee's writing is fast and mean as a chain saw revved to full-tilt boogie."
—Jack Ketchum, author of *Peaceable Kingdom*

"Lee pulls no punches."
—*Fangoria*

"The hardest of the hardcore horror writers."
—*Cemetery Dance*

"Lee excels with his creativity and almost trademark depictions of violence and gruesomeness."
—*Horror World*

THE UNSEEN

Something grabbed her. Not hands, not a person, but something only semi-palpable, as if she'd been seized by the air. When she snapped her eyes open, she saw only a tulle-like veil of black.

Then she could see nothing; her eyes seemed to close on their own, that or something like a hand slipped over them. Chuckling tittered about her head, dark, throaty noises of glee, but they were muffled as if through closed mouths. Then, blind, she was jerked off her feet, back arched, tousled around. Now she was afraid. She tried to scream and release the salt-fumes in the same action but—

Not fast enough.

Something slammed her chin up, something else pinched her lips closed, then something like an awful mouth full of dead breath but totally lacking substance sealed over her nose and sucked all the fumes out of her.

More guttering laughter flitted around her and the ghost-mouth sucked and sucked, stealing all that was left of her breath and everything that breath contained, harder and harder until she grew numb and the reversed pressure threatened to collapse her lungs....

EDWARD LEE

FLESH GOTHIC

LEISURE BOOKS NEW YORK CITY

For Michael Slade, an utmost inspiration.

A LEISURE BOOK®

February 2005

Published by

Dorchester Publishing Co., Inc.
200 Madison Avenue
New York, NY 10016

ISBN 0-8439-5412-4

The name "Leisure Books" and the stylized "L" with design are trademarks of Dorchester Publishing Co., Inc.

Printed in the United States of America.

Visit us on the web at www.dorchesterpub.com.

ACKNOWLEDGMENTS

As always, I am in debt to more people than I can sufficiently thank, but I'll try: First and foremost, Tim McGinnis. Dave Barnett, Rich Chizmar, Doug, Don D'Auria, Thomas Deja, Dallas, Teri Jacobs, Tom Pic. Bob Strauss and John Everson for grueling proofing burdens, and Erik Wilson for the outstanding artwork on the hardcover. Kathy Rosamilia, for lasting not one, but two novels—a record. Amy, Charlie, Christy and Bill, Darren, Jeff, R.J., and Stephanie. Archie and Mike, from *Header*—thank God there are still some Yankee fans....

FLESH GOTHIC

Prologue

"You should've just killed me," the girl said.

The man was shocked. These strange words were the first she'd spoken in . . .

Nine months . . . , he remembered.

"And I know you thought about it," she continued from the lumpy bed. Her voice lowered. "I know you have that gun. I know you've thought that maybe you should just shoot me in the head and in the belly . . . and leave."

Had he really? He wasn't consciously aware of it, and he tended to be the kind of man who was always honest with himself. *You can lie to other people, but you can never really lie to yourself. The lies always catch up.*

My God. I hope that's not true.

He'd come all this way, covering all this time, to *not* kill her, hadn't he?

The image of her was shamefully erotic. Spraddled on the bed so cumbersomely, her nineteen-year-old flesh fresh and shining. All she wore were panties and a bra. He could see the plush tuft of her pubic hair pushing outward against the panties' fabric. The bra was too tight, given the extra expanse of pre-natal growth; her breasts threatened to break out. Her stomach distended pin-prick tight, large as a basketball, belly button popped out like a little white hazelnut.

The man averted his eyes from this glaring image, as he had for all these months.

He spoke to the wall. "You're talking now. That's wonderful. Do you remember the last time you spoke?"

"No."

"After all this time . . . what do you have to say? What do you have to tell me?"

"Nothing," she said.

"Nothing?"

"All I remember is the house."

Clear across the country, he'd taken her. Anonymous buses and fly-by-night motels. The man had never felt at ease with her, even before she'd started to show. The looks people gave him, the desk clerks in the middle of the night, their raised brows, as if to say, *What's a man your age doing with a girl not even twenty? Why are you bringing her to a place like this, at this hour?* They were in Seattle now, the Aurora Motel; their room looked like it was worth what he paid: $25.95 per night. He knew that he had to keep it anonymous, places where no one cared what name you wrote down in the check-in list. All they wanted to see was cash. The looks were worse now. People looked at him as though he were the worst kind of pervert. One night not too long ago, he'd checked them into a room in Needles, California, which turned out to be a flophouse for drunks, prostitutes, and drug addicts. He'd been getting sodas from the Coke machine when a disheveled bald man in a crumpled suit approached him and said, "Hey, man. I saw that cute little pregnant chick you brought in. I'm into that too, you know? What's she charge for an hour?"

"Get away from me or I'll shoot you in the face . . ."

The response sufficed.

It was just that the world, now, after all he'd seen, made him absolutely sick to his stomach.

The world, he thought now.

He looked at the girl.

The whole world . . .

"I'm sorry this place is so shabby," he said. He was ironing their clothes on the patch-burned board he'd found in the closet.

"They've always been shabby." Did she smile? She hadn't done that in nine months either. "But I understand. You talk to yourself a lot. You can't use your credit card, and all that."

"Yes."

"And you're pinching your pennies."

He smiled over a shirt. "That too."

"You're hiding me, aren't you?"

The man's smile wilted. "Yes."

"From them, right? From the people at the house."

He'd never slept in the bed with her, even though he thought nothing would happen. He'd never done anything to her, he'd never even thought of it. He'd never done anything wrong—

—except abduct her.

He'd sleep on the couch, or on the floor if there wasn't a couch. The room he'd gotten in Seattle had a pull-out couch—a luxury as far as he was concerned. Springs threatened to spear him through the mattress, and it stank. *Thank*

God I'm not picky, he thought. The first night he lay awake listening to the rush of traffic on the main road, and the rain. He'd pulled the drapes closed; the room was nearly lightless, and for a moment that sheer *blackness* made him think of the past, of the house. If evil had a color, he knew what it was.

He didn't sleep even though he was exhausted. Instead he lay back on that beaten mattress, looking up at the ceiling. From the bed, he could hear the girl's rhythmic breaths. It was hypnotic.

Then the breaths stopped.

The man's eyes froze open. He was about to lurch up but then her voice grated out of the dark:

"I want you to kill me. Please do it. Wait till I fall back to sleep. And do it."

The next night, she said this single word in her sleep:
"Belarius."

"Blonde hair doesn't work on you," she said the next morning. He'd brought coffee, sodas, and donuts from the 7-Eleven several blocks down the hill. She ate leisurely on the bed, watching TV, childlike in spite of the filled breasts and distended belly.

"Why?" he asked, turning.

"You *look* like someone trying to not look like himself. The hair color looks fake. It's too light."

He appraised himself in the mirror. "Really?"

"Really."

The man sighed. He pulled on his jacket. "I'll be back in a little while."

"Where are you going?"

"To get a different hair dye."

* * *

Would they really be following him? *Maybe we're both just paranoid,* he considered. The bus jostled through rain. Beyond the dotted window, he saw drab gray buildings. A man in glasses and another man wearing a hard hat both looked at him at the same time. *Yeah, I'm just paranoid, or maybe she's right. I used the wrong color hair dye and I look like a horse's ass.* Several kids in the back were getting rowdy, profane even, but he scarcely heard them. Then a black man sitting in the front stood up, looked directly at him, and said, "It was me and Lou Rawls. They stuck us in that cage and didn't give us nothing but milk bottles and soup." Then the doors popped open and he stepped off the bus.

He could've laughed. *Lots of homeless people in big cities, lots of schizophrenics.* It was sad.

At the next stop a blind man got on, tapping his white cane, eyes clouded over. He sat right next to him.

"Hello," the blind man said, staring straight ahead.

"Hi."

"I . . . have psychic powers. Do you believe me?"

"I'm not sure."

"Do you believe that some people do have such powers?"

"I do. I believe that very much."

The blind man chuckled. "I'm a seer who can't see." The clouded-over eyes turned. "You have a troubled aura." A pause, a sigh. "My Lord . . . it's nearly black."

The man had no response, for he did indeed believe in such things. How could he not, after a week in that house?

The blind man's hands were trembling. His lower lip quivered. One crabbed hand reached over his head, desperately feeling for the bell-cord. "I-I have to get off, I have to get off."

The other man just looked back, astonished. "What's wrong?"

"None of it's your fault, so why are you jeopardizing yourself?" When the bus lumbered to a halt at the next stop, the blind man teetered up, cane tapping for balance. He looked at the other man again with those dead eyes and said, "You don't have much time."

"For what?"

"To kill the girl." He tapped away toward the open doors. "Kill her."

Then he got off and the doors closed.

He was never bothered by the prospect of leaving her by herself in the room for a few hours. She didn't talk about it, of course, but she seemed to know what might be out there. *How much does she remember?* he wondered, walking down the aisle of a CVS store. Worse questions occurred to him. *What did she go through? What did she feel and see? What did she open her eyes to and look at?*

What looked back?

The man could only pray that her trauma blocked out the memory.

Damn it . . . The pistol in his pocket had worked its way up, the tip of the handle sticking out. He pulled the side of his windbreaker over, then shoved the gun all the way back down. *I gotta be more careful.* He would never leave the gun back in the room whenever he had to go somewhere. He didn't want to leave her there alone with it.

He bought a darker hair dye and a pack of cigarettes. The steady drizzle had never ceased. When he left the store he pulled up his hood. Across the street stood an Irish pub. The man felt locked in place, staring back at it.

Damn it, he thought again.

"Just one," he muttered to himself. "Just one would be so good . . ."

"There's no such thing as just one," a voice peeped from behind him. He turned and looked down.

What he believed was a young woman sat huddled in a brick cubby beside a fire hydrant. She was drenched, drizzle pattering on a holey rain jacket, whose traditional bright yellow had long-since turned brown. The man could barely see her face as she peered up at him, her open eyes half hidden by the hood. Rotten teeth like corroded pills showed through her smile.

"One becomes twenty real fast," she said.

"I know."

"But you should go in and have one anyway, to celebrate."

"Celebrate what?"

Dirty hands outspread in the strangest glee. "This beautiful day!"

"Oh, yeah? I'm from Florida so I guess I'm not really able to appreciate Seattle's brand of beauty."

"It's a beautiful city if you look hard enough."

"I'm sure it is," the man said.

"I used to be beautiful . . ."

He could think of nothing to say in response, her plight obvious. She couldn't be more than thirty, but who could tell? Cheeks bloated, a splotched pinkness blending over the yellow of jaundice. *Clinical alcoholic,* he knew at a glance. *She's turning yellow because her liver's shutting down . . .*

"Where do you live?" he asked.

"The King Street Shelter. When I can walk."

The man faltered, fumbling in a pocket. "I have some money I could give you—"

"No. I won't need it. I need a drink. Get me something to drink."

The man felt wilted. "I . . . can't do that. I'm sorry."

"That's okay." The soiled smile still shone upward, her head craned. "But if you do go into that bar across the street, and I think you will—"

"I won't," he said.

"But if you do, drink one for me."

Again, the man had nothing to say.

Her expression changed, that exuberance-in-ruin darkened to something lusterless. "There's someone else inside me."

"What?"

"I'm supposed to tell you something."

The last legs of the chronic drunk. Reduced oxygen to the brain, blood full of toxins, then psychosis. He humored her. "What are you supposed to tell me?"

Her voice clicked. "Walk away. Leave her."

The man's teeth came together. "Leave who?"

"Don't kill her."

The man stared.

"Just go away somewhere. If you do that, you'll be rewarded."

The man could say nothing. He simply continued to stare, rain tapping his hood.

"Leave the rest . . . to us."

Then her face changed for the briefest moment, something that was no longer a face at all but just a tremoring black hole within the hood.

The man couldn't move.

Her real face returned, the dying smile and eyes with no life left behind them. "'Bye," she said, and then produced an old-fashioned straight razor with which she calmly cut her throat to the bone.

The man turned away as blood poured at his feet. Cars honked when he stepped off the curb; bloody rainwater splashed up on his jacket. He crossed the street and walked into the bar.

"Come in here."

The man wobbled in the doorway, rain teeming. Behind him, cars tore by on the highway, each a long, wet hiss.

Her warm hand grasped his wrist, urged him back into the motel room, then she shut the door, sealing out the incessant noise of rain and cars.

"You're drenched. You're . . . "

The man was nearly insensible, barely able to stand. All he could do was look back at her with huge, shamed eyes. He couldn't say anything, but he thought, *I'm a disgrace.*

"You'll be all right," she assured him.

The television was on, the sound low, stiff-faced CNN newscasters reporting another U.S. Army helicopter being shot down by Iraqi partisans. Twenty-one dead.

"Did you . . . throw up on yourself?"

The man didn't know. She peeled off his jacket, sat him down on the bed, then began to undress him. She said nothing when she removed the pistol from his pocket. She laughed. "Didn't you go out for new hair color? Where is it?"

"I—" He pushed wet hair back off his brow. "I left it in the bar."

"You're such a goof."

His vision was shifting, blurred around the edges. Her pretty face hovered like a warped bubble before his eyes. When she pulled off his sneakers, she paused, looking at the red tint. "Is that . . . " but she didn't finish. She peeled off his socks, his jeans, his t-shirt. "Come on, help me. We've got to get you in the shower."

"I don't think I can make it."

"Yes you can, yes you can." She stood him up and without hesitation peeled off his boxer shorts. His brain buzzed; he was scarcely even aware that he was standing naked in front of her.

"One step at a time." She held his arm, guiding him to the bathroom where he stood blinking in harsh white light. The light hurt his head. Shower water hissed. Steam rose.

Her hands gripped him tight around the waist. "In you go," she said. "Take your time. Left foot first."

His own hand shot out to brace him against the tiled wall. Shame continued to seep into him. "I don't think I can make it."

"Help me! I can't do it by myself!" Her patience finally lapsed. "You're not an invalid."

He steadied himself, sat down on the edge of the tub, and carefully lifted each leg over. The water spraying down was hot, reviving. Jags of reason began to surface. More awareness and more shame.

"Now stand up and wash yourself!"

Careful, careful! he ordered himself. He couldn't have felt more embarrassed: a pale, naked middle-aged drunk. When he tried to stand up, he immediately slipped. His butt thunked the bottom of the tub.

"Oh, Lord . . . What am I going to do with you?"

She slipped off her robe and stepped in wearing only bra and panties. He looked up like a disillusioned child as she bent over, grunted, and stood him up in the spray. Her hair fell down at once, to wet black lines. Expansive nipples darkened when the water drenched the bra. The large milk-laden breasts wobbled erotically. The image blared, the great gravid belly full of life, the breasts, the dark tuft of pubic hair printing against wet panties. Her fecundity was truly beautiful yet he was at least happy with himself for feeling nothing erotic of his own. No lust, no desire, not even as her soft hands soaped him down.

She got him out, dried him off, struggled to help him get his robe on. Then she walked him out, step by step, and sat him back down on the bed.

By then the man felt a little bit better than dead.

"I'm sorry," he said.

"It's all right."

The news continued on the TV. Children snatched in front of a Maryland schoolyard. Federal agents raid an underground fetal brain-tissue lab. A catastrophic-care nurse admits to murdering a six-year-old retarded girl after making a deal with the girl's father to split the insurance money. Rwandan soldiers burn down a United Red Cross hospital, killing sixty.

"There's evil everywhere," the girl said.

"I know."

She turned off the television and sat next to him. "I'm more afraid than you. Do you understand what I mean?"

Through the fog of alcohol poisoning, the words cut through like a strong beam of light. "Yes. How could I not?"

"I don't know what's going to happen."

"Neither do I."

An audible click as she swallowed. "My water's going to break any day now, maybe any hour."

The man nodded. He didn't have the heart to tell her what he was already certain of. *It will be tomorrow after midnight.*

"I want you to kill me. Shoot me with that gun and leave. I'll forgive you," she said. "So will God."

"I'm not going to kill you," he croaked. "If I was going to do that, I'd have done it a long time ago."

She turned off the light. "Then let's go to sleep now."

He started to get up, but her hand pulled him back. "Sleep here in the bed with me. After all this, everything you've done, don't you think I trust you?" A grim chuckle. "If you wanted to do something perverted to me, you'd have done that a long time ago, too."

He settled back against her, drifting. He still felt awful, and knew he would for awhile, but lying with her like that—in perfect trust—gave him a sense of comfort that seemed priceless to him. She fell asleep quickly, while the man was still experiencing the twirls, but after a time they abated. He listened to her breathe, her hand resting on his chest.

When his eyes grew accustomed to the dark, he could see her outline. The breasts settled to one side over the massive belly.

Before he fell into his own stupor-like sleep, this is what he thought: *No, I won't kill you. But I swear to God on High that I'm gonna kill whatever comes out of you . . .*

Part One

•

Slaughter Night

Chapter One

Nine months previous . . .

I

Faye didn't really know if she dreamed anymore. What went on in her head most of the time seemed like the most vivid nightmares, and nightmares were dreams but she never remembered sleeping. She liked the door locked, though, and she liked the way the moon sometimes shone in through the window at night.

Faye, do some more . . .

If I do anymore I'll be wrecked!

We . . . want you wrecked. We want you out of your mind. And you know you like it anyway. You like it all. Let me put it this way. Unless you're out of your mind, you're of no use to us.

She sat fat and naked on a red-velvet Edwardian-era couch that she knew cost more than she made in two years. Fat and naked, and sadder now in her stimulated exhilaration than when she was sober and alone. Hildreth was right: this was all she was here for. Groundskeeper? It was a joke; she knew that now. *I'm their Pillsbury Dough Girl.* She was there to be laughed at and abused and humiliated. When they were shooting one of the movies at the house, they called her "The Fluff Pig."

Brawny men stood on either side, naked and aroused by either Viagra or evil. She took oral turns with them without even thinking, an automatic impulse now. Two rough fingers twirled a lopsided nipple as if taking a screw out of a wall.

This pig does it DAMN good . . .

Probably been practicing since she was four.

And instead of crying or screaming or even biting them, Faye chuckled in her throat. It was awful what she'd let them turn her into.

I'm awful, she thought.

One man pulled out.

Stick out your tongue.

Faye did so, and on her tongue the man placed a heather-green pill embossed with a Playboy Bunny.

Another man shoved a bottle at her.

Swallow. That's something you're good at.

She slugged the rich wine, oblivious to its faded label: MONTRACHET 1888.

The stouter voice spoke across the candle-lit room. *Janey, why don't you come over here and indulge Faye with some of your own skills?*

A starkly beautiful woman sat nude in the center of the handmade Kashmiri carpet. She looked up, distracted, as she intricately wielded a syringe, about to inject something into a vein in her foot. *Oh, Reginald, please. You know, I only like to play around with hot girls. She's too ugly . . .*

Oh, I will! another naked woman consented, eagerly scurrying across. *I don't know why, but I've always had a thing for ugly chicks!*

You don't know why? someone else said and laughed. *You think maybe being nuts has something to do with it?*

Oh, shut up, Three-Balls!

The woman crawled between Faye's lumpy, rice-white legs, the workings of her tongue immediate, ravenous. Faye shimmied at the jolt of pleasure. A metallic clicking resounded, the woman's tongue-stud laving up and down over the rings of Faye's forced piercings. More warm, pulsing things filled her mouth, shoved in with no regard. She simply did it, without objection, because she knew it was her only acceptance. So much overwhelmed her now: musky scents, churning sensations, drug toxicity, more groins in her face and more things slipped into her mouth.

Gentlemen, please. Save it for later. You mustn't be greedy.

The men all stepped back in obedience, candlelight flickering on their sweating, muscular chests, prongs of flesh sticking up.

The other woman delicately raked her tongue-stud a few more times over Faye's labial rings, then tended the exposed clitoris directly.

Faye was awash in insane pleasures that were about to break.

Look, she's about to get off!

Give her a hit right when she comes.

Faye's legs quivered as more pleasure surged. She panted, her heart racing. The crack-pipe was put to her lips.

No, I can't do anymore, she pleaded against the waves of ecstasy.

A lighter flicked, tinted her deranged face. Then a hammer cocked, a gun was put to her head.

Smoke it all up . . .

Faye inhaled the metal-like fumes as her climax broke. Then she rolled off the couch with a plop, delirious and immobile.

There. Now the fat sack of shit can't say we never did anything for her.

Laughter, as Faye lay like a dropped sack.

The stout voice again: *That was amusing, it always is. Let's adjourn now, to the Scarlet Room.*

Svelte, nude bodies traipsed away, bare feet padding, contours of erotic shadows disappearing through the flickers of candle-flame.

Faye lay drooling, hoping she'd die. She knew what was happening; she knew what it was time for.

Get out! They're all in the other room!

That was her instinct, at least, but she knew that such instincts, such as self-preservation, didn't matter much to her now. Back out in the normal world? How long would she last? They'd addicted her to everything by now, to make their human pinata more compliant and more fun to laugh at and piss on and humiliate—all because they were purely and simply evil. She'd last a few days, run out of drug money, take one last look at her crumpled life, and then blow her head off.

So what did she have to lose?

It took a half an hour of breathing deeply and focusing on calming her heart down before she could get up. The candlelight licked over her flabby body; her head still spun but somehow she'd regained some control over movements and train of thought. She'd come all this way. She just wanted to see.

She wanted to see if it was true and then die.

What room am I in? She focused her eyes. One of the upstairs parlors, she guessed. She couldn't even remember. She
pushed open high, ingrained doors, teetering in the frame
for a moment, then stepping out into the hall. When she got
to the banister and looked down, she saw hundreds of flickering dots of lit candles.

As she trudged for the stairs, her ears detected mutters
and sighs and death-rattles. Every so often there came a
shriek deep from within the mansion's guts. When she
looked in one of the bedrooms, she saw a nude woman
hanging from a rafter by a meat-hook caught in the roof of
her mouth. She twitched a little, gargling. Someone had
carved all the meat off her calves and feet but placed tourni-
quets above her knees to prevent her from bleeding to death
outright. Faye closed the door and walked on. In the next
room, three more women lay dead, but not movie girls.
They were pale as paraffin, emaciated as if starved, bony pubic bones jutting below stomachs that seemed sucked in.
Their throats had all been cut.

Faye knew where she was going. More atrocities greeted
her during her trek. Once her bare foot stepped in a pile of
still-warm human innards. A few steps later, something hard
and wet printed against her sole: a testicle shucked from the
scrotum. At the top step one of the movie girls—one of the
few who'd been nice to her, in fact—lay dead and glass-
eyed, her hip joints broken to spread her legs wider than nature allowed so that the first person to come up the stairs
tomorrow would see what had been jammed up into her
vaginal vault: a human arm.

But Faye was beyond being appalled. These were the
trimmings of Hildreth's madness, his offering, his gesture of
beckoning and worthiness. Faye knew that what he solicited
would indeed find him very worthy. And she knew this

too—from this point on, if she continued to search the house instead of escaping, the things offered for her to see would only get worse.

When she found the door she was looking for, it seemed to be no door at all but instead an oblong orifice rimmed by something lip-like. The drugs made her see things all the time, but was she really just *seeing* this?

When she touched what should've been the door frame it was soft, warm, wet. It was not wood.

Total silence stood before her. More candles flickered here, revealing inklings of the horror that had taken place. She looked, vision surveying Hildreth's precious Scarlet Room, and then she thought: *They did it.*

Some of the bodies remained whole, others in pieces. The center of the room was a pile of butchered nudity. Limbs, heads, hands, and feet lay about the bloody accrual in the middle: bodies. Faye could easily see the work—ax-holes in faces, ax-holes in stomachs. It occurred to her that the bodies had been stacked deliberately for effect: a heaped offering, a plea for invitation. Closer to the door at the rear several buckets lay on their sides, glistening scarlet within. And laying aside was the ax, as if dropped there.

Leave, she told herself.

But she couldn't.

When Faye finally stepped through inside, something squished, something warm under the bottoms of her feet. At first she thought it must be the carpet soaked from so much blood but a downward glance showed her something else altogether.

It wasn't a floor she was walking on, it was raw meat, akin to a vast slab of porterhouse. Veins branched out, thick as garden hoses, and she could see them pulsing. Then she stuck her hand out to steady herself against the wall but what her hand touched was not a wall anymore. It was skin.

Hot, sweating, and flushed, skin full of excited nerves which cringed for sensation. Faye walked along the wall, running her hand, and as she did so it seemed to swell in her wake, as if trying to touch back. She also felt subtle protrudements: open eyes, faces, mouths with licking tongues. They blinked at her wantonly. One mouth's tongue desperately shot forward, then the lips sighed and whispered, "Please, please! Let us taste you!"

Faye's long fat breasts hitched and her flab jiggled when she stepped unbalanced toward the room's center. She needed to see one more thing...

The other door.

It stood there, indeed, where it should be. Rimmed with drooling flesh.

The Rive, she thought.

Yes, they'd really done it.

But where was Hildreth?

Then she looked in there and saw him grinning back.

The police found her hours later, sitting at the end of the mansion's twisting, mile-long driveway. Gibbering. Naked. Insane.

Faye sat now much in the same way, only in a different place. No, it wasn't a nightmare. It was worse because it was memory.

The moon glazed the floor and a wedge of the bed in its soft, ice-like glow.

Movement caught her eye; when she looked up to the little window, a face peered in. They did often, never smiling.

The door opened with a heavy click.

"Come on, Faye. Time for your meds."

II

Patrick Willis never traveled on planes. He'd stopped years ago, when his mentalism peaked. It was mostly tactility which triggered him, but packed so close, so close to all those passengers—sometimes it was too much.

Sometimes it was madness.

That close to so many auras, he didn't need to *touch* them. Too often their horrors came to him with hands of their own.

So it was Greyhound from now on. At least the fares were cheap.

Half of the East Coast rolled by in the large window, like a bright movie. *All that beauty out there,* he thought. Then he looked around at the dozen or so passengers sharing the coach with him. *Yeah, lots out there but not much in here.*

Several bums, several obese welfare recipients, a straggle-haired twenty-year-old white girl sitting stone-faced beside a grinning black man in his forties. A sleeping drug-addict here, a talkative mental patient there. All hard-luck cases. Mostly people whom life had consigned to society's trenches.

So where does that leave me? he asked himself.

Willis looked back out the window. Even looking at people from a distance of ten or so feet could bring on a touch, that is if he looked hard enough. What existed beyond the window was better.

He hoped to view more of the countryside beyond the glass, but eventually—and as usual—he just wound up seeing more of his own broken life. He'd never been materialistic—he'd actually been a good person once. After graduating from medical school, he'd had no desire to pursue a future in private practice—where his additional skills as a tactionist could certainly bring him up to a seven-figure salary in no time. Instead he'd worked at the state health center, helping mostly rape victims and battered women. He'd always been altruistic; working for a much lower salary helping people who couldn't help themselves seemed a noble cause. *It let me give something back to the world.* It wasn't idealism, either. He knew it came from his heart.

The job lasted five years or so, his "gift"—as with so many others who were psychically inclined—became his curse. He hadn't really even known he'd had it to any extent until he'd gotten out of med school (this mode of psi tended to peak in one's late twenties to early thirties). He'd noticed it, for sure, and always with women, all throughout college and med school. Touching. Any direct skin-to-skin contact. Sex trebled the intensity of what he referred to as a "backwash," and since sex existed as the most direct manner of skin-to-skin contact, Willis' romantic life never got past that first night in bed with a woman. There was always something—something awful or dark—that would wash back into his head from hers. Indeed, Willis was cursed.

But I made it, didn't I? he reflected now on the rumbling bus.

By thirty, he knew he'd simply never be able to have an intimate relationship with anyone. He sought his own sexual satisfaction by his own means—as introverted as it seemed—and still did the world some good. This was harder to reckon with sometimes since Willis, by most standards, was an attractive man. At the clinic, his nickname was "Dr. Cutie." But still, he had his resolve, he had his ideals, and he knew that he had genuinely helped a lot of people before he'd lost his license.

Just don't think about it now, he groaned to himself. And another thing he didn't want to think about was the complexity of what he was encroaching. He'd never even heard of Vivica Hildreth but he most certainly had heard of her husband's "entertainment" business, T&T Enterprises, and the one other name in the solicitation letter, too. The letter that came with the package read: *The object in this box is a bracelet that belonged to a woman named Jane Scharr. Her stage name was Janey Jism, a porn star, obviously.* The coincidence was uncanny; Willis was well-familiar with Ms. Scharr's work. The letter continued, *Please consider testing your skills on the bracelet. If you decide that you'd like to further investigate the entirety of the night in question, with other professionals in your field, please know that you will be paid ten times the amount of the enclosed retainer. Contact my office if you'd care to proceed further. Travel arrangements and accommodations will be provided. You may keep the retainer regardless of your decision.*

Sincerely,

Vivica Hildreth

"Jesus," he muttered now at the memory. Willis' little excuse for an office didn't exactly haul in the money; he was lucky now to make twenty grand a year. Vivica Hildreth's retainer was $10,000.

What could he do? He needed the money.

He shook the tiny Express-Mail package once, heard the links of the tiny bracelet rattle a little. He contemplated taking it out of its velvet sack again—just to look at it—but rejected the idea at once and just peered inside. It was an attractive bracelet, a silver chain dotted with tiny amethysts. A crystologist would assert that amethyst and silver would protect the wearer from evil. *Sure didn't work for her,* Willis thought, holding the sack. Sure didn't protect Jane Scharr from anything. When he'd first held it, the day he'd gotten the package at his squalid L.A. apartment, he'd almost fallen on the floor. He'd seen image-fragments of muscular men, their naked bodies glistening as they calmly cut the throats of several women to then drain their blood into buckets.

Candles flickering as an orgy ensued, then a tall, lean, and somehow distinguished-looking man axing the sexual participants down, burying the blade one swipe after the next into backs, heads, and groins. And there, in the corner of a room that seemed to be sweating blood, was Jane Scharr aka Janey Jism, oblivious as her drug-glazed eyes looked up from the female crotch she had her face buried in just in time to catch the blade between the eyes. Then, in silent thunks, her hands and feet were summarily chopped off. Her body was lifted up twitching and tossed onto a pile of still more hacked bodies. Meanwhile, the woman she'd been orally indulging picked up her severed hand and used it to masturbate...

That had been enough for Willis.

And here he was now, on his way to see more, simply because he needed the money.

What a whore I am, he thought to the window.

California long behind him now; the states were blurring by. He hoped the bus would arrive before sundown.

The intercom crackled, the cheery driver's voice announcing, "You can start packin' your gear, folks. Ninth Street North, St. Petersburg, Florida is just down the pike. We'll be pullin' into the station in about fifteen."

Thank God, he thought.

"'Cuse me, sir," a huge, destitute woman said by surprise. "We're almost ta St. Pete and I'se broke. Could'ja spare a dollar'n a quarter for bus fare, please? Got my daughter to see," and then she touched his hand.

Willis flinched back, almost shouted. That single touch, that single *taction,* shot a bolt of utter, silent blackness into his spirit, the feeling in a mother's heart when the police tell her that her son, as he was walking home from high school, had just been shot in the head in a drive-by shooting. And it was more than the feeling, it was a glimpse too: a head erupting, vaulting brains into the air—

"Don't touch me, don't touch me!" he exclaimed and jerked back as far away from her as he could.

"Good Lord, all I'se asked was—"

Willis slammed it out of him; he'd learned to recover quickly. "It's okay, it's okay, I'm sorry," he blurted and feigned a smile. "It's-it's just that you startled me. Here," and then he gave her a twenty-dollar bill.

Her broad face looked astonished in its confusion. "Why, thank you much, sir. God bless ya."

Willis sighed and closed his eyes. "God bless you too."

III

"We're rich," Straker said with no enthusiasm.

"Rich? Are you kiddin' me?" Walton said back in a light North Carolina drawl. "Sure this was a great chunk of change—"

"A hundred grand for three weeks' work, split two ways? Yeah, I'd call that a chunk of change."

"Still can't believe the nutty bitch paid us that much. We'll have to pay taxes on it, though, 'cos I'm sure she reported it."

"Yeah. Shit."

For two men who just earned $100,000 in a few weeks, Walton and Straker didn't seem to have much enthusiasm. They both sat on the front step of the great house, exhausted, dejected, and . . . something else.

"It almost wasn't worth it," Straker said next. "If I had it to do over again, I just might say fuck fifty grand and go to the bar."

"I know."

Early morning seemed entirely inappropriate for the scenario; they should've finished the job at midnight—a proper regard for effect. Dragging their tools back out to the truck under the full moon, then driving away into the humid night.

Their appearances couldn't have been more inappropriate, either: two decidedly grim-faced men wearing goatees, Walton in a black cowboy hat, Straker in a ball cap with an upside-down Buccaneers insignia. Straker smoked, Walton pinched himself a dip of Skoal. And there they sat on the front step of this grand house. So what might seem inappropriate about their appearances? Two guys just getting off a job, one in a ball cap, one in a cowboy hat?

Because they were still wearing their shiny yellow hazmat suits, hoods pulled down, gas-masks and Scot Air-Paks resting at their polypropylene boots.

"I guess the stink was the worst part," Straker mused, smoking. "That first day?"

Walton spat some juice. "Naw, it was just the feel of the place that bugged me. Or maybe it was just psychological, knowin' what happened there."

"I mean . . . who'd have thought, something like that? All those people . . ."

"Guys takin' the carpets out said it was close to twenty. Didn't know exactly how but . . . shit, there were ax-marks all over that room."

"And then there's all that porn shit," Straker added. He wanted to get out of there but he was simply too tired to get up just then.

"I guess that's what ya do when you're that rich—buy a porn company and move it into your house. Fill the place with hot chicks—"

"And then kill them," Straker finished the perplexity. "And you wanna know something? There were times when I was inside, I'd walk into a room, and all of a sudden I'd feel—"

"Like you're in a graveyard and someone's watchin' ya . . ."

"Yeah, that happened all the time, but that's not what I mean. There was a bunch of times when all of a sudden I'd feel *horny*."

Walton chuckled. "Shit, you're always horny."

"I'm serious, man. I'd be standing there scraping dried blood and guts off the floor in a room where a bunch of people were murdered, and I'd pop a woody."

"Yeah, well I guess you must be sick in the head."

"I was disgusted, nauseated, I got maggots squirming on the floor and all I wanna do is stick my head out the window and hurl . . . but I've also got a fuckin' boner and a half."

Walton shook his head, adjusting the brim of his black cowboy hat. "Let's go to the bar, you need a drink."

They both groaned as they stood, grabbed their gear, and trudged to the van full of wet-vacs and chemicals. The side of the van read:

WALTON'S CRITICAL CLEAN-UP
(CRIME SCENES, FIRES, DELAYED DISCOVERY)
WE'RE BONDED!

Another big van pulled into the front courtyard, and out tromped several men dressed in similar protective gear.

"Who're these guys?" Straker asked.

"Fumigators . . ." Walton turned to the lead man. "Have fun, boys."

"Is it bad?" the guy asked, gas-mask in hand. "The lady sure as shit paid enough."

"It's bad," Walton answered, "and it's all yours."

Neither Walton nor Straker said anything when they got into the truck. Walton turned on some twangy Country & Western tune, put the truck into gear, and pulled away.

The only thing Straker was happy about was that the bodies had been removed before they'd been hired. But part of his mind tried to sort through the possibilities. *What really happened in there?*

In his rear-view he could see the immense mansion shrink and then disappear around the first bend. It would never fully disappear—he would discover in the years to come—it would never ever be gone from his memories.

"Wait a minute," he said. "What happened to the guy?"

Walton spat again. "What guy?"

"The rich guy, Hildreth?"

"Shit, I . . . I don't know."

IV

Adrianne Saundlund looked blearily at the faces filing by. *Please, DON'T sit here,* she thought. She always flew with carriers that offered first-available seating, for her luck was generally bad; she'd always get that stinker sitting next to her, or the mother with the squalling baby. At least this way she had a chance, always arriving early to get a seat with the first boarding group. Then she'd plunk down at the first window and would try to look as unpleasant as possible so as to urge potential seat-takers to sit somewhere else. Adrianne didn't want to be near anybody. She didn't really like people.

She preferred window seats because looking into the sky reminded her of her own style of flying—out of her body.

The whine of the backup turbine calmed her along with

the barbiturates she'd become addicted to. Adrianne just
wanted to be calm . . .

She flipped idly through this month's copy of *Paranormal
News,* and stopped at a picture of a pleasant, librarianish-
looking woman with autumn-leaf eyes and a faltering
smile, a choppy bob of ink-black hair. A distant, knowing
yet distrustful expression. The article read "Remote Con-
trolling by Adrianne Saundlund: Techniques and Philoso-
phies of Remote-Viewing." Adrianne was forty but she
thought, *Shit, I'll have to get them to use a new picture. That one
makes me look like I'm fifty.* She wrote the bi-monthly column plus a small amount of freelancing for other magazines
in the field for side money and to keep her abreast of the
business. Her Army disability pension paid her bills.

And look at this floozy. She's forty and looks thirty. A twinge
of jealousy then, when she turned a few pages and saw another column by someone a bit more famous than her. *She
should've gotten smaller implants,* she criticized this other
woman's flawless bosom. Shining hair the color of beach
sand seemed to sweep around, arctic-blue eyes peering intensely back at her, as if enjoying a secret delight. This column read: "Para-Erotic by Cathleen Godwin: Sexual Desire
& The World of Psi." Adrianne looked at the photo of the
woman's face for another second, then suddenly put the
magazine down and shot a glance upward. The same face
was looking right at her from the aisle.

"Hello, Adrianne. Do you mind if I— Oh, I'm sure you
don't mind," the voluptuous woman said and plopped
down in the next seat, a cased laptop on her knees.

"Hi, Cathleen." *Damn!* "I guess this is a coincidence, if
there is such a thing with people like us."

Cathleen Godwin appeared fatigued but not unhappy to
see Adrianne. They weren't enemies really, or rivals, just dis-

tant; paranormalists rarely trusted each other. When she sat down a gentle waft of herby soap scents hovered over to Adrianne.

More trace resentment itched. *She even looks elegant when she dresses like shit,* Adrianne thought. Cathleen wore a t-blouse with flowers and stars that was so faded it must've been ten years old, and just-as-faded jeans.

"I *don't* have to be psychic to know where you're going," the blonde woman bid. "Let me see... Tampa International, then a cab to downtown St. Petersburg. You got an investigation offer from a woman named—"

"Vivica Hildreth," Adrianne verified. She was genuinely surprised, and now even more jealous. Not that Adrianne cared, but she knew that other psi-investigators would be there, some of them men, which meant that Cathleen would be slutting around as always, displaying herself. Adrianne wished she could condemn the woman as a tease but she knew Cathleen Godwin was much, much more than that. "Or maybe I'm just going for a suntan," she said as an afterthought.

"We're two of the top-ten psychics in the country, Adrianne, both on a plane to the same place on the same day, to a house that's verifiably charged."

"How do you know it's charged? You've been there?"

"No, but come on. How many people was it, sixteen, seventeen, all butchered in the same room by a satanist?"

"She didn't say he was a satanist. She just said he was eccentric."

"Oh, sure, I'd say that qualifies as eccentric—a ritual murder, almost like a transposition rite."

Adrianne smiled very thinly. "I don't believe in transposition rites."

"No, but you believe in God." Cathleen sighed, lazing

back in the seat. "I guess we all do in one way or another. People in our business."

Guilt, Adrianne thought. It brought a secret satisfaction. *Shame. She knows her life is a festival of Christian sin . . .*

"And then the guy disappears, almost as if the rite succeeded. Almost like he opened an egress and went in."

There was some fire in Adrianne's objection. "He didn't disappear," she said, flipping through the front pocket of her own carry-on. "He committed suicide after the fact. The body was recovered from the house and autopsied. He hanged himself."

Cathleen just kept looking straight ahead, eyes closed. "There was only one obituary in the very back of the local paper. You found that?"

She flapped her a photocopy. "I have this, and I have the police report and the preliminary of the post."

Cathleen took the sheet, looked at it with little interest, and passed it back. "Don't be naive."

"How do you know?" Adrianne exclaimed, this time almost to the point that her voice could be overheard.

Cathleen sighed wearily, still with her eyes closed. "Adrianne . . ."

"What? You've had a contact?"

"Relax. You're always so hyper . . ."

Adrianne fumed in silence. *Damn her. She probably didn't have a contact but just wants me to think she did.* It infuriated her, but the only thing that infuriated her more was how this stunning, beautiful woman could bring out all her inadequacies at once.

"Let's just wait till we get there. Maybe you're right. Maybe the whole thing's a sham, and if that's true . . . so what? We're just doing a job. People pay us to do a job because they believe in us. If we knew in advance that this was

just some kooky woman with a ton of money and that this
Hildreth house was uncharged, totally cold, and totally ordi-
nary, what would we do?"

Adrianne admitted it. "We'd go anyway, for the money."

"Yes. Of course we would. Because we're mercenaries
just like anybody else with a skill. If somebody hires a roofer
to put on a new roof, but the roofer can see that the old roof
is fine, then he puts on a new roof anyway ... because that's
what the customer wants."

Is that really what we are? Adrianne wondered. She didn't
dwell much on the answer.

"I read on a website that all your PK is dead," Adrianne
said next, to change the unpleasant subject. "That's not
true, is it?"

Suddenly Adrianne's plastic meal tray flapped down in
her lap. She pushed it back and slid the clip back over.
"Funny."

"I just *don't* do it anymore, I just tell people I can't,"
Cathleen admitted. "It's too much of a headache. Especially
since the accident. I'm sure you heard about that."

Of course Adrianne had—everyone in the field had. A
TV documentary on psychic power. Several strong men
lifted a two-by-four wall frame off the ground to waist
level. Another man—the show's producer—crawled under
it, and then the others let go of the frame's edge. It hovered
in mid-air for several seconds, then fell. The producer got
several cracked ribs and a broken nose.

"I guess this sounds terrible, but I don't feel that bad
about it," Cathleen went on. "About the guy who got hurt,
I mean. I was just dating him—well, I mean I was cheating
on my husband with him—and the son of a bitch actually
threatened me. Said he'd tell my husband about our affair if
I didn't do a spot on his dumb TV show."

"Some people get what's coming to them," Adrianne agreed. "They treat us like we're animals in a petting zoo."

"Mm-hmm. Sometimes it's hard not to resent just about everybody." Cathleen turned suddenly, touched Adrianne's arm. "Oh, but here's a story you haven't heard—at least I hope not. A couple of years ago I was dating this guy who was a professional bowler. He'd just barely made the cut to get on the PBA tour. So all of a sudden he starts throwing these really great games, beating everybody—"

"Was it really you?" Adrianne asked.

Cathleen nodded, grinning. "I was sitting in the audience. Any time he needed a strike, I'd push the ball or knock the pins that didn't fall. For about six weeks, this guy was the best bowler in the world!"

"Did you tell him?" Adrianne leaned over and asked.

"Oh, of course not. He thought it was him. He made hundreds of thousands of dollars because of me and set a world record for strikes. Then he started to get big-money endorsement offers. So you know what he does? The son of a bitch was sleeping with some trashy *bowling groupie* behind my back."

"I hate to ask but . . . what did you do?"

"Nothing. I left him and the next year he got kicked off the tour because he couldn't qualify. No more perfect games for him, the prick."

Adrianne laughed.

"What about you? Still working for the Army?"

I'm . . . retired," Adrianne mulled over the answer. "They still call me up sometimes when something hot's happening, but usually I'm not up to it. I can still RV without much problem—it hurts sometimes."

"But you don't OBE at all anymore?"

"I can but I don't, haven't in a long time." She knew that

Cathleen knew about the accelerant drugs, and the barbiturates she was addicted to as a result. "It hurts too much afterwards. I knew one man who got a brain tumor because of it. And there are always the strokes. Occupational hazard."

"The Army hounded me for a long time. I can't imagine what they wanted *me* to do."

"Oh, I can. You'd be surprised. Them, and Navy Intelligence. There're these other weird people out there too, IGA. Stands for Inter-agency Group Activity. They even scared *me*. I know a few people who worked for them—never saw them again."

"Creep me out." Cathleen checked her fingernail polish, then groaned. "I remember reading an editorial in one of the mags during the Iraq war. The editor said that the government should recruit experients like you and Peggy Falco to go out-of-body and look for Hussein, and the whole time I'm thinking *I know damn well they've been doing that since before the war began*."

The details of the comment gave Adrianne call to pause, and in the pause she may have fractured her response into a giveaway. Cathleen was probably playing her.

"Then I saw in a chat-room one night some 'anonymous' source saying that three times when we almost got him, it was you who saw him while you were RV-ing Baghdad from some Army base in Maryland." Cathleen blinked at her. "Is that true?"

Damn it... She was playing her, all right. And it was all quite true but more than three times. The closest she'd come to finding him was the empty apartment building on al-Mu'azzam Square, near Sa'dn Street, downtown. Adrianne had seen Hussein being rushed inside. Then she RV'd back out, got a description of the building and the street, and gave the information to her case officer at Fort Meade.

Twenty minutes later, several thousand-pound, satellite-guided bombs brought the building down. But Hussein had left in a jeep five minutes previous. "Cathleen, you know I can't talk about anything I may have done or may not have done for the Army. There're a few little things called the National Classified Secrets Act and the Federal Secrecy Oath."

Cathleen grinned. "I know. I was just toying with you. Actually, I'm envious."

The remark shocked Adrianne. "What on earth for?"

"I don't really contribute anything. You do. All I do is bend spoons and scry crystals. By the way, how *is* Peggy Falco? Haven't heard from her in years."

More darkness sifted into Adrianne's mind. "She committed suicide last Christmas. She couldn't walk, had no sensation on the left side of her body for the last two years."

"Oh, God. I'm sorry."

"She was greedy. She was too into the power trip, and maxed herself out. But she was the best in the world."

"Now you are."

"Uh-uh. You should see some of the kids they're bringing in now. There's one boy who's only fourteen and he can..." but Adrianne cut it off there. She knew she was talking too much.

"Sorry. I shouldn't have pried." She shot the first bright smile since she'd sat down. "It's good to see you, though. I didn't mean to run at the mouth. I know you don't like to be bothered and to chat much and all that. It's just nice to . . . sit next to someone I know."

"Yes, it is, and it's good to see you too," Adrianne replied.

Cathleen let out a long breath, rubbed her eyes. "God..."

"Rough night?"

"Yes," was all Cathleen said.

A stilted stewardess squawked through the always-ignored pre-takeoff safety instructions. Adrianne let it go out the other ear, preferred the steady whine of the turbine. She didn't care where the exit door was because she genuinely wasn't afraid to die. She knew there was a Heaven because she'd gotten to see it several times.

And once she got to that house in Florida, she wondered if she'd get to see Hell.

V

Clements couldn't say why he would describe the mansion in this way; it was just a feeling in him, a throb in his gut.

The mansion looked maniacal.

Its front must've been fifty yards long. Gray stonework raised the outer walls five stories. The severely inclined roof was covered with gray slate, gutter lines and parapets running with intricate cast-iron crestings. Even the drainpipes and rainwater heads sported pointed arches and fleurs-de-lys.

All gray.

If disconsolation had a color, this was it.

The front existed as a plane of gun-slit windows with pointed-arch transoms and filled with lead-lined stained glass, most of the panes of which looked black. Two cylindrical brick chimney stacks poked up atop the center rampart, like horns.

Clements shivered.

"You don't mind if I toke up, do ya?" the girl asked. She held up a crack pipe.

Clements' eyes bolted from his binoculars straight to her face. Just the idea soured him, made him want to rage. "Yeah, I mind very much."

"Why?"

"Because it's against the fuckin' law."

"So is picking up hookers."

His lips pursed. He'd never hit a woman in his life but just that second, without thinking, he felt the impulse to crack her across the face as hard as he could. "That's different—"

"Oh yeah," she laughed, slipping the pipe back into her shorts.

"The people you buy that from are the same people selling it to nine-year-olds on playgrounds. The same people who want to keep the poor stuck in their ghettos, the same people who've enslaved you. And you know what, *those* people buy their supply from cartels in South America who give hundreds of millions of dollars to the people who brought the World Trade Center down and killed four thousand some odd people. So just think about that. Any time you buy yourself a twenty-rock, a penny or two of that twenty goes to psychos who love to murder women and children."

She didn't listen to half the diatribe, her bloodshot eyes looked back out into the night.

Clements brought his own eyes back to the Zeiss binoculars, watching the front of the house. The sun was going down now, painting the front face of the edifice with edges of orange, as if its framework were aflame. Soon, he suspected, the outdoor floodlights would come on. If they didn't, Clements also had an infra-red monocular and a Unertl low-light scope. He wanted very much to see if the men brought anything out.

"Who're those guys?" the girl asked.

Clements had forgotten her name because they were all the same: Snowdrop, Teardrop, Candy, Kitty. He wasn't even doing a trick tonight; usually he paid more attention. "Fumigators," he answered, still staring at the house through the bright, infinity-shaped field.

"So you're waiting for them?"

"Yes."

"Why?"

"You ask too many questions."

She was a half-starved urchin like most of them but beneath the hollows of her cheeks and sunken eyes and the zero body fat physique, she hadn't lost all of her looks yet. *Tramp appeal,* was how Clements thought of it in his own mind. He just had a thing for it, like the girl's own addictions only his wasn't smoked out of a pipe. He couldn't help it. He was always good to them, and always dropped them off where they wanted, and he even paid a little more than the going street price for services, which was low anyway. Street whores were *his* jones.

She rubbed her upper arms, itching for the pipe. "Look, you gave me a hundred for an hour, and that's good money but—" She pointed to the clock in the dash. "—you've got fifteen minutes left so if you want any action on that c-note, we better get started."

He put the glasses down a moment to light a cigarette. "I told you, this one's not a trick, I just want you to talk." He looked back to the house. "About there."

"I've seen you cruising all the time but you've never picked me up. Then the other chicks tell me you're a great john—"

He almost laughed. "Thanks."

"Now you got me and you don't want nothing."

"I just want to know about the house, and the girl in the picture."

"I told you pretty much everything..." Her attention

seemed to slip. "How did you even know I'd been to the house in the first place?"

Clements spewed smoke, ghost-like, out the window. With no breeze at all, it seemed to hover as it spread—a dis-embodied face looking back. "One of the other girls told me."

"Which one?"

Clements sighed. "Teardrop, Snowdrop, Candy—something like that."

"Well, I told ya, I saw the girl, Debbie, one time."

"*This* girl?" Clements made her clarify and showed her the picture again. "You're *sure?*"

Her eyes dragged back. Now she had her hands on her knees, rocking them back and forth. "Yeah."

"What was she doing? Was she doing sexual stuff?"

"Nope. It was weird. So many people walkin' around in there naked, or barely wearing anything, but then I saw her come down the hall, wearing business-chick stuff."

"Was she affiliated with the Hildreth's porn business?"

"I don't know."

"You see her do drugs?"

"No. Not the one time I saw her. One of guys was tak-ing me and the other girls—"

"The other hookers?"

"Yeah, he was taking us to our room. He called it the something-or-other parlor; it had a name, a lot of them rooms did, and it was upstairs on the third floor. Then the girl—Debbie—stops us and asked if we needed anything. Seemed kind'a nice. She brought us some bottled water, and that was it. That was the one and only time I saw her."

"How many times were you in the house total?"

"Six, seven."

"How'd you hear about the place, the gig?"

"Brandy."

One of the three, Clements realized. *One of the three who got their throats cut.* He snorted a laugh. "You're a lucky girl."

"I know. I was supposed to be there that night but I was in county detent. A plainclothes U.S. Marshal busted me on 34th Street. Can ya believe it? And I'd have been there, too, in a heartbeat. Something even told me in my gut—had a bad feeling, you know? Told me if I worked 34th Street, I'd get busted. And look what happens. I spend the night in jail, and my three friends get killed." She glanced anxiously back out the window, not at the house, at the night. "Maybe there really is a God."

Clements dragged his cigarette. "Yeah. Maybe there is." When he looked back in the binoculars, he kept talking. "What were you saying earlier, about another door, a special entrance?"

"It's way over on the side, it was between two windows, and didn't really even look like a door. That's where they'd park the limo, and it was a different road to the house, not this main drive out here."

Hmm, he thought. "I didn't know that. I'll need you to show me that access when we leave."

"Yeah, sure, when we leave in—" She looked at the dash clock again. "—in five minutes. But that side door? It wasn't just the hookers they'd bring in that way, it was everyone."

"I wonder why."

"I don't know. Maybe they were worried about someone watching the house."

"Why would someone watch the house?"

She stopped wagging her knees enough to laugh. "Man, what are *you* doing?"

"Oh, yeah," he muttered behind the binoculars. He had

to think a minute to get his mind back on track. The girl was distracting him—scratching at that innate, desperate lust—but he was determined not to do that tonight. This was his investigation. This was business. "Everyone, you said? I heard the movie girls *lived* in the house."

"They did, the guys too. But whenever they'd go out, I mean. Sometimes they'd go out to dinner downtown, and that side door's where they'd leave and come back in later."

"I guess they just didn't want anybody seeing," Clements said.

"Sure, whatever. Hey, man, your time's up. Take me back now. A deal's a deal. I'll show you that other road out of here through the woods, but I need to get back."

Clements gave her another hundred. "I want you with me for another hour. I want to wait till the fumigators leave."

"Oh, man, come on!" she objected.

Clements didn't get it. "That's two hundred bucks I've given you for two hours. You're not going to make that much on the street on a week night. What are you complaining about? You don't have to strut for it, and you don't have to sweat cops."

Now she was squeezing her knees till her knuckles turned white. "I'm going nuts here, man. Don't you understand?" For a moment it looked like she would break out into tears. "I'm a crack addict. I gotta fire up."

Clements smirked, as much as he truly felt sorry for her. It wasn't the users, it was the dealers, the suppliers. *Line them all up against the wall and machine-gun the motherfuckers. I'll even volunteer to mop up the blood . . .*

"Outside," he said.

In a half-second she was out of the car. He could hear her lighter flick.

Movement caught his eye in the binoculars. *Finally, they're done!* He squinted. The sun was gone now and just as he'd suspected, the outside floodlamps flicked on. Four weary men in hazmat suits came out of the house. *Damn, nobody carrying anything,* but then what did he expect? Dead bodies? The police took all of those. Some occult relic? *No, they're just there to fumigate the house.* The four sat on the long stone front step, and Clements was curious about their facial expressions when they pulled off their gas masks. Deadpan. Faraway eyes. None of them were even talking.

"Looks like your guys are out," the girl said when she got back in the car. She sat in her stifled, keyed-up bliss.

"Yeah. You should see their faces. They all look really disturbed. Something about that place must've really spooked them."

"You don't have to tell me about that. It's the creepiest place I've ever been in my life. Just walking around inside."

"Yeah?"

"Like walking around a graveyard where all the bodies were just buried a day ago. I sure as shit never want to go in there again."

I do, Clements thought. He'd already been in once.

The fumigation crew was just sitting there. *Maybe they're not done,* he considered. Of course it would be a *big* job, and he presumed that Vivica Hildreth had paid them *big* money. Were they waiting for someone else? No, he was certain there'd been only four of them, just after the clean-up crew had left.

"So it was pretty much just orgies going on there, huh?" he continued to prod.

"I mean, I guess. That's what it sounded like. Lot of hootin' and hollerin'. Big party going on somewhere—downstairs."

"Maybe they were shooting movies for the porn company."

"Maybe. With all the naked people walking around, I can believe it. Really good-looking people too. Most of the men were all buffed up, and the women? There were beautiful women all over the place, not junkies, either. These girls were tan, implants, great bods. Shit—what I wouldn't give. And they seemed normal too, party girls, sure, but not whacked out. At first I thought they were just big-money call girls, but then I started hearing about the porn company that Hildreth owned. Then the last few times I was there..."

"What?"

"Shit, we could see them walking around, me and the girls I was there with. We'd open the parlor door a crack and look out. Really freaky shit—satanic stuff."

This verification perked Clements up. "Why do you say that? Did you see them doing an occult rite, a black mass, something like that? Why exactly do you think it was something satanic?"

"The girls, man. The way they looked."

"But you said they looked normal. Beautiful, like pin-up girls."

"Yeah, earlier. But later on, after midnight, we'd look out that door, and none of the lights were on anymore. Just candles. All through the foyer and downstairs. And the girls would walk by our door sometimes. Black lipstick, black fingernails and toenails. It looked like fuckin' Halloween, man. Oh, and the piercings."

"What piercings? Body-piercings, you mean?"

"Yeah. One time—the last night I was there—one of the girls saw us looking out so she stood there and kind of giggled, and posed for us. Her nipples, bellybutton, and clit were pierced with rings, and hangin' off each ring was a little black upside-down cross. Earrings like that too." The prostitute rubbed her face. "Now, if that ain't fuckin' satanic, I don't know what is."

Clements nodded; it was a fulfilling enlightenment. And he'd seen a pilfered autopsy report on a few of the girls: they'd all had piercing holes in their nipples, navels, and clitoral hoods.

"Did the people at the house—these men—put piercings on you and the—" He stopped, almost having said, *And the other crack whores?*—but he recovered. "Your three friends?"

"Hell no, man. I mean, we would've done it probably, 'cos Hildreth was payin' out the ass, plus all the crack we could smoke while we were there. With these guys? It was strictly scat stuff with them."

"Scat?" Clements didn't know the term, which surprised him. Given his experience, he thought he'd heard all the darkest and most obscene street slang and underground lingo that was out there.

She sighed, her bony shoulders dipping in what could only have been shame. "The gross stuff. Golden showers, Hershey showers—hell, one night they gave us each a spoonful of this awful tasting shit and made us puke on each other."

Clements felt crushed by a sudden press of darkness in his heart. *How could people do that? What could possibly be the turn-on in watching a bunch of desperate girls shit and piss and vomit on each other? What* mental perception could urge a very rich man to manipulate a group of victimized drug addicts to do these things? Clements was beginning to see that answer more and more.

Maybe it really was evil.

Her final note was worse.

"Oh, and animals, too," she said.

Clements spewed more smoke out the window, numbed. Her tone of voice was turning brittle, sardonic with resentment and self-loathing. "I know what you're thinking. You're thinking how could she do disgusting shit like that? Only a complete loser, a complete white trash piece of shit could do stuff like that..."

He turned and grabbed her shoulder. "That's *not* what I'm thinking. Nothing like that at all. All I'm wondering is what kind of piece of shit could *make* somebody do stuff like that." He kept staring at the house. "And you know what? I wish I'd been there that night because I would've gone in there and killed them all, and I wouldn't care about taking the rap. It'd be worth a death sentence to take out a bunch of scumbags like those guys." Yes. He really could've done it.

The girl was wiping tears out of her eyes, the meager remnants of the real her—the real person with a soul and a life and dreams—leaking through the rents that the world had carved into her.

"Tell me about Hildreth. How many times did you see him?"

"Five, six," she said. "Just coming and going. It was the other guys I saw all the time, the beefcake guys. Hildreth was always nice to us, even though we knew what he was all about before long."

"So something else was going on in the house, while you girls stayed upstairs?"

"Yeah. Some kind of freaky ritual, I guess."

"But you and the others never went to one of the rituals?"

"No. Never. They kept us upstairs for their little pre-game show or whatever you want to call it. The men'd all stand around and watch while we did the scat stuff."

"And then you'd—"

She knew what he was going to ask. "No, that's the weird

part. Hildreth and his guys never laid a hand on us, never wanted us to get 'em off. They'd all just stand around, buck naked, watching. We'd do it with men sometimes, just not Hildreth's men. They'd bring people in—crackheads, bums, rednecks all fucked up on PCP—and *those guys* would do us. A lot of times it was just plain rape. These guys would smack us around and rape us, while one of Hildreth's people would film it. It was pretty sickening sometimes, but the rock was so good—all we wanted when we were done. You'd have to be hooked to know what I mean. And the whole time, Hildreth and his guys would watch. Sometimes they'd say weird shit, like we were being *seasoned*. We needed to be *debased*. How do you like that shit? I remember one night one of these boneheads looked at me and said 'You're not soiled enough yet.' Then he—" Her eyes went back to the window, as if there were safety out there. "Then he brought in a goat."

Yes. Clements knew that he could easily have killed them all. *Just walk in there with the Remington . . . and start pumping.* He needed to change topics, for this one, as informative as it may have been, was making him too depressed. "And the pay was—"

"A grand apiece, each night, for each of us. And all the crack we could smoke before sundown. When we were done doing the scat stuff, Hildreth would bring in a *bowl* of it, like someone would put out a bowl of fuckin' after-dinner mints. They'd go downstairs for their little devil party and we'd sit up in the parlor and crack it up till dawn. Someone'd drive us back in the limo in the morning."

"But you say you never saw Debbie—" He held up the picture once more. "—you never saw *her* doing any of this freaky stuff?"

"No."

Clements had a good feel for this sort of girl. Crack addicts were consummate liars; they could beat polygraphs sometimes because their devotion to the addiction overrode physiological responses. *But this one's not lying. There's no reason why she should. There's no one to protect.*

A welcome breeze blew through the car's open windows. Clements looked up when he heard some hollow thunks in the distance.

"Looks like those guys are finally leaving," the girl said. She was rubbing her knees again already.

One last glance in the binoculars. The fumigation van was pulling around the estate's great circular entrance drive. Clements watched them disappear as the road was swallowed by the woods.

"What now?" the girl asked.

I want to go in there, the thought popped up instantly. He had his lock-picks with him, and his gear. But—

Don't be stupid.

"You must really want this Debbie girl bad. What is she, your daughter?"

"No. Her parents hired me to keep tabs on her. Then I started snooping around, and the parents wound up murdered."

"That sucks. So you're a PI?"

The house loomed in its curtain of floodlights. "I used to be," he said.

"So where's Debbie? Is she dead, too? Did that Hildreth kook kill her like all the others?"

"Nope. All the bodies were accounted for, and she wasn't one of them."

"Then where is she?"

Clements started the car up. "I can't explain why I feel this way, but I just feel it in my bones, I can feel it all the way at the back of my heart, that she's still in that house."

Chapter Two

I

Westmore felt less than confident when he hopped off the #35 trolley at the Baywalk shopping complex. In the front of the window of some ritzy designer purse boutique, he could see himself. *Jesus Christ, I look like a tourist . . .* White slacks, loafers, and loose blue and yellow Hawaiian shirt with pineapples on it. He'd have worn his suit, but . . . he didn't have one anymore. It was part of his paring down process when he'd quit the *St. Petersburg Times* to go freelance. Move into a really small, really cheap efficiency, sell the car (not that he could drive legally anymore anyway), and give all the clothes he didn't absolutely need, plus any other clutter to Goodwill. The white slacks and pineapple shirt were all he had clean at the last moment.

And ten grand in an Express Mail package is one hell of a serious job inquiry.

He'd done a quick Nexus-Lexus search on Vivica Hildreth and found nothing of consequence. Plenty on her husband though, the recently deceased Reginald Parker Hildreth—mostly links to adult DVD distributors, but the wife was the goose-egg, which would've made him suspect were it not for . . .

Ten fucking GRAND in an Express Mail package, he reminded himself. Cash, too, not even a bank check. A very loud hello.

Tampa Bay past the Pier shined like lime-green ice in the blaze of sun. The sunshine and the fresh, salty sea-scent off the water reminded him why he'd moved to Florida. Several stunningly attractive women in provocative bikini tops and sheer sarongs provided another reminder. Westmore hadn't cut his hair since he'd left the paper; now it was a shoulder-length dark mane, and when he stepped across 2nd Avenue, a breeze stirred round his head and blew it all back in his face in a tangle. When he reached for his comb, he frowned, realizing he'd forgotten it. *Yeah, I'm gonna make a great impression, all right.*

Before him, downtown St. Petersburg stood clean and uncrowded. It was a small and diverse metropolis but with a big city feel somehow. The restaurant block reminded him of slices of other cities all amalgamated into one: a little bit of Bourbon Street dropped into Rodeo Drive peppered with specks of Baltimore's Inner Harbor. Westmore liked it—classy but unpretentious eateries, sophisticated but genuine people, and upscale bars. But when he walked past one of those same bars, his heart twinged. Yes, Westmore liked this area but he didn't come here anymore. He couldn't trust himself.

The glowing neon light in the front window of the martini bar could've spelled his name. That sadness, that loss of part of himself—however bad—never went away.

He crossed the next block, exiting the sun into a wall of cool shadow thrown by downtown's tallest buildings. Next thing he knew he was standing in front of his favorite oyster bar, watching the skilled shucker effortlessly peel the tops off bivalves larger than his hand. Westmore ate here a lot when he was on the paper. He also did something else here a lot, and he remembered that with a jaded fondness now as he stared through the window and saw rows and rows of top-shelf liquor.

He turned away.

The street's shadow covered him. He'd seen the Strauss Building countless times in the past: sleek, narrow, forty stories high. It looked like a massive rectangle of perfectly smooth, perfectly black volcanic glass—for the darkly tinted windows that formed its skin. He'd seen it a lot, yes, but never knew that it was a residential condo tower; he'd always thought it was an office building. *Maybe Vivica Hildreth has an office,* it occurred to him, or maybe she was using her late-husband's business office for the interview. But then he remembered the rest of her letter, inviting him to her "home."

This is some home, he thought when he entered the posh lobby. A security guard signed him in, even scrutinizing him with a metal-detection wand. Rich people were often paranoid. As he approached the elevator, he spied the parking garage through a door's chicken-wire window, noticing a Rolls, several Porsches, a Ferrari, and a multitude of Mercedes. Just as the elevator opened, a woman stepped out and said, "Mr. Westmore, I'm sorry I'm late."

He was taken by surprise. The short, well-built woman

with the reserved smile couldn't have appeared more prim in a black-leather half-shirt over a sheer gray turtleneck, black skirt, high heels—a high-class sort of sexy office-manager look. Razor-straight bangs and flawlessly straight strawberry-blonde hair to her neckline. She looked forty but was probably only thirty—the Florida sun did that to women, roughened the skin just a little, but an exemplary tan forgave it all and somehow enhanced the harsh attraction.

He'd seen a picture of Vivica Hildreth. As he shook her hand, he said, "You're not—"

"No, I'm not Mrs. Hildreth. My name's Karen Lovell. I'm . . . currently engaged as Mrs. Hildreth's personal secretary."

"Pleased to meet you." The way she'd phrased the statement seemed peculiar, as though she'd been something else until recently. *Until Hildreth's death?* he wondered.

"And now if you'll come with me," she went on, "Mrs. Hildreth is anxious to meet you."

He stepped into the elevator with her, watched the door close without a sound. "I've got to be honest with you," he tried to start some conversation, "I'm an investigative reporter, and I've been in the area for quite a while. But I've never heard of the Hildreth Mansion."

She looked at him with the same repressed smile, burning-blue eyes intensely magnified behind the petite glasses. She didn't say anything in response.

Yeah. "Where exactly is it?"

"I'd prefer not to talk about the house at this time, Mr. Westmore. Mrs. Hildreth will be happy to tell you everything you need to know."

"But I presume she's hiring me to disclose some things that she *doesn't* know."

No response as the lift ascended. Baroque muzak played almost inaudibly from unseen speakers.

Do I need a fuckin' crowbar to open your mouth so you'll talk? "At least that's usually how it works. When somebody hires me to write something for them, it's also to find things out."

"You haven't been hired yet—"

I like a woman with a positive personality, came the irresistible sarcasm. Westmore shrugged it off; the cold shell was often his turf because nobody ever really trusted a reporter. She was probably afraid he'd dig up a lot of bad info on the husband, or maybe even Vivica. An over-protective employee.

She turned an unmarked keyhole on the button panel as the elevator continued to go up. Some scent off her hair smelled intoxicating. "But don't get me wrong, I hope you do get the job," she eventually offered. "Mrs. Hildreth is a very complex woman obsessed with detail. It would do her a world of good to find out exactly what happened out there. It's unpleasant information, Mr. Westmore, but it would at least give her some peace."

Now we're getting somewhere. The statement alone told him a lot. "I'll do my best. I'd like to think I always do."

Westmore was looking up at the lit floor indicator. The top floor was 39. 38 lit and went out, then 39 lit and went out. The lift continued to rise one more floor—to what he presumed was the penthouse—then it stopped and the doors slipped open.

"I'll leave you now, Mr. Westmore. I hope you have a good interview."

Westmore shook her hand. "You're not coming in?"

"No. The security guard and the housekeeper are gone,

too. Mrs. Hildreth prefers to speak with you in total confidence. You never know who might overhear something and run their mouth."

Hmm. This was getting more interesting by the minute, and he hadn't even met the woman yet.

"I'll be waiting for you across the street at the oyster bar. Come over there when you're done, and I'll drive you home."

"Great, I don't have to take the trolley back. It was nice meeting you," he said, but the scent off her hair was driving him nuts. *Honey, you are one cold stick in the mud . . . but your hair smells so good I just wanna lean back and do a rebel yell!*

"See you shortly, Mr. Westmore," she said as the doors were closing.

Wow, there's a live one. Now he faced another door that appeared to be a composite imitation of black marble. A gold plaque read V. HILDRETH, and above it hung the strangest gold knocker: an oval plate depicting a morose half-formed face. Just two eyes, no mouth, no other features. The eyes seemed to appraise him. When he raised his hand to knock, though, the door clicked and swung slowly open on its own.

He stepped into the foyer and found no one there. *Must be some kind of electric lock or something . . .*

The look of the foyer stunned him. Were the walls made of black Plexiglas? Shiny black and white tiles composed the floor, and the ceiling was a mirror. Wire stands housed funky silver vases full of artificial flowers that were disproportionately large and black. *Total Art Deco,* Westmore thought. A far cry from her husband.

"In here, please, Mr. Westmore."

The demure voice drifted out to him. An awesome sitting room opened out from the foyer, but there was no one sitting in any of the Warholish wire couches or chairs. Rich blue-violet wallpaper shot up to a rounded ceiling. On one wall hung an abstract-expressionist painting he remembered from college art-history class: a smeared face in pastel streaks, a face that looked hopeful and crushed and hideous at the same time. It was called *A Study of Woman Number One* by Willem deKooning, and it didn't look like a print. *If that's original,* he realized, *that's ten million fucking dollars hanging on the wall.*

Through a curiously narrow doorway, he saw sunlight.

"In here. I promise I won't bite."

Westmore stepped into an enclosed balcony that was ablaze with blurred sunlight; he almost had to shield his eyes. *This is one strange place,* he thought. It was not open-air at all; instead it was completely enclosed by transparent security bricks.

"You're in the penthouse but you don't want the view of the bay?" he asked without thinking.

The woman looking up at him was intensely pretty in a seasoned, mature way. Late forties but well, well-kept. Vivica Hildreth sat in one of the familiar silver-wire chairs that appeared to hover in mid-air. Westmore expected someone matronly but this was the opposite. *Casual attire for the rich, I guess.* She sat with her legs crossed, wearing black cashmere shorts and an intricate dark-Paisley shawl around a black t-shirt with white block letters that read ROTHKO. The t-shirt was knotted to expose a flat and very tan abdomen. Black flipflops with—*Good Lord!*—diamonds studding the straps. Finger- and toenails shined with a polish flecked with gold leaf. *Man alive,* Westmore thought.

"I love the sun, Mr. Westmore," she said of the clear security blocks, "but I don't like to be seen."

"Will people see you on the fortieth floor?"

"Those awful beach planes! With the ad banners? God!"

It was an amusing comment, but . . . *Is she serious?* "Then how did you get the tan? A salon?"

"I have a tanning bed here." She looked at her legs, then her arms. "It works well. And at any rate, I hope you like my home. Most people find it refreshing."

It's a fuckin' eyesore. "It's diverse and unique," he said instead. Her elegant hand bid him to sit. The wire rocked when he put his butt down on a clear plastic pillow case full of brightly dyed goose feathers. "And thanks for inviting me here . . . and the money, too."

"So you need money," she said rather than asked. "I guess everybody does." Her voice was a cold yet gentle lilt. Soft-blonde hair hung straight to her collarbone. She sat gracefully, her face calm yet her myrtle-green eyes intense. It all gave her an exotic cast, not an aged one; she was high-bosomed, striking in her funkiness. Westmore thought of a Lauren Hutton or a Jacqueline Bissett dressed for a Goth club.

"I'm not poor but—"

"But you don't have a deKooning on your wall," she finished, smiling.

He chuckled. "No, ma'am, I definitely don't."

"I saw you looking at it—" An elegant finger pointed upward, to the mirrored ceiling in the sitting room. "—in the reflection. If you're an art enthusiast, feel free to look in the den before you leave. It's stuffed with wonderful art."

"I'll do that," he almost stammered. This was off to an odd start. "But your decor surprises me. The little I've read on your late husband tells me he was quite a fan of Gothic Revival architecture and design. Yet this is as opposite as you can get from that."

"So you've seen the Hildreth Mansion?"

"No, I haven't. I'd never heard of it until I got your letter. But I do remember reading about something very brief in the paper about it, when . . . when the tragedy happened several weeks ago. Murders in Prospect Hill. As I recall the article didn't refer to the mansion by name."

"No, I paid them not too."

Her directness stilled him. Even in this day and age, the rich had their back-channels to keep details of familial crimes out of the limelight.

When she turned, her chair squeaked. She pointed behind him. But in the process, her pose elucidated more of her physique, the twist of her waist which pulled the t-shirt tighter to her bosom. Westmore—in the brief glance—was taken by her. The crossed legs, her shorts straining at the crotch, the breasts obviously bereft of a bra standing out in a dizzying vision. The $20,000 flipflop hanging off the tanned, perfectly manicured foot. Westmore felt a ludicrous arousal. Even the thread-thin lines of her inclined waist were attractive. Some women wore middle age well; this one wore it like a mink coat. *I'll bet she paid more for plastic surgery than she did the deKooning.* But she was pointing behind him, so he had to take his eyes away. "I'd offer you a drink but my people tell me you're a teetotaler."

There goes one grenade. He never lied about it. "I'm an alcoholic, Mrs. Hildreth. I always will be. But I haven't had a drink in three years." She'd been pointing to a bar stand, a glass counter on a silver wire stand. Black shot glasses stood in a row before bizarre, twisted bottles. "I love those shot glasses, though."

She got up, walked as demurely as one could in flipflops, and picked up one of the glasses. Westmore kept stealing glances at her physique, the meticulous lines of her shoulders and back, the swell of her breasts. All that tight, tan skin—shining. The butterflies in his belly were sinking to his groin, then he snapped, *What the hell is wrong with me! I'm lusting after a woman fifteen years older than me who's also a free-lance prospect! See if you can get more unprofessional!*

She smiled thinly, and placed one of the shot glasses in Westmore's hand. "It's onyx. And I'm glad you quit drinking, I did too. It's best to redirect destructive pursuits for pleasure . . . to natural ones."

Wow, was all he could think. *Yeah, you're right. I haven't been laid in a year . . .* He watched the backs of her calves, that feminine flex, as she walked back to her seat. "Thank you for the glass. It's beautiful."

"My husband was the same way. He never drank, never used drugs. Sex was his intoxication."

Wow, Westmore thought again. He began to say something but she cut him off.

More overt directness. "I'd like to buy your confidence, Mr. Westmore."

Baby, it's for sale. "I can guarantee my discretion, ma'am. This is a private job. I'm not a news hound anymore. But I'm still not sure what you'd like me to do. You'd like to hire me to write a book about your husband's mansion? You want me to write his biography?"

"Nothing like that. But first I want your confidence." She leaned over, bosom swaying, and handed him a fat envelope.

He could tell it was money just by feeling it. "You've already paid me a generous retainer."

"Open it."

Westmore almost toppled out of the chair. More bands of cash.

"That's twenty-five thousand dollars, in addition to your retainer. You can keep that envelope, too, even if you don't take the job. I need to tell you something right off the bat, that you must agree to not repeat."

Westmore couldn't take it anymore, so he simply said what was on his mind. "Mrs. Hildreth—look. I want money as much as the next guy but . . . This is crazy. You don't know me from Adam. Theoretically I could say yes, take this money, and still talk."

"Don't be silly! There's a non-disclosure agreement in there too!"

"Oh." He looked, pulled it out and read it. *Pretty cut and dry. But this woman is definitely serious.*

"Sign it, and the money's yours. And if you repeat what I'm about to tell you, you'll be very very sorry."

He couldn't resist grinning. "Is that a threat?"

"That is a stone-cold promise, Mr. Westmore. I don't simply have a lawyer. I have a law *firm,* and if you break this confidence, they will bury you so deep that you won't see light for a hundred years."

She wasn't smiling.

"I believe it," he said, and signed the agreement. He set the money down, numb in the disbelief.

Vivica was looking at him, her eyes suddenly far away.

"I'm ready," Westmore said.

"Several times already, you've referred to my 'late' husband. Well, Mr. Westmore, I don't believe that he's dead. There's no evidence to that effect."

Westmore frowned. "I read the obituary. Suicide."

"It's fake."

Westmore sat up more alertly. "You mean you—"

"Money talks. I paid the right persons to manufacture the obituary and the police findings."

"So who's in your husband's grave? There was a service listed about a week after the suicide."

"Not my husband. My people assure me of it."

Westmore rubbed his face. "The rumor is that your husband killed a whole bunch of innocent people with an ax—"

"No one is innocent, Mr. Westmore. Believe me, *none* of those people in that house were innocent."

"Fine. What exactly do you want me to do?"

"Find out what happened on that night. I believe that my husband is still alive. I believe that he's still in that house."

Westmore's gaze felt just as far away as hers now. He could only look at her through a blur.

"You're a reporter. Report. To me. And I want you to monitor the other people who will be there."

"Be *where?*"

"The Hildreth Mansion. I've hired some other people to investigate the events of the night in question."

Other people? More reporters? Christ, I hope not. He could see a bad scene coming already. "It was a couple weeks ago, right?"

"Yes. The night of April 3rd."

"And you think your husband's *still* in the house?"

"I believe that he may be." She gave him a card. "This is my cell phone number. You can call me anytime, and Karen will be at your disposal too. There's also a lot of visual evidence, still in the house. Take your time examining it. It will be a bit grueling, but . . . that's what I'm hiring you for."

"What kind of visual evidence?"

"DVD's and digital master tapes. My husband owned an adult movie business. He bought the company outright some time ago, and relocated its studio and offices to the mansion. I'm talking about pornography, Mr. Westmore. My husband was a very sexually obsessed man. He surrounded himself with sexual energy."

Yeah, this is crazy, all right. This woman's paying me a ton of money to . . . watch porn?

"Don't share anything exclusive you discover with the others; that's essential. I only trust Karen, and Mack, my security man. The others I'm not sure about. I have no reason to trust them. They're all a bunch of writers, too."

I knew it. "What can you tell me about the mansion?"

"It's . . . indescribable. It's like nothing you've ever seen. And it has . . . a rich past, which I'm sure you'll discover along the way." Then she smiled.

This was too many curve balls too fast. "Mrs. Hildreth, you're paying me an awful lot of money, and I'm still not exactly sure what you want me to do."

"Ultimately, I want to know where my husband is, and beyond that, I want to know the limits of his obsession. My husband was preparing for something he thought would occur in the future. I want to know what—exactly—it was he was preparing for. And I want to know when. Remember that above all else."

At this point all Westmore could do was slump back in the wire chair. He put his hands up. "I don't know what you mean."

When Vivica Hildreth turned her head slightly, her angle shrouded her face in darkness.

"I don't believe in the Devil, Mr. Westmore. But my husband did."

Chapter Three

I

Nyvysk had no sensitivities, and he was grateful for that. He'd seen enough to believe it all, though. How could he not? In Nineveh he'd been sent to the site of the Library of Ashurbanipal—in the '80s before the Iraq wars—and had failed in exorcizing some *thing* out of a local woman who was speaking what sounded like Zraetic, the first protodialect of the Tabernacle of God. It was supposedly the language that was spoken before Adam and Eve. Nyvysk had stood there in his Catholic raiments, *The Rites of Exorcism* limp in his hand, and then watched a young Kurd in his twenties channel out a noxious endoplasm from the woman's eyes after which she vomited up a pile of live frogs. Nyvysk remembered the young man's name—Saeed—and remembered the effect of his ministration. The local woman had been cured on the spot, leaving Nyvysk to stand there, a fascinated failure.

He'd seen all that, and a lot more.

He pulled the van into a Citgo station once he'd gotten off of 275. *I don't know where I'm going,* he realized with a chuckle. He wouldn't have even taken this job; he liked to think of himself as a part-time retiree. And he didn't really need the money—he made plenty of that with his books, even after the fifty-percent he gave to the Church. But there'd been something about the woman's invitation . . .

And Nyvysk, in all truth, was bored.

He drove a long Ford step van, white, innocuous. He'd taken the wrong turn-off and wound up in this frowzy beach town. Several construction workers were filling up their trucks, one nodded to him as though they were comrades of the same trade. Of course, right now, with the banged-up van and scruffy beard, Nyvysk could pass for a blue-collar redneck himself. The thought amused him: *Your truck's full of tools. Care to guess what my truck's full of?*

His first name was Alexander. He was six-foot-five and sixty years old. So much field work for the Diocese had left him rugged, tough. Not your typical priest. *If they could see me now,* he thought, catching his reflection in the gas-station's plate glass. *I look like somebody in ZZ Top.* Gray hair down to the bottom of his ribs, and a grayer beard to his sternum. Workboots, faded jeans, baggy t-shirt. He tended to dress like this most of the time; a counselor at the mental health rectory in Richmond had told him that it was proof of his repentance, a concerted effort on his part to appear unattractive "to other—er . . . to those who might be attracted to you in a prurient sense," a sideswipe reference to his weakness. The beard and the long hair, too. For decades he'd had a buzz-cut and been clean shaven save for a moustache.

I guess I'm a pretty content mess, he thought.

The only thing that didn't look the part was the large black cross around his neck.

A middle-aged couple crossing the lot on foot were arguing, a blonde wearing an amethyst necklace and a goateed guy in a t-shirt that read JOY DIVISION. They held hands but looked like they couldn't stand each other. *I better not ask them,* Nyvysk thought. Inside when he paid for his gas, an old man at the counter, wearing a cross, gave him the eye when he asked, "Could you tell me how to find Prospect Hill? I'm looking for a place called the Hildreth Mansion."

"I've no idea. Next in line!"

Ah, yes, Nyvysk thought, and reflected the first Book of Peter. *"Honor all men. Love the brotherhood." God be with you anyway.* Back outside, the couple stood by the pumps, embracing, kissing fervently. "I fucking adore you," the goateed guy whispered to the woman.

That was quick. Love is everywhere. Nyvysk asked, "Pardon me but have you heard of Prospect Hill? I'm trying to find the—"

"Hildreth House?" the woman asked, green eyes shining like emeralds.

"Yes," Nyvysk said. "Good guess."

The goateed guy pushed wire-rim glasses up his nose. "It's a pretty famous place . . . and it's the only building on the hill. Take a left onto Prospect Hill Road off 66th Street, and that'll take you there. But once you get there, you'll never be seen again."

Nyvsyk's brow ridged.

"It's haunted," added the girl.

"We're kidding!" the guy said. He had a tattoo on his

forearm that read NARRATION IS YOUR ENEMY. "There was a mass-murder there last month. Kooky rich guy cut up a bunch of house guests with an ax."

Now Nyvysk smiled. "So I've heard. Thank you for the directions." Nyvysk unconsciously diddled with the large cross around his neck. "Let me leave you now with this: 'Fear ye not, stand still, and see the salvation of the Lord.' Oh, and Go Devil Rays."

"Cool," the guy said.

"Why are you going to the Hildreth Mansion?" the girl asked.

"I'm a demonologist and a technical paranormal investigator," Nyvysk said, and got back in his van and drove away.

Five miles and a bridge behind him, Nyvysk spotted a tiny roadsign on the thoroughfare for Prospect Hill Road. Then he winced over a pot-hole, heard something clatter in the back. *Probably the influx tubes of the chromatograph,* he feared. *Or my $50,000 barometer.* Then he saw another sign: JCT - STATE ROUTE 666. *You've got to be kidding me,* he thought. He peered incredulous at the map and saw that the road did indeed exist but thankfully led elsewhere. Then he slowed in the right lane, watching for his turn.

A Muslim—nineteen or twenty perhaps—was hitchhiking. Nyvysk's eyes locked, and he felt something tighten in his chest. The hitcher reminded him of the young Kurd who'd exorcized the woman in Nineveh, the boy named Saeed. The memory seemed to fog about his head: how, when the rite was over, the boy smiled at the younger, slimmer, and much-less-shaggy Nyvysk. How their eyes had locked. The silent invitation mouthed on the Kurd's lips and how hurt those eyes had appeared when Nyvysk sighed and turned away.

Nyvysk touched his cross. *Thank you, God, for giving me the strength to never break my vows . . .*

He knew it was completely disconnected but it seemed that his quelled libido had been raging over the past few days—since he'd gotten the letter from Vivica Hildreth.

Everywhere he went now it seemed that lust was being aimed at him from so many wide-open eyes.

He bit his lip and drove on, watching the boy fade in his rearview.

He blanked his mind for quite a while.

"This can't be it," he complained to himself later but took a hard left turn anyway. He knew the interstate north was coming up, and it didn't look like there was room for too many more turns. The road wasn't on the map, either, but there was a listing in the phone book. *Maybe that couple at the gas station are having a laugh on the old guy right now . . .* But just as he'd lost his faith, less than a hundred feet up the gravel road he'd just turned on to, the bent sign stood: PROSPECT HILL RD. *Why put the damn sign here! It should be on the corner—you know—where people can SEE it!* Then another dissociated thought flicked in his head.

Maybe they didn't want people to see it . . .

The road wound through a dense forest full of weeping willows and very strange, very tall pine trees. He noticed not one of the palm trees that Florida was known for. Spanish moss hung off branches of the trees which lined the road, creating a green curtain. Who would put a house—a *mansion* no less—in the middle of the woods? The road kept winding upward, and seemed to grow more narrow. Branches, like skeletal hands, scratched against the van's side panels, and overhead, more, broader, branches reached across the road, joining, forming a webwork tunnel that filtered out the sunlight. Nyvysk soon felt certain that he was on the wrong road when he was at last emptied into a green clearing surrounded by a ring of trees.

And there the Hildreth Mansion stood, as if in wait.

My God, it's huge . . .

Nyvysk slowed, then stopped to stare at the place. What faced him was a Gothic immensity, five stories of gray brick staring back. Stained-glass windows glittered like bizarre dark gems; oddly placed stone verandas seemed ensconced into the heavy walls. Were the high corner-posts of the building made of iron? Things he guessed were decorative gargoyles sat perched on intricate cornices like transfigured crows. Bow windows with sloping, slate half-roofs extruded from the first story's east and west wings, and stained-glass windows—these diamond-shaped—were set along the sides of the mansion's central structure. Parapets on either side extended over sloping dormers of the fifth floor, rung with spiked crestings.

Nyvysk—though he wasn't psychic at all—could feel the ill-omen hovering over the place, like a murky cloud.

He actually got out of the van to look further, still a hundred yards away. The feel in his gut, and simply the way the sun was half-blocked by the mansion's highest peak, reminded him of a time when he was in Jerusalem, just north of the Damascus Gate. Here, he'd succeeded in an exorcism—an infant—and when he'd looked up he saw a similar murkiness just over the area where Christ had likely been buried. He closed his eyes now but could still see the sunlight through the lids, and he prayed, *Yes, God, I'm really going to need courage this time. Please give me courage.*

When he opened his eyes again, he noticed that the house's massive arched doorway stood open now. Someone was standing under the keystone, waving at him.

II

"I'm flattered that you find me attractive," Vivica Hildreth said, her eyes narrowed. She uncrossed her legs, then recrossed them in the wire chair. "Everybody likes to be admired, even if they act like they don't."

Westmore nearly fell out of his own chair; the suddenness of the comment—a total shift in subjects—threw him for a loop. He blushed, because he knew why she'd said this. "I . . . apologize. I guess I've been . . . staring at you. I didn't mean to."

"Not staring—appraising, maybe. Don't worry, Mr. Westmore. It makes me feel better. Most men are put off by me."

By now, Westmore was growing accustomed to the awkwardness of the day. "I don't know why. You're a very interesting woman."

She took off the Paisley shawl, her breasts blooming beneath the t-shirt. He guessed she was teasing him now, overtly. "You're a very intriguing man. It's regrettable that we don't have anything in common."

Now all Westmore could do was shake his head and laugh. "Come on! DeKooning?"

"Not to mention that I would never cheat on my husband. If you are able to discern that he's dead, though . . . who knows what the future might hold?"

I do not believe this . . .

Her voice edged down. "Do you know what the future holds?"

"No, I don't."

"Well, then. Time . . . will tell." Her breasts, standing out, preceded her words—the bright-eyed pop baroness in flipflops. "Strange day, huh, Mr. Westmore?"

"Yes."

She stood up, and bid the exit with her hand. "You're about to walk into a very strange week. Good luck."

I guess that means I'm leaving. He rose and shook her hand again, felt a static charge crackle when their skin made contact.

"As I've said, there will be others at the house with you, but remember whom you're working for."

Westmore raised a brow. "I thought I was working for you."

"You are, and anything you discover while you're staying at my husband's house—anything *sensitive* . . . you're not to share that with anyone else. Report, in private to me. I can be reached on my cell phone at all times. You're not to give the number to anyone else."

"Understood," Westmore said, but he still didn't really understand much at all. *I guess she wants me to find out everything I can about what happened that night, and find out where her husband is.* It was a trick-bag, though, and he knew it. Right now he knew essentially nothing about Reginald Hildreth . . . except that his obituary was faked. And he couldn't tell a soul unless he wanted Vivica's lawyers to drop a depth-charge into the middle of his life. She'd said it all a minute ago: it would be a very strange week.

She walked him to the foyer. "I'd like you to start tomorrow. Is that acceptable to you?"

"Sure."

"I'm glad. Then go now, to prepare. Karen will be driving you home. She'll give you some things when she drives you back, and any cursory questions you can ask her. She'll be staying at the house, too."

"What about you?" Westmore asked next and then wished he hadn't. His reactive flirtation was amateurish, nothing like hers. "Will you be at the house?"

"I've never set foot in that house, Mr. Westmore," she said, then walked away.

Walking across the street, Westmore remembered what she'd said earlier, the theme of his job: *My husband was preparing for something he thought would occur in the future. I want to know what—exactly—it was he was preparing for. And I want to know when. Remember that above all else.*

"What the hell could this nut have been preparing for?" he muttered to himself. Then he patted the envelope in his pocket, the sheaf of money, and lots more to come.

Who cares? He was not terribly discontent with that acknowledgment. *At least I'm being honest when I don't deny that I'll do pretty much anything for money.*

"I'm really in need, brother," a very rough voice said. "I could use anything you can spare."

Westmore looked around, didn't see anyone. It was getting dark. Then he looked down and saw a filthy, straggly man sitting behind the garbage can next to the bus shelter that Westmore was grateful he wouldn't have to stand in today.

Rheumy eyes beseeched him. "Got my leg all shot up in Iraq."

Westmore doubted it; the leg jutting from stained shorts appeared infected from dirty needles. "Sure," he said, and reached into his pocket. *I've got a shitload of money on me,* he reminded himself. Then he gave the bum a $100 bill.

"Is that all ya got?"

Jesus, Westmore thought and walked on.

Let's see, she said she'd meet me in the oyster bar, of all places. He peered through the dark plate glass and saw Karen sitting up at the fine cherry-wood bar. It occurred to him then that he hadn't walked in here in three years. He'd al-

ways loved the place because of its posh interior darkness—
it was harder for him to see his reflection in the mirror behind the liquor shelves.

A few tables were full but the bar itself stood empty save
for Karen. *Oh, that's just great, she's tying one on,* he thought.
She tossed back her blonde bangs and took a slug from a
preposterously large martini glass full of glowing-blue ice.

Westmore winced when he saw what rested just next to
her: two glasses, a Dewar's on the rocks and a ginger ale.

Now how the hell did she . . .

Karen seemed to be staring at space as she sipped the
massive drink.

"I'm back," Westmore said.

"Did I get it right?" She pointed to the two glasses next
to her.

"Yes, but I don't drink anymore."

"Oh, I know that. But you always order a scotch and
don't drink it. At your neighborhood bar where you live?
Every night? The Sloppy Heron, the place is called. But
several years ago, you'd skip the ginger ale and drink eight
or ten Dewar's. Same thing here, too, right? This oyster bar
we're sitting in right now? You used to come here a lot,
didn't you?"

"Yeah. And I used to get *thrown out* of here a lot. I'm very
happy that I quit drinking." Westmore sat down with a sigh.
For some reason or other, the meeting with Vivica—however thrilling—left him exhausted now.

"So if you're trying to quit drinking—"

"Not *trying*," Westmore corrected her. "I *did* quit." He
knew what was coming next.

"Then why do you still go to bars? Why put a drink in
front of you? I'd think the temptation would be over-
whelming sometimes."

"It isn't. And I do it because it helps me think. I'm a writer. Writers have weird self-rituals." He picked the glass up, peering into its amber. "I like to look at it. I like to hear the ice clink. I like to sniff it. It clears my head." He smiled at the glass. "It's my abstraction. It's my crystal ball."

"It's interesting that you should say that. One of the people at the house is a crystal gazer," she said.

"Really?"

"Perhaps she has her self-rituals too." Karen twirled a finger in her drink, then pointed to Westmore's scotch. "Have you ever seen the future in it?"

"Not now. But I used to. I used to look in these glasses of eight-dollar hooch, and see my death. Right outside by the bus stop there's a homeless bum. He looks like he's rotting. I used to see a guy like that a lot in my future."

"Well, that's cool. I can control it, though. I'm not an alcoholic. I believe that anything in moderation makes you a better person."

Baby, YOU'RE an alcoholic, he thought when he saw her finish the martini. "There's no such thing as moderation, not for me. The clinical addiction rate for alcohol is about fifteen percent. I'm one of those fifteen."

She looked away wistfully. "A false romanticism, though, right? Like Hemingway? All creative people have a demon that's more powerful than them."

"That's an interesting observation."

"And let me guess. You're a drinker with a writing problem."

Westmore smiled. "Hey, that's a great line!"

She ordered another martini. "Blue cheese in the olive this time," she said rather testily to the keep. Then, to Westmore: "I'm glad you can refrain from temptation. You're going to need that power."

Westmore sniffed his drink. Sharp vapors titillated him. "Where? At the house? Or, excuse me, the Hildreth Mansion?"

She didn't say anything. She just smiled to the mirror behind the liquor shelves.

Westmore ordered a dozen oysters on the half-shell, then pegged her, "So you guys put a tail on me, hired an investigator? Can't imagine how else you'd know that I used to come to this bar, that I always order a Dewar's and don't drink it, and the name of my local hangout."

"Of course we did," she said. "Vivica is a cautious person. She's also a determined one."

Westmore remained quietly bewildered. The herbal scent of her hair kept drifting over, distracting him. *It's a good thing I like puzzles,* he thought. When his plate of oysters arrived, Karen smiled and said, "Is there something you're not telling me?"

"What?"

"Oysters. It's true what they say."

"Oh, yeah?"

"Yeah." She snorted a laugh. "They make me horny as fuck."

The abruptness of that particular word jolted him. It didn't sound right coming out of the mouth of someone he perceived as a stiff, proper business woman. Even stranger was that after she'd made the comment, she returned to sipping her drink and looking straight ahead. *I guess I better not offer her some,* he thought as a joke. Instead, he sucked a few down and said, "It's probably all just psychological."

"You don't know the meaning of the word psychological until you spend a night in that house. The place will . . . make you take a good, long look at yourself."

"I don't know what you're talking about but I guess I'll

find out tomorrow. So you'll be picking me up? I'd take a cab but I don't know where the place is."

"I'll find you." She turned and leaned over, reaching for something on the floor. Westmore looked at the wide tan thighs spreading the black skirt, the dip of the obviously implanted breasts as gravity pitched them forward. *This is one hell of a day for innuendo. First, Vivica practically comes on to me, and now I've got this sexual fireplug getting hammered and talking about oysters as aphrodisiacs.*

She handed him a small briefcase. "Here's some info on the victims, if you could call them that. Resumes and stage photos, police reports—mostly drug-related—and autopsy reports. They're all pretty much the same."

"And most of the victims were—"

"Porn stars, yes. Two men, the rest women—all very attractive. Mr. Hildreth liked to surround himself with what he called 'positive visual energy.' That's why he bought T&T Enterprises. He saw the people in it, liked the way they looked, so he bought the company. Then he re-based it in the mansion."

"A porn studio in a Gothic mansion?"

"Yes."

Westmore had to ask. "Where do you fit in here?"

"I was the company's accountant."

"Well, you kind of have that 'accountant' look. Kind of."

Karen got it. "Yes, Mr. Westmore, I used to be one of his movie girls, too. From age twenty to about twenty-five. After twenty-five, in that business, you're considered old news."

More interesting information, but Westmore wondered what use it would be. "Tell me about Hildreth. Did he and Vivica have any kids?"

"God, no. I can't imagine a couple less cut out for children."

"How old was he? What did he look like?"

"He was about sixty. And he was tall. He was a strikingly handsome man."

Westmore was careful to use the past tense because he wasn't sure if Karen knew Hildreth's obituary was fraudulent. This was a crux.

She slipped out a glossy eight-by-ten and passed it to him. "Meet Reginald Hildreth."

Almost a cliche. Longish, swept-back dark hair, "distinguished" gray at the temples, obviously a good dye job. Searching eyes, thin lips, long thin face. *Debonair but tainted,* Westmore perceived. *He looks like a rich phony.* "And you think this guy murdered all those people? With an ax?"

"Yes."

"Why? Because he was insane?"

"I don't believe he was insane," Karen stared straight ahead and finished her next martini.

"I don't know, and forgive me for being judgmental, but if a guy chops a bunch of people up with an ax—to me, that's a pretty good sign of a mental instability."

Her ice-blue eyes slowly turned to him. "You don't know what instability is." She maintained the deadpan expression for several seconds . . . then smiled.

Wow.

Westmore shook his head when she ordered yet another martini. "Mr. Hildreth didn't kill all of them, of course—he just had the denouement, his final act. Somebody else killed the prostitutes."

"Prostitutes?"

"The crack-whores upstairs." She pointed to the briefcase. "It's all in there. I think it was Three-Balls who killed them."

"Three-Balls?" Westmore made a face. "That's somebody's *name?*"

"Yeah, one of the . . . *actors*. He had three testicles, some genetic thing. Perfect for the porn business."

Westmore's mind raced to assimilate the information but before he could ask his next question, she pointed to the briefcase again. "His fingerprints were found on the knives in the parlor. It's all in there, in the cop reports. Hildreth's were found on the ax."

"Where," he began, then thought, *Careful!* "Where was Hildreth buried after his suicide?"

"The cemetery on the property."

That's rich, Westmore thought.

"The other guy was Jaz."

"The other—oh, the other male victim?"

"You'll see. Jaz was another natural. Had a cock on him like a knockwurst."

Another jolt.

She continued: "It was almost funny how you could tell who was who just by their body parts—a lot of them were beheaded, dismembered, like that. The girls weren't as easy, of course, but you could tell by their tit-jobs and pussies. And the guys? One had his head cut off, and the other was cut in half. But you could tell which body was which by their cocks."

Westmore sat stunned, by the combination of the horrid imagery and her sudden shift to slutty anatomical nouns. He couldn't respond for several moments but the obvious occurred to him rather quickly. "How did you know that?" he asked very slowly.

"I was the one who discovered the bodies," Karen said. She didn't flinch at the acknowledgment. "I drove into work the next morning, like I always do. Right after sun-up. I walk into the house, and there it was. Everyone dead, everyone butchered. There was blood everywhere, and it was still wet."

Westmore's mind reeled. *Hildreth turned the place into a slaughter house, and I'm supposed to find out everything that happened that night.* Kind of like being sent into a death camp after all the prisoners had been incinerated. All of a sudden this dream job was losing its luster, even in spite of the money.

Silence. It was awkward, there in the dark bar, and all this looming ahead of him. The barkeep stood at the other end, talking to the oyster man. Westmore felt isolated from everything, as though the few people around him existed in a different plane of existence, and he was somewhere else looking in. His eyes fell on the full glass of scotch—his crystal ball—and in that gold-tinted ice he saw something chaotic yet undefinable.

He shivered when Karen's hand touched his thigh. Her fingers squeezed, then slid an inch toward his crotch.

"What are you—"

Her drunken gaze looked faraway yet very focused, burning. *Of course she's drunk,* he rationalized. *Of course she's gonna be half out of her mind for a while. She's the one who discovered the bodies . . .*

"What's wrong?" she asked.

He was going to grab her hand, urge it away. He felt embarrassed, on edge . . .

"Don't worry, no one can see." Fingers worked higher on the inside of his thigh. Then she said, "Look."

Westmore looked down. She'd hitched the black skirt up, parted her own thighs more. No panties down there.

Fantastic. A drunken nympho.

"Let me drive you home now. We'll do it at your place."

Finally words ground out of Westmore's mouth. "This is crazy. What are you doing?"

"I'm coming on to you. This is Florida, remember? All men are cockhounds, all women are sluts."

"I don't ever remember seeing that endorsement at the Florida Department of Tourism." Again, his thoughts told him to push her hand away but instead, he just sat there. Now she was openly caressing his crotch. Westmore's gut squirmed in a mad arousal.

"What's the matter? This defies your sense of morality?" she joked, her voice a lulling whisper. "You've never picked up a woman in a bar and fucked her?"

"Plenty of times, and it's always a mistake." Still embarrassed, he glanced over and saw the barkeep and oyster shucker still too far away to see or hear.

"Let me blow you in the car . . . "

Common sense propped up as fast as his erection. He grabbed her hand, placed it on her own thigh, then hitched the hem of her skirt down.

"We both work for the same person—"

"Moral turpitude?" she slurred a laugh.

"Yeah." He left money on the bar and rose, grabbed the small attache case she'd brought. "I have some research to do tonight."

"Of course. The dutiful reporter."

"And I'll grab the bus back. You're too drunk to drive me or yourself anywhere." He pulled out his cell phone. "Let me call you a cab."

"Not necessary." She looked idly at her drink, which was almost done. "I'm staying in Vivica's guest room tonight. I'll pick you up tomorrow and take you to the mansion."

"Great." The wake of the uncomfortable situation left his words stilted, phony. He just wanted to get out. "See ya tomorrow," and then he shook her hand quickly and walked out.

Unbelievable, he thought. *I'm flypaper for whackos.*

A gust of relief when he looked at his watch: the trolley home only came once an hour down here but he'd only have a five-minute wait. The city was cooling down as the sun sunk. Very few cars could be seen. The streets seemed pin-drop quiet.

The scene with Karen bothered him; in his drinking days, he'd have been all over it. But all he was left with now was the numb arousal and a primal regret. Bar pick-ups weren't his style anymore; it seemed vapid, juvenile.

"Somebody else is gonna fuck her," a voice rattled.

It was the bum, still essentially collapsed in place by the bus-stop garbage can.

"You a faggot or something? That bitch is a hot number. You should'a seen her in the movies."

"How do you know she was in movies?" Westmore blurted in irritation. Out here, the man couldn't possibly have heard their conversation at the bar.

"I know lots of shit, man." His face was a shadow, below the level of Westmore's waist. "Someone tells me things sometimes."

"Yeah? Who?"

"Your father."

Westmore squeezed his eyes shut for a moment. "My father's dead."

"I know."

Sure you do. "I'm surprised my mother didn't tell you—she's dead too."

The bum paused. "I didn't know that."

Westmore let it pass. His mother was alive and well and living in San Angelo, Texas. "Look, man. I know you need help. I'd be happy to call the county and find out where the nearest shelter is."

"Fuck that. Gimme more money. You've got a shitload on you."

The homeless crazies always seemed to pick Westmore out—they always had. But there was nothing he could do for this one. The downtown trolley squeaked up, its doors flipping open. When Westmore stepped aboard, the bum kept croaking, "Hey! Hey!" but it sounded more like a dog barking.

Westmore got on and paid. The bum kept yelling.

"More and more of these crazy guys keep landing here," the driver said. "Each year there's more."

"Mmm," Westmore murmured. Now the bum was practically hysterical. "Can't even understand the poor guy."

"You're going to a house?"

Westmore stalled in the aisle, turned. "What?"

The driver was pulling away. "That crazy. He was yelling 'Have fun at the house.'"

Westmore sat down, feeling sidetracked and ill. He glanced back through the window, stared, and blinked.

In the shadow, the bum didn't appear to be the bum anymore. The face within the hood seemed highly angled—a wedge—with a hole for a nose and teeth gleaming through a lipless mouth. Darkness blacker than the shadow radiated in eyes like knife-slits in meat. The arms rose, a taloned finger pointing back at Westmore as the bus rumbled away.

Chapter Four

I

"Father Nyvysk?"

"Just . . . Nyvysk," Nyvysk corrected.

"Oh, right. Thanks for coming. Most of the others are already here."

Nyvysk knew most of them, except for this much younger man who'd shown him in.

"I'm Mack Colmes," came an enthused introduction. "I'll be taking you to the South Atrium now. The mansion is big, and confusing at first. But you'll get the hang of it. I'll bet this whole thing turns out to be a blast."

A youngster, Nyvysk thought at once. *Fire in the eyes. He thinks this is a field trip.* "You're a psychic?" he asked but seriously doubted it.

"No, sir. I'm just the security guy. I'll be staying at the house with you guys, just to check the grounds, the alarm, stuff like that. I work for Vivica. The psychic stuff—that's your turf." Short-haired, muscular, a fast bounce in his step. The FLORIDA STATE muscle shirt, knee-length shorts, and expensive sneakers with no socks made him look like a typical spring-breaker. "You've got your equipment outside, right?"

"In the van, yes."

"And there's another truck coming?"

"Yes, hopefully within the hour. Bunks, partitions, supplies. I ordered it all with Mrs. Hildreth's permission, on her account."

Mack nodded. "Yeah, Vivica said that you'd kind of been appointed as the boss of the operation."

"Not the boss, the coordinator," Nyvysk corrected. He'd been on jaunts like this before, and without someone supervising domestically, bedlam soon ensued. *Especially with this group,* he realized. *The craziest of the bunch, at least in this country.*

The inside of the mansion stunned him more than the exorbitant exterior. Trimmings of a thousand-square-foot black-marble foyer made him feel as though he'd just stepped into a cross between a museum, art gallery, and antique exhibition. Handsewn Tablez throw rugs with Byzantinesque patterns lay arranged around the foyer's perimeter, while a dozen foot-tall granite statues stood in the center. Nyvysk—a historian—didn't recognize the brooding, long-coated figure. "Who's the sculpture? Klinnrath?"

"Oh, I don't know," Mack answered. "I'm not into it."

"It's Edward Kelly," a voice informed him from the short banistered galleria overlooking them a story up. "Dr. John Dee's apprentice in alchemy and sorcerial science."

"Willis," Nyvysk greeted when he raised his eyes. He knew the tactionist from a previous outing and some documentary shows. The man was as real as they came—too real, actually. Nyvysk was surprised Willis hadn't committed suicide by now. "How have you been?"

"Lousy, until I got this invitation."

"It should be an interesting junket, or we can at least hope so."

Willis' appearance had worsened since their last meeting—a secret appreciation of Nyvysk's—handsome but haggard, older than his years, a man who'd seen too much from the inside out. Yet he smiled down genuinely in spite of the psychical corrosion that his talents had exacted on him. He pointed to the statue. "If you're interested, Hildreth's main library has some Dee translations—originals—and some letters from Kelly."

"You're joking."

"Nope. There's nothing fake in this house," and then Willis glanced to Mack. "Right, Mack."

The young security man frowned, which Nyvysk found interesting. The two couldn't possibly know each other.

"Yeah, that's right," Mack snapped back.

"We're down here," Willis redirected his attention to Nyvysk. "Come on in."

Willis disappeared through an inlaid walnut door.

"I don't know where you want all your gear set up, but let me know and I'll get it moved in," Mack offered.

"Thank you. I'm too old to do much lugging." Nyvysk paused a moment. "You seem to be acquainted with Willis."

"Don't know him," Mack said, then walked on. "Follow me."

Before Nyvysk could speculate further, his curiosity was hijacked by more of the mansion's nearly sinister splendor. Great arched doorways with wood-carven faces peered down from each point. Most doorway transoms sported a small brass plaque: THE CAGLIOSTRO PARLOR, THE BONNEVAULT SITTING ROOM, THE BRUHESSEN HALL, each room named for some wizard, astrologer, or metaphysical scientist. Rich veneered wood paneled most rooms; a variety of dark imported carpets changed the tone of each area they passed through: a vast dining room, some sitting rooms, a smoking parlor, and then a brightly lit morning room whose exterior wall was all bizarrely etched with lead-seamed glass, some panes with tiny octagon inlays of vermillion or amaranth crystal. Sideboards, armoires, and ball-footed drop-leaf tables lined more walls, over which hung dark oil paintings of solemn, intent faces, centuries-old portraitures of the most famous, and infamous, figures of paranormal and occult arts. Obscure crystals looked back at him like unblinking eyes from high-mounted trivets and gem-mounts: the rare ones such as amethyst, white-lapis, Anpiel Stone. Ornately framed mirrors, some occupying whole sections of wallspace, hung in abundance, too, and more, smaller oculi and lunette windows shot narrow lengths of sunlight across walking areas, an interesting effect. But even the well-windowed rooms held on to spots and corners of murk that shouldn't be there, as if refusing to release that darkness that this house must be so used to.

Next, a long windowless hall—THE BUGUET WALK, named for the French spirit photographer—and Nyvysk was starting to get queasy from all the plush decor, like after eating too much of a fine, rich dinner. More portraits, gemlike knickknacks, granite busts and sculpture—and expensive antiques. The walls of this corridor were covered in leather and onyx-button studs.

The next inlaid door had no title, just SOUTH ATRIUM. When Mack went to reach for the iron latch-hasp knob, Nyvysk asked, "What's that?" and pointed to a covered wood panel at the door's side.

Mack slid it open, revealing a small screen and some push-buttons. "Videocom. They're all over the place. You'll need to know how it works so I might as well show you now."

Nyvysk watched.

"East, north, south, west, in that order," the young man said, and hit the #3 button. "Three is south and we're in the south wing of the house. And because we're on the first level . . . ," he pushed #1. The small LCD screen lit up. "Now, listen." He pushed another button which read TRANSCEIVE and held it down. "There's microphones in every room, and video cameras too."

"It seems excessive for inside. I take it Mr. Hildreth was very security conscious . . . or very paranoid."

"No, but he was a pervert and a voyeur," Mack responded without pause. "He liked to hear what people were saying when they were f—" Mack's eyes stole a glance to Nyvysk's cross. "Sorry, I keep forgetting you're a priest—"

"No, not anymore. Just a writer and researcher."

The security man seemed confused. "But anyway . . . Mr. Hildreth liked to listen to people when they were—you know."

"Of course."

"And he liked to watch."

Nyvysk wasn't surprised, based on the little he'd learned so far of the billionaire. "Well, I just hope that the bathrooms aren't similarly equipped," he joked.

"Actually, they are, but they're not accessible from the door units, just the communications room, which I'll show you later."

Nyvysk surveyed Mack's face. *He's serious!* "I . . . can't wait for my first expedition to the toilet."

"Nobody will be looking." Mack smiled and went on with more instructions for the videocom, keeping his finger on the transception button. Nyvysk heard voices and saw on the screen a numbered list. A red light blinked at one listing: 7) SOUTH ATRIUM. "The red light means people are talking there, so you—" then he pushed the #7 key. "There. See?" The screen changed to video; Nyvysk could see Willis and the others, sitting on several long, gold-velvet scroll-armed couches. "And if you don't know where the South Atrium is—" Mack pushed another button which read MAP. The screen now showed a map of the mansion's south wing. "The system covers the entire house and parts of the grounds. Just like Windows XP!" Mack joked.

Nyvysk was impressed, and already considering an essential modification for their stay. "This is an impressive system. It must have cost—"

"Couple million. Chump change to Mr. Hildreth."

"I'd like to see the communications room."

"Sure. But let's go to the South Atrium first, get stuff settled."

Mack pulled open the doors and showed Nyvysk into what was easily a five-thousand square-foot room. More imported oval carpets covered a shining hardwood floor. Long tables, scroll-top desks, and meticulous stands and day-beds filled the vast space. Heavily draped bow windows lined one wall; banistered stairs cut diagonally up another. A number of chandeliers glittered from oak rafters above, a prism-angled vaulted ceiling which rose thirty feet. Above the rafters, Nyvysk even noticed veneered catwalks with long mahogany rails, leading to small door-like panels, each marked by a carved lion's head. *The House of Seven Gables,* Nyvysk thought. The overall effect seemed focused on the ambience, which he guessed was what Hildreth wanted.

Then Nyvysk winced.

Two main walls were paneled to dado level; from the molding up, then, the walls were covered in a rich avocado-green velour that shimmered depending on the angle one stood. A bas-relief pattern of minutely detailed shield-shapes (scutations) printed against the velour. Three couches provided the room's point of congress, and what totally spoiled the effect for him was an immense flat-screen television before which the other members of the party sat, drinking coffee and sodas.

They were watching the Food Network.

"Nyvysk!" exclaimed Cathleen Godwin, sitting up alertly. "Your beard's longer!"

"I suppose it is, Cathleen. Good to see you."

Cathleen dressed provocatively as ever in stonewashed skirt-shorts and a clinging raspberry scoopneck, long legs crossed and a transparent slide-sandal—luminous pink—dangling off a foot. Slouched at the other end of the couch was Adrianne Saundlund, the telethesist. Her eyes drooped at the TV. *Probably on downers,* Nyvysk speculated. Her slim body looked tiny in the denim overall shorts and baggy green t-shirt beneath. *Dead to the world, or at least this one . . .* Nyvysk knew her story from a variety of sources. "Hello, Adrianne."

She didn't even notice him until his voice dragged her eyes up. "Oh, hi. Sorry—I'm just out of it right now, really tired."

"Well, perhaps this little excursion will perk us all up."

"I could use that."

Willis rose from the other couch. "She's engrossed in the Food Network, which might do us some good, 'cos we're going to need someone to cook."

"I *can't* cook," Cathleen asserted.

Adrianne half-laughed. "Neither can I, but the kitchen and pantry are incredible here."

Willis came over and shook Nyvysk's hand. Nyvysk knew that Willis didn't really have friends—he avoided proximities as much as possible—but now he seemed less down-trodden than when they'd spoken in the foyer. Perhaps he was happy to see a familiar face. "This was some rabbit out of the hat, huh?"

"It could wind up being more than a rabbit," Nyvysk said, not surprised that the man wore gloves. Tactionists entering middle-age often wore them, since the "current" possessed by tainted objects and people were more perceptible at this time of life.

"Sure, it could be a monster." Willis laughed. "But I gotta be honest, I need the money so bad I'll take the chance."

Mack offered a comment. "Really? I heard you were a successful doctor," but there was an edge to the words, a buried snideness.

"I'm not a doctor anymore," Willis said, smirking.

"And Nyvysk's not a priest anymore, and Adrianne's not a party animal anymore," Cathleen laughed. "And, me? Let's see, I'm not . . . twenty anymore."

"Looks like everybody here used to be something that we no longer are."

"I'd rather look at it as evolvement," Nyvysk offered. "It's not what we aren't anymore. It's more important what we've become."

"Thank you, Aristotle," Adrianne said.

But Willis was casting a darker eye toward Mack. "What about you? What *aren't you* anymore?"

"I'm what I've always been, *Doctor* Willis. A security manager."

More indecipherable barbs. *I'm going to have to find out about this,* Nyvysk thought. He'd never been interested in gossip, but mental hostilities—especially among paranormalists—could effect scientific sensors, sometimes drastically. *Why do these men dislike each other?* he asked himself.

"Have you seen the rest of the mansion?" Cathleen asked.

"No, I just arrived."

"There's thirteen bedrooms," Willis informed.

"Mr. Hildreth liked that number," Mack said. "But there are sixty-six rooms in the house, all told."

"Jeez," Adrianne said. "I'm already thinking the guy was an idiot. I'll bet his hero was Anton LeVey."

Nyvysk chose not to guess this early. Ninety percent of the time there was nothing genuine behind any so-called occultist, but Nyvysk had seen that other ten percent too many times. *And so have they,* he reminded himself, looking back at the others.

"Have you seen this?" Willis asked. He'd drifted back toward the entrance, was looking at the videocom. "The whole mansion's wired. I'll bet your brain's already ticking on this one."

"Of course it is. Depending on the central system's specs, I should be able to monitor EVP on it without having to set up my own network. IR, thermal, and magnetic-mass sensors might work too."

"Ever the ghost buster," Adrianne said. "We bring our bodies, he brings his toys."

"I brought some toys, too," Cathleen remarked, then laughed. "Oh, *those* kind of toys."

"You probably have a whole suitcase of them," Willis said.

"Or maybe a steamer trunk. Adrianne the born-again celibate is here. She might need a little plastic boredom relief."

"That's not true celibacy," Adrianne reminded. "Right, Nyvysk?"

"Quite true. Constantial celibacy is the willful abandonment of all sexual release."

Mack smirked. "If you guys are talking about vibrators, there's a parlor upstairs full of them."

"That's right, this place used to be a porn studio," Willis remarked.

Cathleen stretched her legs across to a rosette-engraved ottoman. "That's enticing. I wonder what's left over from that."

"That's part of what we're here to find out," Nyvysk said.

The jokes about vibrators, etc.—Nyvysk knew—were meant as good-natured humor. But it wasn't coming off. Already, there was something in the undercurrent here. *People like this, in close quarters, always start tearing each other up eventually,* Nyvysk realized. He suspected that some fuses had already been lit.

"Look at Willis," Cathleen said. "He's staring at that awful bust of Copernicus."

The blank-eyed statue of white, unpolished stone sat on a carved pedestal, a determined looking man in a cloak and fur-minivered cap, a book clasped to his chest.

"That's Copernicus?" Willis asked. He touched it—unafraid—with his gloved hand.

"No," Nyvysk said. "It's Julian the Apostate. He was an anthropmancer—he read the future by the casting of human entrails."

"Oh, that's just lovely," Adrianne said.

"At least I think that's who it is . . . Cathleen, you should know."

She looked at the bust and shrugged. "I don't know. But don't laugh at divination."

Willis shot another cryptic comment to Mack. "Mack probably thinks it's Ron Jeremy."

Mack exchanged a glare, and some confusing moments ticked by, in silence.

Adrianne scratched her head. "Who the hell is Ron Jeremy?"

Nyvysk had no idea.

Cathleen glanced at the TV. "Well, Martha Stewart's over now so I guess Adrianne's back with us. Instead of sitting around, why don't we all go choose our bedrooms?"

"We're standing in our bedrooms," Nyvysk said.

"What?" several people said at once.

"Our client, Mrs. Hildreth, agreed that I should be the coordinator—"

"Bullshit!" Cathleen objected.

"Not in charge, per se," Nyvysk hastened to quell her ego, "but the domestic coordinator during our stay. She agreed to that, and I think we should all go by it."

"That's fine with me," Willis said.

Adrianne shrugged, but Cathleen said, "Why? Why you?"

"Because it makes more sense from a practical standpoint."

"Just like a man!"

Adrianne looked bored. "He's right, Cathleen. He's just a technician. You, Willis, and I aren't exactly stable in certain circumstances. This place could be charged."

"You all have psychic sensitivities. I don't," Nyvysk finished.

Cathleen lay back on the couch, head staring up at a curious brass chandelier. "Okay, fine. But what's this about bedrooms?"

Nyvysk addressed them all. "I feel it's essential that we all sleep in the same area. This South Atrium seems perfect. It's large enough that we'll all have privacy when we need it. We need to be together when we're asleep—especially psychics, and especially if this house *is* charged. We're all more vulnerable in a sleep-state. Sleeping in separate rooms could be a catastrophe. The Suit Manor Case, Wroxton Hall in Maryland, the Immanuel Rectory in New York City. All of those places had serious accidents that could have been prevented had the investigators not slept in separate rooms."

Cathleen conceded. "As usual, you're right. But—damn it—I had my heart set on that huge suite on the fourth floor with the dark-blue wallpaper and crystal crosses."

Mack suddenly looked pale. "The, uh, that would be the Aldinoch Suite. That's where Mr. Hildreth had his autosexual asphyxia parties."

Cathleen blanched. "Like I said, this room is perfect."

"But where will we sleep?" Adrianne asked. "On these couches? The daybeds?"

"A delivery truck should be here any minute. Beds, partitions, nightstands, everything we need." He pointed toward the north wall and its green-velour wallcovering. "We'll set up the sleeping area over there, and over here—" he pointed to the windowed side of the room—"this will be our meeting area. We might have to bring some extra tables in, and move some of this furniture, but I doubt that Mrs. Hildreth would object."

"You can do anything you want," Mack said. "You guys have free run."

"When will we actually get started?" Willis asked Nyvysk. "With a game plan, I mean?"

"Tonight, maybe. I need to get my equipment set up. But I don't see any reason why the three of you can't start any time, with your own brand of preliminaries."

"I'm not doing *anything* today," Adrianne said. "I'm tired, and—Emeril's on, and he's doing fried turkeys."

Cathleen grinned. "Adrianne, *you* are a fried turkey," and then she shoved the other woman's shoulder. "I'm kidding!"

"I'll go check on my gear and wait for the delivery truck," Nyvysk said. He looked up at the pendulum clock by the fireplace. "Let's all meet again around seven and get something together for dinner."

"I'm all for that," Cathleen said and bounced up. Her large breasts bounced too, which was likely intentional. "Right now I'm going to find the fanciest bathroom in this whole place and take a bubble bath." She strode out of the room.

"What about you, Willis?" Nyvysk asked. "What are you going to do now?"

"I'm gonna start right now; I'm getting . . . feelings." He looked at Mack. "Which room did the murders take place in?"

"There were dead bodies on the stairs, in the first parlor on the second floor, and some of the guest suites, also on the second floor. But the majority of the people were killed in the largest suite of the fifth floor. Mr. Hildreth called it the Scarlet Room. You can find it on any of the videocom maps."

"Right." Willis hesitantly took off his gloves and left the room.

"I'll be back in a couple hours," Mack said. "If you need anything . . ." He held up his cell phone.

When Mack left, Nyvysk felt odd, alone with Adrianne. She stared at the TV, but he had to wonder how much of it she was really watching.

"When was the last time you OBE'd, Adrianne?"

"About a month ago. It was an Army check-up at Fort Meade."

"You still work for them?"

"Almost never. They consider me retirement-disabled. Now I get a check every month instead of orders."

"How did the OBE go?"

"All right. They were just testing my responses on lower doses of Lobrogaine."

Nyvysk held on to a concern. One way or another, they were all damaged. But Adrianne had the worst fears to face if this mansion was for real.

"You're still a Christian, aren't you?"

"Yeah," was all she said.

"Be careful."

"I will." She looked up suddenly, curious. She blinked out of her laze. "There's somebody else coming, too, right? A local writer?"

"I think so," Nyvysk said.

"I wonder where he is."

Chapter Five

I

The cover photography blared: white background behind a long, lean brunette with bright blue eyes and a big white smile, skintight t-shirt adhered to erect, 34C breasts. The t-shirt had a Viagra pill on it, and the words GOT WOOD? The top of the box read: T&T ENTERPRISES PRESENTS: GABRIELLE COX IN GABRIELLE'S BIG BANG. The brightness of the cover, that crystal-like clarity, seemed to hypnotize Westmore for a moment. But it wasn't just the obvious beauty of the woman, nor the glaring sexual provocation. *It's her reality,* he thought. *That's a real person on this cover.*

A dead person.

He recognized the woman's face at once, matching it to the mug-shot and the post-mortem shot from the records that Karen had given him. And her real name wasn't Gabrielle Cox, it was Jane Johnson, five-six, 119 pounds, twenty-four years old, born of a solid middle-class family from Green Bay, Wisconsin, quit college after two semesters to follow the yellow-brick road to Hollywood stardom. The pretty face and stunning body was contracted posthaste by a mediocre Redondo-Beach-based adult video company called T&T Enterprises. Shortly thereafter, she acquired a $4,500 breast-implant job, developed a mounting addiction to cocaine, had three abortions, engaged in sex acts with over 500 men and a 100 women, and appeared in 106 hard-core adult DVD's, until her career ended three weeks ago in an eccentric's mansion located on the other side of the country.

And now this is all that's left of Gabrielle Cox aka Jane Johnson of Green Bay, Wisconsin, Westmore thought, still unable to take his eyes off the cover photo. *A piece of paper on a plastic box.*

Her body had been found in the Hildreth Mansion on the morning of Saturday, April 3rd. Hands and feet severed, evidence of vigorous sexual intercourse with multiple partners. Cause of death: "strike-trauma by six-inch-wide lower-abdominal impactation," the autopsy report coldly informed—an ax buried in her belly. "With possible peri-mortal transvaginal evisceration."

Westmore closed his eyes and took a deep breath.

The place was dark, smelled sweet with something—some fashion of air-freshener. Westmore had only been in this porn shop once—oblivious—in order to buy an appropriate gag gift for a friend's bachelor party. He was as familiar with pornographic videos as he was with Euclidean geometry. He'd read somewhere once that the porn business comprised a multibillion-dollar-per-year industry now. And now, in the shop, he looked around at wall after wall of X-rated videos and DVDs. *It's a world to itself. An underworld,* he thought.

A rough but feminine voice drifted across the shop. "We've got more of hers."

Westmore saw the proprietor, from a high checkout area. "What's that?"

"More films by Gabrielle. I can check on the computer to see which ones are in stock."

Westmore walked over. A large-breasted woman with awful-looking dirty-blonde cornrows, weathered and chunky. *Rode hard and put away wet,* he deduced. "I'll take this one, and, yeah, could you check the computer for more films by T&T?"

"Sure." She was smoking a black cigarette. Stapled to the wall behind her were scores of ad posters sporting more preposterously attractive woman in striking poses, either naked or barely clothed. A stark sign at the top of the wall read ASK ABOUT OUR LINGERIE MODELS! Westmore didn't get it.

"Yeah, Gabrielle was cool. You want me to run just her films or—"

"Anything by T&T," Westmore said. "You sound like you knew Gabrielle."

"Not well. Every now and then she and the other T&T girls would come to the store to do autographs." She pointed behind her, to a poster bearing several signatures, four nude woman in a *Charlie's Angels*–type pose "Wild bunch but they were all cool. You may not know this but all their main stars were murdered early in the month."

"Yeah, I . . . heard about that. Some guy named Hildreth."

"Um-hmm."

"But explain something to me." He was looking at the back of the first DVD. "T&T Enterprises is a Florida-based company, according to the papers. Why does this disc say Redondo Beach?"

"That's where they were based before Hildreth bought them. Psycho billionaire. He bought the whole company because he saw one of their DVD's and liked their looks. Moved the company to his house, for God's sake. Before the buy, T&T released fifty movies a year, but since Hildreth bought them out, they only release a few." She paused. "Er—well, now they don't release any."

"Why is that, though? It doesn't make sense for a rich guy to buy a successful porn company and then not capitalize on its value. When rich guys buy businesses, it's for a return on their investment."

"It didn't matter—that's how rich Hildreth was." She clicked down on the computer screen, the black cigarette hanging unbecomingly off her lips. "It was an impulse-buy—seriously—because he liked the look of the girls. He moved them all into the house to live for free, like the damn Playboy Mansion. Gabrielle said he was obsessed with beautiful women, they were his furniture."

Furniture, Westmore thought, depressed by the notion. *And then he put an ax to it all.*

He wound up taking four more DVD's, T&T's final releases, which all starred most of the victims from the murder. He pulled out his wallet. "How much are these each, by the way?"

"$49.95."

Westmore about had a cow. *DAMN!* The five discs wound up costing more than half of his rent. He looked at the last one she'd taken out. Another stunning woman—a redhead with a tongue stud—standing with nothing but whipped cream over nipples and pubis, while four muscular men grinned behind her. CREAMING ON JEANNIE, it was called. He recognized the cover-model's face from a police post-mortem photograph of her severed head sitting on an autopsy table.

"Thanks. Come back again," the woman said. She'd put his purchase in a black plastic bag.

Unlikely, Westmore thought.

"Oh, and if you're interested," she added. She pointed back to that sign: ASK ABOUT OUR LINGERIE MODELS.

Confusion. "What *is* that?" he asked.

"Thirty bucks for a half hour, fifty for an hour . . ." She stood on her tiptoes, leaning over the counter, looking out. On the side of the store was a black-curtained doorway. "Hey, Natalie?" Then, to Westmore, "She's probably in there crashed. We're both pretty hungover from last night."

Westmore had no idea what was going on until the curtain parted and out stepped a Gothy young woman with black bowl-cut hair tinted by metallic pink and purple highlights. Dark eyes and eyeshadow, red lipstick. She was large-boned but not overweight, and when she came out and looked right at Westmore, she offered him a wolf-like smile. Fresh white skin radiated around lacy black lingerie.

"What, I go in there and she poses or something?"

The woman laughed. "Well, yeah, if that's all you want. But she's got a lot of repeat customers."

A stiletto heel tapped when she parted one leg. A hand drifted up to a lace-cupped breast and unseated it, showing a pert nipple.

The woman continued, "You tip for whatever extra you want. She's pretty reasonable. Handjob, blowjob, straight lay."

Westmore looked back at the woman, astounded.

"Or if I'm more your type," she finished.

This place must get busted a lot, he thought. "How do you know I'm not a cop? Just because I bought some DVDs? I could be undercover. Are you nuts?"

The woman laughed. "I know you're not a *cop.* I used to see you all the time, couple years back."

Westmore was sure this couldn't be true. "Where did you see me?"

"Pretty much any bar around here." She smiled. "Any guy who parties that hard *can't* be a cop."

Jesus. She remembers me from the bad old days. Probably saw me passed out in half the neighborhood bars . . . He was standing in a porn parlor, being propositioned for prostitution, yet *he* was the one who felt morally bankrupt. "Well, I'll pass on the offer." He held up the bag of DVDs. "But thanks for your help."

He turned to leave. He took a last look at the model in the curtain and smiled, embarrassed. She nodded, put her breast back in the bra. Then his eyes shifted in a vertigo. He stopped, focused. He knew it was just a trick of dim light but when she smiled, her face seemed to broaden and form grooves. Her mouth looked full of fangs . . .

I never should have taken that LSD in college. He rushed toward the entrance door, gratefully winced at the explosion of sunlight when he finally got back outside.

"You're the last person I'd peg as a porn-addict," someone said the second he stepped through the door. A black silhouette stood before him, forged by the glare of sun. Westmore shielded his eyes. It was Karen.

He didn't like not being able to see her; it unnerved him. He walked to the side to get the sun out of his eyes. "How the hell did you know I was here?"

"I'm psychic," she said baldly.

A moment ticked by. "Come on! Are you serious?"

"Well, no. I was a little early on my way to pick you up so I went over there." She gestured to the coffee shop across the street. "Saw you walk in." She chuckled. "You're really funny."

He felt doubly embarrassed now. "I went in there to pick

up some DVDs by Hildreth's company. Most of the girls in these are all victims of the murders. I don't know much about the adult video industry, kind of wanted to see what it's all about."

"Hardcore sex is what it's all about. But you should've saved your money. There're DVDs all over the house—you can watch 'em till your socks blow off."

Westmore felt perturbed by her tone. "You don't understand. I don't *want* to watch pornography; I'm not interested in it, and I didn't buy these to blow my socks off. I wouldn't want you to think I'm some pervert who's obsessed with that kind of thing. I bought these DVDs just to have a better understanding of that whole scene."

"Sure," she dismissed and turned. "Go get anything you want to bring. I'll wait for you in the car."

Westmore ran across the street to his cottage, grabbed his travel bag and laptop, then jogged back. Only now did he take any detailed notice of Karen, a delayed reaction—perhaps from the jolt of being caught walking out of a porn store. Her sandy-blonde hair was tied back now; she wore a field-gray tube top and black-leather jeans which, if anything, were too tight and bordering on more trampish than enticing. Sunglasses somehow de-personified her, made her appear even more stolid. But Westmore dragged his eyes away from her tube-topped bosom and the ghosts of nipples shadowed by the tight fabric.

He frowned when he noted the car she was getting into: a brand-new black Cadillac ETC convertible.

"That's funny," he joked away his jealousy. "I have the exact same kind of car . . . in the shop."

They got in, thunked the doors shut. "Really, Mr. Westmore. One of the first things we learned about you was the fact that you lost your driver's license for driving intoxicated."

"It was just a joke," he groaned. The car's passenger seat felt more comfortable than any chair he'd ever owned. "None of my business but—well, judging by these wheels, I guess Hildreth paid you pretty well."

"You're right. It *is* none of your business, and, yes, he did." She pulled out of the lot; Westmore jerked in his seat when she accelerated through a yellow light and soared over the bridge. "Mrs. Hildreth will retain me—if I'm lucky. I know she's keeping me on for a little while, at least."

"You're an accountant," he said. His hair was blowing around in the wind. "You'd be able to find work anywhere."

"I'm not an accountant, I'm a washed-up porn star," she clarified, looking ahead. She drove fast but not cockily. "I only learned how to do T&T's books by looking at them enough times. Years of doing fuck-flicks doesn't look great on a resume."

"I'm sure you'll do fine," he said for lack of anything else.

"Oh, and I'm sorry about last night," she added, and changed lanes around a slow truck.

"Sorry about what?"

"About coming on to you. You must think I'm a total tramp. I can tell you're pretty business-oriented, no non-sense. It must've made you very uncomfortable."

"My fragile psyche's not injured," he said. "It made me uncomfortable and it made my day."

She didn't laugh. "I was drunk and depressed. I always drink too much when I'm depressed."

Westmore found her sudden openness inspiring. "We all get drunk on occasion—take it from a guy who spent most of his adult life in the bag." He thought about it, then de-cided it couldn't hurt to ask. "What were you depressed about?"

Her lips seemed pursed as she drove. "I can't say that I was really friends with any of the girls who got murdered. But a lot of them were nice, and now they're all dead."

"What about Hildreth? Were you friends with him?"

"Good question." She seemed the most unreadable now, the sunglasses camouflaging her thoughts. "Before he bought T&T, we did a lot of movies and barely held our own against the competition. Nobody made much money. Next thing we know all that's changed; we're living here, the company's revitalized, new equipment, new studio, and all of a sudden we're making great money and living the high life. So when a person does that for you, you consider him a friend . . . but . . . "

"But something wasn't right," Westmore concluded.

"*Nothing* was right, and we all chose to not face up to that. We weren't really even a movie company anymore; we'd do a few releases a year because it's what Hildreth wanted, and nobody asks questions when the bills are paid. They shot enough footage in that mansion to make a couple hundred flicks a year, but almost none of it was ever distributed because Hildreth didn't seem to care much about it. He didn't want a *porn company* as a business investment. He wanted us for something else and we never acknowledged that. We were too busy partying and not seeing the light. So, yeah, we all wanted to think of him as our best friend because he gave us a new life. Then we all found out the hard way that the new life was phony. He was just an eccentric psychopath with a ton of money who was using us for his madness." She paused, stared dead-ahead. "He seemed like the nicest guy in the world, but in truth he was the most evil man I've ever met."

Westmore was intrigued by the information. "He wanted you for something else? What?"

"I'm not sure. Imagery, I think. He was always talking about imagery, the imagery of the flesh, the energy of lust—a stimulated environment. It sounds crazy, doesn't it?"

"Sure, and he *was* crazy."

"I don't know about that."

"You just said he was evil, he was a psychopath."

"Neither of those things has to mean he's crazy. He was . . . something else. You'd have to have been there to get it. I guess Three-Balls and Jaz got closer to that part of him—the men."

"But they're all dead now. No one left to tell the tale."

She didn't say anything, her sullenness casting a shadow over her.

"The imagery of the flesh?" Westmore went on. "A stimulated environment? Sounds crazy to *me*. What's all that mean?"

"Only Hildreth knew."

"Yeah, but what do *you* think?"

"All I can say is, wait till you get to the house. Wait till you've spent your first night in that place." Her voice roughened. "It'll start to seep into you."

He didn't want to press her anymore; he'd burn her out. The subject by now had drained her, and probably just kept reminding her of what she walked into on April 3rd. Instead, he said, "I'm looking forward to it. You've got my curiosity stoked."

More silence. Westmore let it go. Strip malls and traffic passed in a blur. He tried to relax, tried to clear his mind and closed his eyes to the sun.

Miles later she laughed faintly and said, "Earlier you asked me if I was psychic."

"Yeah?"

She was pulling up now, onto a long wooded road.

"I'm not, but the people you're about to meet are."

II

After her shower in one of the luxurious third floor suites, Cathleen walked the grounds. She'd always thought of herself as practical in such situations but now . . . she felt uncomfortable. She didn't tell anybody—she'd feel weak and silly, and she mustn't present that appearance. But she could feel it; she could feel it on her skin:

There's something about that house.

Standing in the sun, she glanced back at the mansion. A car engine could be heard, then she saw a black convertible cruising up the road to the outer court before the front doors. For the hell of it, she quickly plucked some petals off a lone rhododendron and dropped them in the grass between her feet, keeping her eyes on the car. It was an ancient but simple augury dating back to the Aztecs. If two or more petal-stalks pointed away from her, that was considered a positive omen; if they pointed toward her: ill omen. She took her eyes off the car and looked down. *Oh, great,* she thought. The stalk of each petal pointed toward her. She squinted a last time at the car and thought she saw a blonde woman driving and a man with glasses in the passenger seat. *I wonder who they are . . .*

Cathleen was multifaceted; she was "into" many things. Personally, she considered herself a medium—since she'd long ago abandoned further pursuits in telekinesis—but she also possessed other sensitivities: crystology, divination, palmistry. At the height of passion—or lust—she could read thoughts. But she was mainly a medium—nothing very complicated. Sometimes things came to her. Sometimes they acted through her.

She worshiped God and Buddha, Nergal and Ra, Mohammad and the Earth Mother . . . because she knew they were all the same.

Her only major problem was sin . . . but that was another story.

God, it's beautiful, she thought, traipsing past the grounds proper. The mansion behind her, she proceeded into the woods, barefoot, a pale-lime sundress hugging her body. The sun played in her blonde hair but its heat dropped drastically when she stepped past a bordering weeping willow that must've been a century old. She didn't notice a single palm tree up here on the hill, just hundred-foot pine trees and the sprawling willows whose branches hung draped with Spanish moss. Deeper in the verge of woods she found herself walking on beautiful beds of wildflowers—carpets of pyxies and pink and white matts of arbutus. *Look at me, I'm the Nature Girl, I'm the happy sprite of the forest,* she thought, and then she thought: *Fuck!* when her bare foot landed on a stem of sand spurs. She hopped away, feeling ridiculous, to lean against a tree and pick them out. *God, those things hurt!*

Beyond, the forest seemed to grow more dense, kudzu and other vines stretching across trees like twisted cordons. The forest's aromas enticed her but at first she didn't see a point in going on—the vines too thick, the overgrowth too wild, but then she noticed a pass, and what seemed to be a gate.

Perhaps her inclinations had brought her here, for she wasn't just out for a walk.

She was looking for something.

This is it . . .

The oblong shape of land looked carved into the forest's denseness: a graveyard. A spiked iron fence encrusted with rust formed the perimeter. Uneven ranks of stones pegged the rust-covered ground. Some stones dated back to the mid-1800s, while the markers in the rear appeared to be a haphazard cuttings of granite with hand-chiseled names that could no longer be read. Cathleen crunched back to the furthest corner, and noticed a date from the 1600s.

This place went WAY back.

She wondered what else did.

Back toward the front she found what she'd come for.

REGINALD HILDRETH read the new but simple black-granite. D: 4-3-2004. Cathleen wasn't puzzled by the exclusion of a date of birth. *Hildreth liked to keep people wondering,* she suspected. *A phony.* It was the house that bothered her, not the man—at least at this point.

I came here for this, so let's do it, she told herself. She knelt six feet from the stone, set her bag down. From the mansion's pantry she'd brought some things, and she removed one now: an egg. Nothing special, just a Grade-A Large, no doubt from the nearest grocery store. With a sandstone spike—a relic given to her from an archaeologist—she gently tapped each end of the egg, breaking a hole. Then she tipped her head back, brought the egg to her lips, and blew. Its contents splattered upward in a plume, then the plume inconveniently landed in an angled line to her right.

Half-assed, she realized. She believed in divination and had used it successfully many times, but she knew she still hadn't acquired the right frame of mind. *I'm not taking it seriously.*

She stood up and tapped another egg with the countersink-like nail of sandstone. Then she thought about . . .

Sex.

She closed her eyes and filled her mind with it, imagined herself naked and sweating and mad with lust as some faceless man pushed her knees back to her shoulders and penetrated her right here in the woods, her bare rump grinding in the dirt. She imagined his weight pressing down, his skin sliding against hers. The simple image excited her in seconds; she felt her nipples tingle as if tweezed by hard fingers. She began to feel flush. Sexuality was her charge—it stoked her predispositions. It solicited the spirits.

Sweating and short of breath now from all the lust in her head, she kept her eyes closed and blew the insides out of the egg, aiming toward Hildreth's grave.

When she looked, she couldn't believe it.

The viscid plume had flown wildly to her right, *away* from the grave.

"Okay, okay," she whispered to herself. "Time to try an alomance." She stood up, looked without much concern toward the pass which led to the graveyard. She saw no one.

Then she pushed off her shoulder straps and let the sundress fall to the ground, totally naked beneath. Her innerself felt something stir at once, something beyond her. *Seikthas* or *Lieppyas*—benevolent spirits which inhabited trees or congregated near graves—or simple curious wraiths attracted to her sudden nudity. Ghosts, or even buoyed souls. It didn't matter what; she knew something was there because she could feel it in her blood.

From her bag she withdrew three more things: a cigarette lighter, a two-by-two-inch square of aluminum foil, and a small baggie containing some sea salt.

"Damn," she was caught by surprise. A sudden breeze blew the piece of foil away. It landed ten feet from her.

Without even thinking, she looked at it, held her breath for a moment, and willed it back. As if blown by an identical reverse breeze, the foil sailed back into her hand.

It was easy. It wasn't even something she gave much thought to anymore.

All right . . .

She formed the foil into a crude cup, then sprinkled a pinch of the salt into it. She cleared her mind of distractions, walked slowly around the cemetery grounds. She thought only of physical desire, and spirits. She was beseeching them, drawing them out. Her feet crunched quietly over the underbrush. Her skin shone in a mist of sweat, and she felt her heartbeat pick up, and as she walked she brushed the tips of her fingers up her thighs. Over her stomach . . .

She returned to the foot of the grave, focused, pin-point. Her bare breasts rose and fell with her quickened breaths. Envisioning herself on the supplication platform of the highest ziggurat, she whispered a prayer to Ea, the god of the sky and of forests, then held the lighter flame beneath the foil cup of salt.

The salt crackled minutely, began to sputter and burn. *Great Ea,* she thought. *Hear me . . .* When a pale tendril of smoke rose from the cup, Cathleen inclined her head and inhaled it.

She fought not to cough, held it in. But before she could search her mind for a portent—

Something grabbed her. Not hands, not a person, but something only semi-palpable, as if she'd been seized by the air. When she snapped her eyes open, she saw only a tulle-like veil of black. *Mesoplasm?* she wondered, not afraid yet. She'd be afraid in another moment. Whatever it was, it lacked luminosity so it couldn't be spirit-based. *What is that?* she thought peering into it.

Then she could see nothing; her eyes seemed to close on their own, that or something like a hand slipped over them.

Chuckling tittered about her head, dark, throaty noises of glee, but they were muffled as if through closed mouths. Then, blind, she was jerked off her feet, back arched, tousled around. *Now* she was afraid. She tried to scream and release the salt-fumes in the same action but—

Not fast enough.

Something slammed her chin up, something else pinched her lips closed, then something like an awful mouth full of dead breath but totally lacking substance sealed over her nose and sucked all the fumes out of her.

More guttering laughter flitted around her and the ghost-mouth sucked and sucked, stealing all that was left of her breath and everything that breath contained, harder and harder until she grew numb and the reversed pressure threatened to collapse her lungs.

When it was finally released, she was slammed down hard on her bare back. Had she been hovering in mid-air? The back of her head hit the ground so hard her consciousness drained. She still could see only blackness, but then that blackness grew even darker. She felt things feeling her, pinching her nipples, plying her breasts and buttocks like dough. Some intricate force yanked her naked legs out straight by the ankles and wishboned her quivering legs, and then more things began to play with her sex, and that's when she passed out.

When Cathleen awoke, she found herself sprawled on her side, arms disarrayed, one leg kicked forward. Bits of leaves and twig fragments flecked her blonde hair. As her consciousness rekindled, she had the sense of rising rapidly from an abyss full of hot, black water.

Oh . . . shit . . .

She lay still for a moment, catching her breath, exhausted.

When she glimpsed a ladybug crawling up one breast, she flicked it off and then noticed the faintest bruises, finger-marks, but they seemed much longer than any conceivable fingers. Trace bitemarks on her abdomen and thighs, and one nipple had a threadlike black and blue ring, but again, the mark seemed a much wider oval than human dentation. She knew instantly what had happened:

Para-planar rape . . .

She maintained her objectivity, though; she'd seen all this before, and had even experienced it a few times, her excessive sexuality seeming to taunt wayward spirits more than most. The only thing that bothered her, though, was the emotional aftereffect. She didn't feel raped or exploited or victimized.

Jesus, I'm so screwed up in the head . . .

She felt satisfied, her rampant yearnings for ecstacy and release fully satiated. Then she thought:

Hildreth.

It had to be. It had all happened right at the foot of his newly dug grave.

Or so she thought.

When she sat upright to brush the forest debris from her bare skin, she expected to find herself facing Hildreth's black gravestone. Instead she found herself outside of the cemetery altogether, ten feet at least past the iron fence.

To the extreme right of the grave.

Part Two

•

Carnal House

Chapter Six

I

"Poor Mack's probably getting sick of being the tour guide," Karen said amusedly. "You're the fifth person he's had to show around today."

"Oh, it's no trouble," Mack said, showing them down the windowless Buguet Walk. "I like showing people around . . . as long as I don't think too much about what happened here."

Westmore followed them in an awed daze through the museum-like mansion. Mack Colmes had been the first one that Karen had introduced him to: young, enthusiastic. Seemed like a perfectly nice guy. Mack stopped a moment and repeated his instructions on how to use the videocoms and house map, which set well with Westmore because he couldn't see himself *not* getting lost in this immense, dark place. Next, they pushed open the door to the South

Atrium, a huge chamber full of odd brightness and a sickly green-velour wallpaper. He looked at the room's structure, its frieze-work, carved wall moldings and paneling, and spire-like medieval bookcases and thought, *Yeah, this place has the word Gothic nailed*. Then he squinted at the obviously out-of-place office cubicles situated about the room's nexus. And more peculiarity: a mousy but not unattractive woman lay asleep on an antique couch watching what appeared to be *Emeril Live*.

"That's Adrianne," Mack pointed to her. "She's out of it right now, as you can tell. Sleeps a lot. And that's Nyvysk . . . "

A large bearded man with hair longer than Westmore's had just exited one of the cubicles, walked right up with a preoccupied smile. "You must be the writer," he presumed and shook hands. "I'm Nyvysk, the technician of the group."

The man shadowed Westmore. "Westmore. Pleased to meet you." *Seems pretty squared away,* he thought.

"Nyvysk is also a demonologist," Karen said.

Westmore was about to laugh at the joke but he could see by the bigger man's face that it was no joking matter. "Wow, there's a loaded one."

"Let me hazard a guess," Nyvysk said, his smile more puzzling now. "You're a journalist and therefore an atheist. You don't believe in demons."

Now Westmore did laugh. "I have no idea how to answer that."

"Good. Perhaps you'll find some answers, during your stay here. I see you've brought some things. Ready to check into your bedroom suite?"

"Sure," Westmore said. He was about to turn for the doors, presuming the bedrooms would be upstairs, but Nyvysk, with his maintained smile, intervened, "Right over here."

He took him to one of the makeshift cubicles. "Looks

like my office at the *Times,*" Westmore observed. "This is the *bedroom?*"

"We'll all be sleeping here, in this atrium. Safety in numbers."

Westmore looked past the curtain of his "suite." A single bed and a locker. He set his bags down. He sighed, imagining a plush Gothic bedchamber with drape-canopies, thick carpets, and curtains billowing from opened veranda doors. "I guess this'll do."

"Charges change at night," Nyvysk said, "especially in a house full of people who *attract* charges. Exterior forces are more eager to be active when such people are separated and in their most vulnerable state: sleep."

Westmore hadn't a clue. "Charges?"

"Have you ever been to a charged location?"

Westmore came back out of the cubicle. "Well, I've been *overcharged* on my Visa at certain locations, particularly when I've been drunk, but beyond that I don't know what you're talking about."

"Certain places have a *charge,* Mr. Westmore. Positive, negative, grounded, and . . . other. We believe that the Hildreth Mansion is probably one such location."

"Actually, Nyvysk, *we* do not necessarily believe anything of the sort." It was the woman on the couch, Adrianne, who'd just roused from her sleep. She introduced herself to Westmore with a meek smile and nod, then furthered her complaint. "We don't know anything about this house yet; we've made no conclusions. Don't delude this man right off the bat." She looked at Westmore, then very strangely asked, "So you're not a Christian?"

"I never said I was an atheist," Westmore answered.

"Well, hypothetically," Nyvysk said, "*if* this mansion is charged, the exterior forces I mentioned earlier have a tendency to manipulate agnostics and atheists. Faith can be a weapon. Lack of faith can affect the opposite. Adrianne and I, for instance, are the only true Christians. The other paranormalists here are multi-denominational. So, if in fact you don't have any religious beliefs . . . I suspect you will by the time you leave this house."

Adrianne rolled her drooping eyes. "Oh, would you stop! He's so overdramatic. He's supposed to be a scientist but he's always pushing people his way."

"We'll see."

Westmore was at a confusing loss. "So there are two other, uh—"

"Paranormalists," Nyvysk said. "You'll meet them by dinner time. Cathleen's exploring the grounds, which, by the way, I'd recommend that you avoid after dark."

"There he goes again," Adrianne complained, then settled back to the scroll couch. She was hugging a velvet pillow.

Karen grabbed his arm. "I second that motion. Don't go outside after dark."

"I'm not saying I'm an atheist, but I *am* saying that I don't believe in ghosts," Westmore asserted. "As far as I'm concerned, this place is just a big, overdone house."

Karen had wandered to the TV, not listening, while Adrianne remained dull-eyed on the couch. Nyvysk just kept smiling.

"As for the accommodations," the bearded man continued, "we only ask that you sleep in this room with the rest of us. I noticed your laptop, so feel free to choose any other room in the house for an office. The rest of us will base ourselves in here for the most part. Anytime I'm *not* here, you'll probably be able to find me in the security and communications room upstairs."

"Works for me," Westmore said. He turned to Mack.

"Any objections if I just kind of snoop around, check the place out?"

"Feel free," Mack invited. "And there's a big bathroom and shower next to the kitchen any time you want to get cleaned up, or use any bathroom you want—they're all over the place."

"Just not at night," Nyvysk insisted.

Westmore smiled. "Understood. See you all later."

As he was heading out, hard-pressed not to shake his head, he heard Karen say, "Where's Willis?"

"He said he was going to the room where the prostitutes were murdered, didn't he?" Nyvysk said.

"Yeah, a couple hours ago," Adrianne said.

Westmore pushed through the palatial double doors back to the main hall, and he could hear Nyvysk saying into the videocom: "Willis? Willis? Where are you?"

II

Willis was on his knees, dry-heaving, in the Jean Brohou Parlor on the second floor, blind from his visions and sickened unto death. He was too insensible by what he'd seen to register anything in his mind that might even be considered rational or reactive. Just *Get out . . . Got to get out of this room . . .* He heard a long, ear-rupturing scream, then a sound like something cutting through gristle.

Then a splattering gush of some thick liquid.

He couldn't breathe; instead he gasped, knees and palms squishing through thick, drenched carpets, death-rattles gurgling behind him. He'd thrown up spontaneously upon entering and now, as his stomach continued to spasm, there was nothing left to come out. Escape was his only instinct but he'd mistakenly closed the door when he'd come in. He reached up, gagging, fingers desperate for the brass door-latch, and for a moment he thought he might actually die before he could open it.

Dark, amorphous *things* looked down on him, leaning closer. When he reached out to push them back, his hand pushed into something that wasn't solid flesh; it was only semi-palpable, like a gas so thick with soot one could feel something. He noticed facial features—or the lack thereof—no noses, eyes, or ears, just great wet mouths full of roving tongues . . .

When he finally did manage to touch the latch, he shuddered and saw another man's hand open the door, a naked short-haired man with streaks of blood on his arms and legs. He carried a bucket out of the room, and a second nude man carried two such buckets. Then a third man left, just as naked, who paused at the open door and looked down at the helpless Willis with a grin.

Willis knew that the man was Reginald Hildreth.

When he fell over, his hand shot out to break his fall and landed on a woman's severed head. Was the mouth still moving? Willis didn't want to know.

Then he vaulted forward and tumbled out of the parlor.

A man in the hall ran forward: "Shit! Are you okay?"

Willis reeled, disoriented and still sick. He wasn't in control of what he was saying—"Jesus, don't go in there, don't go in there!"—and then he yelled and shrugged away when the other man grabbed him in an attempt to help him up: "Don't touch me!"

"All right, all right . . . " The man stood aside. He looked late-30s, had long and rather straggly dark hair. Willis struggled to regain his breath and recompose but he wasn't quite there yet.

"What happened?" the other man asked.

The images still flooded Willis' mind. "Heads, bodies. Blood all over the place . . . "

The other man looked in the room, then came back out. "Man, there's nothing in there except a bunch of great furniture and an expensive carpet that looks thrown up on."

Calm down, calm . . . Willis took more breaths. *Passive revenantial activity. It's nothing.* But it had been so strong. And now that he thought of it he had to consider that maybe the images had been active rather than passive. That last man leaving—Hildreth—had looked down at him.

"Want me to call Mack? Maybe you need a doctor."

"No, no." *Oh, shit. What did I say?*

"What were you saying? Something about bodies, blood?"

Willis only needed another minute before he'd regain coherence. A few more breaths, then, and a sigh. "I'm all right. Forget about anything I said. I was—I was in what you can think of as a state of shock."

"Here, lemme help you up."

Willis pulled his gloves out of his back pocket and slipped them on, then stuck out his hand. The other man helped him to his feet, whereupon he leaned against the banister.

"I'm Richard Westmore. You're Willis?"

Willis nodded.

"Why the gloves? You a germiphobe, something like that?"

Willis smiled, wiped his mouth and brow with a handkerchief. "Long story, I'll tell you later. I guess you're the fifth member of the actual assignment. The writer?"

"Yeah. Downstairs, they told me we'd all be sleeping in the atrium, but Nyvysk said I could pick my own workroom."

"Whatever you do, don't choose that room," Willis advised, pointing wearily to the Jean Brohou Parlor.

Westmore laughed. "It's a damn nice room, but since you threw up in it, I guess it's ruled out."

"There are several studies in the house, and a big library on the first floor. I'm sure one of those would work better for you."

Westmore leaned back, then jerked a thumb toward the parlor door. "What did you really see in there?"

"Nothing that you can see . . . "

"Psychic stuff, huh?"

"It's much more complicated than that. You'll figure it out as we go along."

Westmore seemed to catch on that it was a bad topic for the moment. "So what's with all the names?" He looked at the parlor's brass plaque. "Who's Jean Brohou?"

"A french astrologist. A lot of the rooms here are named—one of Hildreth's many eccentricities, and a pretty tacky one, if you ask me. Clairvoyants, augurs, mesmerists, alchemists, sorcerers. It gets worse as you get to the higher floors. The biggest bedroom is called the Loudun Suite, named for the possessed nuns. The chapel turret on the fifth floor is the De Rais Chapel. You've probably heard of him."

"Satanism, the occult. So you think Hildreth was really into that stuff?"

"Yes," Willis said.

"Well, I don't believe in any of it, but I'm not so close-minded to say that I disbelieve it either. I only believe what I can see."

Willis nodded. He was exhausted. "Then consider yourself blessed, and thank God that you can't see what we can," he said and walked away.

III

Some study, Westmore thought. They were all the same: over the top. Each one seemed a nice, quiet place to work, with exorbitant furniture and beautiful appointments. Until he looked at the bookshelves. He looked at one book after another, frowning at the titles.

The Synod of the Aorists, The Red Confession, The Secret Utterance of Joseph of Arimathea, and on and on. Westmore had never heard of any of them, in spite of a respectable education. Another peaked bookshelf offered worse selections, perhaps flagging more of the real Hildreth: *The Grimoires of the Black Blood, Modern Teratology and Other Biological Accidents, The Field Investigator's Photographic Guide to Gunshot Wounds, Stab Wounds, and Traumatic Rape.* One glance at the photoplates of the latter sent him reeling, and in another, an untitled large-formatted book in a red leather binding, nearly made him throw up: old black-and-white pictures of men having sex with handicapped and deformed women.

"Fuck the study," he said aloud, thoroughly disgusted. *Hildreth was one sick puppy.* He left in long strides, mentally gagging at the images. "Shit . . ." At the end of the hall he noticed some oddly placed drapes that couldn't possibly be covering a window; he looked behind them and noticed a narrow stairwell, so he took them up. *I've only been here an hour and I'm already sick of this nutty place and that pack of weirdos downstairs.* But his bad mood, he knew, was only a sign of his professional confusion. He was being paid to write an account of the coming week and he still didn't know how to go about it.

The third floor seemed darker and more cramped, less

space in the hallway. Darker portraits of obscure men and women glowered from meticulous frames. Tasseled drapes adorned narrow stained-glass windows that allowed very little light to pass. The atmosphere, which Westmore at first found interesting in its novelty, now aggravated him.

"Mr. Westmore. Come in here a moment. You might want to see this."

Westmore hadn't even noticed Nyvysk in the corridor's dimness. From that distance he looked like a tall, shaggy shadow, and as a silhouette from the stained-glass at the end of the hall, he looked momentarily menacing. Westmore followed him into a room blossoming in white fluorescent light.

"Man, this is some shift away from the Gothic," he said.

"Yes, clashes with everything else, but perhaps that's a sign of more of Hildreth's falsehood; he kept his materialisms secret."

The room was full of computers and monitors, and all manner of audio-visual equipment. A central console allowed one to observe multiple camera displays, plus audio transmissions from the intercom. But the small room was made more cramped by a flank of packing boxes stacked behind them. "What's all that?" Westmore asked.

"That's *my* equipment," Nyvysk explained. "From a technical standpoint, this mansion is a dream; every room is wired for camera and audio. All of my detection devices can be piggybacked into any room I want, through the wiring that already exists. And the digital camera system is ideal; I can connect some of my sensors to them from this central location."

Westmore was already confused. "Sensors? Detection equipment? To detect what? You're going to try to take pictures of ghosts?"

"I'm going to try to make photographic and audio readings of various atmospheric *signatures* of presences that may be thought of as ghosts."

Westmore frowned. "Like what? Temperature?"

"Drastic fluctuations of temperature, yes, barometric discrepancies, gauss readings for divergences in trace radiation levels and electromagnetic field configurations, ion-field conversity. One of the simplest detection measures is one of the most useful: electronic-voice phenomena. I'll be able to monitor most of these things from this room. I'll be able to pinpoint times and locations of high activity, even when I'm not here." Then he pointed to a rank of digital recorders.

"Oh," Westmore said. Everything he'd been told was almost instantly over his journalist- and English-major head. "When are you going to start taking readings?"

"I already have."

I can't wait to see what happens here, Westmore thought. "Knock yourself out. I'm gonna go find a place where I can write."

"See you at dinner," Nyvysk said, busy reaching into a panel access with a screwdriver.

Westmore left, confounded as ever, and getting used to that state of mind. Back in the dark hall he checked more ornate doors only to find that most of them weren't to bedrooms or parlors but to offices, supply rooms, and utility rooms. Westmore guessed that these served as T&T's administrative facilities. A larger door was more declarative; STUDIO A, its plaque read. The walls must've been knocked out of the rest of the rooms on the floor from this point on. Several sets could be seen, with various fake backdrops; another set was a bedroom, another a living room, all equipped with lights. *Oh, Christ,* he thought when further back he discovered a padded GYN table on which rested a scene-clapper that read GABRIELLE'S GONZO GANGBANG

(SCENE IV, DAY TWO). *I guess that one wasn't a print,* West-more concluded. *She got butchered before she could make it to Day Three.* Supply shelves housed dozens of different types of vibrators and other sexual aides, rubber phalluses that looked distressingly real, and bottles of lubricant. Westmore's nose crinkled; the place stank. "I don't think I'll be using this smut-hole for a workroom," he muttered and left. He felt dirty just being there . . . and knowing what the room's original purpose had been. Maybe he'd go back to the big library downstairs, even though he didn't like the idea of be-ing in such close proximity to the others—and he didn't want them snooping either. He sighed with relief, though, when he opened the last door on the wing and found a plush office with a big teak desk, a quality leather armchair, and french doors leading to a sunny veranda. *This works . . .*

He set his laptop up on the desk, adjusted the light, ab-sorbed the creative atmosphere, finding it acceptable. He turned the computer on and started a new file entitled VIVICA HILDRETH JOB, and when he was ready to start, he did what most writers do on the first day of a writ-ing job: he turned the computer off and decided not to write. *I'll start tomorrow,* he decided and got up to look around. He went out of the veranda and smoked a solitary cigarette, enjoying the sunlit view of the woodline and the estate's west end. At a great distance he thought he saw a woman coming out of the woods, staggering a bit. *Maybe that's the other woman,* but he couldn't remember what Nyvysk had said her name was. He squinted until she dis-appeared and decided that she was indeed staggering, as if fatigued.

Back in the office, he browsed around more. He didn't need to mind his own business now; Hildreth was dead and so was his company and his employees. He looked through some file cabinets, eyed tax records and supply invoices. Nothing of much interest there, but maybe later a closer look at the books would produce some information Vivica might find useful. He had to keep reminding himself that he was working for her and not necessarily *with* the others. *I guess I'm her paid spy . . .*

A little framed picture on the desk displayed a picture of Karen and Hildreth, both smiling at the mansion's entrance pillars. *I guess this used to be Karen's office,* he reasoned. He looked in the desk drawers and found them relatively uncluttered, but in a multidrawered Windsor highboy he found stacks and stacks of adult DVD's, all T&T productions, and only then, on the desk blotter, did he notice yet another DVD—classily entitled GOO-GUZZLING GO-GO GIRLS—that Karen had used as a coffee coaster. *Now that's what I call respect for the company's product.*

He opened a plain door next to the highboy, expecting a closet, but found another, even posher office. Oddly windowless and full of half-burned-down candles. Behind the desk occupying much of the paneled wall hung a grandly framed oil portrait of Vivica Hildreth, posing in a period depiction: hair in a jeweled bun, fan in one hand, dressed in a Victorian bustle dress and a sashed bodice. The image was jarring, after meeting her for real in the pop-trash fashion she'd worn at her penthouse. Westmore opened the desk's drawers and immediately found—

Oh, terrific.

—a small revolver.

Not that big a deal, really, especially not in Florida where handguns were not taboo; it just shocked him, that first sight of a gun sitting there. He picked it up, sniffed it, and only detected machine oil. *Probably never been fired.* But Hildreth's weapon of choice had already been made clear: an ax.

You've got to be shitting me, he thought next when he pulled the drawer out further and found a banded stack of $100 bills. *Most people have paper clips and staples in their desk. Hildreth's got ten grand.* Maybe it was a test—because he knew the room had a camera in it somewhere. But Westmore's corruptions had never involved dishonesty anyway—just alcohol. He put the money in his pocket, knowing he'd turn it over to Mack immediately, and report the discovery to Vivica.

The top drawer on the other side of the desk was empty save for one item: a small framed picture face down. Westmore flipped it over and found himself looking at what must be a high school yearbook picture.

Pretty girl, he thought at once. The ultimate girl-next-door, big white smile, big innocent eyes, a sweep of shining brunette hair. *Did Hildreth have a daughter?* But, no. Karen had told him he and Vivica were childless.

So who's this?

It seemed that his work was being cut out for him on its own. He left the picture and searched more drawers, these at the other side of the room in a Chippendale roll-top, just as the door opened.

"Everything all right in here?"

It was Mack, leaning in.

"Yeah, I was—"

"Nyvysk said you were looking for a place to write, and it looks like you picked the right place. This was Hildreth's office."

"Yeah, I kind of figured. Any objections to me using it?"

"None at all. Feel free to use the computers or anything else you want, and lemme know if you need anything."

"Thanks—" Then Westmore remembered. "Oh, wait. I

did find this. I guess you should secure it or turn it over to Vivica." He passed Mack the band of bills.

Mack laughed. "Not surprising. That's pocket change to Hildreth."

The comment spurred Westmore. "How did he become so successful?"

"Mainly international bond merchandising, global municipal bonds, stuff like that."

"A Wall Street wizard?"

"That or he ripped a lot of people off. He never talked much about it. He made a billion dollars by the time he was fifty."

"Who managed his personal accounts? Karen?"

Mack laughed harder. "No, no, she just kept the books for T&T, small-time. T&T wasn't a business to him, it was a hobby. I'll be the first to tell you, Hildreth was a perv."

"The proverbial dirty old man?"

"The proverbial *rich* dirty old man, I guess. But he was also a very, very smart guy. It's hard to really peg him quickly. Somebody could write a whole book about the man, and it couldn't possibly tell the whole story." The security man paused. "For all I know, that's what you're doing."

Westmore shook his head. "I'm just writing up a chronology for Vivica, an account of what goes on with all these—"

"Psychic whackjobs?"

"I guess that term could apply."

Mack leaned against the doorframe. "You believe in any of that stuff?"

"I don't know," Westmore said.

"Me either. I guess we'll see. Well, I gotta run, see ya later."

"Sure—oh, and Mack? One more question."

"Yeah?"

"Did Hildreth have any kids, with Vivica, or anyone else?"

"No way. He couldn't stand kids. He was a real curmudgeon when it came to children."

"He have any relatives with kids?"

"Nope. Hildreth was an only child."

Mack rushed off after that, obviously in a hurry, but Westmore felt satisfied by his answers and good nature. *Oh, shit, I should've given him the gun, too,* he remembered. If these "psychics" were whackjobs, a pistol sitting around might not be a good thing, but then he knew he was overcautious. Best to just leave it there, and it was best, he knew, not to make judgments about any of the others at least before he'd gotten to know them.

Instead, he went back to snooping.

He thought of Poe's "Purloined Letter" when he saw it right there in front of him. The broad, leather-cornered blotter on Hildreth's desk. It was an April calendar, the sort that was intended for people to jot notes on, appointments on certain dates, etc. But there was no writing on this one—

"Wait a minute," he muttered, squinting.

—save for one pen-mark and a scribble.

A red X on the box for April 3rd.

A shudder trickled up his spine. *The date of the murders . . .*

None of this was very telling, yet it seemed utterly macabre. *It definitely wasn't spur-of-the-moment,* Westmore realized. *He knew he was going to kill those people on April 3rd. He even wrote it down.*

More to contemplate. *I just got here,* he reminded himself. He had a tendency to project questions faster than he could think. *Be a journalist. Accrue facts, and assimilate them when you've got enough to make a conclusion.* And he knew this: he had very little in the way of facts just yet.

He browsed around, opening another highboy cabinet. No money this time, just several stacks of DVD's, a hundred perhaps. He flipped through a handful, expecting to see more vivid, sexual cover photography but instead found dates for the past year handwritten on each disk's label. At first he was surprised the police hadn't confiscated these, along with the gun in the desk and the money and much else, but then he recalled what Vivica had mentioned. She'd paid a lot of money to jink Hildreth's death-report, and had probably paid a lot more to the proper sources to ensure that the house wasn't searched. He dreaded what lay ahead, though, an obvious task: *I'm gonna have to sit and watch all these DVD's, at least scan over them.* It didn't matter how attractive the women were; porn was essentially the same thing over and over again. *Gee, I can't wait,* he thought and dragged the stacks out, then promptly dropped one. "What a putz!" he yelled at himself. The discs lay like a dropped deck of cards. But when he got down to his knees and began picking them up, one caught his eye.

The was no date but scribbled on it was HALLOWEEN PARTY.

This one might be VERY interesting . . .

He made a mental note to watch that one first, then, before he could get back up, he noticed something else.

Four indentations in the carpet, right next to the highboy, which seemed to match the length and width of the highboy's legs. It was too obvious when he took a second glance.

Someone moved the highboy from there to there. Recently.

When Westmore tried to muscle the large piece of furniture aside, his exertion reminded him of one reason he'd chosen to be a writer instead of a manual laborer; he wasn't exactly a physical specimen. His long hair dangled annoyingly in his face as he shoved and shoved, thinking *God damn! This big piece of shit weighs more than a fucking piano!* But after some sweat and what would undoubtedly result in a sore back tomorrow, he managed to nudge the highboy back to its original position, and that's when he saw—

The plot thickens, he thought.

What the highboy had been covering was an oil portrait of the girl whose picture he'd found in the desk, the bright-eyed brunette. "All right, Hildreth, you're intriguing me now," Westmore talked to himself. He looked closely at the painting, which was obviously very new yet admirable in the way its dark swirls and brushstrokes duplicated High Renaissance style. A pastoral scene at night, trees edging around a cemetery. The girl looked contemplative in a broad ruffled blue dress with white-lace cuffs and neckline.

And she was pointing straight ahead which, from where he stood, made it look like she was pointing straight at Westmore.

Interesting, he thought. *And weird, like everything else in this house . . .*

Then he considered something.

Did the artist craft the painting to appear as though she were pointing at anyone looking at it, or did he—

Westmore did an about-face. With no one standing there, she was pointing to the other side of the paneled room, and there, exactly in line with her painting was another picture in an identical frame.

He walked over. This one wasn't a painting, it was an engraving; it looked old, the work's single subject more like Michelangelo than Raphael. Hunched over an angled table was an old man with flowing long hair and beard; he was writing on a scroll of paper with a stylus pen, and somehow the engraver had captured the most unique contradiction of expressions—in the eyes—a look of dread but also a look of rapture. In the corner the artist had left his name (which appeared to be Albrecht or Albrekt) and a shocking date: 1610. Words in Italian had been etched across the bottom, and a clearly much more recent translation could be found on a small gold plate.

ST. JOHN THE DIVINE SCRIBES THE HOLY REVELATION AT PATMOS, CIRCA A.D. 90.

Westmore squinted closer, and noticed the intricately engraved stippling which spelled the word *REVELATIO* at the top of the scroll, and just below it: *CAPIT 13*.

Chapter Thirteen of the Book of Revelation, Westmore thought with a frown. It was a benchmark for hokey Christian-mysticism and apocalyptic study, and—

And for these freaks into the occult and devil worship, Chapter Thirteen is the "Biggie," Westmore knew, where John reveals the cryptic number of the Beast: 666.

It was all hokum; Westmore was confident of that, and he also felt confident that it divulged more of the real Hildreth—a crackpot.

Somebody should've told John that the real number of the beast is George Steinbrenner's phone number, he joked and went back to the desk. He took out the snapshot of the brunette again, then held it up right next to her painting. Now it was easier to see that whoever Hildreth had hired to do the painting had used this photograph as a model for the face. The artist's name was in the corner, very small, with a date: about a year ago. For no reason he pressed a finger against the paint and of course found it dry.

But something seemed odd.

The painting didn't move, as any painting would if hung in the traditional fashion: string and a nail in the wall.

He pressed the corner of the frame. When he tried to lift the painting off the wall, it didn't budge at all at first. He exerted more strength, felt it give, then pulled harder, and it began more or less to slide away from the wall. *Somebody mounted this with pegs,* he saw when he looked behind the picture's frame. And he saw something else, too. *What the hell is that?*

A few more tugs backward, and the painting came away from the wall, to reveal—

Another painting in a frame.

It was set back several inches into the wall, obviously via some custom woodworking. Westmore tilted the desk lamp to shine directly into the large, square indentation, then saw that what hung there wasn't a painting but another engraving that, if anything, looked older than the other one. Its frame was actually box-cased and covered in Plexiglas.

Westmore examined the work. Instead of a decidedly old St. John wielding a stylus pen, the subject of this engraving was another engraver, younger with short, curly hair, a largish nose, eyes intently slit as he manipulated the burin of an engraving plate: the likeness of a monstrous face. Westmore noticed the autograph. Albrecht—*Same as the other one*—and the date: 1599.

Words in German this time traced along the bottom. Westmore didn't know any German, but a convenient plate translated: MY SELF AS I DARE TO REFASHION THE COUNTENANCE OF MY VISION: BELARIUS.

So Albrecht engraved his own self-portrait, Westmore thought. *And Belarius?* He squinted further. *That ugly-as-shit face that he's engraving.* A picture in a picture.

And all meaningless to him. He could only presume that

Hildreth had hidden the engraving because it was valuable, but why hide the painting of the brunette? Thus far, she was the best thing he had to go on, even though he believed that she *wasn't* Hildreth's daughter.

So who was she?

"It's a start," he mumbled, not altogether unhappy with the day's discoveries.

Then: *I wonder . . .*

Excitement gripped his heart when he pulled on the engraving and felt it give in stops just as the painting had. But when he lifted it away—

"Oh, Christ. Not more DVD's!"

Another short stack of discs sat in the compartment which existed behind the engraving. Westmore groaned and withdrew them, then noticed something else.

A seam in the black-velvet backboard, as well as a tiny silk ribbon whose purpose was instantly recognized.

They're doors . . .

He pulled the ribbon and the black board separated, revealing a wall-safe of serious quality. *A picture in a picture . . . and a big-ass safe in a fuckin' wall.*

Brushed stainless steel gleamed back at him. From the center protruded a brass combination knob sided by a steel latch-handle. Perhaps it was the most basic human impulse but Westmore instantly burned to know what was inside, imagining gems and stacks of cash.

But what else might be in there?

Now all I need is the combination . . .

"I'm not aware of any safes," Vivica Hildreth was telling him a minute later over her cell phone.

"It's hidden behind a painting and an engraving, up in his office on the third floor," Westmore clarified. "You're sure you've never seen it?"

"I've never been in the mansion, Mr. Westmore, which I told you when we met."

"Oh, yeah, that's right. But did he ever mention a safe?"

"No."

"Well, I'd really like to know what's in that safe, and I'm sure you do too. Would Mack know the combination?"

"He must not know about the safe, either, and I'm sure that Karen doesn't. They would've mentioned it."

Shit . . .

Vivica didn't seem like the excitable type, but the long pause over the line verified her concern.

"I'll ask Mack."

Now her voice flirted with anger. "Ask Mack and Karen."

"But you just said they didn't know—"

"I don't care *what* I said. Ask them, and if they don't know the combination, break into it."

Westmore stifled a laugh, eyeing the safe. "You don't understand, this isn't a piggy bank. This is a serious safe. I'd have to—"

"Do anything necessary to get that safe open. I authorize any expense. Tell Mack. And tell Mack to call me; he's supposed to call me several times a day."

"I'll tell him. He was just here." Westmore was going to mention the ten grand but instantly nullified the idea. *Let's wait and see, instead. See how long it takes him to tell her about it.* Did he think Mack would keep quiet and pocket the money? It seemed the fastest way to gauge his character, especially given Vivica's sudden outpouring of neglect. "I'll find him right now."

"You do that. You tell that cocky punk to take his hand out of his pants long enough to do his job."

Ooo-eee, is she pissed! "Yes, ma'am."

Another hissing pause. "I want to know what's in that goddamn safe, Mr. Westmore. I'm trusting you to find out."

"Understood."

click

What a scene that was . . . Then he groaned; he'd forgotten to ask her if she knew anything about the brunette in the snapshot, and given her mood, he wasn't about to call her back now.

Instead, he hailed Mack on the videocom, found him in the South Atrium. "Hey, Mack. You know the combination to Hildreth's safe?"

"There is no safe."

"I'm standing here looking at it."

"In the office?"

"That's right."

"I never knew he had a safe. Kind of ticks me off. I thought he trusted me."

"All that aside, there's a safe, and Vivica wants it open."

"You told her about it?"

Westmore smirked. "Of course. And she wants it open, any expense, she said. She also wants you to call her."

"Shit. Was she pissed?"

"I'd say that's an accurate description."

"Shit. Okay, okay, take care of the safe."

"How?"

"Call a locksmith, and I'll take care of her."

"Okay. Oh, and could you ask Karen if she knows about the safe?"

But Mack had already hung up.

"Ask Karen about what safe?"

Westmore spun, startled. "Don't sneak up on me like that."

"Why?" Karen asked in the doorway. "Nervous? Squeamish?"

"In a mansion where over a dozen people were butchered only a few weeks ago? Yeah, maybe just a tad."

"I didn't know Hildreth had a safe in here," she stated and drifted in, still wearing the tight leather jeans. The image of her figure sculpted by the jeans and gray tube-top distracted Westmore nearly to the point of annoyance. She had a drink in her hand, twirling the ice. She was looking at the safe.

"Who's that girl?" he asked, and stuck a finger at the painting.

"I don't know," but she didn't seem to look very hard.

"How about this girl?" He showed her the snapshot.

"It's the same girl," she noticed. "I've never met her." She kept peering at the safe. "That pisses me off he didn't tell me about the safe."

"Mack said the same thing. Maybe you guys weren't as 'in' as you thought."

"I never thought I was in," she said, as if the remark insulted her. "It's a good thing you don't drink. You should see the liquor bar downstairs." She held her glass up. "This is twenty-four-year-old Glenlivit."

Westmore ground his teeth. *Thanks a lot, God . . .*

Karen picked it up at once: "So this painting was behind the cabinet, then you moved the cabinet away?"

"Yeah."

"And she's pointing to—" She turned. "St. Johnnie writing the *Book of Revelation*. That would be too easy, wouldn't it?"

Westmore just got the gist and felt immediately stupid. He rushed over, grabbed the safe's knob.

Karen watched, bemused, reciting, "'And the Kings of the earth drank the wine of her wrath and her fornication—'"

"What?"

"Just dial the number."

He dialed in 6-6-6 on the combination.

Nothing.

Then 13-18, and variations of those numerals.

Nothing. "You're right, that *is* too easy." Next he called the nearest locksmith in the phonebook, noticed Karen dully examining the second engraving, the self-portrait.

"Is it wired?" a rocky-voiced man on the line asked.

"I . . . don't know."

"Any lights on it?"

"No."

"Does it have a keypunch or any kind of buttons on the door?"

"Nope."

"Then it ain't wired, and if it ain't wired, we can open it. I'll be there in the morning."

Westmore frowned. "How about tonight? Your ad says twenty-four-hour service."

"Extra charge for that."

"We'll pay. I need it opened as soon as possible."

"Okay. I'll have one of my people stop by, say ten p.m.?"

"Perfect! Thank you."

"What's this?" She'd picked up the engraving.

"That was *behind* the painting of the girl. Kooky, huh?"

"There's always been a lot of kookiness in this house." She sat up on the desk, thighs parted. "Looks like we're getting a fair dose today."

"What? The safe?"

"No, I mean downstairs. They were getting on my nerves

so I split, started looking around for you." She finished the scotch, then leaned back on her hands. The pose was nearly lewd, and Westmore guessed she was doing it on purpose, to rile him up.

He looked away, flipping through the stack of DVD's. "Something happened downstairs?"

"You might say that. Willis saw something on the second floor and about keeled over—"

"He *did* keel over, and he threw up. In one of the parlors. I helped him up."

Now she was wagging her feet back and forth, as a toddler might, sitting on a ledge. "That's the thing about him that bothers me. I think he's for real."

"What about the others?"

"I don't know. I've read about the geeky chick. And there's something about her that seems genuine."

"Maybe she's just a genuine drug addict."

"Maybe. And Cathleen got raped."

Westmore dropped the stack. "WHAT?"

"Says she was touched sexually by a 'subcarnated spiritual agency,' which I guess means a ghost."

"For God's sake . . ." Westmore lit another cigarette, lusting more after Karen's empty scotch glass than her parted legs. "You think she's a genuine psychic?"

"I doubt it. She seems like a phony, but—Christ—what a body. Makes me jealous . . . like Vivica. Some things just aren't fair." Now she lay back flat on the desk, sighing. "And don't worry, I'm not coming on to you by lying down like this. I'm just . . . really tired."

"I understand."

"And you're the only person in this kook-house I feel comfortable around."

I guess that's a compliment. Westmore did what he always did when he was uncomfortable. He changed the subject. "And Nyvysk? Real or phony?"

She shrugged, flat on her back and eyes closed. "Nyvysk doesn't claim to be psychic. He just does tech stuff. And exorcisms."

"You're pulling my leg."

"Wish I was. We hired a research consultant to background all of these people before Vivica hired them. I got to sneak a peek at the bios. Nyvysk is an ex-priest who did exorcisms for over twenty years. He went all over the world."

"Ex-priest? Why the ex?"

"Sex stuff. A lot of sex stuff with all of them. I'm sure you'll get all of their full stories soon."

Westmore was dumbfounded. *Sex stuff . . .* He didn't even want to know. Then he looked glumly at the DVD's that awaited his attention. Sex DVD's. Hours and hours of it.

"It's almost time for dinner," Karen said, rousing herself from the desk. "Let's go downstairs and see if the freakshow has calmed down."

Westmore followed her out, his puzzlement churning. As they moved down the dark hall, it seemed that the faces in the oil portraits and statues were different from earlier, but he knew this was just imagination.

"I guess Nyvysk already went downstairs," Karen said, and pointed to the door of the communications room. It stood closed.

"No," Westmore said, stopping mid-stride. "I hear him talking in there." He stood at the door, and very faintly could hear voices.

"Quit eavesdropping, and let's go," Karen urged. She grabbed his arm and pulled him away. "I'm starving!"

But as Westmore was tugged toward the stairs, he thought, *I wonder who he's talking to,* because he was sure he heard more than one voice in the room.

Chapter Seven

I

Nyvysk felt no shock, no overt impact, just something subtly awful deeper in his heart. He had eight V/A digital recorders running through the intercom microphones in random rooms, which he chose only for their likelihood that the other members of the group wouldn't enter, mostly rooms on the fifth story. EVP was always a reliable gauge, and the easiest to implement, even though the exact science was confusing as many different aspects of electronic-voice phenomena existed. Many's the time he'd sat in rooms himself with recorders running, often for hours, and heard absolutely nothing. Later, he'd play the tapes back through sequential equalizers and hear an array of voices. Who knew why? It simply worked.

And it was working now.

And he recognized one of the voices.

Positive meter-spikes had alerted him for EVP in three rooms: the Chapel, a bedroom suite, and Hildreth's so-called Scarlet Room.

On the Chapel disc, he heard this:

"Yes. Oh, yes." A male voice.

Then a female voice, very distant. "Look at them fuck. Let's do that."

The male voice: "No, I mostly just love the blood. I like to see it . . ."

Next, the bedroom, a bending, warbling utterance of varying sonic densities, what sounded like a woman: "Oh my God, stick it in, stick the knife all the way in . . ."

Certainly these recordings could be a trick. No one had been in the rooms during the times the voices had registered; he knew this because he had the room cameras on the display monitors, but he supposed someone could easily be hiding in the rooms, out of the cameras' view. Or hidden speakers could be playing the prerecorded voice back. It would appear authentic but still—a trick. Nyvysk, however, doubted that this was the case here. He could feel it.

The third monitor spike had occurred in the Scarlet Room.

"Alexander," the wan voice slipped through. A Middle-eastern accent. "Are you . . . there?"

Nyvysk sat motionless. Listened.

"I know you're there. Someone told me."

The voice was male yet gentle, even impassioned. It sounded lost but somehow hopeful.

"I know you remember me, and I remember you. I remember the look in your eyes . . . on that day."

Nyvysk's sensibilities struggled with logic and the simple responsibility of his job. Still, his *il*logic forced him to ask, *What . . . day?*

"I could see your love. I wished you'd come with me—I know you wanted to. If you had, I'd still be alive. I went home through an alley by the street market, and got murdered by thieves. But we did well that day, didn't we, Alexander?"

A roll of dead air. Nyvysk could hear himself blink.

"Alexander? Didn't we?"

Dread crept up his skin, while his eyes welled with tears.

"We cured her, Alexander. The woman speaking the devil's words in Zraetic. That day so long ago, in Nineveh."

Nyvysk knew who it was, even before those details. The boy named Saeed, who'd exorcized a possessed woman near the ancient Library of Ashurbanipal.

The boy he'd fallen in love with, and had thought about every day for nearly the last twenty years.

Nyvysk left the recorders on and left the room.

II

"So where is everybody?" Westmore asked.

Karen glanced about the sumptuous kitchen. "Yeah, and where's dinner?"

Westmore was relieved by one thing: the kitchen was the only area of the house that did not conform to the rest of the mansion's ubiquitous Gothic motif. It more resembled a kitchen in a high-end restaurant, with multiple ranges, ovens, roasters, and a large reverse-air grill. The pantry was as large as a two-car garage, and there was a walk-in refrigerator and freezer.

But where was everyone? The dining room was empty and so was the atrium.

"Did everybody leave?" Karen asked.

Just as Westmore would start calling for people on the videocom, the kitchen doors pushed open. It was Mack, looking a bit harried.

"What's wrong?" Westmore asked.

"Nothing, really. Minor crisis with the rest of the crew."

"Where are they?" Karen asked.

"In the library, kind of having a pow-wow."

This didn't sound right to Westmore. "Did something happen? It sure as hell sounds like it."

"I'm not sure," Mack said.

"And what about dinner?" Karen complained, starting another drink.

"Well, we were kind of hoping you guys could cook dinner. We'll be about an hour."

Karen groaned.

I can't cook for dick, Westmore thought. *But—* "We'll whip something up. And then you're going to tell me what's going on, right?"

"Sure, when I find out myself." Mack was rushing back out. "Oh, oh, there's New Zealand lobster tails in the freezer," and then he was gone.

"I don't know how to cook lobster tails, but I guess I'm about to find out," Westmore said.

"You're supposed to be Vivica's chronicler. It almost sounds like they don't want you to know what's going on. Shouldn't you be in there, too?"

"Yeah, but I've got a better idea; discretion might have some advantages, especially with this crowd. I don't know what to make of anybody yet." *The library,* Westmore thought. He punched up the floor index on the videocom, then hit the right wing and room button. Voices etched through the speaker.

"The psychometry of the room was dizzying," Willis' voice asserted. "It was like *my psyche* was seized by the revenant–environment."

"Was there visual?" a woman asked.

"Yes, a long stream. I'm pretty sure it was active, and I'm *positive* it wasn't hypnagogic or pompic."

The other woman again. "Are you sure you didn't touch anyone before you went in?"

"Who's that?" Westmore asked. "It doesn't sound like Adrianne."

"It's Cathleen Godwin," Karen said, "the one who claims she was assaulted outside. She's the one you haven't met yet." She pushed the video button. "There."

Westmore had forgotten. The display screen was now a tiny television, and he could see them all sitting solemnly around a long William and Mary trestle table. A blonde in a soft-green sundress was the one Westmore hadn't met yet. She listened and talked with her fingers steepled, her eyes either grim or very focused.

Nyvysk sat at the table's head. "All right, so Willis and Cathleen have already had positive contacts. And so have I."

"What?" Adrianne said, sitting further away across from Mack. "Gauss? Imagery?"

"EVP, from three different targets."

There was a long silence.

Nyvysk continued. "It looks like we've found a charged house."

"Don't jump to conclusions," Adrianne said, chin in hand.

"Three out of four? With *us*?" Willis remarked. "It's hard to be skeptical with a percentage like that."

"What about you, Adrianne?" Cathleen asked in a way

that sounded like a challenge. "Are you going to sit around the whole time you're here, or put that bottle of pills away for a couple of hours and help us out?"

Adrianne didn't seem affected by the slight. "I did some RV-ing already."

"And?" Nyvysk asked.

"Nothing. Just that writer guy. I don't know if I like him."

Westmore frowned, could hear Karen chuckling behind him. "See what eavesdropping can do sometimes?"

"There's no reason for her to dislike me, for God's sake," he complained. "I don't even know her."

"These are some of the most psychic people in the country. They're also the most paranoid."

"Great."

"I don't trust that blonde," Cathleen said. "She's a floozy, and I swear she was shit-faced before she even walked in."

"What did that bitch say?" Karen exclaimed. "I'm gonna tell her to stuff her implants up her—" Karen impulsively reached for the intercom button, but Westmore snatched her hand away.

"*Don't* do that," he said. "We'll give ourselves away. I don't know about you but I kind of like the idea of them not knowing we're listening." Now it was Westmore's turn for a laugh. "See what eavesdropping can do sometimes?"

"That tramp . . ." Karen went to pour herself another drink from the small kitchen bar. "I'd like to slap her silly."

Nyvysk maintained his place as moderator. "Let's stick to business; we're here to do a job, and I agree with Willis. This house is a charged target. But what were you saying, Adrianne? What did you see in your RV?"

"The writer. He was upstairs, and he found a safe hidden in a wall, but he doesn't know the combination."

Mack, in the screen, looked dismayed. "How did you know that?"

"Trust me."

"That's a good question," Westmore said to Karen. "No one's been in Hildreth's office—Christ, we just left there a few minutes ago."

"I told you, this is a freaky bunch."

"And what the hell did Nyvysk mean? Something about an RV? I got a funny feeling they're not talking about recreational vehicles."

"It stands for remote-viewing. According to her bio and resume, Adrianne can see things from a distance. She can sit in a room and focus, and then see things in other rooms."

"Bullshit," Westmore said.

"How'd she know about the safe?"

"I don't know. Maybe Mack told her in confidence and that whole thing was a con game to convince the others she's for real. Or maybe—maybe she did the exact same thing we're doing. Watching on the videcom without our knowledge."

"Hildreth's office isn't wired. No intercom, no camera."

Westmore shook his head. "Look, I know I can be gullible sometimes but not *that* gullible. I'm not convinced."

"I'm not necessarily convinced either, I'm just telling you what's in her bio. She claims she can do the remote-viewing thing, and also some other, freakier things."

"I don't even want to know . . ." Westmore was trying to keep hold of his journalistic roots, *black and white* roots. He wasn't ready to even consider anything beyond that yet.

"I don't even know what she's doing here," Cathleen said at the table. "I think she's just jealous of me. Frowned at me when I met her at Vivica Hildreth's."

"She's talking about me again!" Karen railed. "Jealous? Why would I be jealous of that over-the-hill whore!"

"Calm down," Westmore said, amused.

"I've got no problem with her," Adrianne said. "But she drinks too much, that's for sure. When I was RV-ing, I saw her at the liquor cabinet twice."

"That *bitch!*" Karen exclaimed again.

"She's a drunk and a half." Cathleen again. "But somebody answer my question. Why's she even here?"

"To snoop for Vivica, I'm sure," Mack contributed. "Karen doesn't act like it, but she loves to snoop . . ."

"*Prick!* Turncoat son-of-a-bitch! Who's he to talk? He's the biggest brown-nose I ever met in my life!"

Westmore just shook his head, listening.

"We're getting off track," Nyvysk suggested. "Forget about the others. It's *us*. The four of *us*. No offense, Mack, but in this situation you're an outsider, too. The four of *us* need to make a conclusion. Three of us have."

Every head at the library table turned to Adrianne.

"I will. Tonight," she said, as if fatigued or dreading whatever it was she vowed to do. "After midnight's always better." She rose from the long table. "I'm going up now to get ready. I have to be by myself, so I'll use one of the bedrooms."

"Aren't you going to eat?" Cathleen asked. "The writer and the drunk girl are fixing dinner—"

"That *bitch!*" Karen fumed, wobbling with drink in hand.

"No, no, I never eat beforehand." Adrianne set a bottle of pills in front of Cathleen. "Watch those for me, will you? And I'm sorry about what happened to you earlier."

Then she walked shakily out of the library, leaving them all, especially Cathleen, to their own contemplations.

"She'll be all right," Nyvysk assured. "She's been doing this for decades."

Doing WHAT? Westmore thought, irritated.

"I'm not really hungry myself, come to think of it," Nyvysk said, and rose. "I'm going to start hooking up some thermal units upstairs, and charge the gauss meters. Tell the writer to leave something for me in the fridge."

What am I, the mansion houseboy? Westmore thought. On the screen the others were getting up. "Shit, help me," he urged, flicking the videocom off.

"Huh?"

"We're supposed to be cooking dinner. Gimme a hand, will you?"

"Sure," Karen said. "I'm going to get another drink first . . ."

III

She stripped down to her panties and bra, already aglint with sweat since closing the room's air-conditioning ducts. Higher temperatures, for whatever reason, seemed to aid Adrianne's psychic endowment, her "jaunts," as she would call them. She chose the smallest bedroom she could find on the fifth floor, preferring a base that was cramped because returning from a jaunt felt less wild: siphoning back from expansive and often barely definable perimeters into a relatable containment. *I doubt that anyone out there can see me,* she figured with some insecurity. Way up here on the fifth story? But she *did* feel self-conscious about her body. *Between Cathleen and Karen, I'm the last person anyone would want to peek at.* Several lights were on in the bedroom, which afforded her an unwitting glance at her reflection in the oblong dressing mirror: arms and legs too skinny, small breasts, an abdomen losing some of its elasticity. She had no tan, but at least hoped to work on that during her stay. She groaned at her jutting hip bones. The Lobrogaine provided an essential advantage to OBE-ing but one side effect was faster-than-normal fat metabolization; she could eat like a pig but not gain an ounce. Such was her multisided curse.

That and total abstinence from sexual contact, the only way she could maintain control . . .

The pills she'd left downstairs with Cathleen were strong barbiturates; the ones that remained in her pocket were her secret. She sat on the high four-poster bed for several minutes, breathing slowly, absorbing the room into her senses. As an experiment, she needed to calm herself and fall into what she thought of as her zone. Then she got up, parted the veranda drapes, and opened the french doors, unconcerned by her near-nudity. The hot night rushed in, caressing, bidding more perspiration and the tacky calm she needed. She looked down the vast hill, and saw only dark woods and a yellow moon rising.

It's time, she thought. She knew she was procrastinating . . . and she knew she was afraid. She could sense the house, too, just like the others, but she hadn't said anything because she needed the safety of remaining objective for as long as possible. She turned all the lights off in the room except the small lamp on the nightstand. The room's midnight-blue wallpaper with cruciform symbols of various sizes appeared multidimensional; her Christian roots found solace in them. Next she poured herself a glass of water from the bedside decanter, and withdrew her other bottle of pills.

Lobrogaine was a psychoactive by text definition, and possessed some minor analgesic properties in low doses.

FDA had long-since banned it for fear of misuse, because in unmonitored doses it could produce psychedelic hallucinations and, in some cases, psychosis. The Army's Telethesia Program had adopted it to accelerate the proficiency of persons with Adrianne's talents, citing the benefits for national security outweighed the risks. Adrianne had since become at least psychologically addicted to its morphine-like properties and hence required even more habituating barbiturates to keep functional. "Just remember what you're doing for your country," her clinician at Fort Meade always reminded her. "Psychics like us are pretty much washed-up in the regular world, or condemned to freak-shows and tarot parlors. We save so many lives by using our gifts as we do here." Adrianne supposed he was right, and she also knew that she was flushing her own life down the toilet for her "duty." Now it didn't matter.

She popped one vanilla-colored capsule and lay back on the bed. When she took the drug she "slipped" out so much faster to the point now that such slips often occurred against her will; hence the barbiturates to counteract the effect. She knew she could go now if she tried but she opted to wait a half-hour for full absorption. She lay in a cruciform shape of her own, toes pointed, arms outstretched, breathing deep and slow. With her eyes closed, her vision was nothing but a scape of dark grain.

First, she tried some remote-views, easier still. Concentrating on a simple target-thought let her mind's eye start to draw "snaps." It wasn't like an OBE at all; there was no roving, no sense of movement or disembodiment. She thought *South Atrium,* and then saw it, spotted Cathleen watching television, legs crossed, something clearly on her mind. Then, *Kitchen,* and saw Karen and the writer busy preparing dinner. She saw their lips move as they conversed—Karen seemed upset about something—but couldn't hear what they were saying. While remote-viewing all she could ever hear was a drone in her head, and her field of vision differed from stereoscopic eyesight, instead more akin to viewing something through a slit. She thought of the several areas she'd seen outside, then "snapped" onto them: the front cul-de-sac, the back gardens, some of the woodline. At one point she thought she saw a small sports car but nowhere near the parking court; instead it sat as if stowed in the woods. She could see no one inside. Then, further afield, *Another car?* Yes, an old, long sedan with a landau roof, and some dents. Exhaust from the muffler floated upward, the engine obviously running. A man and a woman inside but she couldn't see their faces. Had she remoted off the grounds? Sometimes that happened. She tried to redirect herself.

She recalled Cathleen's encounter at the graveyard, and then she saw it: the overgrown perimeter hidden in the woods, surrounded by a spiked iron-crested fence. She saw tilted gravestones, some very old, but even in the dark she managed to read the name on one of them: REGINALD HILDRETH.

Okay . . . Now . . . Push, she told herself.

Down.

Deeper and *down . . .*

The "snap" grew murky. She couldn't see.

Down. Deeper.

She was through the ground, she was seeing inside the coffin but nothing plainly visual, just cold traceries of a death-eminence.

She saw a body but no face.

Out, out!

She snapped out, acrawl from claustrophobia. *Yeck!* She hated seeing bodies.

One more thing and then she could move on to an OBE; she remembered her first remote-viewing earlier: the writer snooping in the office on the third floor. He'd found a safe hidden in the wall.

Safe, she thought.

And there she was, looking right at it.

Through, through . . .

Reading tag numbers, street names and addresses, and information on documents and computer screens was the ultimate value of remote-viewing, at least for military and law-enforcement purposes—Adrianne had been trained well. But today she struck out.

Her vision could detect nothing inside the safe. Just darkness.

Give it up, she advised herself. When she forced her vision out of the safe—an image like a camera in reverse zoom— she saw one last thing: a framed picture that looked quite old, an engraving. In her mind she squinted, and the slit of her viewing field homed in—on an inhuman, empty-eyed face, then lower, to finely chiseled words: MY SELF AS I DARE TO REFASHION THE COUNTENANCE OF MY VISION: BELARIUS.

The words and the engraving meant nothing to her. It was time to end this now, but the practice had fortified her; she hadn't remote-viewed in a while, and she was glad to discover that she hadn't lost her touch; if anything she felt even more attuned—

—which would be good for what came next.

She opened her eyes on the bed, found herself looking straight up at fascinatingly detailed tin ceiling tiles. She brought her hands to her face, then down to her bra'd breasts, her abdomen, and thighs. Sweat saturated the bra and panties, and her skin felt glazed. Heat always invigorated her, and heightened her perceptions further.

The Lobrogaine had kicked in, it left her smiling dopily. Perhaps it was the drug's most paramount side effect—a greedy satiation much like orgasm—that attracted her most to it. Was she subconsciously using it to replace genuine sexual release? The two weren't the same but this was awfully close, and her dependency made more sense given the fact that she'd abstained from sex for almost a decade now. She couldn't even masturbate. It was an indulgence she longed for.

But she was too afraid to do it now . . .

She relaxed, reclosed her eyes, maintaining her position of crucifixion. She prayed to herself, *God, I know that what I am is part of You. Release me in the midst of this evil place and keep me safe . . .*

Her abdomen tightened and her face seemed to bulge, as if something bigger than her physical form was exiting her, which in a sense was true. She was out in an instant.

The best way she could ever think to describe an OBE was having your eyes and brain inside a transparent helium balloon. She felt buoyant and barely stable, a row boat on an ether sea but with a faulty rudder.

She looked down, and saw her body lying still on the big bed.

Adrianne was apart from her body now, connected to it only by some aeriform nerve that out-of-body-experients sometimes called their "soul-tether."

Then she backed away, and was gone, out of the room.

She had no hands now to touch with, no feet to run; instead the urn of her spirit *flew.*

Through doors, through walls. Through life-size statues of solid marble. On the third floor, she wisped through the door of the communications room and found herself hovering over Nyvysk who tinkered with one of his detection machines. When she guided herself through his solid body, he flinched, welping, "Damn, that's cold!" He looked around, looked up, shaking his shaggy head. "I know you're there somewhere, Adrianne. But *please* don't do that!" She laughed to herself and drifted out of the room, then down, through the carpet and floor-studs, and the next ceiling. She rocked the vessel that she could only think of as her head and saw Cathleen looking in rooms, carrying her tote bag. When she chose a room and entered, she closed the door behind her, but Adrianne pushed through its oaken panels.

She hovered and watched, an otherworldly spy, a mystic candid camera. Cathleen seemed pent up about something, murmuring, "Oh, God, what is wrong with me?" and then she lay down on a high-post bedstead plush with a thick-quilted mattress. *She's insatiable!* Adrianne thought when she saw what the lusty blonde was doing. From her bag she'd withdrawn some implements: two nipple-clamps and a frightfully realistic vibrator. In a desperate second, her breasts were popped out of the swells of her top, her nipples clipped hard by the clamps, the hem of her sundress dragged up. She wasted no time in placating herself with the vibrator, teeth grinding and eyes squeezed shut. Adrianne felt embarrassed but also infuriated. Cathleen whispered, "Please, please, please. I just . . . can't . . . stop . . ."

The vibrator hummed, delving in and out. If Adrianne had had a mouth, she surely would've frowned. *I've seen about all of this that I can stand*. She was glad she couldn't read minds, for Cathleen's was likely full of sexual garbage right now, the images she summoned for her pleasure a kaleidoscope of all the countless men she'd let herself be used by in the past.

But Adrianne at least was honest enough for this single

thought: *Oh, what I wouldn't give . . .* before she zipped out of the room.

Up through more ceilings and flooring boards, and she bobbed into the middle of a dimly lit hall on the fifth story. The chapel stood eerily silent, its hardwood walls utterly black. There was no crucifix, naturally, but a single underlit sconce before a black altar whose rear panel was carved with a simple inverted cross. A black pulpit faced a few rows of black pews and black kneelers. The environment upset her, so she backed out but not before spying a cistern whose silver bowl sat empty. Next to it stood a racked stand containing several stoppered glass flasks which, in a church, would be full of holy water. These flasks, however, appeared to be full of semen.

Adrianne exited, revolted. She'd sensed nothing para-active in the room, nor even residual. The place simply made her sick.

The Scarlet Room, she thought next, trying to focus. She hovered before the veneered doors. On the floor, she noticed several of Nyvysk's things, which she instantly recognized as new-generation gauss screens. They detected increases in ion activity, a supernatural presence-signature. *But they're not even hooked up,* she could see. *Why didn't he put them in the room?*

It didn't matter; the tech stuff was his business, and Adrianne didn't have much faith in it anyway. She was just testing the waters right now, having a look around. She floated through the door.

And stared.

The Scarlet Room was indeed well-named. Everything was red: the wallpaper, baseboards and half-paneling, the carpet. A variety of rod-back chairs, Edwardian cloak-stands, gateleg tables—all in red veneer. In the center of the room stood nothing, which seemed strange. It reminded her of a stage. *Why have all that empty space in the middle?* she wondered.

She roved around, examining the fine, intricate wallpapering and woodwork. After a moment, though, just when she was getting bored . . . she started to feel sick.

Not physically—for she had no physical body. Instead, her buoyant spirit felt nauseous. Her vision dimmed.

Was she falling?

A second later, she was somewhere else . . .

Something dark yet impossibly light-like accosted her psychic senses. Her soul felt surrounded now, by humid heat. A long spell of vertigo unwound, and when she was able to focus her vision—

What in the name of Christ is that?

Figures moved before what could only be described as a temple, but instead of pillars and stone, the temple was constructed of . . . flesh.

Fluted columns sided a wide, corniced archway, where each stone was a block of some flesh-like substance. Steps rose to a closed entrance; Adrianne could tell it was a doorway because she could see a seam between two high panels, and some indescribable wavering in the seam. Was it light?

A colonnade with thinner pillars sat recessed behind the main archway, these columns too composed of palpable flesh. Figures stood between the columns.

Adrianne was aghast when she looked more closely. Wide-jointed but thin-limbed things looked back at her through faces with no eyes or noses. Bald-lumpen heads sat tilted on plops of shoulders, and the faces had only mouths rimmed by narrow lips the color of garden slugs. They were naked, and seemed teeming in sweat or oil, the flesh that composed their bodies semitranslucent. Malformed genitals hung like flaps of pale meat at their groins.

"A traveler," came a voice from aside. The voice radiated,

like raving light in this dark place. "Meet the sentinels of the Chirice Flaesc."

Adrianne shrieked psychically, turned her spirit about. Facing her now was something different from the repugnant creatures that prowled the colonnade.

It was a man, or something akin to a man, for he had a face, a stunning, handsome face with burning eyes like melted emeralds and a smile that burned similarly. He wore a tunic over sculpted muscles, but Adrianne felt instantly queasy when she realized the tunic was fashioned from veined skin that appeared identical to the skin that covered the entire, hideous temple.

"You're enlightening," he said next, stepping with interest past the column. "We have so few travelers here."

Who are you? Adrianne asked with her mind.

"Jaemessyn," he said, the strange word rolling from his mouth.

And, and—what did you call this place?

"The Chirice Flaesc." The eyes smoldered at her. Adrianne shuddered when he extended a hand—no normal hand at all. She saw now that the limbs attached to his magnificent torso were dissimilar—they weren't human. They were runneled and darkly splotched, heavily sinewed. More revolting were the hands themselves: each finger was a stout, tumid penis.

He gestured the figures in the colonnade. "And these are the Adiposians. They guard this temple . . . and wait."

"Wait for what?"

"For the very rare chances, to venture out and taste the Living World—the world of *your* God. But *this* . . . is the world of mine."

Adrianne tried to focus on Jaemessyn's face but found it difficult. She sought more detail. Each strain of her out-of-body vision, though, caused an annoying series of shifts, like trying to look at something through jerking blinds.

Several of the things—Adiposians, he'd called them— peered facelessly out at her, from behind the flesh-columns. The one that stood closest stepped out, and Adrianne gasped, sickened, to see the vaguely featured genitals, like a sausage skin filled with lard, grow aroused.

How can it see me? she asked Jaemessyn. *I have no body to see, and that thing has no eyes.*

"It senses your desire," the penis-fingered being told her. "That's what this place—and our Lord—thrives on. Desire. All the desire of history. And you are . . . *drenched* with it."

Adrianne gasped again, and actually hovered higher at the start, when a set of skeletal wings spread behind Jaemessyn's back, a complex webwork of bones. "No, I'm not a demon, as you can see. I'm one of the righteous Fallen."

The bones of the wings were pitted and charred black.

"The Adiposians aren't demons, either. They're crafted, by our Warlocks. They're soulless; they're made from rendered fat and shaped, then animated by spells, to serve, to protect, and to rape. All in the name of my Lord. And like yourself, they're venturers. A soul in Hell can't ever leave, but what of something that *has* no soul? They can venture out, I cannot."

And they can go . . . to my world?

"Yes, that delicious sphere of sin and failure. Once every eon or so, someone on your side is smart enough to open a Rive, and a few Adiposians depart. They don't last long over there, but long enough to send some visions back. To be suckled by the lord of the temple."

If Adrianne had possessed a throat, it would've been parched when she asked, *What's your lord's name?*

"You're not worthy to hear his unholy name. But he is Lucifer's third-favorite, and he is known as the Sexus Cyning. This is his church, where he is revered. And *this* . . . is how we revere him . . ."

A muffled peal resounded then. Was a bell ringing behind the closed doors to this temple of skin? Was it a clock?

The Fallen Angel stepped back behind the column where, set into the temple's main sidewall there appeared to be a tall narrow panel. Veins throbbed beneath the panel's sheen of skin. Jaemessyn whispered something and the panel opened. What hung there, in the coffin-shaped depression, was a woman, or some facsimile thereof: a thin, voluptuously curved but horned demonness with canine-like fangs and skin pink with rash. Elegant, long-fingered hands twisted against wire bonds which tacked her wrists together. "One of our courtesans," the Fallen Angel said, producing a pair of iron pliers. "They can be irascible, though." The demonness jerked on her mount as Jaemessyn manually extracted the longest of her fangs. Blood much thinner than human blood poured down her nude body, some of it actually flying off her convulsing belly in crimson plips. Adrianne couldn't help but notice large breasts that were each almost entirely nipple. Then the Fallen Angel lifted her out of her containment, from barbed hooks, and threw her down at the feet of the Adiposians.

The slug-rimmed mouths gaped—mouths with no teeth but only broad, foaming tongues. The gelatinous things fell on the female, and began . . .

"Watch," Jaemessyn said. "This is what we do here."

Adrianne watched . . . the unwatchable. Her spirit floated dizzily; during an OBE, she couldn't close her eyes because her vision was lidless. Jaemessyn supervised as the female was primordially raped on the temple's peristyle. *I can't stay here,* Adrianne thought, dismal. It was time to end the OBE, go back to her physical body where her mind would be safe. She willed herself to move off, to return, but . . .

"Not yet," Jaemessyn said.

Adrianne couldn't move.

"Behold the wonders that take place here in the Chirice Flaesc." Jaemessyn's luminous voice crackled. "Stay and watch awhile. Let these beauteous images be branded into your mind . . . Something to take back and tell your friends."

Adrianne squirmed as she hovered. The demonness was mauled in place, flipped over, contorted about, to afford the sex organs of her attackers every conceivable purchase of coitus and sodomy. Eyes the size of peaches and clear as glass bulged forth as she was taken and taken again.

But the creature had never screamed, and when the things were done with their rut they left her calmly limp and gratified in spite of the ravenous degradation. Then the ten stout penises of Jaemessyn's hands lifted her up by her throat and squeezed, squeezed, squeezed some more, until her back arched backward in midair, and—

CRACK!

—her neck broke.

The body dangled flaccid now in Jaemessyn's grasp, but when he set her back up on the hook, Adrianne noticed her face: a serene and very sated smile.

Ecstasy in eternal death.

The Fallen Angel's gaze moved back up to Adrianne. "Go now, traveler. Go back to your domain and speak of what you've witnessed here."

Again, Adrianne tried to move off, to flee, but couldn't.

"And if you have the will to meet my Lord—and I think

you do—then visit me again"—he pointed to the archway—"and I will open those doors for you. You're not ready now, you haven't gone far enough. But I think—I really think—you soon will."

Adrianne stared back at the flawed but grand being.

"I know that my Lord would love to meet you."

Adrianne soared away, her ethereal exit followed like a flapping banner by the darkest scream. That scream still filled her head when her soul-tether constricted and dropped her spirit back into her physical body with an effect like a rock being dropped into a lake.

She felt dead as she lay on the bed. For minutes she could barely move, could only stare upward. The bedroom's darkness seemed to churn at first, like something alive. Her heart was racing—*Calm, calm, calm,* she ordered herself—and her hands shook. When the rush of adrenalin began to dissipate, subtle pains became apparent. Her nipples felt chewed on, her stomach and thighs bitten. And something worse:

Her sex ached.

When she pressed her hands down against the mattress, they flinched back. The bed was *drenched.* Most experients perspired heavily during a jaunt, and Adrianne was no exception. But *this?*

I couldn't possibly have sweated this much . . . could I? she wondered, patting more of the mattress. It squished, as wet as if whole buckets of warm water had been dumped on it, and on her. Or perhaps something else had.

When she finally leaned up and looked down at herself, she thought very dismally: *Oh, no . . .*

She lay nude on the wide bed. She wasn't positive but she was almost certain that she'd been wearing her bra and panties when she'd begun.

Chapter Eight

I

"Here comes somebody," Clements said, eyes pressed to the binoculars. "Who the hell . . ."

"It looks like another van," the girl said. She squinted more out of boredom than interest. "Maybe it's another workman."

"No, not now. Vivica had the place cleaned up before any of that crowd arrived. You saw them, the fumigators, the disposal crew. There were more last week. Painters, paperhangers, carpet-layers. I don't know *who* the hell this is. And at this hour?"

The girl squinted through the windshield and shrugged.

The girl called herself Teary but she'd eventually told Clements her real name: Connie. Twenty-five years old but looked thirty-five. She'd been addicted to crack since she was fifteen, when she first started turning tricks. It had been her mother and step-father who'd hooked her and put her on the street. Clements' attraction to such girls was pretty concrete—something about the look and the attitude, the late-night car-rides, prowling around alleys and looking for that image in his headlights. They were all the same, except, evidently, this one. He was starting to actually like her.

He'd paid her again just to drive out here with him, for a closer look at the hidden access-road, which was where they sat parked now. Since that first night he'd picked her up, he hadn't laid a hand on her.

"It's a locksmith," he said, finally getting a glimpse of the van when it turned into the mansion's front floodlights.

"Guess they need something open," Connie remarked. But she looked out the open passenger window instead as if studying the forest might take her mind off how badly she needed to light her pipe. She brushed a straggle of hair off her brow. "When are you gonna tell me what you're doing out here? You just sit here, watching. Hildreth is dead. Everyone who was there that night is dead. There's nobody in that house right now who had anything to do with Hildreth—"

"Actually there is. A woman named Karen Lovell, who did all the paperwork for T&T Enterprises, and a guy named Mack Colmes, who works for Hildreth's wife—"

"Okay, great, but neither of them were in the house on the night of the murders. So what are you doing out here? I know it's got something to do with that girl in the picture—"

"Debbie Rodenbaugh, yes."

"She sure as shit ain't in there, and you said she wasn't one of the bodies. She probably split when all the shit went down. What good is sitting out here going to do?"

"I'm . . . not sure," Clements admitted.

Connie squinted out of her withdrawal for enough time

to really look at Clements. "She's not the daughter of a client, I don't believe it—"

"It's true." Clements shrugged. "Her parents hired me over a year ago to keep tabs on her once she started working for Hildreth—"

She chuckled. "Yeah, and junkies never lie. I think I know what it is. She's some young chick you had the hots for, fell in love with—"

Now Clements laughed to himself. "No, nothing like that at all. I never even met Debbie Rodenbaugh."

"I don't get any of this. You rich or something?"

"Not really. I have a pension from the Navy and retirement from the police department. I've been a private investigator for two years—something to do."

"I ain't complaining," she said, scratching her knees. "This is three nights in a row you're paying more than I'd make on the street, and you don't even want any action." She sighed and looked at him again. "You're such a nice guy, which is weird. Most johns are pricks."

Clements' brow rose.

"Oh, I'm sorry," she said, half-heartedly. "You're offended if I call you a john?"

"No," he answered. How could he be? He'd picked up countless hundreds of prostitutes in his life.

"Lotta time tricks and cops call me a whore, and you know what? It doesn't piss me off because I know that's what I am."

The comment barbed him. It was tragic how she had no positive concept of herself and never saw anything beyond this in her future. "I'm a john—I admit it. A bigtime john."

"Then how come you never buy any action from me? I know you trick all the time with the other girls on the street."

"Let's talk about something else."

"Okay. What time is it?

"About ten o'clock."

"Your time's up then, right?"

Clements nodded.

"So why don't you take me back now? Unless you wanna pay me to sit here with you for another hour and not even give you head. Don't get me wrong, it's fine with me if you do. I've never said this to a john in my life but I'm starting to feel like I'm ripping you off."

Clements laughed at that one. Of course, he knew how strange this situation must seem to her. "How about tomorrow? Same thing. I need to come back out here, and I want you to come too."

She frowned. "What time?"

"Around noon—"

"Noon! I *get up* at noon, man."

"I'll pay you five hundred bucks—"

"You're so fuckin' weird . . . But, yeah, of course."

"Great. I guess it's time for us to go home—"

He put the binoculars under his seat. He leaned back.

"Well?" she said.

He sat a moment longer and lit a cigarette.

"You just said it was time to get out of here," Connie objected. "What gives now?"

"How much . . . ," Clements faltered, "for you to go home with me?"

She twirled in her seat, almost astonished, put her hand on his leg. "I was wondering when you'd finally come around. You must know some other john who's had me, right? And he told you I was good?"

"No, I don't know any other johns." Her hand on his leg

confused him. "And I don't even know if *that's* why I want you to go home with me."

She was shaking her head again but before she could speak, Clements put his arm around her and kissed her. She didn't retract at first; after a moment, though, she put her hand against his chest and pushed him back.

In the moonlight, her face looked very sad. "What are you doing?" she whispered. "Nobody *kisses* us, ever."

What could I possibly be thinking? "I like you," he groaned.

"We're just meat. We're things johns fuck or get head from—that's all. Nobody ever *likes* us."

Clements pulled her close to him, and her arms slipped around his shoulders, and then they kissed for a long time.

He wanted to fall into her right now, forget about everything else: Hildreth, the mansion, Debbie, the murders. It felt so good, in fact, to just be with Connie and clear his mind of all those other things.

He'd worry about those other things tomorrow, when he'd sneak into the Hildreth Mansion.

II

Westmore didn't like the mood of the house when he and Karen cooked dinner. Something felt wrong, too much silence, something. "Are we just going through the motions here?" he asked Karen, who had just finished preparing a make-shift cob salad. "Dinner's ready but no one's around."

"I don't know. This place screws with people's moods." She listlessly lit a cigarette, sitting bored now on the kitchen's expansive butcher-block table. "And don't forget the mentalities of the others."

"What do you mean?"

"They're all half-nuts. They're a bunch of paranoid, scared-shitless *psychics.*"

"Oh, that," Westmore said. "At least the dinner we busted our butts making *looks* good." He picked up the tray of grilled lobster tails and put it in the oven to keep them warm.

"I guess there's no reason why we shouldn't eat," Karen said, getting some plates. The plates were shiny-black. "The others can get theirs when they're ready."

It sounded like a good idea to Westmore. He was about to get a plate for himself when the doorbell rang, a bright clanging bell.

Karen and Westmore looked at each other. "Who's that at this hour?" Karen said.

"Vivica?"

"She never comes here . . ."

The bell rang again.

"Who knows where Mack is?" Westmore took off his cooking apron. "I guess I better answer it."

He strode to the foyer, still addled by the mansion's damped silence, and unbolted the doors to find a robust, attractive brunette in a blue jumpsuit standing on the stone stoop. She held a clipboard close to a sizeable bosom and gripped a black toolbag in the other hand.

"I'm here about the safe," the woman said in a tired but seductive voice.

Her sexy curves and contours—contrasted by the slovenly work clothes and clunky boots—sidetracked Westmore. In the cul-de-sac sat a van: PINELLAS LOCK & KEY. "Oh, the locksmith," he finally snapped to. "It was a guy I talked to on the phone."

"That was my boss. I was coming back from another job when he dispatched me." A patch on her top read: Vanni.

She either seemed peeved by the late call, or just disturbed by the ambience of the house; she didn't look happy—something else to contrast the stunning body and very feminine face and hair. Westmore let her in and when he turned after closing the door, he saw her staring up along the curving stairwell. At once, she shuddered.

"The a/c too cold for you?" Westmore asked.

"No, I'm fine. What a strange place. It's gorgeous but . . . well, strange, I guess."

"I suppose it is." Did she know about the murders? Whether she did or not, he could tell at once that she didn't want to be here. But he *was* curious about the safe. "The office is on the third floor. Sorry, there's no elevator."

"That's fine, I need the exercise."

She didn't need any exercise, not in Westmore's view. He followed her up the stairwell, gritting his teeth at the shape of her rump as she rose. *This is all I need, another bombshell walking around this joint.* By now, between the porn and all the attractive women his vision had been inundated with—it was all starting to get on his nerves. *Oh, great,* he complained more to himself when they got to the office. Plump breasts strained against the jumpsuit top. *Of course she's not wearing a bra.* Westmore admired attractive women as much as the next guy, but this was getting to be too much.

"You said the safe's not wired, right?"

"It's not wired." He let them in, first, to Karen's former office, then to Hildreth's office behind it.

"Good, 'cos if it's not wired, I can open it," she assured.

"Your boss said the same thing."

He took her around to the oddly placed space behind where the cabinet had been, which reminded him of the strange way Hildreth had hidden the safe: pictures beneath pictures, old engravings, and the pastoral oil painting of the young, dark-haired women whose snapshot he'd also found in the desk. "There it is," he said, and pointed to the safe.

Vanni looked right at it, slumped, and said, "I can't open it."

Westmore was bewildered. "But you just said—"

"Sir, that's a custom Sec-Lock safe. Same company that makes bank vaults. I couldn't get into that with dynamite."

"What? Dynamite?" Suddenly Mack was in the room, his youth clearly perked by the sight of the attractive locksmith. "I heard the bell and saw the lock van outside. Hi, I'm Mack."

"Vanni." She shook Mack's hand with little interest.

"She can't open it," Westmore said. "It's a special kind of safe."

She looked back at it. "I'll bet that thing cost twenty or thirty thousand dollars. And guess why it costs that much? So no one can crack it."

"There must be some way," Mack said, idling about the office. He appeared more interested in the safe-cracker than the safe.

"Can't you use a stethoscope, like on TV?" Westmore suggested.

Vanni frowned hard. "That's a myth. The pins on the combination don't make noise anyway, and they're mag-pins, not gravity pins. It's biradial, the most advanced pin-tumbler system made. Nothing will drill through it, and if we tried to cut through it, the temperature would go so high that anything inside would be burned."

"So it's impossible?"

"Maybe."

"Maybe means maybe you *can* open it," Mack said.

She set her bag down. "Yeah, *maybe*. It could take all night, and there's no guarantee."

"We need this safe open," Westmore stated.

"And we don't care if it takes all night," Mack added.

She turned to them both. "I'll be honest with you, guys. I got two kids and a mortgage, I need the money in a big way, and I charge a hundred bucks an hour for special jobs like this. You want to pay me that kind of money for no guarantee, then great. I'll do my best. But I'd feel almost like I was stealing from you. You could have the manufacturer open it for a lot cheaper. It might take a week for verifications but you'd save yourselves hundreds of dollars."

Mack whipped out the $10,000 stack Westmore had given him earlier, peeled off a thousand, and gave it to her. "Go to it. If it turns out you need more, that shouldn't be a problem."

Vanni tried to subdue her disbelief. In her eyes, though, she looked overjoyed. "I— Okay." She glanced to the CRT behind the desk. "I'll need to use your computer to go on-line. I need to get the basic specs of the box and try to find out how many numbers the combination might have. Probably either three, five, or nine."

"We'll leave you to it, then," Westmore said. He turned to Mack, "Let's go back down while she's working. Dinner's ready."

But Mack was hovering over Vanni where she sat. "Can I get you something to drink?"

"Uh, sure, thanks. A Coke would be fine."

He touched her shoulder. "How about something to eat? I think we're having lobster for dinner. I could bring you up some."

"Well, if it's no trouble, yeah. Thanks."

Westmore withheld his amusement when he and Mack left the office and proceeded down. "So, what? You're putting the make on the safe girl?"

"Are you kidding? That body on her could start a riot in

a seminary. I don't know about you, man, but I haven't had any action in a week. I sure as hell don't want to mess with any of those weird chicks downstairs."

Westmore couldn't believe his audaciousness. "The woman came here to open a safe—she's not a *date*."

Mack chuckled, eyes thinned with male arrogance. "She's hot, and she's hot for me. We'll see where it goes from there."

Westmore lit a cigarette. "Oh, so she's *hot* for you, huh? And you know this . . . how?"

"It's in the eyes, man, the eyes." Mack slapped him on the back, as a linebacker might slap the quarterback after a sack. "Hey, no hard feelings. I can't help it that she was scoping me out instead of you. But I'll bet you could score with Karen."

Westmore had to laugh. "I didn't come here to *score*, Mack . . ."

Back downstairs, Nyvysk, Willis, Cathleen, and Karen had already set dinner on the study table in the atrium.

"It's happened to me before—not a big deal," Cathleen was saying over her plate. She looked disheveled and tired. "Just not with this intensity. God, it was just so *precise*."

"What was precise?" Westmore asked, sitting down next to Karen.

Nyvysk filled him in. "It's been a trying day for some of us, Mr. Westmore. Earlier, Cathleen suffered what we call a transitive paramental contact—or a para-planar rape. Willis, whom you assisted after his ordeal in the parlor, experienced what he describes as the most intense taction transference of his career. And I experienced positive EVP activity—all within the last several hours."

Westmore's mind held onto the first mention: "Para-planar. From another plane of existence is what you're saying? You were *raped* by something from another plane?" he asked Cathleen.

She finished chewing some lobster, and answered: "I thought it was Hildreth—because when I began my divinations I was right in front of his grave. But when I came to . . . I was outside of the graveyard fence."

"You're saying you were raped by Hildreth's spirit?"

"Yes . . . or . . . I think so. I'm not sure."

Westmore rolled his eyes. He retraced his steps to something more objective. "You found Hildreth's grave?"

"Yes," she said. "There's a clearing in the woods right behind the house."

"I'd like you to show me where it is later, if you're up to it."

"Oh, I'm fine. I'm used to transitive contacts."

Westmore wasn't even sure what a "transitive contact" was; still, he was surprised by the casualness of her regard to an apparent trauma. *For a girl who was just sexually assaulted, she's taking it well.* Cathleen was eating voraciously, finishing the entire lobster tail and knocking out her salad and potatoes.

Willis, on the other hand, looked starving yet didn't seem to notice that there was food in front of him. He sat slouched at the table, circles under his eyes, depleted. "Well, I'm *not* fine. This house is definitely charged. We all know that by now."

"I agree," Nyvysk said.

"What exactly does that mean?" Westmore inquired.

"That's our way of saying haunted," Nyvysk offered. "It's a technical reference. A bunch of people sitting in a house, for example, each emit a trace electromagnetic field. Anything alive, including plants. Detection equipment, such as ion sensors, thermographs, and radiometers, can detect the presence of that field. Even though you can't see it, it's there, it's measurable and therefore verified. Now, if you take all the plants and people out of that house, and there's still evidence of that electromagnetic energy—you've got a charged house. People with psychic acuities such as Cathleen and Willis, have their own sensors, if you will, in their minds. They can feel and see aspects of that charge."

"What about you?" Westmore asked.

"I don't have those same sensitivities. That's why I have my equipment, to provide another avenue of verification."

"No, no, I mean what you said a minute ago," Westmore backed up. "You said you experienced something too."

Nyvysk diddled at his food too. "Positive EVP activity. Audio recordings."

"Of ghosts, you mean."

"Yes."

Westmore looked at him. "And you actually *have* these recordings?"

"Oh, yes. I've been getting readings all day."

No one else at the table seemed alarmed, which bothered Westmore. "I want to hear them." Westmore looked around at the others, dismayed. "Excuse me, folks, but this sounds like kind of a big deal to me. Doesn't anybody else want to hear these tapes?"

Willis seemed not to even hear him, and Cathleen simply shrugged. "We've heard them before," she said, eating more salad and potatoes. "It really *isn't* a big deal."

"It provides a necessary scientific authentication," Nyvysk said. "Helpful because it establishes more quickly that the mansion is charged and we're not all wasting our time."

"And I'd recommend that you *not* bother listening to any of the tapes," Willis said. He was fiddling with his fork, still wearing his jersey gloves.

"Why?" Westmore asked.

"Because sometimes the voices tell you things you don't want to hear."

The response made Westmore feel excited and suddenly apprehensive at the same time.

"I'd like to hear the ghosts," Karen finally spoke up, spinning her ice cubes in her glass.

"Later tonight," Nyvysk promised. "Let me finish setting up."

Westmore tried to eat but scarcely tasted the food, wondering about all of this. The room's odd, low-key vibe hung over the table like a very low ceiling.

"Where's Mack?" Karen asked if only to break the silence.

"I think he took a plate of food up to the locksmith."

"What's the status on the wall safe?" Nyvysk asked.

"She says she might be able to open it, might not."

"*She?*" Karen questioned. "The locksmith is a woman?"

"Yeah." *Just ask Mack,* Westmore thought in jest. "She said it might take all night."

Nyvysk pinched his chin through his beard. "I'm very interested in what might be in that safe."

"It's nothing alive or dead, that's about all I can tell you," Adrianne said, drifting wanly into the room. She'd obviously just showered, her ink-black bob wet and haphazardly combed. She clutched a white bathrobe around herself. "I remote-viewed and OBE'd into the safe. Couldn't see what's inside, but it's nothing with a life- or death-force."

"You were expecting a severed head?" Cathleen asked.

"In this house?" Willis contributed, "I probably *would* expect that."

"How was your jaunt?" Nyvysk asked her.

"Valuable, but . . ."

Everyone peered at her.

"I RV'd first, to the cemetery, found Hildreth's tombstone, then looked in his grave—"

Westmore recalled Karen's earlier explanation of remote-viewing, didn't know if he believed any of it, and didn't ask for details. But he was very interested in the grave simply because of Vivica's secret—that Hildreth's body was never actually recovered. "Was there a body in the grave?" he asked.

"Yes, a solid cold spot."

"Was it—"

"I couldn't see the face."

Yes, Westmore was *very* interested. *Mental note: find a shovel.*

"Oh, and there's an abandoned car out there in the woods," Adrianne added, brushing wet spikes of hair off her brow. "I'm not sure where but I know it's on the grounds because I could see the mansion in the background. And there's another car with people in it, two people, I think."

"On the property?" Westmore asked, slightly alarmed. "Right now?"

"As of about an hour ago, at least. A big sedan. It looked old."

"The house is elaborately alarmed," Nyvysk said, sensing Westmore's concern. "I wouldn't worry about it. We don't want to be calling police—they'd want to snoop around inside, and we can't have that kind of interference."

Karen leaned forward, elbows on the table and clearly bored. "It's probably just some kids parking in the woods, getting it on."

Westmore supposed he could go with that . . . but he still wanted to see. And the abandoned vehicle? *I gotta get the tag number run . . .*

"But there's something else, isn't there, Adrianne?" Nyvysk prodded. "You're obviously distraught about something."

She nodded, pulled the collar of her robe closer. "I'm pretty sure that I was molested, too. Like Cathleen."

Cathleen stiffened up in her seat. "At the cemetery?"

"No," Adrianne said, a grimness in her tone. "In the house."

Everyone stiffened up at that.

"Another para-planar rape?" Nyvysk asked, eyes open on her.

"I don't know if it was para-planar, discarnated, revenant." Her head drooped. Her hands shook a little, and when she looked imploringly to Cathleen, her unspoken need was re-alized. Cathleen passed her the bottle of pills, which West-more understood were barbiturates. Adrianne took one with some water and continued, "I based myself in one of the suites, then I OBE'd pretty successfully. I roved to the Scarlet Room, but I'm not sure what happened after that. I may have been misdirected, because when I started to re-ceive some direct sensory-responses, it felt like I was pulled off. As if *I* was guided to the target instead of me guiding myself."

"You were commandeered?" Nyvysk asked.

"Something like that, maybe."

"What did the location look like?"

More grimness mixed with confusion. "It must've been hallucinotic—I think I was in Hell."

Westmore listened, still skeptical but captivated.

"I need to think about it more to remember everything that happened," Adrianne went on. "After a jaunt I always need a little time for—"

"Memory refraction," Nyvsyk said.

"But when the OBE was terminated, my body was in a different position on the bed, and I was naked. I almost never OBE naked, usually just underwear."

Now Nyvysk was jotting notes down in a pad. "Usually? This is very important."

"I'm ninety-percent sure I had a bra and panties on when I started. That's the best estimation I can give."

Cathleen asked, "Was there any—"

"No semen. I was drenched but I'm not even sure it was sweat. It may have been something mesoplasmic or residual. It was gross—it almost smelled like urine. Light bruising, and I'm still pretty sore."

Westmore could barely comprehend what she meant; the only thing more shocking than what Adrianne reported was the attitude of the others. *They're not batting an eye at what she's saying . . .*

"How many of them molested you?" Cathleen asked next. "Mine was multiple."

"I don't know," Adrianne expressed, "I have no idea. I wasn't there. Only my body was there, and I really don't like the idea of that. That's never happened before." She took a sip of water from an etched goblet. "Somebody playing around with my body when I'm not even in it . . ."

"An element of transposition?" Willis guessed. "Something came out when you went in?"

"An interplanar agency crawling back here on your tether while you were elsewhere?" Nyvysk added.

"I never heard of that happening to anyone in my field, and it's never happened to me," Adrianne dispelled them. "It must've been something that was already here. OBE-ing tends to activate discorporate activity, so do vulnerabilities—discorporates can smell it a mile away. Same as when it happened to Cathleen—she was in a divination trance."

Westmore slammed his open hand down on the table so hard the silverware clattered. He stood up, tempering his outrage. "Sorry, folks, but I've had enough. I do a pretty good job of keeping an open mind and always considering every side of every story but this is past the line."

"Mr. Westmore?" Nyvysk looked up. "Is there a problem?"

Westmore snorted. "A problem? Yeah, we got two women here who claimed to have been raped, and everybody's sitting around trying to figure out what kind of *ghost* did it. I guess I'm just old-fashioned, huh? I guess I'm just not *hip* to this stuff. Did any of you people consider for even a second that these girls may have been raped by, uh, you know—a *rapist?*" He frowned at Adrianne. "For shit's sake, you just got done telling us that you saw an intruder on the property!"

"Relax," Cathleen said.

Willis lit a cigarette. "You don't know about this stuff. It's confusing at first."

"If we'd been molested by real men," Adrianne explained, "there'd be physical evidence. There'd be semen."

"Ever heard of rubbers?"

"It's not the same," Cathleen said.

Nyvysk was getting annoyed. "Really, Mr. Westmore, you must leave this to us. We understand your reaction, but what *you* must understand is that we have to remain focused. We respect that you're here as an observer only. *We're* here for another reason. We can't have any interference from you."

"Fine. I won't interfere," Westmore said. "You know what I'm gonna do? I'm gonna get a flashlight, go outside, and LOOK FOR THE RAPIST!"

"That's highly inadvisable," Nyvysk told him. "There are things about this place that you simply don't understand."

Westmore stormed off.

When the atrium doors slammed behind him, the others all looked at each other.

"There's one in a every crowd," Nyvysk remarked, and they all began to laugh.

III

Jeez Louise! Make my life easier, why don't you! At least they were paying. Vanni couldn't believe the money Mack had laid on her. Car doors and disk-tumbler deadbolts comprised ninety-percent of her work, and she was good at it. She could open most locks in not much longer than it took to open with the key. But this safe?

A tough job.

She went to the manufacturer's website and found the model number of the safe. The general specs were listed, including information about the combination, and that's when the job just got harder. It was a rare nine-number combination series, which meant that even if she *could* get the safe open, it would take three times longer.

The food that Mack had brought her earlier was great—she hadn't had lobster in a while—and then he'd plugged in the office coffee pot and started it for her. She opened her bag and pulled out the Stiles GMR (gravity-motion reader). It was simply a box with a meter on it, and this she plugged into the wall. Two other wires plugged into the front of the box. At the end of one wire was a heavy, cylindrical magnet; at the end of the other was a square counter-magnet which she taped to the left of the safe's combination mount. The magnet and counter-magnet created a simple magnetic flux which the meter measured. When a tumbler moved into sequence alignment, the device could detect that movement. In all, GMR's worked about half the time, and it could take several hours per pin. *And I've got NINE pins here,* Vanni reminded herself. She opened her pad and began.

An hour and a half later she'd gotten a total of five pins. *How do you like that? This might not take as long as I thought. Only four more to go . . .*

She left the GMR on and got up. She called her sister, who was watching the kids, and let her know she wouldn't be home for awhile, then poured some coffee. As she sipped she noticed the two paintings on the floor leaning against the wall. A young girl in a billowing dress, a painting like a romance cover. Then the odd engraving. *Weird,* she thought. But it was a weird place. *Someone must've spent millions on this joint—multiple millions. Must cost ten grand a month just for the power bill.* Five floors? All those rooms?

Without thinking about it, she left the office and found herself walking down the hall. More weird paintings hung on the walls, and for some reason she was grateful it was too dark to make out much detail. There was absolutely no sound. *I guess they don't mind me looking around,* she hoped. She didn't even know who "they" were, but it didn't matter. When you had kids and an ex-husband who'd fled to Thailand to avoid child-support, money was pretty much all that mattered.

Christ, I haven't even been on a date in six months . . . She worked at the bank during the week, and took night calls and weekends with the locksmith. So as for romantic prospects, where was the time? There was certainly no shortage of interested men. She had a healthy self-image, and when she looked in the mirror she not only knew that she was looking at a motivated, responsible woman, she knew she was looking at an attractive one. She'd get a lot of calls to construction sites, where foremen lost keys to houses being built. No, no shortage of interest there. Lots of whistles, lots of long looks. And from all those tough, brawny hardhats? Sometimes she fantasized about frenzied quickies in pickup trucks, just some rough, horny, and very nameless man hauling her boots and pants off and simply *doing* her without a word. Yes, sometimes Vanni thought about things like that—and a lot more—and she guessed that all women did, to themselves. But they were just fantasies. The reality was the workaday world: feeding the kids, paying the rent. Sometimes it just didn't seem very exciting.

A brass plate on a door read: THE LADY OF KADESH SITTING ROOM. *Yeah, this place really is too much,* Vanni thought, not even knowing that the Lady of Kadesh was purportedly history's first prostitute. Lots of the rooms were named. Why? The door was open a crack so she saw no harm in entering.

"Some sitting room," she muttered to herself. It was a gymnasium! Padded bench presses, racks, and cabled pulleys filled the center of the room, but . . .

Wow . . . This is outrageous . . .

Large oil paintings hung on all the walls. Unlike those in the halls, though, these depicted explicit scenes of sex. Orgies, mostly, in—

Vanni looked closer.

Orgies in the midst of demons. One stunningly realistic portrait showed a wide-eyed blonde wearing a crown of thorns, lips parted in bliss, face glazed by what could only be semen. Scaled demon-hands with red nails cradled her breasts. Another depicted group sex in the chancel of a cathedral, partially disrobed priests and nuns the participants. Another group-scene blazed, naked celebrants with scarlet eyes demonstrating more sexual positions than Vanni knew existed, all in a flaming grotto while horned monsters looked on.

Vanni turned away. She could never imagine such artwork. And in a gym?

"Crazy."

Beside a cabinet stood a small liquor bar topped by racks of glasses. *This is the weirdest gym I've ever seen,* she thought. *Booze? Porn?* Next she examined the gym equipment and found it all equally perplexing. In fact . . .

It wasn't gym equipment.

How could it be? She walked around, dismayed. Several padded benches, with thinner benches branching off at adjustable v-shapes. Pulleys which appeared to be able to raise the levels of each bench. Seats which seemed to be raised in the air. But there were no weights, no cables or Soloflex-like power bands. *What is this place?* she asked herself.

"I see you've stumbled on the playroom," Mack said curiously at the open door.

Vanni looked up, uneasy; he'd caught her by surprise. Would he be mad? After all, he was paying her a lot of money to open a safe, not dawdle around the house. "I wasn't snooping, I just decided to take a short break and . . . I thought this was a gym. But I've never heard of a gym with liquor and dirty paintings."

"It's no gym." Mack came in. "What you need to understand about the guy who owned this place is . . . he was a nut. A sex freak."

"I guess so," she said, looking at the paintings again. "What are all these weird benches?"

"Playthings, for his parties. How about a drink?"

"I really shouldn't. I'm on your clock. You're paying me

to do a job, I really shouldn't even be in here. Like I said, I was just taking a short break. And I got the first five numbers of the combination, I think. The total's nine."

"That's great," he said but didn't seem terribly interested. "What are you having?" He walked to the bar, got some glasses.

"How about a little something to jazz this up?" She held up her coffee, and he poured some Irish whiskey in it. Then she squinted at herself. It wasn't like her to drink on a job; she rarely drank at all.

Even before she took a sip, though, she was beginning to feel odd. Something about the house? It felt heavy with something. It was an overload of the senses. Her eyes kept straying to the paintings . . .

One robust woman lying naked, surrounded by monsters appraising her. In the distant background, behind a veil of smoke, she thought she saw a temple of some sort.

He opened a cabinet to grab a bottle of vodka. On the bottom shelf she noticed several large bowls full of . . .

"What's in the bowls? Mints?"

"No, I'm afraid not. It's dope. I haven't gotten around to throwing it away—it's all over the place."

Vanni stared at the bowls. One was full of pills, the other—"Is that *crack cocaine?*"

"Yeah. If you're into it, go ahead, I won't tell."

"I don't smoke crack!" she said, shocked.

He shut the cabinet, stirred his drink. "Don't worry, nobody here does drugs. It was the previous owner. He'd always keep dope in the house, for his party guests. He'd have parties all the time."

"I hate to think what kind of parties."

"Well, the paintings should give you a clue. This house was a non-stop orgy. Take a look—" He went to one painting of a woman's splayed buttocks, grabbed the frame, and pulled. The painting was a hinged door, and behind it—

Vanni may have blushed. *God!*

Behind the painting was a pegboard rack hung with a dozen vibrators, ben-wa balls, and rubber phalluses.

"And all this stuff?" Mack pointed to one of the benches.

Vanni looked more closely. *They're for women to lie on,* she realized. Something else, dangling with an array of cables, sported a pair of padded harnesses, a third larger harness behind it. Now she saw what this place was about, and could picture what had gone on here. For the briefest moment, she even pictured herself in the thing. Hovering in mid-air, legs spread, back arched, as one man after another stepped up to take a turn, while another woman, perhaps, would dangle from a higher harness behind her, to precisely position her crotch above Vanni's mouth. *This place is obscene,* she thought, mildly revolted. *Rich people, Jesus*—

Mack sipped his drink, looking at another painting: nude women levitating before a chasm of flames, their faces delirious with ecstasy. What Vanni wasn't acknowledging to herself yet . . . was a growing sexual excitement.

She went back to the picture with the temple. It seemed multi-dimensional the longer she looked at it. The woman lay in obvious angst, eagerly waiting to be taken by the monsters . . .

She didn't know how much time had passed while she'd been looking. She flinched at the next contact: Mack's hands on her hips, standing behind her. Any other time, she knew, she'd bolt. He was just some rich punk thinking he could use her for some fun because he'd paid her a lot for a job.

But it never occurred to her to leave. She didn't want to.

It didn't take long, his hands sliding up and down her breasts, stomach, and hips. Without any reservation at all, she was reaching behind her, to caress his crotch . . .

What am I doing! This wasn't her style at all—it was tramp-morality, the same as a fly-by-night screw with some guy she might meet in a bar, or actually responding to the whistles at a construction site. Mack's groin rubbed her buttocks from behind, his large hands now intent on her breasts, shucking them from her jumpsuit, then peeling the entire suit off.

No morality now. She turned, kicked out of her boots as she let their mouths suck together. She didn't even consciously know what she wanted but the crudest impulse, way down deep, pulled his shirt over his head, dragged his tennis shorts off, and urged him to the harnesses . . .

She was aloft in a minute—Mack obviously knew the system. He stood between her floating legs, lowered her head back further from one pulley, parted her thighs wider with another, and was penetrating her at once.

It was all so perfunctory and animalistic; it didn't even last long, just a minute or two, but in that short period, Vanni's entire body flexed in the air, and her orgasm rolled over her. Mack paused momentarily, his muscled chest straining as he bucked, didn't make a sound, and finished.

He left her exhausted, floating on the harnesses. She could hear him dressing but didn't move; instead, she lazed there as if on clouds. Behind her, her head was upside-down, and when she stared beyond, she was looking right at the painting of the woman being watched by demons.

"That was great," Mack said. "I gotta go now, but lemme know when you get the safe open. Just call around on the intercom."

She couldn't respond, her bare bosom still heaving in the

aftermath. When she inclined her head, she could see him, already back in his clothes. He was leaving.

What did I expect? Cuddling? She was as guilty as he. *He came onto me and I went for it.* Without a second thought.

But she didn't regret it, either, so why did she feel dirty now?

She looked back at him through her obscenely spread legs. What was he doing? He seemed to be getting something out of his pocket.

On her stomach he tossed down a stack of bills.

"Hey!" she finally objected.

"Relax, it's for your kids. You said you had kids, right?"

It looked like a lot of money but still. She hauled her back up higher by grabbing a cable. "I'm not a prostitute," she said, disgusted. Mack held a blank gaze, then half-smiled, and walked out of the room.

Damn him! She felt humiliated now, hanging there, with money on her belly. When she counted it, it was a thousand dollars.

Then she sunk in further humiliation, because she knew she was going to keep it . . .

She didn't know what was coming over her; taking the money was bad enough, but what came next was even more inexplicable. She got out of the harness and presumed she was going to get dressed. She picked up her jumpsuit, though, and just stood there, staring at nothing. Change and keys spilled out of her pockets . . .

She never put her clothes back on. She walked back to the hinged painting. *What . . . am I doing . . . now?* the thought groaned in her head.

She looked at the assortment of toys, bewildered at herself. Why did they look enticing now? She'd never been into such things but she took several down, fingering them, feeling their surfaces. Some were riddled with bumps and rings or two-pronged, another had rubber feathers branching out, while another's tip was shaped like a small fist. Several of the phalluses were so large she couldn't imagine any woman putting one in herself . . .

Next she took down a phallus that looked like a row of rubber balls connected to each other.

This is the one I'll use . . .

She was back in the harness, splayed again in the air. She felt so keyed up she couldn't stand it. Mack had left her dizzy for more contact but when she thought back to him, pretending he was with her again, the fantasy did nothing. She blanked her mind, easing the balled phallus slowly in and out. The sensation was nerve-racking and delicious at the same time. Faster, then, and deeper . . .

At one point, panting, she opened her eyes and was looking absently at the painting of the woman over-watched by monsters. Immediately, the image trebled her excitement. Was there something she didn't know about herself? Was she subconsciously attracted to women?

No, she was looking at the monsters.

Her pleasures were mounting, threatening to crest. Had the demons in the painting moved closer to the subject? Of course not, but they'd seemed to. They were pallid things like skinny sacks with arms and legs, the color of butter. She noticed something else, too. How could they be watching the woman when they had no eyes? No eyes, noses, nor ears—just gaping toothless mouths.

Hideous, she managed to think, but that didn't slow her progress with the dildo.

A more pointed glance: was there a figure standing at the distant temple? She didn't care . . .

She closed her eyes again and imagined . . . the demons watching *her*. They were reaching out with hands that appeared boneless, caressing her, playing with her as she played with herself. She could feel them now, padding her skin, squeezing her breasts. Was it in her mind or was the room cloying now in some rich meaty smell? In the fantasy, many hands were on her some monstrous and others soft and intent but very much human. Women's hands? In fact, Vanni even thought she could hear feminine whispers now, and something darker, like heavy guttural groaning. More fantasy hands glided up her breasts to trace gingerly around her throat.

A snapping sound. An impact. Something was jerking her up as if on a hoist. The dildo flopped to the floor and when Vanni reached to her throat, she found no hands there squeezing off her screams; it was a strap.

One of the harnesses.

Which now served as a hangman's noose.

Her eyes bulged. Pulleys squealed as she was jerked higher, the motion slipping her legs out of the harnesses she'd been using. She was jerked higher and higher, feet kicking. In only a few moments, all that raw, hot desire that ran through her veins had been replaced with raw, hot terror. She worked her fingers under the strap around her neck, to relieve some of the strangling pressure. In gun-shot glimpses she glanced down . . .

Several women were looking up at her: stunningly beautiful women with perfect centerfold bodies, all nude, all grinning. But they were streaked with blood. Black nail-polish and lipstick, vulpine eyes. Tiny ornaments dangled from rings which pierced their nipples and navels: upside-down crosses. And behind them . . .

Worse things stood in attendance.

Vague pale shapes with eyeless faces. Somehow they looked eager, in wait for something.

Vanni's ankles were grabbed by two of the grinning women, her legs parted. Then, inch by inch, she was lowered several feet on the cable. Vanni hoped she'd die before the things got their way with her. Her vision was already dimming from strangulation. The last thing she saw before the festivities began was an additional figure, a tall, lean man with long wavy hair standing beyond the others, watching . . .

IV

"Where are the girls?" Westmore asked. He'd just come back down to the atrium. Mack was watching ball scores on the TV with the sound down, while Nyvysk scribbled in a notepad.

"Adrianne and Karen went to bed," he said quietly. He pointed to their curtained cubicles. "They were both very tired."

"Tired?" Mack chuckled, an imported beer between his legs. "Adrianne tranked herself up, and Karen was hammered, as usual."

It didn't matter if it was true; Westmore was perturbed by the young man's flaring cynicism.

"Cathleen's somewhere," Nyvysk said. "Wandering the house, I suppose."

Mack looked over his shoulder from the couch. "And the safe-cracker girl told me an hour or so ago that she was making headway." Then Mack winked at him.

Westmore didn't get the wink. "What?"

"She's good at more than opening safes."

Westmore rolled his eyes. He didn't want to know. "I guess she'll come down when she's done. If we're not all asleep."

"I'm sure I'll be up. I never sleep much," Nyvysk said. "I'm a night-owl, and so's Cathleen."

Several clocks chimed distantly. Midnight. "I need to find her. I want her to show me the cemetery, where this psychic rape or whatever supposedly took place."

"Discorporate sexual assault," Nyvysk corrected.

"Sure. And Adrianne said something about several cars on the property."

Nyvysk sighed. "Please do me a favor, Mr. Westmore. Don't go onto the grounds at night."

Mack laughed. "Maybe Westmore needs a little of that ghost action."

Nyvysk ignored the remark, continuing to Westmore, "You're not used to a place like this. You're very subject to suggestion. And anything that might be out there *can* manipulate you, especially at night."

"What, the Witching Hour and all that?"

"Just don't go onto the grounds at night," Nyvysk stated more firmly.

"Okay, okay."

"And I need your help with something now if you don't mind."

Westmore had nothing else to do. *Except begin writing whatever it is I'm supposed to write.* "Sure."

"Let's go upstairs to the Scarlet Room."

Mack jerked a more concerned glance at them this time. "You guys got balls going in there at this hour."

"Why, Mack?" Nyvysk challenged.

"It's creepy enough during the day. You wanna give yourself nightmares, go ahead."

Westmore followed Nyvysk up five winding staircases. From behind, in the meager light, the man looked like a hulk with the long hair and wide shoulders. Each floor seemed darker, more grainy, with a soundlessness that somehow seemed beyond silence.

"Are you a believer yet, Mr. Westmore?" Nyvysk asked, back still to him. The low voice echoed.

"I'm open minded," Westmore answered. "But I haven't seen any ghosts yet."

"What about Mack? He thinks this is all a joke that he can ride along on."

Westmore shrugged. "He's Vivica's errand boy."

"Is that all, though? I don't know. He appears to have been close to Hildreth, too. He knows all about the house."

"Then he's the *family* errand boy, I guess. I don't much care about him if you want to know the truth. I don't think he likes anybody here, just pretends to be cool."

"Maybe he's Vivica's spy."

Well, that would be me, actually. "Maybe. Or maybe he's just maintaining security like he said, to make sure we don't trash the place. This house and everything in it must've cost twenty million."

Nyvysk turned up the next landing, to the fifth. "I don't trust Mack."

"You trust *me* enough to tell me that?"

"Yes," he said, lower. More to himself: "You might be the only trustworthy one here."

Westmore appreciated the remark but not too deeply. Nyvysk could easily be playing him, just as anyone could here. Westmore was totally blind in the thick of it all. But the implication struck home. Something about this place or these particular people—or both—ignited quite a fire of suspicion. He wished he could tell Nyvysk he intended to dig up Hildreth's grave tomorrow . . . but thought the better of it.

He knew he couldn't tell *anyone* that.

Maybe Vivica's the one being played. By Mack, or even Karen . . .

"Here we are." Nyvysk stopped, seemed unsettled. Just a heavily molded door stood before them. On the floor were three cylindrical implements fronted by grills, that looked like fancy air-purifiers.

"What're those?"

"They're gauss sensors, the newest generation. I need you to arrange them in the room, three wide positions, facing each other. They're a little weighty—they have portable battery packs that I have to charge every day. But when you're done—" He picked up a roll of cable on the floor. "Plug this into the jack on the videocom, please. It shouldn't take more than a few minutes."

"Piece of cake." Westmore picked up the devices and wire. Nyvysk opened the door, then stood back. "Aren't you coming in?"

Nyvysk shook his head.

Westmore's brow lowered. "Something wrong?"

"I'll tell you when you're done. I can't go in the room."

Westmore entered, not at all reading the other man's suddenly weird attitude. *Whatever.* He didn't care. He wanted to see the infamous Scarlet Room.

Low lights from electric wall fixtures filled the room with a solemnness. *This is it. All those people murdered by Hildreth and his boys.* In a second, he understood Mack's observation about the room: even someone who didn't believe in the supernatural would be bothered by coming in here.

But why hadn't Nyvysk come in?

Everything was red. Furniture, carpet, wall-coverings.

Odder was the room's center, which stood empty, where one would expect to find more furniture. Stillness surrounded him with the flickering, tinted light.

He arranged the gauss sensors as instructed, then connected the end-cable to the com-jack. *There. Big deal. I'm done.*

The deepest impressions set in when he crossed the carpet again to get back to the door, his belly flipflopping. *There were bodies lying here, and parts of bodies,* he thought. *Three weeks ago, the carpet I'm walking over was drenched in blood.* When he was back in the hall, he felt normal again.

"All set up?" Nyvysk asked.

"Yeah. Don't you want to go look, make sure they're in the right position?"

Nyvysk shook his head again.

Westmore lit a cigarette, looked at the man. "I didn't mind doing it, but . . . you could've done it just as fast as me. How come you didn't want to go in the room?"

Nyvysk nervously pushed his hair back, led them both back toward the stairs. "I'm too afraid to," he finally said.

Westmore considered the man's size and constitution. "Come on. You don't look like the kind of guy who's afraid of much. What, the ghosts?" Westmore smiled. "There weren't any in there that I could see."

"Let me play some of these EVP's for you," was all Nyvysk said.

Back in the communications room on the third floor, Nyvysk quietly addressed his equipment, and seemed to be clicking on sound files on the big computer. "Listen. These are some voices that were picked up in one of the parlors."

Westmore put an ear to the speaker. He heard nothing but dead air at first. Then:

A scratchy voice from far away, a woman's: "Look."

Another woman: "Who're they?"

Several seconds of silence, then a man's voice: "I wanna cut something up."

Westmore fingered his chin. "Interesting."

"Here's one from the stairwell hallway leading to the stairs to the first floor."

Westmore listened intently, fascinated. He heard faint thumping, like someone walking in a stagger. "Where's my knife?" a man said.

A woman: "I think you left it in the bucket with the blood."

"Where's Jaz?"

"He's bringing the heads down when he's done fucking . . ."

Westmore backed up from the speaker. "When were these recorded?"

"Today."

He recalled the name, too, from his shocking conversation with Karen. *Jaz. One of Hildreth's porn guys.*

"I've got a dozen or so of these just from today," Nyvysk said. "You don't need to hear them all but you get the idea. Oh, and I know what you're thinking. Recordings are pretty weak proof of a haunting."

"That *is* what I'm thinking. That stuff could easily be created or staged."

"Of course, it could. But we're not looking for proof anymore; we're confident that the house is charged. From *our* point of view, these messages serve as an information source. It doesn't matter if you believe it. *We* do, so we're proceeding in a practical manner."

Of course. Westmore was the outsider here. "But I'll also admit, if those recordings are for real—it *is* a big deal."

"From your standpoint, yes. You've never experienced anything like this before. But from a psychic standpoint, or the standpoint of a technician such as myself—we've heard things like this a million times. We're not surprised at all."

"So what's this got to do with you being afraid to go into the Scarlet Room?"

Nyvysk clicked on another file.

"Rejoice in him, rejoice in what awaits," a tiny voice whispered after some silence. "Rejoice and join hands with us . . ."

The voice sounded male, with an obvious middle-eastern accent. "Like this place, my love never dies. I love you."

Westmore leaned closer.

"I await you, Alexander. Don't make me wait too long."

"Who's Alexander?" Westmore asked.

"Me," Nyvysk said.

Westmore stared at him.

"And the voice is that of a twenty-year-old Kurd exorcist named Saeed. I fell in love with him, so to speak, in Iraq, twenty years ago."

"So, uh, you're—"

"I'm gay, if you will. I don't believe that God has a problem with that but the Catholic Church certainly does, which is why I stepped down from the priesthood a long time ago. But to this day, I haven't broken my vow of celibacy."

Here was a bombshell.

"Everyone in this house has a secret, Mr. Westmore. I suspect that you do too. At any rate, the young man on that recording from the Scarlet Room has been dead since the day I met him. I was supposed to see him later that day, but I didn't at the last minute, a moral reluctance, I guess. He was murdered by muggers, waiting for me in an alley near what was once the market square of the ancient city of Nineveh."

Jesus, Westmore thought.

Nyvysk was showing him out. "There's no reason for you to stay here, the tapes are all similar, if not grim. Tomorrow I'll have the ion-sensors working. I'm sure you'll be fascinated by the results."

Westmore took his word for it. He'd be going to sleep soon, and he didn't need those voices in his head. "Let me check on the locksmith while we're up here," he said, looking for a distraction. *Secrets,* he thought. Yes, he supposed there were all kinds of secrets around here.

In the office, there was no sign of Vanni. "I wonder where she is." The safe in the wall remained closed.

"Where is this safe?" Nyvysk asked. "I haven't even seen it."

Westmore pointed. "Talk about a secret. It was hidden behind two paintings and an armoire."

Nyvysk looked down at the two frames leaning against the wall, and picked up the engraving. "Oh, this is *very* interesting right here."

"Why?"

"It appears to be an original work by a German engraving artist named Stettin Albrecht. He was known to dabble in the occult and make custom engravings for rich satanic societies."

"Why's he important enough for Hildreth to hide his picture?"

"Nobody knows how for real Albrecht was, but it's fairly certain that his patrons *weren't* for real, not genuine satanists, in other words. The idle and very debauched rich just going through the motions because a 'satanic' orgy was more interesting than regular orgies. These societies merely looked for an alternate excuse for sex, pretending that their satan-worship was their under-the-table revolution, their rebellion against a very oppressive Church. So Albrecht was hired by these people to render portraits of Lucifer and the other demons. If this is original, it may be worth low six figures."

Westmore shook his head at the engraving. "I don't know from engravings, but it doesn't look that good to me."

"No, Albrecht wasn't known for any great skill or talent, he was essentially a hack with tin plates and a burin-tool. The conditions and age of the piece is what warrants a high sale price. But—" Nyvysk's eyes poured over the plate. "I doubt that its value to a collector was why Hildreth purchased it."

"What, then?"

"This is . . . troubling."

"I don't understand."

"Look at the engraving within the engraving." Nyvysk's big finger pointed.

"A monster, it looks like," Westmore said.

"Not a monster, a demon, and this seems to be the only artistic rendering of it. Albrecht would typically be hired to depict the more well-known demons such as Asmodeus, Baal, and the like. The same way artists at fairs do portraits of famous baseball players. They don't do many third-stringers, do they? This demon here, I mean. Is much more obscure in the realms of the occult."

Now he pointed to the caption: MY SELF AS I DARE TO REFASHION THE COUNTENANCE OF MY VISION: BELARIUS.

"Belarius?" Westmore thought back to old lit classes. "That name rings a bell now that I think of it. A character in Shakespeare, right? *Cymbeline?*"

"I'm afraid this Belarius is quite different from Shakespeare's amorous warlord. Belarius was Lucifer's first servant in Hell, and, according to the compendiums, Lucifer rewarded Belarius for his loyalty. He was made the Sexus Cyning, which is very old-English for something like the Lord of Lust, the magnate of sex, something along those lines. If Lucifer is the Prince of Darkness, Belarius is the Prince of Carnality."

Nyvysk set the frame back down, sullen. His eyes had widened in some knowing dread.

"What's wrong now?" Westmore asked, irritated by the man's sudden crypticness. To him, a demon was a demon. Like Roman gods and other nature-symbols of mythology.

"Follow me."

Nyvysk took him back to the communications room. He clicked on another voice file. "This is from the parlor where the prostitutes were beheaded."

Westmore could only hear a barely audible drone, like listening to a blank tape with the sound all the way up.

Then he heard it, a single group of heavy syllables through a warbling, suboctave voice: "Belarius . . ."

Chapter Nine

I

"Call it," Diane said.

"Heads," Jessica answered. She knew her luck. She caught the coin and frowned. *Tails. I lose.*

Diane was polite enough not to laugh out loud. "Tough luck, sister. This is what we get for dropping out of high school."

"Yeah."

"You get to wash the Sack!"

That's what they'd dubbed Faye Mullins. The Sack. Because that's what she looked like.

Diane was just getting off-shift. "At least she shouldn't be acting nutty today. Didn't make a sound all night. The Prolixin hit her hard this time."

"You probably slipped her a double dose just to keep her quiet during your shift," Jessica suspected.

"Me?" Diane's grin sharpened. "That would constitute an extreme occupational dereliction. Of course, if you think I do stuff like that, you can turn in a written complaint to the ward director."

Jessica got the joke. They all did it sometimes, they had to. Some of these patients just took too much out of you, and no one gave a crap about them anyway. They were lost and had somehow landed here. The families paid the in-patient bills to keep them shut away. Out of sight out of mind.

But Jessica wondered who was paying the Sack's bills. No living relatives were listed on her admittance form. *Doesn't matter to me,* she realized. *I just get paid to wash their dirty butts.*

She trudged into the dorm. That's what they called them. Dorms. Like a college. This was no college. But any employment was better than none. Changing bedpans, mopping vomit, and sponge-bathing bedridden or incapacitated female patients was the most regrettable part of her job description.

In the dorm she wheeled the cart to the bed. "Hi, Faye," she tried to sound cheery. "Rise and shine!"

There was no response from the woman in the bed. She looked dead—eyes slitted, head lolled. Her mouth hung open to show crooked teeth and foamy saliva. But she wasn't dead, she was just zonked. All the better for Jessica; she'd be a lot easier to wash if she wasn't spitting or trying to bite her. So far, at least, they hadn't had to four-point her or put her in a bed-net or straitjacket.

Her cart's casters squeaked when she brought her wash buckets around the side of the bed.

Oh, Jesus. Even Jessica had some remaining pity. Faye Mullins was a wreck of human flesh, insensate. Her hair was a pale-brown tangle, eyes silently delirious. "Come on, hon, hitch it up for me, okay?"

Jessica got her leaned up on the bed and managed to drag her wrinkled white gown off. Long flat breasts sagged like flaps over the stomach roll; hair shot from the creases of her armpits. *Detachment,* Jessica forced the thought. That's what the doctors and RN's always said. Sometimes it was easy, when the patient had lost enough humanity.

Grim-faced, Jessica sponged Faye's body, sometimes averting her eyes.

"No more, no more," the patient murmured. "I don't want to do it anymore."

Nuts. "You don't have to do anything, hon."

"No more crack my God please no more crack . . ."

Jessica wilted, trying not to imagine what horrors the woman had witnessed. At that house?

She'd heard that some satanic cult lived there, and were sacrificing women. Jessica almost wished they'd sacrificed Faye, to avoid the misery, a ruined body and the hell of a pudding brain.

"*Sexus Cyning,*" Faye mumbled next, spittle glazing her lips. "I saw it . . ."

"Hmm, hon?" Jessica said, sponging rolls of belly.

"The *Chirice Flaesc.*"

Such talk was nothing new to a psychiatric janitor. Patients often lived in a delusion, and invented their own words, their own language.

"Don't let them make me go there again . . ."

Slop, slop, slop, went the sponge. "You don't have to go anywhere you don't want, hon. You get to stay here and watch TV where it's safe. And breakfast will be ready soon."

Faye urped up a line of bile.

Great. Jessica plunged the sponge.

Eventually came the part she always put off. She could

avoid it, just *say* she did it, but then the patient could get a rash or something, and there'd be hell to pay.

Oh, God . . . What did she do?

Jessica parted Faye's rice-colored legs, winced as she sponged down the genital region. The doctors and nurses had informed her well in advance that some psych patients mutilated themselves—usually something guilt-driven—and some would even mutilate their genitals. But this was the first time Jessica had ever seen it.

Faye Mullins' pubic region looked gnawed.

Jessica washed it all the same, thinking *Don't look, don't look,* but she couldn't help a glance or two.

"They did that," Faye gibbered. "They did it."

"Who did, hon?"

"Belarius and his friends, in the Chirice Flaesc."

Jessica gagged through the rest of her work.

"It's coming again . . ."

"What's coming, sweetie?" Jessica asked if only to distract herself.

"The Chirice Flaesc—"

Jessica stared.

"—and Belarius. Soon."

Faye giggled faintly, grinning upward with a toothy mouth. She parted her legs more.

Jessica groaned. Yes. She wished very much that she had stayed in school.

II

Westmore awoke groggily at about 9 a.m., squared beams of sunlight cutting into the atrium from odd, high windows.

He'd slept dreamlessly. It took a while before the morning cogs began to turn, and he remembered everything that had happened yesterday.

Belarius, he thought.

It was nearly as eerie now as when he'd heard the strange name on the tape.

I don't believe in demons, he reminded himself, gathering his toiletries from the small cabinet in his cubicle. In a Marriot-Courtyard robe he'd pilfered years ago at a writers convention, he used the large bathroom by the kitchen, showered, shaved, and dressed. Then he was ready . . .

But for what?

He considered calling Vivica but thought better of it. *Later, when I have something to tell her.*

In the office, he typed some notes into his laptop for a few hours, then it occurred to him as an afterthought: *The safe!* But when he looked, the safe was still closed, and there was no sign of the locksmith. Mack had still been watching television when Westmore had gone to sleep. Had she opened the safe and reported to Mack? He looked down from the window and saw that her truck was gone. He had to know.

Back in the atrium, he could hear at least one of the men snoring; he guessed most of this crowd were late sleepers. Then one of the women—Adrianne, he thought—murmured anxiously in her sleep: "No, no!"

Nightmares.

He found Mack's cubicle and tapped on the edge of the partition. "Mack? Hey, Mack?"

"Huh?"

"Sorry to wake you up but what happened with the girl from the locksmith's?"

A grunt and a cough, then Mack came through his cubicle's privacy curtain clad only in boxer shorts. He palmed sleep out of his eyes. "Shit, I don't know. Is she still here?"

"The safe's still shut and her truck's gone."

He went to the bay window and winced when he pushed the drapes back, letting in a block of sun. "Shit," he said again. "Maybe she's not done. Maybe she's coming back."

"Or maybe she just couldn't open the son of a bitch. She did say no guarantees."

"Did you see her at all last night?"

Mack was clearly only half awake. "Well, no. I mean, not later."

"Look, man. What's the scoop with her?"

"Huh?"

"Last night you said something like she was good at more than locks. What's the scoop with that?"

Mack signed in a grog, then shrugged. "I did her, man. I told you she was hot for me."

Unbelievable. "You had sex with the locksmith, you're saying?"

"Yeah. She came on to me, know what I mean? And she's a hot number, too. Killer tits." Mack dragged his feet toward the kitchen, still rubbing his eyes. "Did you put coffee on?"

Westmore shook his head. Mack was probably about twenty-five. *Kids, Jesus. They have sex with people like it's changing channels on a television.* Westmore considered his own morality. *Or maybe I'm just getting old . . .*

"Yes, I think her name's Vanni. She came here about ten o'clock last night," he said later to the man on the phone. He'd called the locksmith's. "Did she say if she's coming back to finish the job?"

The man seemed duped. "I— There's no invoice in the nightbox, and—" A pause— ". . . the truck's in the lot. Lemme get back to you, sir."

"Sure." Westmore hung up, astounded. *Mack gave her a thousand bucks to open the safe and she walked off with it?* Good help was hard to find. Maybe she *had* opened the safe and found a *lot* of money in it. Westmore wondered.

He walked outside into the blaze of the day. *Adrianne said she saw some cars on the property . . .* One seemed abandoned, she'd said, in the woods. Westmore was determined to find it, if it was to be found at all. She'd said she'd seen it during an out-of-body experience, which couldn't have sounded more hokey. There was quite a bit of hokeyness around here but the thing that bothered Westmore most was the casual if not bored regard the "psychics" maintained for each other. *None of it's hokey to them. It's commonplace.* It was like a bunch of Olympic weightlifters hanging around each other. Nobody was the least bit impressed that they could all bench four hundred.

An opening in the woodline led him down a brambled path. Gnats flitted annoyingly around his head as wigs of Spanish moss brushed his shoulders. *The graveyard,* he thought. And here it was, iron-crested fence and all. He noticed a broken eggshell and piece of burned aluminum foil at the foot of Hildreth's tombstone. *She said something about divination,* he remembered. Westmore knew nothing about that save for folklore about people finding water with forked branches.

He looked down at the grave and thought very resolutely, *I'm going to have to dig this up.* It would be no easy task and Westmore was a soft-handed writer, not a ditch-digger. *And I'll have to do it on my own, can't let the others know.*

But not now. There were still preliminaries. Back out on the open property, he began to bake in the sun. The annoying gnats turned into more annoying mosquitoes. At the opposite end of the property, after a sweat-seeping walk, he found a scratch of a foot-trail that stopped at a cramped clearing overhung by tree limbs. Lizards scattered when he wedged his way through brush. Facing him, dusted by pollen, was a relatively new jet-black Miata with a walnut-brown convertible top. Westmore's first impulse, for whatever reason, was to look inside for a dead body, but the vehicle's two bucket seats sat empty. The glove box revealed no title or registration. He jotted down the plates and walked around back, found two long tire ruts, and followed them a hundred yards down the mountainous hill that the mansion had been built on. The heat teemed; spider-webs broke stickily over his face. *Christ, it's like a rain forest!* Soon, though, the tire ruts emptied onto a wider dirt road that seemed to lead all the way down the hill. *To the main road?* he questioned. It had to be. But there was no reason to follow it all the way down.

At least he'd found the car in the woods . . . which made him wonder. *How the hell did Adrianne know about it unless she'd really had one of these OBE's?* Westmore could scarcely grasp the concept much less have faith in it.

Oh, well.

He walked back to the house, smoking in spite of the heat and frowning at himself for wearing long pants on a day like this. Back at the courtyard, he spotted a man getting out of a van and approaching the front door. *The locksmith?* he thought.

No. BAYSIDE PEST CONTROL, the van read.

"Can I help you?" Westmore asked when he got to the porch.

Hair cut very short reduced the obviousness of a bald spot. Dark moustache. The man looked in his late-50s, starting to lose a battle to middle-age. Typical workman's utility dress, a nozzled cannister of pesticide sling over his back. "Hi, I'm Mike, from Bayside. Is Mr. Hildreth in?"

Westmore didn't know what to say. *No, but there's a high likelihood that he's in a hole in the ground a couple hundred yards from here.* "I'm afraid he isn't."

"I'm here for your routine 30-day service."

"Come on in. I'll get Karen." He took the guy inside and down the long hall to the atrium. He knew it was nothing but he also didn't want to give some guy free-reign in a house full of treasures. He tapped on the end of Karen's cubicle. "Karen?"

Eventually, a flattened voice said: "Aw, fuck. My head's about to explode."

"The exterminator's here. I just wanted to make sure it's cool to let him in the house."

A groan. "Aw, shit. Uh . . . That's not supposed to be till the first of the month, I think. What company?"

"Bayside Pest Control."

"That's them. It's Jimmy, right?"

Westmore's brow arched. "No, a guy named Mike."

Cot springs creaked. For the briefest moment, when her hand parted the curtain, Westmore could see in the gap that she wore nothing but rose-red panties. Large white breasts blared from the impressive tan of her shoulders and abdomen, delineated by razor-sharp tan lines. Then she stuck her head out and closed the curtain around her neck. Bloodshot eyes squinted to the door. "You're not the regular guy. Where's Jimmy?"

"Jimmy Parks is in Key West, ma'am," Mike said. "Two weeks off. I'm filling in for him. Your next spraying isn't scheduled till the first, but they sent me out a little early to pick up some slack. Feel free to call my manager, Mr. Holsten, to verify."

"He's fine," Karen said, then disappeared back inside.

"Go do your thing," Westmore told the guy.

"Thanks for your time. I won't be more than an hour. It's just a perimeter spray."

The guy got to it, slowly spraying a line of clear fluid along the baseboards.

Westmore went back to the office, immediately got on-line. He ran the Miata's tags on the DMV website, paid $7.95 on his credit card, and got the owner's name. *Damn. Doesn't do me any good*. The vehicle was owned by Reginald Hildreth. The only thing left to do was go back into the heat and get the vehicle-identification number off the dashboard, if it was even marked on the dashboard, because not all cars did that now. It might be on the engine someplace. But then he thought: *Insurance!* He searched several oak file cabinets until he found a group of folders that appeared to be household. Records, receipts, warranties, etc. One folder read: CAR INSURANCE. The receipt for the last bi-yearly insurance receipt was right on top. *Jesus, this guy owned a lot of cars!* Over a dozen were listed, including a Rolls Royce Silver Shadow which cited the primary driver as Vivica Hildreth.

Eureka! he thought next. A black convertible with the same tag number was there.

PRIMARY OPERATOR: DEBORAH ANNE RODENBAUGH.

There were five Rodenbaughs in the phone book. Westmore called them all. Three answered and had never heard of Deborah Rodenbaugh. The fourth was a message: "Hi, this is Peter Rodenbaugh. If you have a legitimate reason to want to talk to me, leave a message. And if you're one of those goddamn telemarketers, eat shit and die and don't ever call this fucking number again because I *hate* all you annoying pains in the ass. If I need something, I go to the

store and get it. I don't need you assholes ringing my fucking phone twenty times a day trying to sell me cruises or
aluminum siding or satellite tv or basement waterproofing
when I don't even have a fucking basement. I rent an apartment, dickheads. I don't need any of that bullshit you're
trying to sell for some pissant commission. Do the world a
favor, all of you moronic, lazy, unmotivated, no account
motherfucking telemarketers: Get a real job." Westmore,
laughing, left a message, eventually got a hold of the resi-
dent who'd never heard of Deborah Rodenbaugh, either.
The fifth number was disconnected.

He'd have to research more thoroughly, and ask around
some more. Maybe Vivica knew, or Karen. *Why would Hildreth give a car to this woman?* More importantly, why was that
car abandoned in the woods? Later, he'd call one of his
friends at the paper and ask for a full-scale Nexus-Lexus
search.

The house below seemed very silent. Westmore spent the
rest of the day watching DVD's by T&T Enterprises. It was
stupefying. He groaned through one porn DVD after the
other, making active use of the fast forward. The logo
graphic on each DVD's main menu was a Gothic mansion;
Westmore rolled his eyes. Each scene left him numb, the
eroticism of beautiful women gone after the first "wet-
shot," which was followed by even more, hundreds more,
over the course of the day. It was all the same, just different
sets and different women, all of whom he'd seen previously
in their autopsy photos. Many of the men in these films
were fly-by-nights, with ludicrous stage names like Myles
Long and Dick Standing, and finally Westmore met the
cream of T&T's male crop: Jaz and Three-Balls. The latter's
nickname was no joke, and both men's qualifications for the
sex industry couldn't be contested.

The hours stretched by. The scenes were so depressing. But in none of the DVD's did he find anything of interest. Eventually, he plugged in the Halloween disc, which was refreshingly free of sexual activity. Plenty of imagery, though, most of the same girls from the hardcore movies prancing around in the skimpiest costumes. Lacy red-devil outfits, vampires complete with fangs, a nearly nude bride of Frankenstein, etc. Mack dressed as Sinatra (probably a reflection of his self-image) only in this case, Old Blue Eyes sported horns, and Three-Balls was a caveman (not much of a stretch) with his three namesakes gratefully hidden behind a loincloth. Jaz, on the other hand, partied as the Mummy, his occupational attribute similarly wrapped. Karen barged drunk into the frame, an exotic belly dancer. The camera zoomed in and out as she staged a dance. Thus far, though, there was no sign of Hildreth at the party.

"Hi," Karen said, wandering in.

Westmore did a double-take. She wore nothing but a carmine string bikini. "Hi."

"Do I look hungover?"

"Actually, no. That bikini's a very effective distraction."

She leaned against the doorway, arms crossed under her breasts, which propped them up even more than the implants. "Is that your way of saying I look good in a bikini?"

"Karen, you look so good in a bikini that I can't even concentrate on what I'm doing." He leaned back in the chair and lit a cigarette. "And, no, that's not a come-on."

"Damn."

"Did you forget your clothes?"

"I've got nothing better to do so I thought I'd work on my tan in the inner courtyard. Care to join me?"

"No. I'm a journalist. Journalists are supposed to be pale; it's an image-thing."

"Well, at least if I'm by myself, I can sunbathe nude."

Westmore raised a brow. "So. Exactly *which* windows face the inner courtyard?"

"Funny. What have you been doing up here all day?"

"Watching the highly literate and always intellectual productions of T&T Enterprises."

Karen laughed. "Poor guy. Don't worry, I'll turn my head if you stand up."

"You got that wrong. To me, porn's not erotic or stimulating. It's depressing. I'm about brain-dead from it by now. And you're on the screen as we speak."

Karen came around the desk with something like a fret on her face. "The Halloween party, thank God. I thought you meant you found one of my old pornos from the early '90s."

As attractive as Karen was, Westmore squarely *didn't* want to see images of Karen doing the same things he'd just watched the T&T girls do. "Great belly but—no offense—you're not much of a dancer."

"I am when I'm sober, which I definitely *wasn't* during that party." She looked amusedly at the screen.

"I don't see Hildreth anywhere. Wasn't he at the party?"

"Actually, no. He took Halloween *very* seriously."

Westmore smiled at the inference. He could imagine the laughable image, which was probably true nonetheless: Hildreth and cronies chanting in the chapel, wearing ridiculous black capes and hoods. "Of course."

Still, watching the party footage, Karen shot a quick frown. "Oh, shit. You can see my c-section."

Westmore hadn't noticed the scar, and he was further surprised. "I didn't know you had any kids."

"See?" She pulled the rim of the already-minuscule bikini down a hitch, revealing the thin scar. "I had Darlene when I was twenty-one, if you can believe that. It's starting to make me feel old now; she's in her first year of college. I'm really proud of her. She got accepted at Princeton."

"That's great," Westmore said. "But you practically gotta be a millionaire to cover the tuition."

"Vivica picks up what the scholarship doesn't cover."

"There's some good fortune. What happens if she lets you go?"

Karen paused. "Why would she do that?"

"Well, I don't know. You used to work for her husband's company, and now her husband's dead and the company's shut down."

"I guess if she cuts me loose, I'm more fucked than all of the chicks in those videos combined."

Westmore would have to find a polite way to tell her that profanity didn't make her more attractive. But he almost groaned when Karen waltzed around to the coffee machine and bent over the cabinet to get some filters. "Oh, while I'm thinking of it. You ever hear of a woman named Deborah Anne Rodenbaugh?" he asked.

"No, I don't think so."

"She's listed as the driver of the car that's abandoned. Maybe one of Hildreth's porn girls."

"Maybe."

On the screen, a rather dumpy, overweight woman could be seen sitting in the background. Lank hair hung in her eyes; she looked out of it. "Who's that?" Westmore asked.

Karen looked without much interest. "Oh, that's Faye. Talk about a basket case; I always felt so sorry for her. She was the company janitor, and did some groundskeeping."

"She's not even in a costume."

"Not a party-type. More dejected wallflower. She was

just waiting for the party to end, so she could clean up. A lot of Hildreth's porn people would poke fun at her. It was really cruel. She was a closet junkie, is what I heard."

Looks like she was on something. Westmore was about to say something else, when his heart lurched.

On the screen.

He quickly hit pause. Someone else had stepped into view on the party DVD.

It's her. It was the girl from the desk snapshot, and the subject of the oil painting that hung in front of the safe. But she wasn't in costume at the party, just a nice dark business dress and high heels.

Could that be Deborah Rodenbaugh?

"I wish I knew who that was," he muttered to himself.

Karen glanced at the screen. "Never saw her before."

Westmore looked at her with some suspicion. "Yes you have."

"Nope. I don't think so."

He pointed behind him to the floor. "It's the girl in that painting. You said you never saw *her* before, either. And it's obviously the same girl." Westmore didn't even know what he was suspicious of, yet he gave Karen a long look.

"Why are you being a dick all of a sudden!" Karen sniped at him.

"I'm not, I just—"

"I was drunk when I saw that picture, and you're looking at me like I'm lying to you or something!"

"I only meant that it seemed strange when you said you'd never seen her before but you had, in the picture, and here she is at this party that you're also at but don't know who she is—"

"Jesus Christ, what is it you think I'm lying about? People would come and go in this house the whole time I

worked here. There might as well have been a fucking re-
volving door out front. I can't possibly remember every single woman that had the hots for Hildreth!"

Karen was obviously pissed off now; Westmore felt foolish.

"Let me look—Jesus Christ. Let me see if I can remember every single chick to set foot in this fucking house—"
Frowning, Karen leaned over, her bikini'd rump a few
inches from Westmore's sight. She studied the screen. "Oh,
wait a minute, I do remember her."

"Was she one of the porn girls?"

"No, she was one of Hildreth's gofers. He'd take one under his wing every now and then, called her his assistant. Almost never saw her, though, and she definitely wasn't a
party girl. Never even saw her with a drink. And come to
think of it— What was the name you just ran by me?"

"Deborah Anne Rodenbaugh."

"Okay, then that's probably her 'cos I think her name was
Debbie. She drove a little black convertible."

Yes! Westmore celebrated. "Then that's her. I finally
know who the hell it is." Westmore had made a big deal
about nothing, but at least he got the info he needed.

"Why is she so important anyway?"

Westmore scratched his head. "I don't know, but it's her
car stashed in the woods. Knowing who she is is a start."

"A mystery. Is that what Vivica really hired you for? To
find out about this girl? Vivica's not the jealous type, believe me."

Westmore did his best to skirt the question. "I'm
just . . . checking things out."

"Yeah? Checking things out?" Karen put her hands on
her hips, deliberately displaying her body to him.

Holy Jesus. This place is gonna drive me bonkers.

"I'm going to go tan. You can finish checking things

out." She gave him a last amused glance. "You're a real goofball, you know that?"

"Bigtime. But that's what you like about me, right?"

"I guess so," she chuckled and left.

Chapter Ten

I

Westmore was never going to make a play for her. Willis was sexually terrified. Mack didn't like her. Nyvysk was gay. And Adrianne and Cathleen were looney toons. So why should Karen care what people might think?

Go ahead, somebody. Call me a sleaze.

She preferred to think of herself, instead, as uninhibited. It seemed natural and honest. *If someone wants to peep on me, I don't care . . .* She popped off the tiny bikini and stood stark naked in the middle of the sunny inner court. The sun on her skin felt luxurious; it reminded her of why she loved Florida.

She stretched back on a stone lounge chair topped with weatherproof cushions. The fountain had been turned off, a dry-mouthed gargoyle that seemed to leer at her. Beds of day-lilies, touch-me-nots, and milkwort bloomed various shades of orange. Karen could smell the sweet richness in the air. She closed her eyes behind the sunglasses and the world went from radiant to black.

She tried to blank her mind but her thoughts kept turning to Westmore. He wasn't her type at all; perhaps that explained her attraction. After twenty years of sleeping with the wrong guys maybe she was starting to see the light. Somebody decent and smart might be nice for a change. *But it doesn't matter 'cos he's not going for it,* she thought. *Yeah, he's smart, all right. Smart enough not to mess around with me . . .*

She tried but failed to resist the fantasy, imagining Westmore with her right now, right out here, both of them clothed in nothing but sunlight. His mouth was on hers, then began to lower. His hands were molding her flesh. The feel of his body on hers compounded the luxury of the sunlight enveloping her. Karen felt ecstatic . . .

When she drifted to sleep, Westmore came with her. His mouth was between her legs now, laving her. Karen's nerves felt like a network of springs about to snap at any moment.

Then, something felt . . . wrong.

The tongue delving into her felt impossibly long: tubular meat extending. Was it forked? Karen's eyes bulged, and when she snapped them open, she wasn't in the courtyard. She lay on the bare stone floor of some dungeon-like cell, with orange firelight wavering in through smoking holes in the wall.

Where am I? she thought, aghast.

Through one of the broken holes in the wall she saw something in the distance, a temple of some sort, perched on a fog-seeping rise. It was flesh-colored. Arteries seemed to run up and down its front columns and side walls. But as the sensations deep in her loins began to intensify, her attentions pulled away from the temple because that's when she noticed something else.

It wasn't Westmore who tended to her below the waist, it was Jaz.

Karen screamed. Jaz grinned, a grin full of fangs, as he retracted a veined, foot-long tongue that was black as a lizard's and very much forked. His forehead rippled, skin ruddy, with blood-red eyes. A pair of fat knurls protruded from the forehead, and the hands that gripped her thighs were clawed.

"Mom! Help!"

The plea was unmistakeable. It was Darlene, her daughter. Karen screamed doubly hard when her eyes found her: hanging upside-down and naked. Sheer horror flooded her young eyes.

Three-Balls, horned and mutated as Jaz, stood beside Darlene with a sickle-shaped knife.

"Hang her up beside her daughter," another voice commanded.

It was Hildreth, standing alone in the cell's corner.

The clawed hands that had been pushing Karen's knees back to her face now yanked her up by a fistful of hair. In this evil place, wherever it might be, her large breasts were even larger, her hips wider, her curves more extreme. The place, yes. It had re-formed her, but for what?

The thing that was now Jaz shoved her face toward another hole in the wall.

"Take a good look, my dear," Hildreth's voice ground. "Take a look at yourself back in *your* world. Can you see? Can you see what the acolytes of Belarius are doing to you?"

Karen saw.

She saw herself back in the inner courtyard. She was being mauled on the lounge chair by what could only be described as gelatinous shadows. The things were gang-raping her, while a transposition of Hildreth stood aside and watched. He was here and there at the same time.

"And you know what, Karen?" his image in the cell asked. "You're enjoying every moment of their efforts. Such is the nature of true, unadulterated lust."

Karen watched in horror at what was being done to her, as the hand gripping her hair twisted tighter. Below, the gargoyle stooped in the center of the fountain was vomiting blood . . .

"It's lust that summons them. Why else would I choose such a house?"

Karen couldn't cogitate anything he said. Her terror was burning through her. She screamed loud as a train whistle when, next, she was thrown to the floor and her ankles were lashed together by something like slimy rope, and she was hung upside-down on a hook next to her daughter.

Hildreth smiled, a spoiled light in his eyes. "Mother and child. How appropriate a homage."

Darlene was screaming first, a pitiable wail of violated innocence. Three-Balls was sawing into the meat of her neck with the curved knife. The bone-deep wound poured blood like water from a spigot, emptying into a trough which sat below them.

"Don't worry, Karen," Hildreth assured. "This is only a dream that we've hijacked from you. It was your lust that let us in."

Jaz was cutting into Karen's neck. Strangely she felt no pain, only the sensation of being emptied.

"It's just a dream, just a dream. Please, Karen. Help me make *my* dreams come true."

She twitched on the hook as her blood poured into the trough.

"Good, good. Spill forth. It's so beautiful, isn't it?"

When there was nothing left, their heads were cut off and tossed to the floor. Karen could still see, both her and her daughter's headless bodies hanging above. Jaz and Three-Balls were running their hands down the bodies, from ankles to waist, then waist to neck, to squeeze out every drop.

"Good," Hildreth said. "Now paint the walls with it."

Hildreth carried both heads to a wooden table fitted with a hand-crank press. Karen could still see as her head was placed on the pressure plate and the device was wheeled down and down and down, until the skull collapsed and her brains were squeezed through her mouth, ears, and nose, and eventually crushed flat.

II

The girl was asleep in Clements' bed. *The girl,* he thought, frowning at himself. He knew her name now. Connie. And he was even sort of falling for her. *A crack-addict, a prostitute.* He laughed at himself. He didn't care. He'd get her off that shit when this other thing was over. Clements was determined to see it all to an end, even if he had to end it himself. Then he'd get Connie into a long-term rehab, and didn't care how much he'd have to pay. He was either very sincere, or the biggest fool on earth.

She'd helped him earlier at the mansion, with his cell phone on vibrate, watching with binoculars in case Vivica Hildreth dropped by at the house. She was the only one who knew Clements by sight and hence would know the man in the exterminator's uniform was really a commendated ex-cop.

In the atrium, while pretending to spray for bugs, he'd taken the CD's out of the voice-activated digital recorder that he'd hidden under the couch nearest the center of the room, and replaced them with blank recordable CD's. He'd gotten the info on the Hildreth account from the guy who owned Bayside Pest Control. Clements had been the one who—with less than ethical means—had busted the coke-dealer who'd hooked the owner's daughter. Favor time.

Now all he had to do was listen to five CD's worth of voice-activated recordings. It was going to be a *long* night.

Some major conversations took place by the time he got to the second disc. Nyvysk and the three psychics were all there now—a real batty bunch. Cosmic rapes, they'd talked about, as if it were real. Out-of-body experiences. They were convinced Hildreth was a true satanist and the house was "charged," whatever that meant. Clements knew they were coming in advance from the bug he'd gotten into Vivica Hildreth's penthouse. Two employees of Hildreth's were there now, too, and so was the writer.

The weak link was the writer.

But not a peep about Debbie Rodenbaugh.

Yes, it was going to be a very long night. Mr. Johnny Walker Black was there to keep him company, and so was the Marlboro Man. Maybe, just maybe, one of these kooks knew about Debbie and what had really happened to her.

The weak link was the writer, he thought again.

Clements looked at the bio pic of journalist Richard Westmore. He tapped a finger against the photo.

He's the one I go for, Clements thought.

★ ★ ★

It was much later that night when Clements heard one distorted voice which seemed to vacillate in and out, and seemed backed by the most distant shrieks—a voice that cackled and said: "Clements! Come into our midst and be one of us! We know you're listening . . ."

III

Westmore felt sick to death.

He sat paralyzed, watching the screen. *Oh my dear God. What a sick, sick world . . .* How could people do things like this? What could compel the human will to engage in such perversion? How could people even be capable of this?

Westmore could only devise one answer.

It was evil. It had to be. It could be nothing else.

Several of the DVD's toward the bottom of the pile weren't like the others. Not sex frolics with laughable plots and awful dialogue. These movies were *not* the fare one would find in an adult entertainment store.

They were rape movies.

And other things. Beatings. Sadism. Bestiality. The worst that humanity had to offer was right here for him to see, compliments of Mr. Reginald Hildreth. Men in masks were the male participants in these cases, and at least two of them were Hildreth's boys: Jaz and Three-Balls. Younger women—presumably prostitutes or homeless women, street waifs—were being beaten and raped before the camera's cold eye. The women were either gagged, or allowed to scream outright. Often they were blindfolded, to steepen their horror. There were several DVD's like this, and they were all shot in locations that Westmore recognized—various rooms and parlors of the mansion.

Another DVD was a genital piercing—or at least that's what Westmore thought it would be called. A half hour of footage that was one shot: A woman's splayed pubis. One piercing at a time, the woman's vaginal opening was closed by chrome rings stitching the lips together. The woman's face was never shown, nor was the rest of her body. The camera never moved.

Westmore was dizzy by the end of it all. It took several minutes to compose himself, and when he thought he had himself back together, he got up to leave the office but found himself bolting for the bathroom where he spontaneously vomited.

Then he walked back down through the dark house to the South Atrium, a long sightless stare in his eyes, like someone who'd just left the observation window of an execution.

"You look like you've just seen a ghost," Cathleen said when he trudged in.

"Maybe he has," Willis said.

The group was all sitting around the conference table. "I *wish* I'd seen a ghost," Westmore said, seating himself. "I saw something a lot worse."

"What are you talking about?" Adrianne asked.

"I've just spent the last couple of hours watching more of the illustrious productions of T&T Entertainment. Rape movies."

"T&T never did anything underground," Karen remarked. "It was all licensed and legal pornography."

"This stuff wasn't. It was nauseating. Stuff that Hildreth made on the side, for kicks, I guess. I'm starting to finally see the real Hildreth. The guy was sick in the head." Westmore still felt dried out, abandoned by his own spirit. "Only the sickest sort of people in the world could find that stuff arousing. It was criminal."

"Hildreth was a sick man," Nyvysk said. "There are a lot of Hildreths in the world. It's beyond sickness. They exist to perpetuate evil. Pornography, rape, degradation—those are the tools they use to solicit the devil."

Westmore was still too nauseated to reject the theological inference. The images from the discs—the vacant faces and pale skin, the screams and the sounds of fists colliding into flesh—it haunted him at the table. He looked for any distraction . . . and found one. Some sort of a large recording device—the size of a VCR—sat on the table. "What's that?"

"We had a trespasser," Cathleen said, squeezing lemon into some iced-tea.

"We're being bugged," Willis added.

Westmore was flabbergasted. "*What?*"

"That's a CD recorder with a voice activation switch," Nyvysk explained. "It's only on when someone's talking, so each disc can conceivably record everything said in this room for at least a day. I found it under the couch. It's hooked up to an RF transceiver that picks up all the sounds of the room through *that* microphone." He pointed up toward the crystal chandelier hanging above the table.

A studied squint showed Westmore a tiny microphone stuck to the bottom of one of the lamp bulbs. "Who was bugging us?"

Cathleen laughed. "Somebody *you* let in the house today."

Westmore thought back. "The bug guy?"

"The bug guy," Nyvysk said.

"But he was legit . . ."

"If it's anybody's fault, it's mine," Karen admitted. "It wasn't the guy who usually comes out. I should've called the company to verify, but I didn't." She paused, to frown at herself. "I was hungover and I didn't feel like going to the trouble."

Nyvysk walked to the TV. "It was sheer luck on my part. I was in the common room checking my own hookups, when I happened to notice this man walking around down here over the videocom. So I pushed the record button on the camera. This is what I saw him doing . . ." The TV winked on, and there it was. "Mike" from Bayside Pest Control. On the screen he was spraying a line of pesticide along the molding, when he quickly set his tank down, glanced around, to kneel at the couch. He slid the recorder out, replaced some discs, then was back to spraying a minute later.

"How do you like that?" Westmore said, astonished. "Why's he bugging us?"

"Maybe he works for Vivica," Adrianne posed.

Mack scowled at the end of the table. "Why would Vivica bug her own house? I work for her, remember? So does Karen. If you psychic folks pulled anything funny, one of us would tell her in a heartbeat."

"Then it's got to be the police," Cathleen asserted.

"That doesn't make sense, either," Westmore said. "The police have closed the Hildreth case. It was a multiple homicide/suicide. Everybody's dead. So where's the case?" but even as he spoke the words he wondered, *Maybe Vivica's not the only one who thinks her husband is still alive . . .*

"It doesn't really matter who was bugging us, or why," Nyvysk said. "It is curious, though."

"Curious?" Mack objected. "This is a little bit more than curious, I think. It's making me paranoid as shit."

"Nobody's doing anything wrong here," Nyvysk reminded. "We're in the house by invitation of the owner. No crimes are being committed. To novices, we're just a bunch of crackpot ghost-hunters and mentalists. It would be illogical for the police to care, to even waste their time."

"Maybe it's a newspaper," it occurred to Westmore. "*That* would sell some copies. 'Murder House Investigated by Famous Psychics.'"

Everybody looked at Westmore through a long silence. "I didn't even think of that," Nyvysk said. "And it's noteworthy that you're the one who suggested it. So tell us, Mr. Westmore, *which* newspaper is it you work for?"

"Wait a minute!" Westmore hastened. "I don't work for *any* paper now. I'm freelance."

"Could be writing a freelance book," Cathleen added. "It would be a blockbuster!"

My and my big mouth, Westmore thought.

"But again, it scarcely matters as far as I'm concerned," Nyvysk said. "There's little need for Mr. Westmore to plant electronic bugs when he's already in our midst. And it wouldn't make sense to risk sneaking in an outsider to change discs when he could much more safely do it himself."

"Thank you," Westmore said, relieved.

Nvyvsk went on, "We mustn't let this bugging incident distract us from our purpose. Something far more grave happened today, and we need to talk about it."

Westmore looked around. Every face at the table turned grim, especially Karen's.

"Did something happen?"

"I had one of those things that Cathleen and Adrianne had," Karen told him.

"One of *what* things?"

"A para-planar rape," Nyvysk answered for Westmore's benefit. "A discorporate sexual assault."

This again, Westmore thought. But Karen looked sullen, fractured. He knew that she was no great believer in all this psychic stuff—she could take it or leave it—and she didn't at all seem the type to be manipulated by the power of suggestion. She looked truly shaken.

"So where did this happen?" he asked.

"The inner courtyard." She winced thinking about it. "It was probably just a dream."

"It was no dream," Cathleen felt confident. Then she asked a seemingly irrelevant question: "What were you wearing?"

Karen's shoulders drooped. "Nothing. I was sunbathing. No one was around so I took everything off."

"Mobilizing imagery?" Nyvysk asked.

"I think so," Cathleen said. "This house is very sexual. We all felt that the minute we walked in. When I was doing my alomance in the graveyard, I was naked."

"And when I did my OBE, I was only wearing my bra and panties. When I came back, they'd been taken off."

Maybe YOU took them off, Westmore had to think.

"Shortly before this happened," Cathleen asked Karen directly, "were you thinking about anything sexual? Whenever I do a divination, a seance, or try to make a contact, I think back to some pleasurable sexual experience in my past, not because I'm trying to summon anything but it sometimes tunes my psi, makes my receptivity more keen."

"I sort of do the same thing before an OBE," Adrianne admitted. "I've been orgasmically abstinent for years now— I have to be—but sexual thought always primes my senses, helps me slip out of my body easier."

Westmore was stupefied by the talk. *Orgasmically abstinent? Thinking about sex to summon "psi?" Jesus. This isn't exactly small-talk at a Tupperware party.* He couldn't believe this. And they were all *serious.*

"What about you, Karen?" Cathleen asked.

"Oh, jeez." Karen—unembarrassible—looked embarrassed; were it not for the tan, she'd be blushing. "Yes, I was thinking about sex before I fell asleep."

"Sex with anyone in particular?" Willis asked, pouring himself some lemonade.

"Yes."

"Sex with Hildreth, or any of the men who died here, or any of the women?" Cathleen inquired.

"God, no! What difference does it make who?"

"Believe it or not," Nyvysk piped in, "it could be important. In a place like this? Some of the most powerful human emotions are relative to sex-drive, and the same can be true of any corresponding *in*human emotions, or discarnate emotions. This house is charged which, to you, means it's full of spirits. *Negative* spirits, and probably very sexual spirits."

Westmore just sat and listened. Ordinarily he would've scoffed. But now?

"All right," Karen confessed. "I was . . . fantasizing. About Westmore."

Now Westmore blushed. *That's just peachy . . .*

No one else was the least bit surprised. They listened, serious.

"Were you asleep at this point?" Willis asked. He slid the pitcher of lemonade to Westmore, who noticed that the man was still wearing jersey gloves.

"It started out with me just thinking . . . about sex with Westmore. Then it changed to one of those things like you're dreaming, you're seeing the dream, but you're still awake—"

"Hypnapompia," Nyvysk and Willis said at the same time.

Or hypnabullshitia, Westmore considered.

"—then I fell asleep and Westmore continued to be in

the dream, but . . . only for a few moments. Then I was someplace else. In Hell, I think. Hildreth, Jaz, and Three-Balls—but they had demon features. They were killing my daughter, and me."

"The place?" Adrianne asked next. "Was it like a church made of flesh? Something like that?"

"No," Karen said, lighting a cigarette to dispel her discomfort. "It was more like a prison cell, but there were some holes in the wall, and through one of the holes, I did see something like that. A temple that looked made of skin."

"That's what I saw," Adrianne said.

"The Chirice Flaesc," Nyvysk said grimly.

Adrianne was enthused. "That's the term the figure in my vision used."

"The temple of worship for the *Sexus Cyning,*" the older man went on. "According to the Morakis grimoires and other major demonological tomes, it's a church made of flesh, the nexus for the lord of carnality—"

"Belarius," Westmore uttered, remembering Nyvysk's explanation in the office. "The demon in the engraving, and you also have a voice saying that name on one of the EVP tapes."

"In my dream, Hildreth used that name, too," Karen acknowledged. "This is really scaring the shit out of me now."

"Hildreth's pieces are starting to fit together." Nyvysk was absently diddling with his beard. "He may well have been using this house as a power icon, to revere Belarius. Belarius is a very sexual demon, and this is a very sexual house. Orgies, prostitutes, pornography, rape movies. The sacrifices on April 3rd were sexually grounded." He looked to Willis. "Your target-object visions the other day. You said you saw Hildreth?"

"Yes," Willis said. "In the Jean Brohou Parlor, where the prostitutes were throat-cut." He closed his eyes to pause. "Hildreth and two men."

"Probably Jaz and that goddamn Three-Balls," Karen said. "I saw them with Hildreth in the cell, before they made me look at myself being raped."

"But who was raping you?" Cathleen asked with concern.

"No who, what. They were things. They were like shadows—"

"Subcarnates," Willis said. "I saw them in my flash too. Like touching an oily gas is the only way I can describe it."

"And the same kind of things were what molested me near Hildreth's grave," Cathleen said. "Not a revenant of Hildreth. They were like . . . a pack of monsters that I could only partially feel. I've been assaulted by subcarnates before, but never like this."

Westmore interrupted with a smirk. "What the *hell* is a subcarnate? A ghost?"

"Actually, no," Nyvysk said, "and utterly confusing to a novice. A subcarnate is a surviving entity that's trying to become flesh, to become *incarnated*—but can't because its physical body is dead."

"Sounds like a ghost," Westmore said.

"*Or*, if its physical body is somewhere else," Nyvysk added. "Another plane, perhaps. But you get the idea."

Do I? Westmore thought.

"Strong living human emotions as well as revenant residue can summon subcarnates," Nyvysk continued. "And it's really making me think harder about this house."

"Like the house is an antenna," Adrianne posed, "and Hildreth was tuning it, calibrating it, with more carnality—"

"And eventually ritualized sacrifices," Willis said.

"Yes," Nyvysk agreed. "But I don't really know anything about the house since Hildreth bought it."

"Mack would know," Karen said.

"Where is he?" Cathleen asked.

"Probably sluffing somewhere," Karen added a pinch of sarcasm.

"Sluffing? You can't possibly be talking about me." Mack strode into the room, then switched on a television sports show. "I just got back from that damn locksmith company. Says Vanni must've quit on him, 'cos he can't reach her."

"Maybe she . . . ," Westmore began, but thought the better of it; however, Cathleen finished for him anyway: "Maybe she saw something here."

Adrianne laughed. "Wouldn't be the first time a subcarnate scared somebody out of a house."

"Anyway," Mack went on, "The guy who owns the lock place said he'll send somebody else out as soon as he can."

There went Westmore's hopes about the safe. There was probably something in it that was much more understandable and concrete than ghosts, subcarnates, etc. Something he could relate to.

"What do you know about the house, Mack?" Karen asked. "Before Hildreth owned it?"

"Does it have a history?" Nyvysk asked.

"Well, yeah, now that you mention it." Mack sat down at the table next to Westmore. "It's always had a rep that it's haunted. In the early 1900's, it was a sort of a lockup treatment center for the Presbyterian church, for sick priests."

"Ministers, not priests," Nyvysk corrected.

"Whatever. These days if a priest or minister gets caught messing with kids or boffing half the congregation, it's in *Time* magazine. But back then it was very hush-hush. One day the guy'd be in his church doing the sermon and the next day he's history, replaced. They'd shuffle him off in the middle of the night and stick him here, to give him psych counseling and keep him away from the public. Evidently, some of these guys were *really* screwed up."

"Sex-addiction problems, in other words," Nyvysk augmented.

"Yeah." Mack helped himself to some lemonade, then propped his feet up on the table. "And during World War Two, and on into the early '50s, the mansion was a bordello. It stayed open for a long time 'cos the madame had ties to the cops, cut them in on the profits to look the other way, even after the murders."

"Murders?" Karen asked. "I didn't know there were other murders here."

"Yeah, a bunch of them. Especially right after the war. Guys'd come home from Germany and the Pacific theater, all boned up and still salty from killing, and they'd get carried away and wound up killing some of the hookers. There was also a lot of sexual misadventure later, guys getting too rough with the girls, taking the kinky stuff too far, and some girls wound up dying."

"Interesting," Nyvysk commented. "More sexually-motivated murder. A very powerful revenant residue. Sex truly is a component part of the charge of this mansion. There's a full century of negative sexual energy here."

"What exactly does that mean?" Westmore asked.

"We think of any so-called haunted house as a 'charged' location. Charges can manipulate the living, especially to those who are psychically attuned. Take a house where there's been multiple murders. Those murders leave a residue, so to speak, of negative energy, in which discorporates, subcarnates, spirits, etc., gain strength. If a homicidal person enters such a house, the charge accelerates, becomes

stronger. The charge in a house where a suicide occurs becomes stronger when a depressed or suicidal person enters.
And this house?"

"A double whammy," Cathleen said.

"Quite so. Sexually-motivated murder leaves the
strongest charge for they involve two of the strongest human emotions: hatred *and* lust. Such revenant energy is an
ideal environment for the kind of entities we're experiencing here. It's like a catalyst, a summons of sorts."

Karen's eyes glanced up. "That's what Hildreth said in
my nightmare. He said that lust summons them, and that's
why he chose this house."

"Lust summons who?" Westmore edged in.

"Subcarnates, for one," Cathleen offered. "And poten-
tially any revenant entity. Lust, hate, greed, pride—"

"You're saying emotions like that," Westmore deduced,
"combined with tragedies, sex-crimes, and all that, can turn
a house into a culture dish for ghosts?"

"In a manner of speaking, yes," Nyvysk verified. "And
it's a good bet that Hildreth had a very deliberate and specified purpose in choosing this house and turning it into a
pornography den."

"What purpose?" Westmore asked.

"He was making it into a church of his own," Cathleen
said.

Nyvysk nodded. "A church to worship Belarius."

Chapter Eleven

I

The next several days passed without event, or at least with none that Westmore could observe. The only person he felt close to would be Karen, but even she, now, seemed different. Less animated, low-key, bereft of the sharp sarcasm she'd been radiating since they met. And since her incident at the inner court, that overt sexual aura of hers was enfeebled, replaced by a caul. She didn't even dress provocatively anymore—jeans and a baggy blouse most days. And no more nude sunbathing.

He wrote productively several hours a day, though he still wasn't sure what he was writing. But if the others were— and it sounded like they were—then he would have something pertinent to report to Vivica Hildreth. *She wants to know exactly what her husband's last night in this house was all about.*

Now he knew.

It was about Belarius.

But he remembered her most crucial instruction from the day he'd met her at the penthouse: *My husband was preparing for something he thought would occur in the future. I want to know what—exactly—it was he was preparing for. And I want to know when.*

What could he have been preparing for? *The murders were obviously a rite of some kind, a sacrifice.*

To Belarius?

To trigger something, he guessed. In something so senseless, it made perfect sense. The key to it all was in Hildreth himself, who—in spite of his wife's conjecture—was probably dead. That was one grim chore that awaited. Westmore knew he'd have to go into the woods soon and exhume that coffin, and he had to do it without anyone else knowing or else suffer the wrath of Vivica's non-disclosure agreement. He knew she was much more bite than bark.

Over time, Westmore stumbled upon some channels in the house that could only be described as secret passageways—he even got lost a few times. One led to the Scarlet Room, another to the strange, railed walkways suspended above the South Atrium. A third, behind a curtain in Hildreth's office, led to several very narrow stairwells built behind the walls, which eventually ended in a small windowless study that seemed embedded in the house, somewhere on the first floor. The mansion was a strange place that just kept getting stranger. And over the course of those days, he'd found more DVD's which he dreaded to watch but watched nonetheless, hoping for more clues about the mysterious Rodenbaugh girl. But there were none. The discs were either more T&T porn frolic or more nauseating rape and brutality movies. He found a few more snapshots in an otherwise empty bedroom on the first floor, on a shelf in the closet. The dowdy, overweight woman he'd seen in the Halloween disc. *Faye Mullins,* he recalled Karen telling him. *The house janitor.* In the pictures, she posed half-smiling with some of T&T's stars and starlets, but beneath the smile, he could clearly detect a restrained misery. The question begged: *Where was Faye Mullins on the night of April 3rd?*

And where was she now?

Westmore called a private research consultant he knew from his newspaper days, to do some searches on Deborah Rodenbaugh, and he asked for a complete make on the background and financial portfolio of Hildreth himself. *How did he get so rich?* Vivica and others claimed he was a financial genius, yet the basic web searches Westmore had done on his own revealed no traces of the man whatsoever, which seemed very odd . . .

"Did you hear what that kook Cathleen says she's going to do tonight?" Mack asked him in the kitchen. He fixed some espresso, diddling around. "She's going to do some sort of a séance."

Westmore was not surprised. In *this* house? "What, to contact the dead?"

"To contact Hildreth." Mack smiled sarcastically and walked away with his coffee.

"Come in here," Nyvysk said, surprising Westmore. "There's something you might want to see . . ."

Westmore went out to the atrium. "What's this about Cathleen doing a séance?" he asked.

Nyvysk chuckled. "It's not quite what you're thinking. Cathleen's a mentalist—that's a sort of medium—and she can put herself in what we call a theta-trance, which sometimes solicits communication-prone spirits. Some surviving spirits are very talkative, Mr. Westmore, to an annoying degree. But what Cathleen will do isn't like anything you've read or seen in movies. No Ouija boards, no people sitting around a table with their pinkies and thumbs touching."

"Cathleen seems pretty diversified," Westmore observed. "You only do one thing—the tech stuff. Adrianne only does the out-of-body thing. And Willis does the touch thing—"

"Target-object tactionism," Nyvysk corrected.

Westmore frowned. "Right. But I take it Cathleen has a number of skills."

"Oh, yes. She's clairvoyant, she's trance-inductive, she's a scryer—a crystal-gazer, in other words—and quite paranormally sensitive."

"Is she famous?"

"In her field, yes, quite famous. She keeps to herself much more now. You rarely see her on TV anymore. Twenty years ago was another story. Do you know what her claim to fame is?"

"Not a clue."

"She's a psychokinetic."

"She can move things with her mind?"

"Oh, yes. She stopped doing it publicly a long time ago. She got in some trouble; someone was injured. A wall she was holding up—mentally—fell on someone."

"A spoon-bender, you mean."

"Mr. Westmore, there was a time when she could bend a crowbar. She could look at a car-jack, and raise a car." Nyvysk cast an amused glance. "But you don't believe that, do you?"

"Sorry, but I gotta *see it* to believe it."

"Your skepticism is not only healthy, it's crucial. And

now, here's something you can focus more of your skepticism on."

Westmore noticed some computers and screens that Nyvysk had set up on a William and Mary trestle table. Nyvysk explained, "I've set up a small observation post down here so I don't have to keep running up and down the stairs all the time," the bearded man said. "And I thought you'd like to see exactly what an ion signature looks like. The readings thus far have been . . . interesting."

Westmore focused on a flat-panel screen. He saw a blank, black screen.

"Do you know what zeolite groups are?" Nyvysk asked.

"No."

"Do you know what *labile* ions are?"

"That's a big negatory, professor," Westmore admitted.

"Ions are charged sub-atomic particles; they're in everything," Nyvysk began. "What my scanners detect are ions in the air. Any physical body, in any space other than a vacuum, will disrupt the ionic environment, and these disruptions can be monitored. Heat, moisture, movement, minuscular radiation given off by the skin, will cause airborne ions to fluctuate or even reverse their electrical charges. Follow me so far?"

"I . . . think so," Westmore said.

"A human being walks into a room, ions around that physical body change in a detectable manner. But the same is true of revenants, discorporated entities, subcarnates—the manifestations we were discussing earlier."

"Ghosts," Westmore said. "Leftover spirits of dead people."

"Exactly. That's what we're looking at now."

Westmore looked more closely at the screen. "It's just black. Nothing there."

"Wait . . ."

Westmore kept looking and eventually wisps of something luminous, like dandelion-yellow glitter, moved across the screen. "So you're telling me that *that*—"

"—is a revenant. A ghost."

Westmore frowned. "What if a live human being walked into the room?"

"Then you'd see a similar effect."

"All right. How do you know *that's* not Cathleen or somebody?"

"Look."

Westmore's eyes widened. Now the black screen was full of the luminous wisps. *That's a lot of . . . something all of a sudden.*

"Here's the room in normal light, from a patch through the video camera." Nyvysk flicked a switch, and the room stood devoid of any persons.

It was the Scarlet Room.

When Nyvysk put the black screen back on, more ion activity could be seen, off and on.

Then it all dissipated back to total blackness.

"I've recorded some interesting ion signatures in there today, but actually nothing spectacular. Perhaps later tonight, the activity will become more frenetic."

"Oh, sure, it's interesting," Westmore agreed. "But any skeptic could look at that and say it could easily be fake. It could be manufactured with a simple digital editor on a computer." Westmore smiled. "Just like crop circles and pictures of fairies and paper plates for UFO's. They would think that *you* manufactured it. Same thing with the EVP's."

"Of course they would, and of course I *could* easily do something like that," Nyvysk admitted. "But I didn't. I'm not looking for credibility. I'd like nothing more for this house . . . to just be a house."

Now Nyvysk smiled. "I've seen a lot worse."

"Proof of demons?"

"Oh, yes. In Toledo, I helped a monsignor exorcize a ninety-year-old woman and transpose a demon named Zezphon into the body of a mule. The mule lost all its hair at once, turned dark-red, and ran mad through the town square, excreting all of its internal organs through its anus."

Charming, Westmore thought.

"This is an active-element infrared thermograph," Nyvysk said next. He clicked something on the computer and suddenly Westmore was looking at a murky-green screen. Nyvysk went on: "A human being entering this room would generate an orange outline." Then he hit the intercom switch and said, "Okay, Karen. Go on in."

On the screen, a fluctuating orange shape, in a human outline, flittered across.

"That's Karen in the room?" Westmore asked.

"Yes. It's the Jean Brohou Parlor."

Where the hookers were killed, Westmore remembered. *Hung upside-down. Beheaded over buckets.*

"The infrared element picks up confined heat signatures," the older man was saying. "But what would the presence of a discorporate entity register?"

"I don't know."

Another click, and the screen reversed. Karen disappeared, but now Westmore could see gray-blue shapes—on the floor. They were moving.

"Humans give off heat from their bodies. Spirits are the opposite. They're cold. Those shapes are—"

"Ghosts on the floor," Westmore said.

"If you will."

Westmore watched in a macabre captivation. Eventually two of the gray shapes rose—human shapes—dragging two other shapes off the floor and suspending them upside down. The motions which followed were obvious: the two standing outlines slowly cut off the heads of the hanging figures. Blue blobs—the heads—were cast aside.

"Think there are real people in there play-acting?" Nyvysk clicked back to the green screen, showing Karen's outline standing there. Then he cut the IR system, reverting back to the normal video camera. A very normal Karen stood there plainly. No one else was in the ornate parlor with her. She seemed bored, so she walked to the bar and poured herself a drink.

That's definitely not a ghost, Westmore concluded.

"Let me show you something else. We have many tools, as I explained the other day. Manometers and aneroid barometers measure divergences in air pressure, slide-tomographs can sometimes detect incipient presences in walls, cement foundations, etc., resonance imagers similar to those used by clinicians can even detect revenant presences in living beings, as in possession, hygrometers measure variations in humidity. But the quickest and most effective way to tell if a house is charged? A simple thermometer."

"What?" Westmore said dumbly. "How do you take a ghost's temperature?"

"Not the ghost, the room that the ghost is in. I don't like the term 'ghosts' but we'll use it for simplicity's sake. Most types of ghosts will lower the temperature of the area of space they occupy, sometimes to an exact configuration of their spirit-body, sometimes just a spot—because they *have* no bodies. Other ghosts will raise the temperature of that area of space. Psychotic ghosts, in particular. Still others can raise or lower the temperature of that space, often instantly."

Spirits 101, Westmore thought.

"Karen?" Nyvysk said back into the intercom. "I'm turning off the active IR. Turn your probe-stick on and just start walking slowly around the room. Up and down motions."

"Okay." Karen put her drink down and picked up a metal bar with four nodes on it. A handle sprouted from the middle of the bar.

"That's normal video," Nyvysk said. He pointed to another screen, totally black. "That's the feedback screen for the probe. It's four bimetallic platinum thermometers. The readings are sent down to me with a radio-wave booster.

Westmore's eyes peeled on the black screen. Suddenly he saw four blue dots that moved forward, to and fro. At one point, Nyvysk said, "Stop, right there," and they saw the dots moving up and down, changing hues. Some glowed minutely red, yellow, or orange for split seconds. "Right there. Up and down, faster."

"You'd be surprised how often men have said that to me," Karen mouthed over the intercom.

Westmore kept watching: a kaleidoscope of neon-like streaks, most of which were varying hues of blue.

"I'm recording this for a collective playback," Nyvysk told him, then back to Karen, "Thank you, Karen. Turn it off and come back down."

Nyvysk clicked more tabs, but when the footage played back, each sweep of the dots and streaks froze on the screen while further sweeps accumulated as well. Soon, a shape was forming.

"See?" Nyvysk said. "Now you know the process. Keep watching and eventually an almost solid image will form.

I'll be back in a few minutes. Have to make some iced-tea."

"So this is—"

"It's a revenant," Nyvysk said without much concern. "A surviving discorporation—the spirit of a dead person."

Nyvysk walked off.

Westmore lit a cigarette and kept watching as more of the gleaming image adhered to the screen. Alternately, he clicked around the house through Nyvysk's patches into the mansion's normal video outputs. He saw Mack walking down a hall on the third floor, Willis wearing his perennial gloves as he read through some old tomes in the study, Adrianne sprawled on a high poster bed in one of the suites.

Karen walked in and placed the thermometer bar on the table. "What's that? It looks like a painting with fluorescent finger paint."

"It's you. Waving that thermometer thing in the parlor."

"You're . . . kidding . . ." She leaned over to study the screen. Now the image was much more precise. A tall, lean, and very human figure. "What *is* that?"

"I think it's Reginald Hildreth," Westmore said.

II

A theta-trance, the "theta" coming from the Greek word for death: thanatos. Such a trance—almost always self-imposed—would allow the spiritual remnants of decedents to share thoughts and visions with a living medium.

If said medium was good.

Cathleen was, or at least had been, known as very good, and she knew why. She could tune her sexual aura like a radio wave. That aura functioned as a beacon. Her mind was an antenna to the dead.

As fully trance-inductive, Cathleen had an array of options. Each location was different, each surviving circumstance unique. But she didn't have the nerve to go back to the cemetery, especially at night, and the Scarlet Room was simply too scary. Instead, she chose a sitting room on the fifth floor, which was right next to the Scarlet Room and had a stone balcony which faced the graveyard.

It was close enough.

There was no bed in the room; it was more of an anteroom for Victorian ladies to freshen up, Cathleen guessed. Beautifully furnished, crocket moldings, hand-carved corner finials, all surrounding an expansive vanity. A long arched-backed day-couch on mahogany scroll feet stretched across the rear window. The room was half-paneled, with rosette imprints adorning brandy-colored wallpaper.

Cathleen dragged the day-couch across the plush carpet, and stopped before the French doors, whereupon she stepped out on the balcony and let the warm night rush into the room.

Mental priming was always necessary; she had to acquaint herself with her position. The night seemed to hover. She could sense the five stories of height without having to see the ground below; in fact, for a moment before her eyes adjusted, she imagined that there *was* no ground below. Eventually, she could see the opening in the woods that led to the graveyard, and she thought intensely about what had happened to her there several days ago. A chill of dread shot up her back, but deeper down came a shameful glow of excitement that made her nipples harden to pebbles beneath her tank top.

Then she simply removed the tank top and cast it aside, as if to offer her breasts to the eyes of the night.

A warm breeze touched her hair. She looked over her

shoulder to gauge the position of the couch, then agreed with herself: *If someone—or something—were standing in the clearing to the cemetery, they could look up here and see the couch. They could see me . . .*

That's what she wanted.

Only the dimmest lamps lit the room from behind. The day-couch sat in wait for her, for it was on those velvet, buttoned cushions that she would lay when she put herself into theta-sleep.

But she still wasn't quite ready.

She went back into the sitting room, stepped out of her jeans and panties, then walked to the bath.

A spectacular claw-and-ball-footed bathtub sat beneath a curtain ring. The tub itself was made of stainless brass and the tulle curtain glittered from pockets of semi-precious gems. Cathleen turned on the shining faucet and began to fill the tub with cool water. She added High John shreds, jasmine and poppy oil, and lavender extract; she wanted the scent on her clean skin, which was said to arouse male revenants, particularly those guilty of sexual crimes when alive. At the side of the tub she also placed a tiny vial of pulverized pontica stone—a stunning aqua and vermillion—which she would rub over her skin after the bath. She wasn't sure if this actually enhanced trance-reception, but it was a long accepted practice through the ages, so she always did it just in case.

The water was lukewarm. *Perfect,* she thought. She must clean herself first, then go out to the couch and induce the trance. She lowered herself down into the strangely fragrant water and at once felt . . . luxuriously lewd. She was already priming herself in her mind, by exciting her body.

Her eyes closed. The water licked her body from all around. She thought only of dense, pure physical passion, of lust unrepentant and unreserved. Beneath the water her hands stroked upward, over her thighs, over her sex, up her belly, around her breasts. When her fingertips pinched her nipples, she moaned. She pinched and twirled the little nubs of flesh till she squirmed from the delicious discomfort, harder still till she ground her teeth, and her feet churned under the water. The impulse was almost irresistible, then: to bring her hand to her sex and masturbate, to get herself off right now. But she didn't. She wouldn't let herself.

Her lust was the summons, and she was summoning them right now, or at least she hoped.

When she couldn't stand it anymore, she stood up in the tub. Her desires agonized her now, but that's how it needed to be. It was time to go to the couch and induce the trance, and when she pulled the ornate shower curtain back—

Her breath locked in her chest, like a hot stone. She couldn't even scream.

Three *things* stood around the tub: gaseous black shadows, like clouds of soot. But they were alive. They had no eyes yet they looked at her just the same, their auras even blacker than their subcorporeal bodies. Cathleen could tell what charged those auras: the most driven, demented lust.

Discorporates, she realized in her speechless terror. *The things from the cemetery . . .*

They were on her at once, their pad-like hands felt like globs of hot lard. But when she shoved out at them to push them away, her own hands disappeared into the black fog of their bodies. She was up-ended in a split-second, held upside-down by her ankles, then her head and chest were lowered into the water.

The fat hands gripped her body as surely as metal clamps; Cathleen couldn't push up, couldn't even flail in defense. Her face pressed helplessly against the bottom of the tub and she could feel one of them taking her from behind. She was methodically penetrated and humped. Her brain began to fizz out, her lungs expanding. When she was about to lose her air and inhale her first breath of water—

She was yanked out.

"Let her get a few breaths first," a voice ordered. "Then do it again."

Cathleen was too panicked to think, just a basic instinct to drag in a lungful of air and close her eyes, as she was plunged back down into the water. Now it was another one of them taking her—they were taking turns, using her body as well as her horror. By the third plunge, she was beginning to simply give up.

Heartbeats away from dying, she was yanked up again, but this time they didn't re-submerge her. She hacked out splats of water as she was carried aloft out of the bathroom. Her vision was so dimmed by oxygen depletion that she could barely see at all when she opened her eyes. Her drenched body was dropped on the couch before the open French doors.

One of the things was pointing to her.

What are they doing? she thought.

Another had the tiny bottle of pontica dust. It was emptied onto her face and bosom and dropped to the floor.

Now they were *all* pointing at her.

Her heart was still racing, her lungs frantically expanding and contracting, but once some semblance of reason returned to her, she knew what they wanted her to do.

They WANT me to do it, she realized. *They WANT me to induce a trance . . .*

Cathleen let herself go lax on the couch, her bare breasts glittering blue and red from the dust.

She began to put herself into theta-sleep . . .

III

*God, I know that what I am is part of You. Release me in the
midst of this evil place and keep me safe . . .*

Adrianne let the Lobrogaine seep into her brain, then her
nerves. She'd secured herself in the suite she'd used the
other day—the room where she'd been molested while out-
of-body. The drug's lull took her, a wicked treat like the
most selfish sex, then her bare stomach and legs tightened,
and her face began to swell and give off heat, and that was
when Adrianne slipped out of her prone body . . .

She floated upward, a balloon of consciousness and sight.
What she was now—a contained spiritual entity—moved
forward with a thought, and she was soaring through the
ether of the plane she now existed in. She passed through
doors and walls. She didn't even have to first go to the
Scarlet Room to get to where she wanted to go. Perhaps
she wasn't even *going there* at all. Perhaps she was being
taken.

The Temple of Flesh, the Chirice Flaesc . . .

This citadel for the thing called Belarius throbbed before
her beneath the black moon hanging in a blood-red sky.
Veins in the structure's columns and walls of living, skin-
covered meat beat faster as her presence was detected. Adiposians stood like sentinels of rendered fat, guarding the
temple's colonnade. Their eyeless faces looked up when
Adrianne hovered closer, and so did the structure's adjunct,
the Fallen Angel called Jaemessyn, a being with a stunning
humanish body but demonic arms and legs grafted on by
some infernal surgeon. His face seemed grand yet hideously
blank, until he looked up at her and gave away an expression
like approval in his large, supernaturally blue eyes.

"The traveler returns to us," the light-like voice bid to her. He'd been previously occupied, slowly strangling a female imp who hung limp as an empty coat in his grasp. The five penises that were the fingers of his other hand throbbed erect as they stroked the naked breasts and belly of his victim. That's when Jaemessyn noticed Adrianne; the She-Imp wasn't quite dead when he cast it to the floor like a handful of garbage.

"We're glad you've returned," he said. "And the Lord of this place is pleased."

I want to see the Lord of this place, she said back to him in a thought.

"And you shall. I promised you last time, and I never break my word."

The monstrous hand opened toward the temple's closed double-doors. In the door's seam, Adrianne detected fluttering, dark light. The doors began to slide open with a wet fleshy smacking sound.

"Welcome," Jaemessyn said. "I know you want to see the Sexus Cyning."

Belarius, Adrianne remembered. *Hell's monarch of lust . . .*

She floated in with no fear. Bodiless, they couldn't hurt her. Only her psyche was vulnerable, and Adrianne had a *strong* psyche.

The configuration inside reminded her of the De Rais Chapel back at the mansion, only everything here was forged of living meat: the pews, the nave, the altar and presbytery. All that flesh surrounding her shined from profuse sweat, networks of veins standing out, filled with hot blood. Severed hands in organic sconces flicked from fingertips lit like wicks. Throughout, the airless temple smelled like fresh, raw meat.

Her spirit-vision glanced about; there was no sign of the temple's overlord. However, at the structure's deepest recess—

"And there's someone else you want to see," the Fallen Angel added.

—she noticed someone lying prone on the high altar of flesh.

It was human, not demonic. It was a man.

Hildreth, she recognized at once.

He lay in a cloak, atop the altar's offertory slab. Pallid, eyes closed.

Motionless.

Is he dead? she wondered.

"He's never been more alive," Jaemessyn informed her. "But like you, his soul is temporarily vacant from his body. His soul is somewhere else . . "

The mansion, she realized, but before she could calculate anything further, something shrieked in her mind, bolting her with a psychic shudder.

Something shot about the nave, something terrified, and Adrianne knew exactly what it was.

It was the spirit-vessel of another soul, a human out-of-body just as Adrianne was. Adrianne could see it above her, darting back and forth terrified, and she could tell it was a much weaker consciousness than herself—the sign of an untrained experient.

Don't be afraid, don't be afraid, she tried to calm the other vessel and rose upward, but then her own conscious was nearly shot out of the nave by a burst of unadulterated, full-scale terror, and the other vessel's voice shrieked to her:

"Adrianne, my God help me help me!"

Adrianne easily recognized the psychical voice. It was Cathleen.

IV

I must be cauterized by now, Willis thought. He wasn't being incapacitated by what he'd been seeing through his "touches" tonight, awful as those sights may have been. In any number of rooms, or any number of specific target-objects, his mind-sight kicked right in and showed him: visions of murder, satanic ritual, and the most perverse sexual activity. Lots of blood, decapitation, torture. *Nyvysk was right,* he thought after leaving one of the parlors where women were blindfolded and raped by men in black hoods and cloaks. *They were paying reverence to something here.*

This . . . Belarius . . .

In a fourth floor suite, Willis picked up a woman's hair-brush and was sequently jolted by the image of a naked young woman on an altar, in a room shellacked by blood. Not one of these porn girls, either, nor one of the ravaged prostitutes; she looked wholesome and very normal. A peaches-and-cream complexion, long simple chestnut hair. She didn't fit in with any of the others, not the look, not the air. *She looks innocent.* He picked up a frilled pillow off the canopied bedstead and saw her again, her face pinched and tossing in the grips of a nightmare. And again, in the hall, when he ran his ungloved finger against the paneling, he saw her body being carried by several naked men, but Willis couldn't tell if she was unconscious or dead.

I wonder who the hell that was . . .

He saw remnants of Hildreth all over the place, too. Generally standing poised and very still, watching with great attention. Looking at something as if to appraise its value of worthiness for whatever nameless purpose. Regrettably, though, Willis often saw exactly what it was Hildreth was looking at: either a debasing sex act, an overt orgy, or someone being butchered. In one particularly disturbing vision, he saw a dowdy overweight woman with dead eyes injecting drugs into her arm while one of Hildreth's grinning porn-boys held a cocked revolver to her head.

It was insidious. Everything.

This house truly is a place of the devil.

But even on Willis' strongest day, he couldn't take much. The impact was simply too draining. He wandered alone down the main hall of the fifth floor. He passed the Scarlet Room but didn't enter; he'd already tried several tactions there but didn't see anything. Some rooms, like some objects, were only charged at certain times of the day, generally closest to the time that the target-event had occurred. *I think I'll just call it a night.* Most of his tactions had been very clear—and the group would be interested in that—but there was really nothing new to report. He was hoping to see something that might tell them something new. Tonight, though, was just more of the same. More murder, more degradation and sickness. The entire *house* was sick. He knew he couldn't stomach anymore tonight.

On the third floor, he saw a light from an open door, and heard someone tapping on a keyboard. Willis was a loner, but he didn't necessarily like being alone all the time. The house made him feel more isolated, and now, at night, something about it seemed to press down on him. He walked into the room.

"Oh, so this is the office," he said when he saw Westmore typing on a laptop. "How's it going?"

"I'm not sure." The writer chuckled. "I'm not even sure what it is I'm supposed to be writing."

"Same here, different process." Willis walked around, eyeing the room's impressive relics. "I was hired to come here and look for things . . . but I don't know what those things are." Willis lit a cigarette when he saw Westmore light up. He noticed a pile of DVD's on a fancy table inlaid with ingots of gold. "What's all this?" he asked.

"A bunch of porn, stuff that Hildreth's company produced. After about five minutes, stuff like that's all the same."

Willis said nothing of his disagreement. As a sex-addict whose psychic skills prevented him from touching women, he'd long ago become something of a porn addict. More lonerism. Just knowing what was on the discs gave him an anxious urge to watch some of them. But he didn't want to let on—for just as he was sure of his dependency, he was doubly ashamed of it. He turned away from the pile. His eyes fell on the recessed square in the wall that contained the safe.

"And there's the mansion's biggest mystery."

"Oh, the safe?" Westmore said. "Yeah. God knows when we'll get it open."

"Didn't the lock company say they were sending someone else?"

"Sure, but not for a few days. And they were the only company in the book. It's just weird that the woman they sent left without saying anything, and evidently she quit the company."

"You think something in the house scared her out?"

Westmore raised a brow. "By now it wouldn't surprise me. Nothing would in this place."

On the floor, then, Willis noticed a painting: a young brunette in a flowing bustle dress, pointing outward. At once, Willis' gut clenched. It was the woman he'd seen after touching the hairbrush. "What's this painting?" he asked with some reservation.

"Weirdest thing. It was hanging on the wall, over the

safe, and under it was another painting—er, not a painting but this engraving." Westmore flipped it back and showed him. "Evidently that's an engraving of Belarius."

Willis looked at the small, distorted face, obviously quite old. But that didn't interest him nearly as much as the painting of the woman. "What's she pointing to?"

Westmore pointed himself, to the second engraving on the opposite wall.

"The Revelation of John the Divine," Willis read the inscription. He chuckled at the cliche. "Did you try dialing six-six-six on the safe combination?"

"Yeah. Didn't work," Westmore said. He noticed Willis staring back at the painting of the girl. "Her name's Debbie Rodenbaugh. She worked for Hildreth. I guess he had a thing for her, to have this period painting done of her."

"Is she one of the women who got murdered?" Willis asked.

"No. No body was recovered, and she's missing. I'm dying to know where she is."

Willis cleared his throat, uneasy. "I just saw her—in a flash, I mean. When I touch charged objects, I sometimes get a visual flash of the last person affiliated with the object."

"What?" Westmore seemed alarmed. "You saw her in a vision?"

"Something like that. It's called a target-vision. I see the past of objects I touch. And I saw her—back in one of the other rooms."

Westmore's eyes turned distant. "So you think she *is* dead . . ."

"Oh, no, I didn't say that. People like me are called tactionists," Willis explained. "Somebody who sees ghosts sees spirits of the dead—but that's not me. I have no medium talents. If I see someone after I touch something, it doesn't necessarily mean they're dead. The flash I had of her was very obscure . . ." He didn't say anything more.

Karen walked into the room, something inquisitive in her eyes, and a gin and tonic in her hand. "Dinner time, guys."

Westmore looked at the clock in his laptop. "Dinner? It's almost eleven."

"Fine. Call it a pre-midnight snack." The jeans, and bare, flat, and very tan midriff below her knotted blouse made Willis avert his eyes; otherwise he'd be caught staring. "What's on the menu?"

"Cheeseburgers," she said. "I'm starting them right now."

"I think I'll pass—" After some of his target-visions tonight, Willis didn't have much of an appetite.

"Me, too," Westmore said, turning off his computer. "Can I borrow your car? I need to go to my local bar for a little while."

Willis was puzzled. "But I've heard you don't drink at all."

"He doesn't," Karen said. "He goes to bars to *not* drink. It's some screwed up writer thing."

"I go to bars to clear my head," Westmore explained. "It's a long story." His eyes shot to Karen. "So? Can I borrow your car?"

"You don't even have a license."

Westmore sighed. "You know I'm not going to be drinking. If I wreck your car, I'll buy you a brand new one with Vivica's money."

She threw him her keys.

"Thanks. You're a great sport."

"I know."

"See you guys later," Westmore bid and walked out.

She looked at Willis. "The bastard thinks I can't make a good cheeseburger."

"I'm sure you'll make fantastic cheeseburgers," Willis replied. "In fact, I've changed my mind. Fire one up for me, please. Well-done."

"You should see the top-grade ground sirloin that's in the fridge. Sure you don't want it rare?"

I've seen enough raw meat tonight in my visions. "Well-done, if you don't mind."

"You got it."

"I'll be down in ten minutes."

"Cool." She smiled, turned, and left.

The lustful shame reared in Willis' heart when Karen closed the door behind her. He went immediately to the DVD player and television, slotted the first disc he found. At once he was entranced by the images, however unrealistic and overdone they may have been. He clicked through to each new scene, to see each new girl. *God,* he thought remotely. All that bare skin. All those swollen breasts, splayed legs, and lewd grins. The women were beautiful . . .

Just stop, he thought. *This is pathetic.* What could he do here, anyway? Masturbate in secret, like an adolescent hiding in a closet? *With my luck someone would walk in. Wouldn't that be a hoot?*

The next scene showed two girls with Rodeo Drive bodies prancing into an office, dressed as maids. They began to clean the office with vacuums and dust wands, bending over liberally. Soon the scene deteriorated into lesbian frolic, in the middle of which the supposed Office Boss walked in, one of Hildreth's cocaine-tweaked studs. The rest went without saying but the reason Willis kept watching was because something about the scene nagged him. Then he realized what it was.

The office in the scene was vividly familiar.

It was the same office he was standing in right now.

That's what I call filming on location.

A chill crept up Willis' spine; it was simply the notion. The actors on screen, in the room Willis stood in now, were all dead. *It's like I'm watching their ghosts,* he thought and turned off the television.

He stopped before the door, again noticing the safe in the wall. *I'm really not up to anymore of this shit tonight,* he thought, but took off his glove anyway. He wondered what he would see. Certainly not the combination—tactionism didn't work that way. But . . . *What the hell . . .*

Willis touched the knob on the safe.

When he looked over his shoulder, he saw her, sitting at the desk. The attractive girl in the utility clothes named Vanni. She was looking at a small box on the desk, reading numbers off an LCD screen and writing them down on a piece of paper. It made sense, of course, that he should see her; she was the last person to touch the safe. The vision shifted, then, through something like looking through scratched glass, and suddenly they were in another room—the mirror-walled workout room he'd seen down the hall the first day. Bliss strained her face, her nakedness raving as she was made love to on a harness that spread her bare legs wide in mid-air. It was Mack who was having some pretty ravenous sex with her. *That asshole,* Willis thought, and before he could think much more, the vision snapped again, and they were back in the office . . .

The room felt cold now.

The machine on the desk was gone, and so were the rest of Vanni's locksmithing tools. She remained naked standing before him. Hollow-eyed. Deep lines in her face.

She's dead, Willis realized.

Her skin was ashen gray, the large, puckered nipples bruise-purple.

She pointed to the safe.

"They killed me before I could get it all," she said, her breath fogged in the frigid cold.

"Who's they?"

"Those things from the temple . . ." She walked over to the safe and idly ran her finger across its face. Several days of death left her slat-ribbed, bony now. She was beginning to desiccate. "But it's easy . . ."

"The combination?" he guessed.

"You people are supposed to be smart. It's a basic number-letter switch, an acrostic from canonic Gematria." She seemed to frown at him. "The oldest cipher in the world."

Willis didn't quite get it.

Her gut seemed to be sucking in by the minute, the lines in her ribs deepening, veins in her neck and arms growing more pronounced. "Touch me," she said. "Are you afraid?"

"I'm not the least bit afraid," Willis said, and meant it. "And I can't touch you because there's nothing to touch. Your physical body doesn't exist. You're a revenant. I see revenants every day."

Her gray breasts rose and fell. Was she breathing? "So you're certain we're all the same?"

"Yes."

She grabbed his throat and threw him to the floor. Willis couldn't react it happened so fast. His feet flew out from under him, and his teeth clacked shut when his back was slammed to the floor. When his vision cleared, she was straddling him, her bare groin splayed over his stomach, one dead hand still clamping his throat down. Willis couldn't think, and could barely breathe.

"Touch this," Vanni croaked. "Touch my heart and see. I have something to show you that's very important."

Willis mustered some resistance but to little effect. When he reached up to shove at her face, her free hand snatched his wrist. Her crotch ground against him. It was his right hand she'd snared, after which she slowly dragged it to her left breast, pressed it against her. He could feel veins pulsing and a heartbeat. An instant after his skin touched her, the vision sucked him down.

"Look, look. And see . . ."

A chasm below a scarlet sky. A temple standing bathed in an impossible black moonlight . . .

A temple of flesh.

And a man standing before the skin-and-muscle columns on either side of the temple's doors—doors with visible veins that beat in an exact synchronicity with Vanni's heart.

"Do you see it?" the voice ground overhead.

Willis didn't respond, so her hand clamped his throat tighter, cutting off his breath and threatening to vise apart the bones in his neck. Eventually he nodded.

"That's what I have to go back to," he was told. "But my instructions were to show it to you first."

"Instructions from who?" Willis managed to choke out the words. "From Belarius?"

"No. From the man standing before the temple doors . . ."

Willis looked back into the vision and recognized the man. Hildreth.

The hellish vista blacked out. For moments, Willis could see nothing . . . but he could feel. Cold lips sucked his tongue out of his mouth, to be met by an even colder tongue. A bony hand caressed his crotch, fingers fervent.

Then Willis opened his eyes and found himself on the floor of the office.

Alone.

V

Westmore sat downstairs in barely lit darkness, at the dock bar of his favorite hangout—on the wagon and off. The place was called the Sloppy Heron, a massive waterfront tavern on stilts. A pier extended just behind him; he could hear water lapping against the boats moored there. Upstairs, the main bar was too crowded tonight—spring-breakers. It was a packed house full of twenty-one-year-olds guaranteeing poor performance on their mid-terms thanks to seasonal drink discounts. Several bras had already landed in the water before Westmore's eyes. He didn't need the scene—*I'm too old and*—*I hope to God*—*too mature.* Down here was quiet, just a few others sitting over beers and watching sports highlights.

Nice and quiet, he thought.

He was clearing his head, and there was much to clear. Too many things had happened at the mansion for him to calculate, and there were too many more things that he didn't know. *Psychics. Jesus. Gauss meters and EVP and infrared ghosts. I'm just a fuckin' newspaper writer.* But the more he focused on the things he *could* relate to—missing persons, questionable graves, mysterious matriarchs—he found himself even more confused. At one point, he looked down the dark bar where several patrons started to groan. "You heard it first here," a sportscaster on TV announced. "The New York Yankees have just signed a record-breaking contract with superstar Alex A-Rod Rodriguez, which will give the Bronx Bombers one of the very best infields in the history of the game . . ." Westmore didn't know from sports but was amused when one of the patrons walked out onto the pier and threw up in the water. Then his cell phone rang.

"Finally got some poop on your man," came the voice

on the other end. It was Tom McGuire, his friend from the paper who was a freelance research consultant. Westmore'd hired him on the side to run a few names on Nexus/Lexus and some other research sites.

"That was fast, Tom. Thanks."

"Don't thank me yet. There's not much poop. I got stuff on the girl and Hildreth, but it ain't much. Some of it's interesting but there's nothing fishy."

Actually, Westmore was *hoping* for something fishy. "I'm ready."

"Deborah Rodenbaugh, Florida native, 18 years old. Comes from a no-big-deal middle-class family that's clean as a whistle. She was an honors student in high school, got a big history scholarship that a bunch of local papers covered. Sounds great, but then comes the downer. Her parents were murdered a little over a year ago, right after she graduated from St. Petersburg High."

This perked Westmore up. "Murdered? Murder isn't fishy?"

"It was a random break-in, it happens all the time, everywhere. Crackheads bust into a place, the family wakes up, so the crackheads get spooked and kill everybody. Cleaned the house out for valuables, wallets, some appliances, stole the car, and drove away. Treasure Island PD finds the car ditched near the bus stop the next day. The police have it down as a routine drug-related homicide still under investigation. Which is their rubber-stamp way of saying it's unsolved and probably never *will* be solved 'cos like I said, there's a couple hundred murders like that in Florida every year. It ain't just the Sunshine State, it's the Cocaine State. This shit happens, man."

Yeah, I guess it does, Westmore thought. "So where is she now?"

"After her parents were murdered, she was still a minor, so her aunt and uncle in Jacksonville became her legal guardians. The aunt and uncle are clean as a whistle, too. When I talked to 'em on the phone, they told me that Debbie's attending her second semester at Oxford University, in England. They gave me all kinds of contact numbers, school registration ID, her dorm, her classes and teachers—the kitchen sink."

"You check the contacts?"

"Registration, sure. Everything else I didn't bother with, but I'll give it a shot if you really want."

"I want. Please."

A sigh over the line. "Do you have any idea what a pain in the ass that is? The time-difference alone—"

"I told you I'd pay your normal rate," Westmore interrupted. He knew his request was inconsiderate, but he couldn't help it. "I really need this, Tom."

"All right, gimme a few days."

"Thanks," Westmore rushed. "And now fill me in on Hildreth."

A light chuckle. "This billionaire businessman of yours was no businessman."

"What do you mean?"

"He's only applied for one business license in his life. One incorporation, some sleazy outfit called T&T Enterprises. You ready for a laugh? It's a—"

"A porn company, I know," Westmore said. "And I don't even think it ever showed a profit."

"You got that right," Tom told him. "This Hildreth character bought it from some scumbag in California for a million when it was turning a slim profit, then he ran it right into the ground. Barely released any movies, didn't maintain distribution deals, stopped advertising. It's almost like he didn't care that he wasn't showing any numbers in the black."

"He *didn't* care," Westmore confirmed. "He was an eccentric. What I heard is he bought the company because he liked the girls who worked in it."

Tom laughed. "Yeah, I'd say that's eccentric. 'Hey, baby, I like your ass so much, I bought your company. You work for me now.'"

"Something like that, I think." Westmore lit a cigarette. "What about his background?"

"No background. Born in Jersey in 1944, parents moved to Florida in '46—all non-descript. High school education. Haven't dug deep enough to get a work history, deed history, etc. Reginald Hildreth is off the map, like most of us small-time regular people, until the early '80s."

"What happened then?"

"That's when he got rich. The only real trace of him financially are his federal tax records. This is the part that'll knock you over."

"Start knocking."

"Between 1981 and 1983, your man grossed a hundred million dollars. I thought he must be some financial whizkid or a Fortune 500 guy—boy, did I get that wrong."

"So how'd he do it?"

"Gambling."

Westmore frowned. "You can't make a hundred million dollars gambling. That's crazy."

"I know, but tell that to your guy. For those two years he walked into about a hundred different casinos, took each place for about a million, and walked out. Paid his taxes on each hit, and moved on."

"A guy wouldn't last two nights in Vegas like that. They'd bar him."

"He *didn't* last two nights. He took Vegas for a million, then went to Atlantic city, then hit the biggest Indian casino resorts in a dozen different states, then did it in Costa Rica, Monte Carlo, and on and on, like that. Nothing anybody could do about it 'cos it was all legit. And the fucker paid his taxes, so Uncle Sam didn't raise a fuss."

Westmore shook his head at the absurdity. "Was he a mathematical genius or something? Photographic memory?"

"Could have been, no real way to find out, though. Maybe he was just lucky. The guy ran with a streak. Maybe he did what most gamblers never do: walked when the pile got high."

"I don't know. That's a lot of luck," Westmore said.

"The real luck comes later. But this gambling stuff? You read about it all the time. Weird, sure. But it happens. Like that lady in Ohio who won the two state lotteries in the same year. As far as your man goes, the real luck came *after* the gambling streak."

"I heard he was an investor."

"He was—with no educational training to back it up, and no investment background. Any time Hildreth won a jack-pot at a casino, he'd pay the taxes and invest in the stock market."

"Blue Chip stuff?"

Another laugh. "This guy bought shares in every long-shot garage company out there, but pretty much just the ones that hit it big down the road. Microsoft, Apple, Bank of America, the little pee-hole that AOL was before they be-came AOL—there's a long list. They all turned out to be winners a few years later, thousand-percent share-profits and multiple buy-outs and stock-splits. Right now, the guy's worth one-point-four-billion."

Was worth, Westmore corrected in thought. *Now he's dead.* Or was that even true? He was trying to keep profes-sional. He'd taken a *job.* He had a *client,* Vivica Hildreth, yet the harder he tried to remain focused on the responsibilities he was being paid preposterously well for, he had to wonder. *What exactly am I doing now?* It almost seemed he was on his own investigation, for his own curiosity. "That's great work, Tom. Thanks. But I also want you to run another name for me too."

"Oh, no problem, buddy. I'm not busy here, I've got nothing better to do than—"

"I hear you. Bill me double, anything. But when you're following up on Debbie Rodenbaugh, I want you to run a check on the wife—Vivica Hildreth."

A long sigh. "You got it."

Westmore's thoughts strayed—back to Hildreth.

"You there?" Tom asked.

"Oh, yeah. I was just thinking. All that money Hildreth made? *Gambling?* You really think any guy can be that lucky?"

"Some guys got it, some guys don't," Tom said. He laughed dryly. "Who knows? Maybe the guy sold his soul to the devil."

Westmore was staring into space. "Thanks for the help. I'll let you go now, and give you a call in a few days."

"Sure thing."

Westmore hung up. He spewed cigarette smoke, watched it twist into strange shapes and dissipate. *Jesus. What am I thinking?* He picked up his glass of scotch, sniffed it, then put it down, and swigged some ice water.

Someone tapped his shoulder. "This who you're looking for?" and then a photograph was thrust in front of his face. "I heard you mention her name on the phone a minute ago . . ." Before Westmore could look at the man who'd said it, the photo hooked his vision.

It was Debbie Rodenbaugh.

Who the— He jerked around in his seat, glaring up.

And was stunned by the face that looked back at him.

"I guess I better call the police," Westmore said, infuri-ated. The guy who sat next to him he'd seen before. Older guy, buzz-cut with a bald spot, dark mustache.

"You made me that fast?"

It was "Mike," from Bayside Pest Control. Here he wore jeans, beat-up loafers, and a t-shirt with Jane Fonda in rifle cross-hairs.

Westmore was at a loss. "I just saw you on a security video tape, changing discs in your illegal bugging equip-ment while masquerading as a pest-control employee."

"Don't that beat all . . ." He looked at Westmore's scotch. "I thought you didn't drink."

Westmore slumped, groaning. "I don't, long story, none of your business. Two questions. Why shouldn't I call the police right now, and why do you have a picture of Debo-rah Rodenbaugh?"

"Wait on calling the cops. I'd beat the rap anyway. My brother-in-law is the state attorney, and some of my best friends are in the county prosecutor's office. I'm an ex-cop, I did twenty-years with the county sheriff's department. When I retired, I was the commander of the narcotics unit, and I got more commendations than any cop in the history of the department."

"Correction," Westmore said. "*Three* questions. Who the fuck are you?"

"Bart Clements." He passed Westmore his wallet, which contained a retired police ID. *Looks legit,* Westmore thought. *But what do I know?*

"Gimme a minute, and I'll answer all your questions," Clements said. "I came here for a reason—to talk to you. I know this is your hangout. Christ, I've been coming here every night for the last week. It's about time you finally showed." He ordered a draft beer, a Coke, and a basket of onion rings from the barkeep, then took the Coke to a girl who sat by herself out at a dark table overlooking the water.

When he came back, Westmore asked, "Who's that?"

"A friend."

Westmore frowned, looked at the girl again. She looked skinny, trashy, cut-off jeans, flip-flops, tube-top. Stringy dark hair. "What are you, about sixty?"

"Fifty-seven."

"No offense, man, but she looks like a twenty-five-year-old streetwalker."

"She is."

"That's great. Decorated ex-cop . . . picking up hookers."

"I've got a problem with hookers, always have." Clements looked at him. "Everybody's got something, right? Nyvysk quit the priesthood 'cos he was fuckin' falling in love with other priests. Adrianne Saundlund is a drug-addict, and Cathleen Godwin is a sex-addict. Patrick Willis is a porn-addict. Each one of us has our *thing*. Mine's hookers. Can't help it."

Westmore was astounded. "I'd be impressed by how much you know about the people at the mansion, but I guess when you've got bugs in the joint, it's easy to pick up *personal* information. But you don't know me from Adam. Why the hell would you tell a perfect stranger some very personal shit about yourself? Picking up hookers is nothing to be proud of, and for an ex-cop it's an outright disgrace. Why tell me?"

"I want to earn your trust," Clements said, sipping his beer and lighting a cigarette. "I've got a better bug in Vivica's penthouse at the Strauss Building downtown, by the way. A wireless mike. I don't have to go into the place to change discs like the mansion. I've learned more from that bug than the other. And I'm telling you *that* for the same reason I told you the shit about me. So you'll trust me. You could call Vivica right now, tell her about me, about the bug, and that's a *federal* charge. I'd really be screwed on a bust like that."

Yeah, he would, Westmore realized.

"Oh, and the girl?" Clements looked over at the ratty young woman he'd taken the Coke to. "Yeah, she's a street hooker, but I never picked her up for that. Her name's Connie; she's . . . a friend. She's helping me, and I'm helping her. I'm gonna get her in rehab."

"And how's she going to help you?"

Clements shot Westmore a dry smile. "She's one of the last people to see Hildreth or any of those porn nuts alive. She's also one of the last people to see Debbie Rodenbaugh."

Westmore chewed on the information, then it clicked. "She's one of the parlor prostitutes . . ."

"That's right. She got busted the night before the slaughter, otherwise she would've been there too and got her head cut off with the rest of them. She knows more about that house than you and me combined."

Westmore was waylaid. *This is out of the blue, all right.* "And the reason you want me to trust you is . . . why?"

"Because I need your help. And you never know, you might need mine. We're both on the same trek, buddy. We're both trying to find out what happened to Debbie Rodenbaugh. We can help each other."

"What's your interest in Debbie Rodenbaugh?" Westmore asked next.

"She was my last case. I don't like failure, and I sure as shit failed her. It's more than peace of mind. I never met the girl but I feel like I owe her something. Her parents were murdered because I took the case."

"What *case?*" Westmore was aggravated now more than intrigued. "What's she got to do with you? Her parents were murdered in a freak crime, by drug-addicts who broke into their house."

Clements' lips pursed at some distant disgust. "Her parents were murdered by Hildreth's order. Hildreth and that bitch wife of his. They'd already sucked her in, so the parents started asking questions. Where is she? What's she doing at this new 'job' of hers. Hildreth needed her for something. Little more than a year ago, I retired from the sheriff's department so I started my own PI firm. The Rodenbaughs hired me to keep tabs on Debbie, find out why she was spending so much time at the Hildreth mansion. Next thing I know, the parents are dead, and I'm in the county detention center full of scumbags I put there. An ex-cop in the joint is not a good thing to be."

Westmore didn't get it. "What were you in jail for?"

"Possession with intent to distribute crack cocaine. The cops got an anonymous tip and found a pound of the shit in a plastic bag stashed in my house. The bag had my prints all over it. It was lock solid."

Westmore shook his head in complete confusion.

"It was a *set-up,*" Clements said. "Don't you get it? Hildreth hired people to do the job. They got the bag out of my garbage—of course it's gonna have my prints on it. They put it in my house, simple. It was the city cops who made the bust; they didn't give a shit that I used to be a county narc—to them it looked like I was an ex-cop turned bad. No jury would believe me so I pleaded guilty in a swap. My brother-in-law believed me, and so did my pals at the prosecutor's office—shit, those guys have known me for decades. And the judge believed me, too—so I got a suspended sentence, lost my PI license, and got five years of fuckin' parole. The only reason I didn't lose my police pension is 'cos my cousin is an attorney for the LEAA, found a loophole. But the bottom line? I was a pain in Hildreth's ass, so he got me out of the picture. The parents were a pain in Hildreth's ass, so he had them killed. Problem solved, all nice and neat."

Westmore kept mulling it over. When the keep brought the onion rings to the bar, Clements waved the girl over. She came to the bar timidly, all hundred pounds of her. "Connie," Clements said, "This is Westmore. He's the guy who's gonna help us."

Westmore winced. "Hey, I haven't agreed to help you with anything. I'm still not even sure I'm not going to call the police and turn you in, or I still might talk to Vivica about this."

"Don't you get it? Vivica's the one running the show now, while Hildreth is in hiding," Clements insisted. "She's a manipulator, and she's manipulating the shit out of you. But you're starting to see through the stink—you're no moron. If you're not on to her by now, you really do have shit for brains."

Westmore thought about *that,* hard. Something *was* wrong, and he'd always been mildly suspicious of Vivica. *Clements is right, I DON'T trust her. If I did, why would I ask Tom to run a check on her?*

"Something's about to go down at that house," Clements continued. "I don't know what, and I don't know how, but I'm gonna find out. And I know this: it's all got something to do with the disappearance of Debbie Rodenbaugh."

"She didn't disappear," Westmore said without much confidence. "She's attending Oxford University right now."

"Bullshit. Connie saw her in the house less than a month ago. Sure, she's registered at Oxford, but she never showed up."

"I think it's pretty clear that Connie might be mistaken," Westmore put it as politely as he could. The girl was obviously a drug-addict—not exactly a reliable source. "And Debbie Rodenbaugh's legal guardians—"

Clements cut him off with a snide laugh. "What? The aunt and uncle in Jacksonville? People will say anything if you pay them enough—and Vivica Hildreth has a lot to pay."

Now Westmore wondered . . . about himself. Blinded by money that he definitely needed? *The most effective loyalty.* "All right, I'm still listening. You said you want me to do something for you. But what will you do for me?"

Clements chuckled. "In that freakshow house? Something's gonna happen there. It was Hildreth. He planned something—and it's still in the works."

Vivica had implied the same thing, hadn't she? *That's why she claims to have hired me,* Westmore remembered. *To find out whatever it was Hildreth had set into motion before he killed himself . . . IF he killed himself.*

"When the shit hits the fan," Clements went on, "you're gonna need some back-up. You're a fuckin' writer." The ex-cop lifted his shirt, showing two guns in clip-on holsters. "I can pick cherries at a hundred feet with these."

"You're expecting a shoot-out?" Westmore asked, incredulous.

"You keep forgetting where you're at. A *slaughterhouse.* You know that Hildreth isn't dead—"

Westmore's eyes widened. "I don't know anything of the sort. He committed suicide on April 3rd."

"Don't jive me, man. Vivica *told you* she didn't think he was dead. I *heard her* tell you."

Then it dawned on him. "You heard it on the bug you've got planted in her penthouse . . ."

"That's right, brain-child. You don't believe he's dead anymore than I do. That non-disclosure thing you signed with Vivica doesn't mean much now, does it? I know, too. If Hildreth really is still alive and in that house somewhere, *that* might be what he's planning for the future. Another slaughter. If he and more of his psychos come at you with meat cleavers 'cos they want to cut your head off and drain your blood into a fuckin' bucket, what are you gonna do? Use big words? Throw your laptop at 'em?" Clements patted the guns under his shirt. "Me? I'll kill the motherfuckers."

Suddenly it was a sound consideration. "What do you want me to help you with?" Westmore finally conceded.

Clements smiled. "I knew you weren't a moron." He turned to the girl, who was crunching onion rings. "Connie, tell him what you told me. About the door."

She looked at him with bottomless eyes. "On the side of the house. They used it all the time, to bring us in and out—and other people too, anyone, after dark. Hildreth didn't want anyone coming or going through the front door, I guess because he was afraid someone might be watching, police, whoever."

"I'm not following you," Westmore said, but what he didn't say was that now, for some reason, Connie was beginning to look familiar.

"There's a side road through the woods that comes up the hill. Not the main road, but a dirt road—"

"I know where you mean," Westmore said. "I found it the other day. Would never have known it was there if I hadn't stumbled onto it."

The girl went on, "There's a door on the side of the house that faces that road."

"A door?" Westmore thought about it. "I don't think so. I didn't see a door there."

"There's a door," she repeated. "It's part of the outside wall. You can only open it from the inside."

"A hidden access," Westmore deduced.

"And what else, Connie?" Clements reminded her. "Why's that door important?"

"Because it's not connected to the alarm system," she revealed. "I know it's not because I heard Hildreth and some of the men mention that it wasn't."

A secret door, Westmore thought. *Unmonitored.* "Okay. And you want me to find that door?"

"That's right," Clements said and lit another cigarette.

"Are there any clues you could give me?" Westmore asked the girl. "I'll be looking for it from the inside."

"The room that the door opens to is a small library," Connie said. "Not the main library; it's smaller. Lots of old books. And you get to that room through a curtain upstairs."

Instantly, then, Westmore knew. He'd found it earlier when he'd been looking around the house. One of the passages led to it. "I know exactly where it is."

"Good," Clements said. "You find the door, you open it, you let me in."

"Why?"

"So I can search the house for Debbie Rodenbaugh. Is that too much for your college-graduate brain to handle? I believe she's still alive. I believe Hildreth's got her captive in that house somewhere. I want to find her . . . and take her out."

Westmore stared back at him in the dark bar.

"Who else do you have to trust?" Clements asked, polished off his beer. "You can trust me, or you can trust those whackadoo psychics."

"I'll admit, they're a weird bunch, but they're good peo-ple," Westmore said.

"Jesus Christ, they can't wipe their own asses without having a vision or seeing a spirit. You think there's ghosts in that house because you hear voices on some *tape?* Shit, I heard one the other night off one of the discs I took out of there. It's one of Hildreth's people—probably that Mack fucker whispering spook noises. And that shit Nyvysk shows you on his TV screens? Shit, any good movie lab can do stuff like that—and Vivica has the dough to pull it off." Clements grabbed Westmore's arm. "And do you really think those women were *raped* by spirits? Gimme a break. It's either a con-job or they're having fuckin' hallucina-tions. Those chicks think they can talk to the dead and leave their bodies—they're whacked out of their minds. They spend more time on a psychiatrist's couch than they do walking the street."

Westmore kept thinking on it. "I don't know."

"You're gonna trust *them,* or me? Nyvysk can fuck round with his low-light cameras and TV's and ion shit all he wants. I'm gonna find out what's going on the old-fashioned way. With my balls and my brains," Clements said. "Did you ever see any *ghosts?*" he asked Connie.

She sat uncomfortably, pushed some hair out of her eyes. "No, but it is a creepy place."

"Did you ever get *raped* by a ghost?"

Her eyes flicked down. "No, not by ghosts . . ."

"Hear that?"

But Westmore kept looking at her. She was familiar in some unpleasant way . . . "I know I've seen you before," he said to her.

"I usually stroll 34th Street at night."

"No, no, not like that. I mean—" Then it hit him. *The*

movies, he thought with a plummeting stomach. "I found a bunch of DVD's at the mansion, and I saw you in one of them, being raped by a bunch of men. Some of them looked like bums. And there were—" Westmore gulped, remembering the extremity of some of the movies. "There were other things."

The girl just nodded and looked away.

"That's the kind of thing Hildreth had people do to these girls," Clements said. "Rape movies, animal movies—for shit's sake. And you're working for the guy's fucking wife who knew all about it and never did anything. And now you're gonna trust *Vivica* over me?"

Westmore's moment of truth was fast approaching. *If he's wrong, I'll never get the rest of the money Vivica promised, and I'll get sued for every penny she's given me so far,* he realized. *If he's wrong . . .*

"All right. I'll help you."

"Thank God," Clements sighed. "Couple nights from now, you leave that door open for me at a specific time." He gave Westmore a card. "Here's my cell number. Call me tomorrow and we'll work out the details."

Westmore pocketed the card, nodding and still bewildered. "Okay, but I need your help with something *tomorrow* night."

"Name it."

Westmore couldn't believe what he was about to say, but it was something he'd been thinking about since the day he'd entered the house. "Before I believe Hildreth might still be alive, I need to see the proof."

"Yeah?"

"And you're right, I'm just a fuckin' writer. I'm *not* a ditch digger. I need you to help me dig up his grave."

Clements shrugged. "Piece of cake. What time tomorrow night?"

"Midnight. If I find this hidden door of yours, I'll leave the mansion at midnight and walk straight to the dirt road. Meet me there. Bring a couple of shovels."

"You got it."

"And if I'm not there, that means I didn't find the door." Westmore paused. "Or I changed my mind."

"You won't change your mind," Clements assured. "You ain't stupid. You and me, Westmore. We'll find out what's really going on in that freakshow mansion. At least we already have an idea."

"What's that?" Westmore asked.

"You know." Clements pulled a bag out of his pocket, dropped it in front of Westmore.

"I don't believe in the devil, but I believe that Hildreth does. That's the whole show he's got going in there."

Westmore picked something out of the bag: a small, black inverted cross on a silver ring. The image rang a bell. *Didn't I read something in the autopsy reports . . .*

"Hildreth's party favors," Clements said. "That's some madhouse, ain't it? All the female victims were wearing those things when they were butchered on the night of April 3rd, all this weirdo body-piercing shit. The girls had those things on their nipples, clits, and bellybuttons."

"Where'd you get these?"

"The county deputy medical examiner is my best friend from the Navy. He did the autopsies."

Westmore shook his head. "Is there anybody in a position of power around here that isn't either a relative or your best friend? You probably know the county executive."

Clements laughed. "You kidding me? I play cards with him every Friday night. I was best man at his fuckin' wedding. I also went to the police academy with the first responder to the mansion. He saw the bodies in place. All of

Hildreth's porn girls were wearing those." He tapped the bag of crosses. "Upside-down crosses are a sign of the devil. That's what Hildreth was pushing: full-tilt, to-the-max satanism. He was like one of those cult leaders you read about, gets a bunch of kids all fucked up on drugs and orgies, and brainwashes them." He put the bag back in his pocket. "And that's what April 3rd was all about—a satanic sacrifice. The asshole thought he was summoning the devil."

Not the devil, Westmore thought. *Belarius.*

Westmore followed Clements and Connie to the parking lot. Clements had his arm around the girl; they were obviously more than just friends. "So we're on for tomorrow night," Clements verified. "I'll be at the access road at midnight."

"All right." Westmore looked out on the water, thinking. "You know more about the house and Hildreth than I do. What else should I know?"

"Be careful around that Mack fucker, and the girl, what'shername, the ex-porn star who drinks more than a platoon of fuckin' Russian sailors."

"Karen."

"Yeah. Don't trust either of them."

"I'm pretty sure I trust Karen. She's harmless."

"She was under Hildreth's thumb, and she works for Vivica. Don't trust her. She's a mouthpiece to the queen witch."

Westmore squinted a confusion. "What if you're wrong about all this? What if Vivica *didn't* know anything? Maybe she's just a lonely middle-aged woman investigating her husband's death."

"Yeah, and what if I had a square asshole? Could I shit a television? Don't trust anybody. Whatever happened there on April 3rd is *still* happening. Everything's moving toward something, something that's gonna happen soon. That place is about to boil over, and if we're in it when it does, we want to be ready. The more information we have, the stronger we are. Oh, one other thing. You know about Faye Mullins, right?"

The name jogged his memory. *The overweight girl in the Halloween DVD . . .* "Karen mentioned her. The groundskeeper or something. A janitor."

"She's the only survivor of April 3rd," Clements specified. "She was *in the house* when it all went down."

"*What?*"

"You heard me right. I guess the only reason Hildreth didn't kill her was he must not have known she was there. I tried talking to her but she's a headcase now. You might have better luck."

Westmore was mildly alarmed. "Vivica never told me there was a survivor that night."

"There's probably a whole lot Vivica didn't tell you. Faye Mullins is the only living witness."

"Where is she?"

"The Danelleton Clinic, about a half hour from here. It's one of those $20,000-per-week private psych clinics. Go talk to her."

Westmore was doubtful. "A private-care clinic like that? They won't let anybody in there except next-of-kin."

"Go there tomorrow around, say, two. I can pull some strings and get you in."

"How?"

"The head of security at the clinic is my nephew. Trust me."

Westmore sighed. "Yeah, it looks like I'm going to do that."

"And I'll see *you* tomorrow night. Midnight."

"You're gonna be there, right?"

Clements laughed. "With shovels and guns."

He's not kidding . . .

Clements got into a big, beat-up Olds 98 with a landau roof. The girl walked around to the other side, but before she got in, she looked across the roof with a wide, empty-eyed stare. For a second, she shivered.

"Be careful in that house," she said very quietly.

"I will," Westmore said.

Clements rolled down his window. "We're gonna get Debbie Rodenbaugh *out* of that psycho place. And after we do, I'm gonna find Hildreth and blow his brains into the next zip code. Him and anybody on his side." Clements winked. "I'm gonna kill all of those evil, slimy, sick pieces of shit, and I'm gonna love every minute of it." Westmore watched them drive away.

Chapter Twelve

I

The pendulum clock in the foyer struck one a.m. when Westmore re-entered the mansion. He'd called ahead and Mack had disabled the alarm to let him in.

Something, right off the bat, felt odd.

Mack reclosed the door and reset the alarm.

"Something wrong? The house feels . . . weird."

"You could say something's wrong," Mack verified. "Willis had another one of his spells. He and Nyvysk are in the atrium."

Westmore followed him down the main hall. "Where are Cathleen and Adrianne?"

"They're both doing their things."

Westmore guessed that meant Adrianne was OBE-ing and Cathleen had put herself in a trance, trying to contact something in the house.

The atrium stood dead quiet. Nyvysk and Willis sat at the long conference table, Willis wearing his gloves and looking shell-shocked.

"What happened?" Westmore asked.

"Willis had another target-vision," Nyvysk told him.

"When?"

"Right after you left the office upstairs," Willis said.

"Another one of Debbie Rodenbaugh?"

"No, it was the woman who tried to open the safe. Vanni. It wasn't a passive vision—it was active. I believe it was her revenant communicating with me, but it was . . . different. Either that or it was a temporal-lobe hallucination."

"Tell him what triggered the vision," Nyvysk said.

"The safe. I touched the knob on the safe and had multiple flashes."

Westmore's eyes shot wider. "Did you—"

"I didn't see what was in the safe," Willis said in a drone. "I saw Vanni. At first the vision was passive; I saw her as she was when she was trying to open the safe, but then it changed. She was dead, she was a corpse talking to me. And I had a transitive contact."

"What's that mean?"

Willis groaned, obviously wearied.

"It means the vision—or whatever it was—physically touched Willis," Nyvysk explained.

"Which is essentially impossible," Willis finished. "Which is why I'm thinking it must be hallucinotic."

"The psychological factor," Nyvysk speculated. "A serious consideration in a house like this, especially after being here almost a week."

"A place like this can put a whack on anybody's head is what you're saying?" Westmore inquired.

"I hope to God that's the case," Willis said.

Westmore leaned forward, attentive. "But Vanni talked to you? What did she say?"

"A number of things. She showed me a vision herself. She said Hildreth had told her to. Then I saw the Chirice Flaesc, that Nyvysk has already explained—which is just more reason for me to hope it was a hallucination inspired by suggestion."

"What did it look like?"

"A temple of flesh."

"The domain of the Sexus Cyning—Belarius," Nyvysk augmented.

Willis rubbed his face. "It was alive. It was flesh and blood, and it was growing."

"Adrianne and Karen saw the same thing," Westmore recalled. "What else did you see?"

"Hildreth." Willis laxed back, exhausted. "Then the target-vision changed. Vanni implied that the combination to the safe was Gematric."

"What's that mean?" Westmore asked.

"Part of the system of the Kabalistic alphabet," Nyvysk informed. "She said it was *acrostic*, but I'm not familiar with the word."

"And neither am I," Willis said. "Let's find a dictionary—"

"We don't need a fuckin' dictionary!" Westmore blurted and had already sprung up, racing out of the room.

He ran down the main hall, then vaulted up the stairs to the third floor. By the time he got to the office he was winded yet shaking with excitement. He looked at the safe, then looked at the engraving across from it. *Couldn't be,* he thought.

A moment later, Willis and Nyvysk jogged into the room. "What is it, for God's sake?" Nyvysk said.

"Do you know the combination?" Willis asked.

"Acrostic," Westmore said. "I majored in English in college—acrostic is a term sometimes used in symbolic poetry. In the old days, people would write poetry with hidden meanings—ciphers—"

"Vanni said this was the oldest cipher in the world," Willis remembered.

"She's probably right," Westmore said. "In old poetry, sometimes a letter would be used to indicate its numerical equivalent." He looked back anxiously at the safe. "I heard her say it was a nine-number combination . . ." Then he held his hand up, a bid for silence, and calculated on his fingers, counting to himself. Then he grabbed a pen and scribbled something on the desk blotter.

"What *is* it?" Nyvysk raised his voice.

"It's *that,*" Westmore pointed to the engraving of St. John writing the *Revelation*.

"What? 666?" Nyvysk questioned. "We already tried that."

"Not acrostically," Westmore said and rushed to the safe. "S equals 19, I equals 9, X equals 24," he said and starting dialing the combination.

"The same three numbers three times in a row?" Nyvysk said. "Nine numbers in all?"

Westmore dialed the three numbers three times, then—
click
—he opened the safe.

The room hushed. Westmore put his hand in the safe—then felt ripped off. "Jesus! There's nothing in it . . ."

A pause.

"Wait."

He slid his hand along the bottom, felt something tiny. *A piece of paper . . .* He pulled it out.

"What is it?" Nyvysk asked.

Westmore felt let down. "It looks like another cipher." The slip of paper, the size of an index card, read:

INPUT REQUEST: FEED
STRAT APOGEE
RESPONSE: 06000430
ASSIGNMENT POINT: 00000403

What is this pile of crap? Westmore thought. He couldn't have been more disappointed. *But what did I expect? Hildreth's journal? A pact with the devil, signed in blood for shit's sake?*

Nyvysk seemed more hopeful. "Even random numbers are something to go on. And I *do* know what apogee means—"

"Geometry," Willis said. "The highest point, the highest angle of a geometric configuration."

"And from astronomy," Nyvysk tacked on. "As in a lunar apogee—the moon's farthest orbital point."

He's right. It is something to go on. "I think I'll fool around online for a while, see what I can find out," Westmore said. Then, under his breath, he repeated, "The moon's farthest point."

They turned to leave—

"Not just the moon," a voice slipped through the air.

"Cathleen," Nyvysk said, eyes narrowed at her.

Willis stepped forward. "Are you all right? You look—"

"I'm fine . . ." She sauntered into the room, looking around, and the eyes of the three men followed her, concerned. Cathleen was obviously not fine. She wore a black nightgown, nothing more, and she seemed diffuse, distracted, in spite of a catty grin. *Oh, wow,* Westmore thought. *She's ALL fucked up.*

The front of her throat, her bosom, and her face glittered faintly, from shining red and blue dust.

Nyvysk spoke up first. "Cathleen, what's that on your face?"

"Pontica dust," she said, still straying about the room. "It summons eager spirits. It shines through the planes of the dead, and they see it. Like a beacon."

When she passed Willis, her finger coyly slid across his chest, then to Westmore's.

"You been drinkin'?" Westmore asked.

A glare cracked through the sultry smile. "I don't contaminate my body with such things. I never have. The body is the conductant of the soul. I will not taint myself."

Willis spoke up louder, as if to an old person. "Cathleen, are you in a trance?"

Now she'd stopped, to look at the open safe. Her eyes flicked down to the painting of Deborah Rodenbaugh.

She sighed.

"There, people. There is the ultimate untainted body and spirit."

"Debbie Rodenbaugh? What do you know about her?" Westmore shot the startled question. "Why is she untainted?"

"Think about it." Cathleen faced Westmore directly. She put a hand to her thigh and slid it upward, hiking the already very short hem of her nightgown. The gown's neckline plunged to reveal the top edges of her nipples. "She's stainless, bereft of the world's tarnish. Unlike you. A busted, alcoholic hypocrite."

Thanks a lot, Westmore thought. "What the hell's your problem, Cathleen?"

"Westmore," Nyvysk stated. "At this precise moment, it's not Cathleen we're speaking to."

Westmore looked back at him, dismayed.

"Cathleen, wake up!" Willis raised his voice louder. "Come back!"

She turned back to Willis, walked right up to him. "The toucher. Who can't touch *anybody* without seeing horrors."

Willis grabbed her arms with his gloved hands. "What did you mean when you said 'not just the moon'? Did you mean some other kind of apogee?"

"You're a pervert but you can't touch other people," Cathleen said. "You can't touch the women you lust for more than anything. That's glorious. That's *perfect.* What do you see, then, when you touch yourself?"

Willis shook her some more. "Wake up!"

In a snap of her arm, she slammed him back against the wall. "What do you see when you jerk yourself off, feasting your eyes on smut? Hmm?" She slammed him again.

"Nothing," Willis said, gritting his teeth. "That's the way I like it."

"You'll like this better—" and then she grabbed his hand, pulled the glove off, and forced his hand up under her gown.

"Stop it!" Nyvysk shouted.

Willis tried to fight her off but the instant his hand was pressed between her legs, his eyes rolled up in his head and he collapsed.

Jesus! Westmore rushed over, grabbed her from behind, but she snapped around and rammed the heel of her palm up against his chin. His teeth clacked shut, nearly cracking. The force of the blow bolted him across the room where he toppled over the desk.

Now Nyvysk, a much larger man, was trying to pin her to the wall. Westmore got to his knees, looking through stars in his eyes across the desk.

What is going on here! Nyvysk's getting his ass kicked!

"Give me that phony celibacy, you pious queer," Cathleen croaked. In spite of Nyvysk's size and strength, Cathleen had twirled him to the floor and had pinned him down by his shoulders. She straddled him overtly, sexually. "You can get it up for me, can't you? Just close your eyes and think about all those trusting priests and young men you've spent your whole life wanting but never having. For what? For God? Would He do that for you?"

Nyvysk struggled against her but it was as though he'd been shackled down. "Westmore!" he yelled out. "Get Mack, get the others! Get help!"

Westmore jumped to the intercom and yelled for everybody. Now Cathleen was trying to drag Nyvysk's slacks down. She breathed her promises right into his face. "Come with me and I'll take you to a place where you can have them all, forever. And you can have your boy, Saeed. He misses you so much, since you got him killed . . ."

"I didn't get him killed!" Nyvysk choked out.

Westmore jumped on her, tried to pry her off of the older man. "You're the damned exorcist! Exorcize her!"

"It's not a possession! It's just a simple transposition," Nyvysk garbled back.

But none of this seemed *simple* to Westmore. He was wrestling with her and losing. When Mack and Karen rushed into the room, it got easier but not by much.

"Is she crazy?" Karen exclaimed.

"What the hell's going on?" Mack yelled.

Cathleen kicked and flailed as the four of them finally got her to her feet. They had her wedged against the wall; finally her struggles grew feeble.

Thank God, Westmore thought. *She's wearing out . . .*

Cathleen's eyes turned mad. Her smile seemed inhuman.

She looked at the four of them and said, "None of you are going to live much longer. Then I will see you again, in the domain of my king. We'll grind you up every night . . . until the end of time."

Objects began to slam around the room, paintings falling from the wall, books sliding off shelves. The blotter on the desk flew upward, and then a statue in the corner thudded over.

Cathleen went limp, folding up in Westmore's arms. Exhausted himself now, he picked her up and trudged to the couch. "You've gotta be shitting me!" he nearly shouted at Nyvysk as though it were his fault. "What was that?"

"She looked insane," Karen said.

Mack seemed as baffled. "What, did she just go nuts?"

Nyvysk was leaning over Willis, who remained unconscious. "It was a transposition. Cathleen's a very accessible medium. Things like that will happen to her when she puts herself in a trance."

Westmore checked Willis out too. "Is he all right?"

"Yes. He just passed out."

"And how come all that stuff flew around the room?" Karen asked in delayed shock.

"Cathleen's not just a mentalist, she's telekinetic," Nyvysk said. "Some of those powers got away from her when Hildreth left her body."

"That's reassuring," Westmore complained. "What if it happens again?"

"It probably won't."

"Should we call a doctor for Cathleen?"

"Not necessary," Nyvysk said. "She'll wake up in a while and be fine."

"She wasn't even acting like herself," Karen said.

Westmore sat down next to the safe. "According to Nyvvysk, she *wasn't* herself, she was someone else. It was someone other than Cathleen talking to us."

Mack seemed skeptical. "If it wasn't Cathleen, who was it?"

Another figure drifted into the room: Adrianne, in a disheveled robe. "It was Reginald Hildreth," she said. "I just saw him *and* Cathleen at the Chirice Flaesc."

II

"This flesh church," Westmore said when they'd relocated to the South Atrium, "that Nyvvysk told us about."

At the long table, the older man nodded. "The Chirice Flaesc—the Temple of Flesh—the altar of Belarius."

Karen was astounded by what Adrianne had said in the office. "And you saw Hildreth there as well as Cathleen?"

"How could that be possible?" Mack added.

Adrianne sighed. "It's not the first time I've seen Hildreth's spirit-body there. Karen saw it too—"

"And so did I," Willis reminded, "when I saw the revenant of the girl from the locksmith company, before Westmore opened the safe."

But Adrianne specified. "Seeing Hildreth at this place in hell is nothing new now. But when I said I saw Cathleen too I meant that I saw the vessel of her soul. It's almost as if they lured her spirit there to keep it captive."

"I still don't understand," Westmore said.

"Cathleen was out of her body," Adrianne elaborated. "Just like I was."

"An out-of-body experience . . ."

"Exactly."

"That would explain the transposition," Nyvysk calculated. "It was deliberate."

Adrianne nodded. "Those things—those Adiposians—seem to be Hildreth's helpers here—the things that have molested all of the women of our group. They *wanted* Cathleen to induce a trance, so that Hildreth could occupy her body for a while."

Westmore didn't know if he could believe this.

But, at this point, what *else* could he believe?

"It's just so damned frustrating," Cathleen said next. She looked blanched, a blanket wrapped around her. Since she'd roused from the mishap, she'd wiped off the strange pontica dust, but a few traces left the most minute glimmer on her skin. "I don't remember *any* of this."

"That's not uncommon," Nyvysk said.

"Yeah, but it's still maddening." Cathleen looked around, embarrassed. "I'm sorry I put everyone through that."

"It wasn't your fault," Nyvysk reminded her. "You're a very sensitive medium—we all knew that a transposition was possible. Overall, the incident gives us more information about Hildreth and his motivations, however supernatural they obviously are. You, Adrianne, and Willis know full well that your many talents can often go overboard."

"What exactly are your other talents?" Mack asked Cathleen.

Bored, she replied, "I'm a diviner, a crystologist, a medium, and a telekinetic. It's no big deal."

"Sounds like a big deal to me," Westmore had to comment. "A telekinetic? I'm starting to believe this other stuff, but I'm not sure I believe you can move things with your mind."

Nyvysk and Willis chuckled under their breath.

"I pretty much gave it up after the accident," Cathleen

went on. "It's the kind of thing you have to constantly practice, or else you get rusty."

"Cathleen doesn't like to show off anymore," Adrianne told him.

Westmore smiled. "That sounds like an excuse to me, but that's cool."

Cathleen frowned. "All right . . ." She looked at the ashtray that Westmore and Willis were sharing. A few seconds ticked by, then the ashtray turned a hundred and eighty degrees.

"Did you see that!" Karen said, impressed.

"This is bullshit," Mack insisted and looked under the table.

Hmm, Westmore thought.

"Now, don't blame me if I screw this up," Cathleen announced. "I told you I was rusty."

She looked at the pitcher of lemonade at the middle of the table. In increments, the pitcher began to move toward Cathleen an inch at a time.

She reached out to grab the handle but just as it would get close enough—

clunk.

The pitcher fell over.

"Damn!" Cathleen said.

The lemonade spilled. Everyone at the table stared.

"Well, almost," Cathleen said.

Mack was still looking under the table, to see if it had been rigged. "I, uh, I guess it's not bullshit . . ."

"I can't believe what I just saw," Karen said, astonished.

"It's still no big deal," Cathleen repeated, wiping up the mess with a bunch of paper towels.

Seeing really is believing, Westmore thought. The demonstration stunned him. He didn't see how it could possibly be faked, and that made him wonder harder about everything else that had happened here. "All I can say is . . . I'm pretty friggin' impressed."

"Such is the power of the mind," Nyvysk offered. "But I'm sure that Cathleen can tell you, her talents can be quite a burden at times, and the same goes for Adrianne and Willis."

"With every benefit, there's a detriment," Adrianne said.

"What exactly *are* the detriments?" Westmore asked. "You all have incredible talents. Seems to me you have a unique power. How can that be a burden?"

"I can't touch anybody," Willis volunteered an answer. "I'm a tactionist. I can read target-objects. When the target object is a person, I see things I don't want to see. That's my burden."

Strangely, Mack piped in, "Why don't you tell them everything, Willis? You would if you had the balls."

Westmore's brow furrowed. For the entire stay, there'd seemed to be a strained animosity between Willis and Mack that Westmore could never figure.

"We were all born in original sin," Adrianne said. "Not just Willis—*all* of us. It's between us and God . . ."

Another strange comment.

"Indeed," Nyvysk said next. "We all have our secrets. We don't need to discuss them here."

"No, why not?" Willis seemed perturbed yet animated. "I don't care. Mack and I know each other, from five years ago. We hate each other. Now he wants me to tell you all why, so I will." He looked right at Mack.

"Go ahead," Mack said. "And you can also tell them why you lost your medical license."

An uncomfortable silence ticked by, which Willis eventually broke by saying, "I have a *sexual* problem. It's got nothing to do with my target-object abilities—I'm just what you'd call a sex-addict."

"Don't feel bad," Cathleen said. "I am too."

"But you've never broken the law because of it," Willis went on. "Earlier in my career I was a clinical psychiatrist. I chose to work for the state instead of private practice. I wanted to give something back to the world—I'm not materialistic." He shrugged at the table. "Social services seemed ideal for me, but as a psychiatrist—as you can imagine—I got the hard cases. Mostly battered women, rape-trauma victims. Women with drug problems. My tactionism was a great advantage to a point; when I'd touch a patient, I'd see so much of her life. It was all very, very dark, as you could guess, and it was very depressing. I did manage to help a lot of women, but there was a price—all that mental backwash, all that despair and horror: I had to look at it in almost every patient. Over time, I began to medicate myself, so to speak, with sex."

"Sex with your *patients?*" Westmore asked.

"Damn right," Mack said. "Some doctor—he was fucking his patients, and that's not all."

Willis' voice grew grim in this confession. "It's true, I'll admit. Just as I was addicted to sexual release, a lot of my patients were addicted to drugs. I'm not a strong person. There were many times when I was manipulated."

"Bullshit," Mack said. "You're the one who was doing the manipulating. You were taking advantage of a bunch of head-cases."

"That's not true!" Willis snapped.

Nyvysk held his hand up to Mack. "Let him talk."

Willis continued. "Sometimes my patients would seduce me—for drugs." He gulped. "I'd prescribe drugs for them, in exchange for sex. I had many weak moments; I wasn't strong enough to resist the temptation. I was falling apart; the despair was burying me, all those bleak, traumatized lives washing back to *me*, any time I touched them seeking a diagnosis. So, yes, I used some of them—to treat my own addiction."

The room stood in a stunned hush. *Wow,* Westmore thought. *That's some confession.*

"I admit, some of my actions were criminal, and all were unethical," Willis went on. "It didn't last long. Eventually a complaint was filed against me by the husband of one of my patients. The hospital investigated, I confessed, then I was fired. The hospital was sued. My license was revoked."

"Sometimes it's good to talk about things like this," Adrianne broke some of the discomfort.

"Yes," Nyvysk added. "Self-disclosure is therapy in itself. We all have our misgivings and our outright mistakes, or *sins.*"

Mack leaned forward, with a sarcastic grin. "But Willis hasn't told you the best part. He hasn't told you who the husband was that turned him in."

The table waited. Willis took a deep breath and said, "It was Mack."

Another hush bloomed over the table, with some shocked looks.

"I didn't know you were married," Cathleen said.

"I'm not now. My wife went off the deep end and ran off. She went nuts on the dope Willis got her addicted to—"

"That's not true at all!" Willis shouted back. "She was already strung out, long before she ever came to me for treatment. She got into drugs in the *porn* business, where she met you!"

More shocked looks spread across the table.

"You were in the porn business?" Adrianne asked.

"That's how Mack met Hildreth in the first place," Karen offered. "And me too. We were both working for T&T Enterprises when Hildreth bought it." Karen smirked, if only at herself. "Mack and I were both in the movies . . ."

"It's not part of my life that I'm proud of," Mack said. "I came from a shit town, got almost no education. The porn industry was there, so it was a way to make money. That's where I met my wife. She wound up having some psychological problems, so she goes to see Willis and he gets her all fucked up on drugs—"

"I didn't do anything of the sort!" Willis exploded. "I admit, what I did was wrong—"

"Wrong! You were exploiting disadvantaged women, manipulating their addictions, and giving them drugs in exchange for sex! Yeah, I'd say that's wrong!"

"I wasn't the cause of your wife's problems, you were! I *know,* Mack! I saw her entire life every time I touched her!"

Mack jumped up, red-faced in rage. "She fell off the edge of the earth, you asshole! She's probably dead now, and it's because of you!" and when Mack made to lunge at Willis, Westmore and Nyvysk grabbed him, held him back.

"Stop it, both of you!" Nyvysk insisted. "This is accomplishing nothing."

"Everybody just calm down," Karen said.

Mack stared Willis down. "You're a piece of shit." He shrugged away from Nyvysk and Westmore and stalked out of the room.

"So much for self-revelation," Cathleen said when everyone was reseated.

"That was a shock," Adrianne said. "I didn't know you two guys even knew each other."

"It doesn't matter now," Willis said. "It's between him and me. Anyway, I apologize for all that."

Nyvysk looked contemplative now. "It's interesting, though, objectively, I mean. Another sex-connection."

"What?" Westmore asked.

"Everything about this place, and about Hildreth, is sexually rooted. Everyone here has a sexual connection. Karen's been in the sex industry, and tonight we learned that Mack has been in the sex industry. Adrianne is sexually self-repressed; she hasn't had sex in a decade because sexual contact for her triggers involuntary OBE's, while I, too, am sexually self-repressed—I'm a gay yet celibate ex-priest. Willis is a sex-addict who can't touch other people, and Cathleen is a sex-addict who can't function psychically without some sexual motivation. We all have sexual secrets, and it's almost as though those secrets have brought us here." The older man paused and looked at Westmore.

Everyone else was looking at Westmore too.

"All but you," Cathleen said through a half-smile.

"Yeah, what's your sexual secret?" Karen asked. Her eyes glimmered.

Great . . . Westmore swallowed a laugh. "I don't think I have any . . . because I almost never have sex, not since I quit drinking. For all my adult life, I was a one-night-stand guy because my social life was the bar scene. Now I don't drink. I still go to bars but never drink, and when I'm there I'm not interested because I'm the only one sober, and the only available women are drunk. I stay away from them because they'd get me too close to *my* addiction: alcohol."

"Ah, so you're sexually self-repressed too," Nyvysk seemed satisfied.

Westmore frowned. "How'd you arrive at *that?*"

"To you sex and alcohol are synonymous. But you've eliminated alcohol from your life, therefore sex is eliminated by default. Simple."

Westmore threw up his hands. "Whatever you say."

"It's just worth considering as something more than co-incidence," Nyvysk went on. "Each one of us has a sexual quirk or anomaly, and we're all sitting in the middle of this house which used to be a porn studio, a bordello, and a treatment center for clergymen guilty of immoral sexual behavior. Prostitutes were murdered here in the '50s, and adult film stars were murdered here several weeks ago. So far, Cathleen, Adrianne, and Karen have all experienced a discorporate molestation. Willis has target-object visions of the mansion's sexual atrocities, Westmore finds DVD's full of even more sexual atrocities, and I'm getting EVP's of a dead young man I was sexually obsessed with twenty years ago. There's something very sexual about this house, in an innate way. Carnality seems to live in its walls, and there's either an active or passive carnality in all of us. It's almost as though the sexual singularities of everyone here have been magnetized—by the mansion. We didn't gravitate toward the house, the house gravitated toward *us*."

"Like something chose each of us specifically," Cathleen pondered.

"Vivica?" Willis suggested.

"I was thinking more along the lines of something like fate—or providence," Nyvysk said.

Westmore wasn't inclined to believe that. "But it was *Vivica* who chose us, right?"

"Topically, yes," Nyvysk said. "But after all we've seen, hasn't the house *changed* since we've arrived?"

"It's become more overt," Adrianne said, "as if it's grown, as if it's gained something by us being here."

"Energy?" someone said.

Westmore thought more on that, and remembered something Vivica had said. "When I met Vivica, she told me her husband was very sexually obsessed. He surrounded himself with sexual energy."

"Of course," Nyvysk added. "He bought an adult movie company—"

"And filled the house with porn starlets, people whose lives *revolved* around sex," Karen offered.

Mack came back into the room still looking pissed.

Willis: "And the target vision I had tonight in the office . . . It was the most sexual vision yet. The woman, Vanni. I saw her having sex in that mirrored room—with Mack."

Mack smirked, embarrassed. "Well, that did happen, I admit it. She came on to me, and—"

"That's not the point," Willis said testily. "The point is the nature of the vision. It remained very sexual, and it was active, not passive. The locksmith woman *knew* about my sexual addiction—and its specifics. Then she showed me a vision of her own. For me, and for any typical tactionist, we see the past through the objects and/or people we touch. The *past.* But I believe this particular vision was showing me some aspect of the future."

Nyvysk seemed suddenly concerned. "In what regard?"

"The target-object activity began when I touched the safe," Willis continued, seeming fatigued and shaken. "I believe it has something to do with that piece of paper Westmore found."

Westmore's eyes narrowed, mulling this over. *We'll see,* he thought, *when I find out what all those numbers on it mean . . .*

But Willis kept going, to emphasize what he'd revealed earlier, "And I saw that place, the same place Nyvysk defined earlier in the week. The same place Adrianne, Cathleen, and Karen saw."

"The temple of flesh," Adrianne said.

"The Chirice Flaesc," Nyvysk finished.

The group sat in silence for several moments.

Belarius, Westmore thought.

The night grew heavy; most of the group was exhausted and went to their beds. Nyvysk, Cathleen, and Westmore stood out in the inner-courtyard for a final chat.

"And Hildreth," Nyvysk was saying, "when he was speaking through Cathleen, referred to the future."

Westmore was looking up at the moon. "An apogee. If I weren't so damn tired, I'd start doing some web searches tonight."

"Do it tomorrow," Nyvysk suggested. "Get some rest. It's been a trying day for us all."

Cathleen looked worn, pale-faced in moonlight. "It's all about sex. This house, Hildreth, and the thing that Hildreth and his people worshiped. This mansion truly is charged."

"And we're increasing the charge evidently," Nyvysk said. "Hildreth chose this place specifically for its potential revenant energy, and the base of that energy is sexual. An ideal focal-point of worship for an entity as sexual as Belarius. Even in physical death, Hildreth continues to harness more and more of that energy for the system of his belief."

"Decadence," Cathleen said in a low voice. "Unrepentant lust."

"So this Belarius is solicited by lust?" Westmore said. "Am I getting that right?"

"By lust and all sins of the flesh, which is why his very church is flesh," Nyvysk appended. "That energy renders power. The best way to revere the Chirice Flaesc is by homage through a place like the Hildreth House, a place where lust *drenches* the walls, where three weeks ago what took place was a festival of sexually-motivated murder, or—"

"Sacrifice," Cathleen added. "Which only increases the mansion's charge."

Nyvysk spared a rare chuckle. "I get the feeling I'm being manipulated. Do either of you feel that way?"

"Oh, I do," Cathleen agreed.

"Manipulated or paranoid as holy hell," Westmore said, watching drifts of cigarette smoke. *Or maybe the real person doing the manipulating is Vivica.* Paranoid wasn't the word for Westmore now. Between all this and what he'd learned from Clements at the bar, he didn't know what to put the most faith in.

"Time will tell, eventually," Nyvysk intoned.

"I wonder how much time," Cathleen ventured.

"Me, too." Nyvysk sighed, wearied. "I feel very weak saying this, but I'm almost afraid to go to bed, even as tired as I am."

Cathleen made a dry laugh. "I'm not *almost* afraid—I *am* afraid. And that's unusual for me."

Now it was Westmore's turn. "Hey, I'm just a freelance writer. I'm too objective—or too stupid—to be afraid. So if I wake up with my head cut off, I guess I deserved it."

He'd said it as an offbeat joke, to change moods. But Nyvysk and Cathleen both shot him silent, reproving looks. *Shit.* "Sorry."

"Good night," Nyvysk said. "I'll see you *both* in the morning. *With* your heads."

They finished their good nights and turned in.

Back in his own cubicle, Westmore stripped down to his shorts, got under the sheets. One small light remained on in the atrium; he could see it through the gap in his curtains. Ordinarily it might bother him. *But not tonight.* Who'd left it on? Westmore wished that a few more had been left on, in fact. Then he chuckled to himself. *Look at us. A bunch of adults acting like kids afraid of the dark.*

Each time sleep began to claim him, an image jolted him awake with a feeling in his gut like a glimpse off a cliff. Images of Hildreth, of the flesh temple, of the engraving of Belarius. Images of all the pretty faces he'd seen in the DVDs compared to the butchered remnants he'd seen in the autopsy photos.

Images of Debbie Rodenbaugh.

Shit . . .

Was this house really "charged?" *They think it's alive with Hildreth's spirit—an EVIL spirit that's planned something for the future. Do I really believe that?*

He groaned. *Maybe this haunted dump wants to make sure I don't get any sleep tonight.*

He got up and didn't even bother putting pants on. Everyone else was asleep—he could even hear the men snoring—so who would see him if he walked out in his shorts?

I don't care.

Next thing he knew he was browsing the atrium, smoking, restless.

He could hear the clock ticking. Then it chimed 3 a.m. He turned and almost shouted when a figure walked by quickly.

Adrianne, in her robe, looked bug-eyed at him. "You scared the—"

"—shit out of me," Westmore finished, a hand to his heart.

She raised a coffee cup. "I couldn't sleep so I heated up some milk."

"I might try that too. Can't sleep at all." Then the delayed wave of embarrassment rocked him. *Oh, shit, I'm standing here in my fuckin' Fruit of the Looms!* Blushing angrily, he said, "Sorry, I didn't think anyone was awake."

"Relax. Just because I haven't had sex in ten years doesn't mean I'm offended by seeing a man in his underwear. Good night."

"Good night."

She traipsed off and disappeared into her own cubicle. *Smart move, Westmore. What a jackass.*

Between Nyvysk, Mack, and Willis, he didn't know who snored loudest. *Jesus, guys. That sounds like a bunch of chainsaws.*

Then someone sleep-talked: "No . . . God, no—"

And silence. Someone must be having a nightmare. Then, someone else—Willis, he thought: "Stop, stop. Please stop . . ."

This house is spooking everybody. The air felt heavy around him, rich, the way high humidity felt, only the air-conditioners were working fine. The house, at this hour, felt *dense.*

When he was stubbing his cigarette out, he heard feminine moaning. It sounded impassioned, like a woman at the point of climax. *It's Cathleen . . .* Westmore shook his head with a smile. *Either she's playing with herself or she's having one hell of a dream.* Nyvysk and Adrianne, he supposed, would suspect that it was the influence of the mansion rousing Cathleen, stimulating her.

Westmore wondered.

He slipped back to his own cubicle and went back to bed. At first he'd thought Nyvysk's cubicle idea was silly—especially in a house so splendorous. Now, with that inexplicable *denseness* weighing down on him, he had to admit he was much more comfortable sleeping in the same room with the others.

He continued to drift off through veils of vivid, unpleasant shards of dream, then kept snapping awake. Belarius, ion signatures, and infrared silhouettes. Naked women with black, inverted crosses pierced to their nipples . . .

When he next snapped awake, he stared, his heart slowing.

Someone stood in his cubicle, the human outline frozen.

Westmore stared through more seconds of speechlessness, of dread.

"I can't sleep," Karen said.

All that dread poured out of him in a breath.

"Come here," he said.

He slid over on the bed, and she slipped in next to him. He couldn't even see what she was wearing, but it didn't matter. He leaned over her for a few moments, cupped her cheek with a hand, then kissed her. Their tongues touched, and they shared a breath . . .

Then they fell asleep in each other's arms.

Westmore slept dreamlessly.

Chapter Thirteen

I

"Westmore, right?"

Westmore stood duped at the wall opening with a sign that read: VISITORS: REMOVE ALL SHARP OBJECTS FROM YOUR PERSON. THIS IS A MAXIMUM-SECURITY PSYCHIATRIC WARD.

"Yes, I'm Westmore," he said. "I don't have an appointment but I was told—"

"Quiet."

A basket was passed to him, into which he placed his keys, pens, etc.

"Wallet, too."

"My wallet's not what I would call a sharp object."

"There are nut-jobs in here who'd love to get hold of your wallet."

"What for?"

"Credit cards."

Westmore didn't get it. "How's somebody in a locked psychiatric ward going to use a stolen credit card?"

"They cut their throats with them all the time."

Jiminee-Pete. Westmore turned over his wallet, then walked through a metal-detector. Once out of the glare, he finally got a look at the person talking to him, a 30ish guy with a shaved head and all-business face, built like a fire plug. The tag on his pocket read WELLS - DIRECTOR OF SECURITY.

Westmore was led down a silent, shiny-tiled corridor. "So you're the guy who knows—"

"Quiet."

Wells' boot-heels cracked down the hall. "What do you know about Faye Mullins? You know what's wrong with her?"

"Actually, no. What *is* wrong with her?"

"In normal-guy talk? She's all fucked up in the head from dope."

"How about something a little more specific?"

"CDS-aggravated monopolar schizoaffective schizophrenia and symbolized delusional psychosis with occult and sexual ideations."

Westmore nearly hacked. "That's some diagnosis."

"We've got her tranked down pretty well, she's usually docile," Wells informed. "She's usually not coherent, mostly just motor-mouth word salad. But if you're lucky, you might get something out of her."

"She ever talk about anything regarding astronomy? Lunar apogees, anything about the moon or the sun?"

"Mostly just fruitloop stuff about dope and gang-blowjobs. And blood."

"I guess that makes sense," Westmore said. "References to blood."

"Hell, yes it does. She's the only survivor of that psycho-show Hildreth was running up there."

They passed several nurses stations and med stations, all heavily locked. Could there be many patients here? Westmore didn't hear a sound anywhere. He'd borrowed Karen's car to drive down. The outside of the place looked innocuous enough: a long complex of clean brick buildings, one-story each, and a simple entry sign that read DANELLETON CLINIC. The place looked more like an HMO or chiropractor's.

Westmore's stomach jolted when one of the small door-widows they passed was suddenly filled by a face: a man who'd apparently eaten his own lower lip off. Then he screamed blood-curdlingly.

"Lemme eat ya, buddy! Lemme eat ya! Humans taste like horse if ya cook 'em wrong. But I'm a good cook!"

Westmore gritted his teeth and walked on with shoulders hunched.

"Don't mind him," Wells said. "He was the executive chef at a big restaurant downtown."

Westmore didn't want to know which one. Several nurses passed without a glance, then Wells loudly unlocked a door. "You want me to have her restrained?"

Westmore looked at him. "Is that necessary?"

"Probably not."

That makes me feel SOOOOOOOO confident. "No, don't do it. She'll talk more if she's at ease."

"Cool. But I have to lock it behind me. Hit the button if she gets froggy."

"Will do."

Westmore was numbed when he stepped into the stark white room. The face that looked back at him he'd seen before, in the DVD's, but now it looked even more pallid, more plump—a visage of hopeless sadness. Faye Mullins wore a white linen gown, from which pale, heavy legs emerged, ankles swollen from medication-related edema and overall inactivity. Lusterless eyes blinked above drooping cheeks. Drab brown hair looked unwashed for several days, flecked with dandruff.

"I saw you in a dream once," she said a second later, eyes widening on him. "You were getting off a bus, in the rain, and you went into a bar and got drunk until you were *so sick*."

"A couple years ago, that was definitely me," Westmore said.

"No, no," she hastened to correct. Her hands flew in a gesture of animation. "It was a dream of the future."

"Ah, well, that sounds very interesting, Faye." *She seems pretty coherent to me,* he thought. He'd expected a babbling in-patient, drooling, staring off. The room was plain. White walls, white floor, white ceiling. White bed. "I'd like to talk to you if you don't mind."

"There's another woman here who can fly puppies," she replied. "She has a special license to do it. She flies puppies like they're planes."

Westmore's brow grew a serious ridge. "Ah, interesting."

"We have to watch the football game because the future of the world depends on it, and on Slim Jims and wind chimes, the chimes with stars like my mother used to make for craft shows. Oh, and toilet paper. Don't forget! I'm talking the future of the *world*."

Westmore nodded, remembering what Wells had told

him about word salad and incoherence. "Oh, sure, I know. Slim Jims especially. Debbie Rodenbaugh likes Slim Jims."

"No, she doesn't, you liar," Faye Mullins grinned dopily back at him. "She never eats pork or beef!"

"Oh, that's right. But she likes wind chimes. She told me." Faye's voice lowered in tenor. "She only likes the kind with stars."

"Stars, yes. I like them too." Then Westmore thought, *Stars. Astronomy* . . . "Did she like lunar apogees?"

Faye's face lurched forward on the obese, tube-like neck. "Huh?"

"The moon, the sun, stuff like that? Certain points of an orbit? You ever take astronomy in school?"

A pallid stare. Some silence. "I think you're trying to trick me."

"I won't trick you. I'm an honest person, Faye. I'm not like the men at the mansion."

Her stare focused. "What men? The Adiposians? They're not men."

Westmore was thrown for a loop. *Keep her talking!* "No, I mean the men who did bad things to you. The men who raped you."

"They didn't really rape me," she said. Her coherence was sharpening. "They'd make me use my mouth on them a lot." She blinked. "Is that rape?"

"If they made you do it against your will, yes, it is."

A fat chuckle. "Oh, it was against my will, all right. They'd make me do it to get them more excited for what came later in the Scarlet Room. The rituals. They'd hold guns to my head to make me do it, and knives. Yeah, I guess that is rape. But what I meant is they never *had sex* with me."

"Intercourse, you mean."

"Yeah, nobody ever wanted to 'cos they all said I was too fat and ugly. One of them, Jaz, he was the meanest. He'd always call me 'Wood-killer.'" Suddenly she tossed her head back and forth, mimicking: "'I wouldn't fuck you if you were the last piece of ass on earth,' he'd say. Then he'd make me smoke crack or shoot up."

Westmore tried *not* to envision the details of the evil that went on in the mansion. *Just a bunch of evil people . . .*

"But he's in hell now, and I'm glad," she went on. "And so is Three-Balls and Hildreth. They can't hurt me anymore."

"No, no, they can't."

What next? He had to keep her talking or she'd probably lapse back into her gobbledegook. "Faye, do you know where Debbie Rodenbaugh is?"

Then she said the strangest thing, which Westmore recognized, a quote:

"'Let that hath understanding . . .'"

Westmore finished in his mind, "'—count the number of the beast.' I've read the Book of Revelation, Faye. And that line's pretty hokey if you ask me. The combination of the safe is a variation of six hundred and sixty-six."

"So you opened . . . the safe?" she asked with hesitation.

"Sure. I found the piece of paper inside that has the secret on it."

She shot a dirty, nail-bitten finger at him. "You're trying to trick me! You're lying."

"About what?"

"You didn't open the safe. You're just acting like you did—to trick me into saying something I shouldn't."

Westmore took out his wallet. "Faye, if you think I'm lying about the safe, look. Here's the slip of paper we found in it." He passed it to her. "Do you know what those numbers mean?"

She looked astonished at the paper, then—

"Faye, no!"

—she ate it.

Westmore's shoulders dipped in frustration. "That wasn't very cool, Faye. That paper may have had important information on it. I *needed* it."

A broader, dopy grin. "Well, now it's in my stomach. If you want it bad enough, you can come and get it."

Westmore feigned aggravation—of course, he'd previously saved all the information on the paper in his computer. "That was a lousy thing to do. Why don't you just tell me what that paper meant? Why are you afraid to tell me?"

"Because something's going to happen at the house . . ."

"Yeah? What?"

"None of your beeswax."

"Does it have to do with the numbers on that paper?"

"Look at my kitty," she said next and jerked up the hem of her gown.

Westmore dragged his eyes away, appalled. Faye's vagina looked mutilated.

Oh, Christ . . .

He had to grit his teeth to continue talking to her. "Who did that to you? The men at the mansion?"

"It felt good."

Westmore sighed. "Faye, I have to leave soon. Why don't you do me a favor and tell me what's going to happen?"

Now she was masturbating, her tongue stuck out one corner of her mouth. "They're gonna open the Rive."

"When?" Westmore asked, trying to hide his desperation.

"It's on the piece of paper." She patted her stomach and grinned.

"It's all about Belarius, isn't it?"

Faye burst into a high-pitched shriek, shot off the bed, and lunged at him.

Holy CRAP!

She was all over him in an instant, slapping at his face, poking fingers at his eyes. The shriek rose: "You're not allowed to say his name! You're NOT ALLOWED!"

Her mouth snapped open and closed before his face, teeth clacking. Another half inch and she'd have taken off the tip of his nose. Her bulk slammed against him; it was all Westmore could do to protect himself.

"He is the Sexus Cyning! He is the Lord of the Flesh, and you will bow down to him in his holy temple!"

She had Westmore's throat now, thumbs digging in, trying to thrust him to his knees. "Pay homage to him by giving succor to me with your mouth!"

She jerked up the front of her gown, and it was all in Westmore's face at once. Even in his strife, he managed to think, *That's one thing that AIN'T gonna happen, honey* . . .

She was wedging his neck back by fistfuls of hair. She meant to clamp his face between her sagging thighs when—

zzzzzzzzzzzzzzzzznt!

She fell backwards as if jerked, her back slapping the floor like a side of raw beef.

Wells and two of his men had subdued her. When Westmore's vision cleared, he saw that they'd used some kind of stun gun to get her off him.

"Come on, Faye," Wells said. "You know what happens when you act like this."

Her face looked swollen from pain, eyes puffed.

"We're going to get the bed-net—"

"No, please!" She was sobbing, physically and mentally dilapidated in her schizophrenia.

"Then be good, and calm down." Wells' men urged her

to lie down. When she did, she wrung her hands, staring up at the ceiling.

"You ready?" Wells asked.

"Yeah," Westmore said, still a bit winded. *What a day. And it's just started.* He turned at the door. "Good-bye, Faye. Thank you for talking to me."

"Watch out for the Adiposians," she suddenly snapped her gaze around and said. Her eyes were filled with portentous dread.

"The what?"

"They're going to open the Rive again . . ."

Westmore shook his head. "Explain that to me, please."

Now, a huge insane grin. "They're gonna turn that house into a great big mouth that's gonna eat you. It's gonna suck you all down and swallow you."

Westmore grabbed a coffee and cigarette in the security break room.

"I told you, man," Wells said. "Totally nuts."

"But coherent at times. It was a strange mix."

"Some of them are like that. It ain't dual personality. Chemicals in their brains switch on and off. One minute they make sense and you can get something out of them, the next they're living in fantasyland but believe it's real. Like with her—all that occult shit."

Westmore didn't look forward to the next question. "What, uh, what happened to her genitals?"

"Ten to one it's self-inflicted. Sexual self-mutilation. Happens a lot with psych patients. That's how they kill the pain of their abuse or some shit. You should *see* some of the things mental patients do to their works, especially dope burn-outs."

No, Westmore thought. *That's one thing I should NOT see.* He felt horribly sorry for her. Forced into drug-addiction, sexually degraded time and time again. And God knew what her childhood had been like. "Will she ever recover?"

"Naw. Receptors in her brain are burned out. She'll be schizo the rest of her life."

"Thanks for your time," Westmore said, and walked out feeling about as bleak as he'd ever felt.

II

"Has somebody here mentioned a term," Westmore asked behind the bank of monitors in the communications room. "Apidosians, or adiposians?"

Nyvysk looked up from his tinkering, with interest. "Adrianne and Cathleen claim to have seen them—in their *jaunts.* Where did *you* hear the term?"

Westmore lied. He didn't want anyone to know that *he* knew about Faye Mullins. "I heard somebody here mention it, can't remember who."

"Well, they're thought to sexually molest women—*and* men—in a discorporate, or subcorporeal, state. The revenant rapes of Cathleen, Adrianne, and Karen, for instance. Which would make sense."

"Not to me. What are they? Demons?"

"Actually, no. They're significantly less than demons. It's more of a Hex-Entity, if you follow older sources which may or may not be reliable. An Adiposian is one of many such entities. They're soulless but *not* spiritless, if that's not too confusing. According to the *Morakis Compendiums* of the 1500s, Adiposians are fashioned in Hell from rendered fat, and then animated by spells. Supposedly. They're sentinels, so to speak, guardians."

"Of what?"

"Adiposians specifically? They're the guardians of certain domains, or prefectures, in Hell. Domains supposedly granted to hierarchal sexual demons."

"Like Belarius," Westmore said more than asked.

"Exactly. Think of sacks of congealed bacon grease shaped into a humanish form. They have no faces save for mouths. They have tongues. And they have genitals. They can be generated as male or female. Supposedly. Since they're soulless, they can easily pass from the physical boundaries of Hell to our world, as discorporates. Deniere's *Index of Demonographies,* from 1618, claims that sex with a discorporate Adiposian is an opium-like experience. And anyone raped by a physical Adiposian in Hell will experience an eternal climax. Supposedly."

"*Supposedly,*" Westmore said.

"Of course. Who can know for sure?"

Not me, that's sure as shit. But Westmore remembered the other odd reference from the psychiatric ward, yet one he'd heard here too. "What's a Rive? I've heard you use that term. A doorway or something? A doorway to hell?"

Nyvysk seemed piqued by the question. "In a sense. Every religion and counter-religion has something like that. Christians believe that one day a Rive will open in the sky and through it will pass all whose names are in the Book of Life—in other words, those worthy of Heaven. Ancient Egyptians believed that death itself was the Rive through which they'd access the afterlife."

"And satanists?"

"Some believe that a threshold to Hell can be opened by

certain rites, incantations, and gestures of sacrifice. That's probably what Hildreth thought he was doing on the night of April 3rd. Trying to open that threshold."

Westmore looked at him. "Do you—"

"Do *I* believe that such Rives genuinely exist?" He looked right back. "No, of course not . . . And, yes, of course."

"Great."

Nyvysk smiled. "It's founded in myths and legends that go back to cave man days. Later, as mankind learned to leave a record of himself, those myths were written down. Grimoires and compendiums and more occult tomes than you can shake a stick at—from just after Christ's death, through the Middle Ages, and even on into the early 20th Century—these sources are *full* of references to Rives, portals, doors to the underworld, and the mystical secrets needed to open them. In my opinion? Do you want to know the truth?"

"Yes," Westmore said.

"It's mostly poop, Mr. Westmore." Another subtle smile as Nyvysk adjusted a sensor panel. "Ultimately, *faith* is the Rive. I believe in all I need to believe in. I believe in Heaven and Hell. Do you?"

"Man, I don't know."

Nyvysk's smile was gone. "I suspect you will by the time we're all through here."

Westmore worked in the office most of the rest of the day, forgetting to even come down for a meal. He scarcely saw anyone else in the group for more than a few moments. When he'd passed Karen in the hall, she'd merely smiled and nodded, walking on in some buried distress. It was obvious she'd forgotten—probably because she'd been too drunk—their wee-hour kiss and sleeping together last night. It had been strictly platonic yet arousing in some exotic way. She'd left his bed before he'd wakened, leaving only the scent of her hair all over him.

At one point, out the window, he spotted Cathleen strolling barefoot toward the opening in the trees which led to the graveyard. She wore only a white bikini and sarong. She stood at the opening for a moment, hair up in the breeze, the sarong flowing—then suddenly turned and strode away almost at a trot. *Bad memories*, Westmore thought. But it only reminded him that he'd be entering the same graveyard—tonight—with Clements.

If he shows up.

After several more hours of inputting notes, he fiddled with some web searches of the numbers and information on the slip of safe-paper. Only the word "apogee" yielded many results but they were all endless and uselessly basic. Knowing he was out of his league, then, he called again on his friend Tom, who begrudgingly agreed to try some more skilled searches.

Restless, he decided to prowl about. Tonight before midnight he'd have to find the hidden door that Clements' bizarre companion had mentioned. She'd told him how to get there, an area he'd already seen. *And that's how you get there,* he thought, looking at the narrow red-wine colored curtain in the office corner.

He went through, entering the network of shoulder-width passageways lit by tiny mounted lights. The passages seemed to lead around the mansion's outer walls, zigzagging downward via several just-as-narrow stairwells. Eventually he emerged into a plush but cramped library. *This is it, according to the girl* . . . Oak bookshelves lined the wall; he began pushing and pulling on them. Along the way, he noticed the strangest titles on the spines of the books, many of which seemed extraordinarily old: *Cultes Des Ghoules, Terra Dementata, Megapolisomancy,* and many more. "Weird place," Westmore muttered. Something cloyed in the air but he couldn't tell what it was. He felt watched but he knew it was just atmosphere and paranoia. In a far corner, then, he noticed a pale curtain, looked behind it, and saw the heavy metal-braced door.

That's it, he knew.

Simple enough. A carriage clock showed him it was 8 p.m.; he had four more hours. He could go back to the office but all at once, fatigue assailed him. *I guess I'm gonna take a nap,* he realized, feeling old. But where? Not in his cubicle, not with everyone else walking around.

Right here would do.

A long bench with plush upholstery and brass studs sat beneath a framed canvas that was totally black. That would have to do. Westmore lay down and fell asleep at once.

He dreamed that he was awake but paralyzed, on the same cushioned bench he lay on now, in the same library. Figures stood around him yet he couldn't turn his head to get a look. Terror propped his eyes wide open; a figure stepped over the bench—a *naked* figure, he could tell—and—

Oh, shit!

—and sat right on his face. Fat hung down, his face compressed by it. He knew who it was, even before the hand clenched his hair and twisted, and the voice spoke very quietly:

"You're not allowed to say his name."

Over the roll of fat, he could see Faye Mullins' face looking down, deadpan.

"Now pay homage to him by giving succor to me with your mouth. And do it right, or—"

click!

"—you'll meet him sooner than you think."

She'd put a gun to his head and cocked it. Westmore, helpless, did as forced, his tongue roved upward against the shredded flesh . . .

"That's good," she complimented. Her broad hips fidgeted for better purchase. Hands—or things like hands—pulled his pants down on the bench, but he couldn't see who or what was doing it. Then a mouth that felt inhuman. Something much thicker and warmer than saliva worked with the act.

Westmore was repulsed yet his responses would not obey the commands of his emotions. His arousal was instantaneous, a bucking orgasm not far behind. He emptied himself into whatever it was that fellated him, yet as he ejaculated, he began to smother: Faye Mullins' groin completely covering his mouth and nose. Meanwhile, Faye's own responses were cresting, and the basest part of Westmore's fading conscience wondered if he would smother to death first, or have a bullet fired into his brain when she climaxed. His lungs swelled and swelled. He began to convulse.

Long moans swirled around his head as his face was vised tighter but a second later, Faye went lax, moved back a few inches, and his mouth and nose was cleared.

Westmore sucked in breath as she climbed off him. His eyes followed the amorphous, nude bulk. She was walking toward a half-circle table festooned with carvings. She opened a tiny drawer in the table's front, looked in it, then closed it. Then her gaze met his.

"Now you know how I felt every day," she said, grinning.

Westmore couldn't speak.

"Something's going to happen here," she said. Her voice seemed to be reducing to a gurgle.

Westmore stared.

"You better not be here when it does."

Westmore shot awake.

All right, Westmore. Don't lose it. Don't be an idiot. That was not a discorporated molestation, for God's sake. That was not a visitation, a psychic vision or any of that shit. It was JUST A BAD DREAM.

Then he looked in the tiny table drawer and found several DVD's. *No big deal, no big deal. So what? There's DVD's all over this house. Coincidence!*

Nevertheless he pocketed the DVD's. At the same moment, the carriage clock began to chime: twelve times.

Damn! I'm supposed to meet Clements outside!

Westmore rushed through the curtain, turned the lock-latch, and opened the stout door. He stuck a pen in the door's gap once he got outside. Twilight glittered beyond, a bright half moon and stars like diamond chips spewed across the sky. A pleasant heat radiated, but he reminded himself, *It won't be so pleasant when we're behind those shovels.* He walked briskly straight away from the side of the mansion, to the woods, then walked slower toward the access road. He could barely see.

"Jesus, I thought you were stiffing me," Clements said, buried in shadows. Connie stood with him, but Westmore was surprised to see four other men there too, in jeans, boots, and t-shirts. Each one had a shovel over his shoulder.

"Who are these guys?"

When Clements dragged off his cigarette, the heightened glow of the ember tinted his face orange. "You said you needed help digging a grave? There's the help. Younger muscle. You and me both are too old for that shit."

Speak for yourself, Westmore thought half-heartedly. In truth, though, he was relieved.

Clements introduced the others: "Higgins, watch com-

mander for Florida SPD, and my cousin; Butler, assistant
deputy for county public safety, and my nephew; Skibiniski,
with the bailiff's office——he was one of my students when I
taught training blocks at the academy, and my other nephew
Jimmy Wells, who you met today."

The guy from the psych ward, Westmore thought of the latter. He traded nods with the others, then Clements said,
"Lead the way. Voices down, stick to the inside of the
woodline and try not to sound like the fuckin' Germans
marching to Stalingrad."

Westmore carefully led them around the property, to the
other side of the house, crickets trilling about them in a
sound that was palpable as the humidity. "In here . . ." The
night sounds grew louder when they entered the dense
path.

Wells elbowed him. "Your girl was asking about you."

"What? Faye Mullins?"

"Yeah, about eleven o'clock. I was just getting off-shift,
helping one of the nurses give out the night-meds. Mullins
wakes up and looks at me and asks about you."

Westmore frowned. "What did she say?"

"Said she just saw you."

"Huh? Where?"

Wells chuckled. "In some library."

Where I was sleeping . . . Westmore didn't let himself pay
it any mind.

"Then she said to ask you if you found the drawer in the
table."

Westmore's belly jumped.

Wells chuckled further. "These psychos are something,
ain't they?"

"Yeah . . ."

Westmore's eyes were still acclimating. "Anybody got a

flashlight? Can't see where Hildreth's stone is, it's too dark."

But the younger men were already in the gates, combing the stones with small focused penlights. "Right here," one of them said.

"Let's stay out of their way," Clements advised, pulling Connie and Westmore aside. The digging commenced. "I'll bet they have this grave open in ten minutes."

Connie stood rubbing her eyes. She looked twitchy, miserable, her thin face even more pale in the moonlight. Clements put his arm around her, gave her a pill. "Take another one now, it'll take the edge off."

She nodded, swallowed the pill, and washed it down with soda.

"What's that?"

"Some prescription stuff that eases coke withdrawal. I can get 'em anytime I want from my sister's best friend."

"Pharmacist?"

"Naw, she's the senior manager for county rehab services." Westmore rolled his eyes.

It was actually less than ten minutes when Wells announced, "We're down to the lid, Bart. You want us to open it?"

"We'll take it from here," Clements directed. "Leave two shovels so we can fill it in. You guys get your asses out of here and get back to my place. There's two cases waiting on ice."

Westmore distantly thanked them as they filed out of the graveyard and disappeared. Now the three of them stood in a troubling silence. *We're about to open a grave. Who's in there?* Westmore walked to the hole and looked down.

"Connie, hold the light down here." Clements got in with a crowbar while Connie focused the narrow penlight beam. The coffin wasn't latched; Clements opened the lid with ease.

"What do you think? Doesn't look like Hildreth to me . . ."

"It isn't," Connie said, squinting.

Westmore peered in, a tall, lean man in his sixties, grayish hair, flesh sagging from a few weeks of putrefaction. "Same height and weight. Are you sure?"

"It's not him," Connie insisted. "I know that guy—"

"What?" Westmore and Clements said simultaneously.

"Jesus. That's one of the rummies who lives under the 275 overpass. I'd see him all the time walking to the main drag whenever I needed to cop some crack." She turned away, waylaid by the sight. "Look and see if a bunch of his teeth are missing."

Clements pried the jaw down with the tip of his shoe. "About half of 'em have fallen out." He looked at Westmore. "Satisfied?"

"I guess." It clearly wasn't Hildreth. "A substitute body, same basic age, height, and build."

"I'm waiting out here," Connie said, edging out of the graveyard. "This place is too fucking creepy."

Westmore couldn't disagree. "Vivica told me that the obituary and autopsy report were faked by someone she paid."

Clements kicked the lid closed, hopped out. "Fucker stinks."

"But Adrianne said she saw a body in it."

"Huh? You mean she went to the funeral?"

"No, what I mean is she saw a body in the coffin when she was having an out-of-body experience."

Clements grinned his hilarity in the moonlight. "You pin-head. She's probably the one who *put* the body in the coffin."

"She's a one-hundred-pound woman, for God's sake," Westmore countered. "You're saying that she killed a bum to pose as Hildreth's corpse and then came out here, dug open the grave, and put the body in an empty coffin?"

"Somebody did." Clements lit a cigarette. "I told you not to trust anyone in that house, and don't believe any of the psychic hokum they're spouting. It's bullshit."

"The one I trust the least is Mack," Westmore said. "Everyone else seems pretty straight-up."

"Lemme know when you wanna buy the fuckin' Brooklyn Bridge—I can get you a good price. Let's fill this hole in and get out of here." He grabbed a shovel, tossed the other one to Westmore, when Connie said: "Hey, Bart. I-I think there's something here . . ."

She was standing just outside the graveyard fence, to their right. Leaning over, she aimed the light, pushing at something with her foot.

Then she yelped and leapt backward. "There's something there! I think it's a hand!"

Westmore and Clements jumped over the fence, wielding penlights of their own. "Calm down," Clements said. "Where?"

Teeth chattering, she pointing down.

"Ground's soft," Westmore noticed at once. He dragged the blade of his shovel over the leaves on the ground, revealing tilled earth.

"Someone's already been digging here," Clements said. "One of your cronies from that freakshow in there."

Westmore thought back. "Cathleen claims she was raped by something right on this spot, the area right *next* to Hildreth's grave, she said."

"She's fuckin' high. But there is something here. This

dirt's already been turned once." He fished around some more with his blade. "What the . . ."

"What *is* that?" Westmore asked, squinting down.

"It's a hand!" Connie exclaimed.

But was it? In the narrow beams of light, they saw something that looked like a white glove. Clements knelt, picked up the glove, then muttered "Oh, my God," when something long and white came up along with it.

Something like an arm attached to the glove.

No one spoke; instead, Clements and Westmore gingerly dug at the area. Whatever lay beneath hadn't been buried deeply. It seemed more haphazard than a standard grave. A rotten meat-stench rose up, gagging them. All the while, Westmore was thinking: *What are these things?*

They unearthed several bodies, but they seemed to lack features, even bone structures. Arms, legs, and heads, or facsimiles thereof. Westmore couldn't see well in the penlight beams . . . but he didn't need to.

"They're not human . . ."

"Of course they are," Clements said, yet didn't sound convinced himself. "They're rotten corpses, stripped down. They look like floaters. Buried that shallow they'll rot down fast, build up a lot of gas."

When Connie looked into the pit, she turned away, choking.

"And the gas could be toxic," Clements went on, "and we're breathing the shit like a couple of idiots. Let's cover them back up quick." He started re-covering the paraffin-white, glistening corpses.

"How about let's *not* cover them back up," Westmore suggested. "Let's get out of here, call the cops or something."

"Put some ass behind that shovel and help me out here."

Clements frowned, throwing more dirt back into the pit. "We ain't calling cops or nothing like that. They would defeat our own purpose. I'm getting Debbie Rodenbaugh out of that house. You get a bunch of cops up here, then Vivica'll call off whatever it is she and Hildreth are planning. That would defeat my purpose and yours." Clements poked Westmore in the chest. "You and me have a deal. I told you I'd help you dig up that grave, and you told me you'll let me in that house. Stick to the deal."

Westmore saw his point, or at least he hoped so. In a few minutes they'd both re-covered the pit and also Hildreth's grave.

They tossed the shovels into the woods. Connie looked nauseated when they were walking out, and Clements himself looked wrenched, his tough-guy veneer showing a few cracks.

"He's right," Connie said, indicating Westmore. "Those things didn't look hu—"

"They're dead *human* bodies," Clements insisted. "Between this heat and all the rain we had a few weeks ago— they get that way. I've seen 'em. *They're not fuckin' monsters* that Hildreth brought here from some satanic *sacrifice*. The two of you are letting his whole Lucifer-worshiping guru shit bend your fuckin' brains."

Westmore was too wracked by sight and stench to say anything. Of course, Clements was right, but he was still appalled by the look of the bodies.

They traversed the property, back to the service road. "Are you all right?" Clements asked testily. "You look like you're gonna puke."

"I feel like it."

"Don't worry. All this shit's gonna be over tomorrow night."

Westmore popped a brow. "What happens then?"

"That's when you let me in that house, and I put an end to this. I'm getting Debbie out of there, and I'm finding Hildreth and blowing him away. You don't want to get your hands dirty, fine. Just let me in that house like you agreed."

Westmore sighed. "All right. What time?"

"Two a.m. on the nose."

"Okay."

Clements and the girl got into the car. "Tonight'll be the last night you spend in that house." He grinned in the moonlight. "Don't get yourself killed, huh? I don't want the next body I dig up to be you," he said and drove off.

Chapter Fourteen

I

It's going to be a long one, Adrianne thought, wandering the house the next day at noon. At first she'd thought of strolling the grounds—it was gorgeous out—but a few minutes outside offered no release from the mansion's *heaviness,* that feeling of something in the air, something around her pressing down, watching. Outside was just as bad even in the midst of the grass, sun, and sky. Inside or out she couldn't get away from it. *It's just me,* she hoped, and came back in.

Portraits and brooding marble busts stared at her in the main hall. When she got to the atrium, she could hear some of the others talking from the kitchen, proceeding in some semblance of normal social interaction. Adrianne wanted no part of it. She liked the others but didn't want to be around them, couldn't. Other people were a distraction, especially before a jaunt. She had to focus. She had to stay in her zone.

She wandered further up into the communications room, where Nyvysk spent most of his time. Playbacks on certain screens did not enthrall, frighten, or even interest her. Infrared figures and ion signatures of figures in rooms that were physically empty. She jotted a quick note down for Nyvysk, so at least someone would know what she was up to today:

I'LL BE OBE-ING TODAY, PROBABLY ON THE ROOF. NOT SURE WHEN I'LL BE DONE —ADRIANNE

She taped it to a monitor, then left.

When she passed the office, she could hear Westmore in there typing, but she passed the room by without saying hello. She didn't want to talk to anybody right now, at least no one alive or on this plane of existence.

The only entity she wanted to talk to was Jaemessyn, the temple's seeming gatekeeper.

For she knew it was only through the Fallen Angel that she might gain access to Belarius.

This is perfect, she thought awhile later. She'd been wanting to come up here, just hadn't exactly found it until now. After taking further flights of stairs upward, she stepped out onto a roof parapet. There was a sundeck, a lounge chair, and umbrella. *Yes. This'll do fine . . .*

Adrianne lay down on the lounge chair, let herself relax. The umbrella shadowed her. *What I am afraid of?* she wondered after several minutes.

Nothing over there could hurt her here.

She swallowed one Lobrogaine tablet, closed her eyes, and began to say her preliminary prayers.

II

Westmore felt hungover the moment he got out of bed. *Wait a minute,* he thought. *I don't drink.* The awful feeling had to be the bodies he'd seen last night. And the stench, which probably *was* a little toxic, as Clements had warned. But at least he agreed with the older man now: waiting another day to report the bodies would work better. *More time to find out what's really going on in this place.* Westmore, by now, was cringing to know. *Don't blow any whistles yet.*

Words kept nagging at him while he dabbled at his work, the voice of Faye Mullins . . .

They're gonna turn that house into a great big mouth that's gonna eat you.

He cleared his mind. He plugged in one of the DVD's he'd found in the hidden library, stared dully at it. It seemed the same old thing, the same old smut. Men having sex with women for the sake of having sex, to verify the function of ejaculation externally. But more words itched at him:

It's gonna suck you all down and swallow you.

He blinked and was suddenly staring with more intent. In the next vignette, he recognized the male "star" who was furiously copulating with a blonde who looked drugged out.

It was Mack.

There was an initial shock, but— *Why should I be shocked?* Mack had admitted that he'd been more directly involved with this business in the past. Pornography in L.A. *All right. So what? Just because the guy's done porn for Hildreth doesn't mean he buried bodies in the woods. Stay real.* The scene switched, to the foyer downstairs. This time it was sex on the red-carpeted stairs, but when the svelte woman Mack was with turned around, Westmore almost fell out of his chair.

It was Vivica Hildreth.

Westmore needed to adjust to the impact. Seeing her like this—naked, obscenely posed, a patented sex-object—made him feel keenly aroused yet absolutely outraged at the same time. She was indeed a beautiful woman, as enticing nude as he'd imagined when he'd seen her clothed, close to perfect even in her cosmetic-surgery-embellished middle age. Reason returned very quickly, though. Westmore snapped up the cell-phone and dialed her number.

When her voice-mail came on, he said very stoically, "Mrs. Hildreth, this is Richard Westmore. Right now I'm watching a porn disc with you on it. You're participating in an interesting little sex-scene on the stairs in the foyer—with Mack. I want to know why you lied. I want to know why you told me you've never been in the mansion before. I can't possibly do a job for you unless you're going to be honest with me. I want you to call me back and explain because right now I don't know what to think. I feel like a dupe that's being manipulated with money."

Steaming, he hung up, lit a cigarette, and ground his teeth. *What a sucker I am.* But why would she lie about never being in the mansion? He tried to calculate a purpose in the lie but could think of none. When his phone rang, he almost dropped it by picking it up too fast. *That was quick,* he thought. *Let's see what the queen bee has to say . . .*

"Hello?"

"You sound really happy to hear from me. I swear it wasn't me who killed your dog."

Westmore frowned. It wasn't Vivica, it was Tom. "Sorry, Tom. I'm a little jacked out of shape here. Thought you were someone else."

"Well maybe this info will un-jack you. I don't know."

"You find anything else out about Hildreth?"

"Nope, just more of the same stuff I told you the other day. Fuckin' guy pays his taxes and has some serious *luck* in the stock market. As for Vivica Hildreth, she's got no record, nothing in the way of a questionable history. Social climber from Sarasota, Florida. Hooked up with Hildreth in the mid-eighties. She's fifty-two. All she is is a pinkie-in-the-air gold digger. Looks like she found the right guy to dig on. And—"

"And what about Debbie Rodenbaugh?" Westmore rushed.

"Hold your horses, I was just about to tell you. Deborah Rodenbaugh is a freshman right now at Oxford University, majoring in Art History."

"Who told you that?"

"The registration department, two art professors who have her as a student, the director of the Bodleian Library where she has a part-time job, and her."

"What do you mean 'and her?'"

"I just talked to her on the phone, and by the way, the long-distance call to Oxfordshire, England, goes on your bill. Thirty-five fuckin' bucks, can you believe that?"

"Yeah, yeah, fine. But you said you talked to *her?*"

"Yep. It was about seven p.m. there with the time-change but I got her at her dorm, someplace called Lady Margaret Hall."

Westmore felt riveted. "What did she say? What did she say about—"

"Hildreth? She said he was an odd man, but was always very nice to her. Took an interest in her because she was an art enthusiast, like him. She worked for him for a year and a half, office assistant type of thing. She seemed genuinely mournful about his death when her aunt and uncle in Jacksonville told her about it, said she couldn't believe it. In her opinion he wasn't capable of an act like that, and he never seemed crazy. She'll be spending the summer here when the spring semester's over, said to feel free to call her anytime."

Westmore listened, silent.

"You get all that, buddy?" Tom asked. "The girl sounded for real."

"Yeah, yeah," Westmore said. He blinked. "It's a relief."

"In a little while I'm gonna take a crack at that other info you wanted me to do a search on, the numbers you found in the safe. I'll call you back in a few hours."

"That's great, Tom. I really appreciate this."

"No problem. You can buy me fuckin' dinner when I'm all done."

"You got it."

Westmore felt relieved and decompressed. *Maybe I should call Clements?* he considered. He had the ex-cop's cell number. *No, better idea.* There was still the mystery of Hildreth's missing body. Debbie Rodenbaugh was safe but maybe Clements was right about the rest. *Something's still very wrong around here.* He had till two a.m. tonight to glean more information. *Clements thinks that Hildreth's somewhere in this house too. Maybe I can find him myself first . . .*

Westmore left, setting out to do just that. He had all day to search the mansion's every nook, cranny, wall, and room.

He made two critical mistakes when he left the office. One, he left his cell phone on the desk and, two, he didn't consider for even a moment that everything Tom had just told him might be a lie.

III

Three Adiposians stared up facelessly at the vessel that was now Adrianne. She stared back at the grotesque things, safe in her bodiless distance. Behind them, the Chirice Flaesc shined in sweat, its skin moving slightly, the veins running across its walls pulsing with vitality.

I'm here, Adrianne thought. *What now?*

"You've come to test me," a voice resonated. Again, the Fallen Angel's voice sounded like light, which was impossible; hence, this impossible domain. Jaemmysin appeared below, next to his mindless attendants—he'd stepped out from the temple's pillars of tense muscle, the penises for fingers limp from a recent rape of a minor species of demon. Yet as terrifying as the figure was—the angled, beautiful face, and monstrous arms and legs grafted to his angelic body—Adrianne was not afraid. In her out-of-body state, she was a sparrow on a high branch, looking down at the pack of wolves.

I've come to hold you to your promise, she proclaimed. *You're monstrous to look at. But a liar, too?*

The Angel smiled, a rim of bright light within his black halo. *I never lie. I never even lied to God, when I knew Him.*

Adrianne's eyeless gaze gestured the temple's closed doors. *I want to meet—*

Jaemmysin interrupted, pointing a phallic finger upward. "*Don't* say his name."

I want to meet the Sexus Cyning.

"Open the doors for our polite guest," Jaemmysin commanded the Adiposians. "I grant her permission to enter and to come face to face with our Lord."

The lard-colored things trod back, slapped their hands onto tendons that served as handles, and pulled. The temple's doors opened with a sound akin to grinding stone, even though they were composed of hot, living skin and muscle . . .

The Adiposians stepped back, and even if mindless, faceless, and *soulless* entities could not be capable of fear, they seemed terrified. They bowed and disappeared into wet orifices in the wall.

Jaemmysin lowered himself to his knees.

The most monstrous thing Adrianne could ever contemplate awaited, a mammoth penis pointing up from stout legs of gray skin and corded muscle. Adrianne's first impulse was to shoot away, to flee forever and leave the horrid place to its secrets.

"The bold traveler," the strangely tiny voice floated upward. It reminded her of sticks being rubbed together briskly, an etching sound that somehow translated itself into words she could understand. "I am Belarius."

Adrianne couldn't respond. The vision of Lucifer's first servant seemed to vibrate; she was grateful she couldn't focus on details. The face was like a nightmare not quite remembered upon waking up in a sticky sweat. All she could detect was a face that seemed bezeled like a chisel-end, and large eyes that were empty holes in space.

"I welcome you to serve me," this lord of lust said to her. "Few are offered that honor, even those who've ventured as far as you have."

I won't serve you, Adrianne told the thing outright. *I'm not here for that. I'm here for answers, that's all. Can you resent me for that?*

"No. All of life, and death, is a sojourn—for answers to what is not understood."

Thank you, she tried to ingratiate him. *I want to know what's going to happen at the Hildreth Mansion.*

"And your question will be answered, one way or another. Choose to serve me—that would please me much."

I told you, I can't do that. You'll only answer me if I serve you, then?

The etch-like voice reiterated: "You'll be answered one

way or another. I've delighted in your physical body already—through my acolytes . . ." The finger of the lord of lust pointed outward, to the Adiposians. "It's a delectable body. Serve me, and I promise I'll show you ecstasies when you die."

No.

"Then you'll come here when you die anyway. And I'll rape you every day until the stars lose their light."

No, Adrianne said. *But you said you'd answer my question.*

The incalculable face looked more pointedly at her. "Ask my servant Hildreth yourself. He'll be happy to reply."

Adrianne's vision darted off. Next to an altar-like plinth made of flesh stood a tall, lean figure in cloak and hood. The darkest smile glimmered up at her, and the face in the hood's oval was Reginald Hildreth's.

He whispered to her in an etching, barely audible voice, like Belarius'.

My God, Adrianne thought of the words he told her.

"There, you have your answer," Belarius said. "Do with it what you will. You believe you're safe as you are? Your physical body is elsewhere—you're just a spirit now, you can't be hurt here?"

I don't just believe that, Adrianne replied. *I know it.*

"Then go, traveler. Fly away, back to your body."

Adrianne willed herself to do exactly that, but—

What?

When she tried to turn and whisk herself out of the temple, nothing happened.

Belarius was grinning at her. "Jaemmysin," he ordered. "Bring in our next entertainment."

Adrianne felt locked in the air above them, when Jaemmysin entered the temple, followed by two Adiposians who were dragging something curvaceous but of considerable bulk. It was some manner of She-Demon, horned and husky, with sweating skin the color of shale. The breasts, several times larger than a human woman's, rose and fell. The pubic hair between the well-muscled legs looked like black seaweed. The Adiposians spread the creature's legs apart, then walked out of the temple, leaving it unconscious where it lay.

What is this? Adrianne asked in alarm.

"A little more sight-seeing for you," she was answered. "To give you the best taste of this place."

Adrianne tried not to show her fear but knew she was failing. She couldn't move; Belarius had somehow paralyzed the psychic vessel that she existed as. *What's he going to do now?* she thought in the lowest dread.

It was Belarius' infernal grin that began to pull on her now. The harder she tried to pull away from him the more quickly she was drawn down. She wasn't the sparrow safe in the high tree anymore. In a moment, the thing's will had her locked right before the unglimpsable face, and then—

A sound like the wind.

—and Adrianne was inhaled.

It was as though she were gaseous, she was an air-pocket being divided into three streams: two were sucked into Belarius' pit-like nostrils, the third into his fanged mouth. Terror kept her from even thinking. Now she was *inside* Belarius, being processed through his lungs, dispersed into his blood. The monstrous heart pumped her throughout the eons-old body, and somehow she knew she was accumulating at his groin. The sudden frenetic movement told her what he was doing now: raping the husky She-Demon that had been brought in.

The movement seemed to never cease. Adrianne's spirit was blending with Belarius' lust. Then—

A guttural chuckle that rocked the temple's walls of flesh.

Adrianne was ejaculated out with the semen of the Sexus Cyning. She shot through the mammoth penis right up into the She-Demon's cervix . . .

In the act she saw a vision of Hell that had never even *been* seen.

"A lovely union," the voice etched above her. Inside, Adrianne felt the She-Demon's heart stop. The cells of Belarius' sperm swam around her spirit, mixing with it.

Then Adrianne oozed out of the She-Demon's sex and pooled on the floor—a psychic wet-spot.

"Piss that blaspheme off my floor," Belarius said.

Adrianne was only partly cognizant, the ether of her soul trying to re-accumulate. She couldn't really see, she could only sense. Jaemmysin approached the spread legs of the now very dead She-Demon, pointed his ten penile fingers down and washed the smear that was Adrianne out of the Chirice Flaesc, each stream of his urine hard as a blast from a fire-hose. Adrianne was dispersed.

Reforming herself, as she was, could only be described as the mental equivalent to hauling a load of bricks up a steep incline. Her exhaustion threatened to defeat her, but just as she would give up, she gradually became buoyant, began to rise.

"Fly away, traveler," the etchings from within bid to her. The temple doors began to grind closed. "Take your useless secrets back to your world. We'll see you again very soon . . ."

As if fleeing murderers, Adrianne soared off, back to the safety of her physical body.

As always, God had protected her this time . . . but barely. *Maybe He's teaching me a lesson,* she supposed.

But she was intact, and when she woke up later in her physical body, she could tell the others exactly what she'd learned.

She was coming back now to her world, through a crystal night and over gorgeous moon-lit landscapes. The mansion soared into sight . . .

OH MY GOD NO! she screamed to herself when she got back to the roof where her body should be.

Adrianne's body wasn't there any more.

Part Three

•

The Temple
of Flesh

Chapter Fifteen

I

Westmore stopped to take a break on the fifth floor, stepping out onto the stone veranda of one of the master suites. He lit a cigarette and watched smoke sail away. The sun had already gone down, leaving the land before the mansion painted in ghostly moonlight.

He'd searched every room in the house, every closet, every auxiliary passage, plus every attic room he could find. There was no sign of Reginald Hildreth, no evidence of anyone residing in the house in secret.

A glance to his watch showed him 11:59 p.m. *At two I'm supposed to open the side door for Clements.* Westmore wasn't sure what to think now, his moods and his convictions tipping this way and that. *Maybe I should just call Clements, tell him I've searched the house and found no sign of Hildreth.* He'd also want to know about Tom's verification: that Debbie

Rodenbaugh was definitely present at the University of Oxford.

He won't believe it but it's still a good idea. And another reminder. *I should also call Vivica back.* She hadn't returned his not-so-pleasant call earlier, and Westmore found that interesting.

He sputtered at himself when he reached into his pocket and found it empty. *Idiot! She probably DID call back. I must've left the damned phone in Hildreth's office . . .*

He lumbered back down to the third floor, to the office. He picked up his cell phone, which still lay on the desk, but before he could check his messages—

"Everybody!" Nyvysk's voice barked over the intercom. "Come up to the roof!"

Huh? Nyvysk had sounded urgent. Westmore ducked back out, almost collided with Cathleen, who'd been trotting toward the stairs.

"What happened?"

"I don't know," she said.

"How do we get to the roof?"

"I don't know!"

Back up on the fifth floor, the stairs ended. Nyvysk's exclamations could be heard again on the intercom. "Where the hell's the stairs to the roof!" Westmore shouted back into the intercom.

Mack and Karen appeared at the other end of the hall. "This way!"

They rushed after them, up yet another set of stairs. Then the four of them emerged onto a plush overhanging parapet, complete with lounge chairs, umbrellas, planters.

"Adrianne left a note for me in the commo room," Nyvysk told them, leaning against the high, stone wall. He looked defeated. "She said she'd be OBE-ing from up here."

"What's wrong?" Karen asked.

"Look."

Nyvysk pointed down, over the parapet's edge. They all peered over.

"Aw, Jesus," Westmore muttered, a hand to his head.

Cathleen and Karen cried out. Mack and Nyvysk just stared.

Adrianne's naked body lay sprawled on the fieldstone walkway below. The five-story drop left her broken, canted at nearly a ninety-degree angle via a fractured spine. A halo of blood lay around her head.

"Somebody must've thrown her off," Karen sobbed.

"Yes," Nyvysk said, "and no doubt while she was OBE-ing. Her most defenseless state."

Cathleen wiped her eyes. "Well, maybe not. She has been suicidal in the past."

Westmore extended a bewildered hand. "Come on, suicide? She's nude. She was probably raped and thrown off. Why would she take her clothes off to commit suicide?"

"Sometimes experients take off their clothes before they begin an OBE," Cathleen pointed out. "I often do the same thing when I divine or put myself in a trance."

Westmore shook his head. "I can't buy that. It's obvious somebody threw her over the side." An involuntary impulse caused him to glance at Mack. Several others did too.

"Hey, fuck you, man!" Mack objected. "Anybody could've done it. You just want to point to me 'cos I'm not part of this psychic-mumbo jumbo. And where the fuck were *you?*"

"He was coming out of the office, I saw him," Cathleen confirmed.

Mack frowned. "He could've done it any time!"

"Yeah?" Westmore egged. "And what happened to the lock-girl, Mack? You were the last one to see her. You even had sex with her, and then what happens? She disappears."

"You're talking shit, buddy!" Mack lunged, grabbed Westmore by the collar. "I think *you* killed her!"

Nyvysk's height and bulk easily pushed the two men apart. "Nobody's accusing anybody. Let's keep our heads together."

"And where's that crackpot perv, Willis? Huh?" Mack added.

"I think somebody raped her and threw her off," Westmore repeated.

"She was already raped once," Karen reminded. "And not by some*body*. By the same things that raped me *and* Cathleen."

"It's a consideration," Nyvysk voiced. "Discorporate murders are rare but they are documented."

But suddenly Westmore considered something else. *SomeBODY, or some THING? Or maybe Hildreth himself . . .*

II

Willis hadn't heard Nyvysk's intercom call . . . because he was passed out in one of the parlors. Again, his last target-vision seemed to show him the future instead of the past.

A room of flesh. A *temple* of flesh.

A wall. No, a door—a door, too, composed of quivering, hot flesh.

The door was parted to a gap.

Willis' vision suddenly made his brain feel as though it were boiling, pressure rising, his skull fit to burst—

He glimpsed into the gap and saw something hideous behind the door. Then the vision snapped and he saw himself being slowly strangled to death as Hildreth and several unnameable things looked on.

That's when he collapsed, unconscious.

He thought he might've had a minor stroke when he woke up. Pain pounded in his head. *I've had enough of this place,* he decided, on his knees. *I should just leave . . .*

He staggered to his feet.

Yeah. I'm going to leave.

What good was more of Vivica's money if he was dead? He wandered out and down, straggled down some hallways. He supposed he was looking for the others, to tell them he couldn't hack it here anymore. Would they think him a coward for leaving? *I doubt it. Deep down they all want to leave too . . .*

He walked into the office, hoping to find Westmore, but the room stood empty. Aside, something flickered.

He had no choice but to walk over when he realized what it was . . .

Westmore had left one of the DVD's playing on the computer, the sound turned off. It was more porn, more of Willis' curse.

His weakness forced him to watch.

It never ends with me . . . His shame enshrouded him, yet he looked on: scene after scene, one beautiful naked woman after the next.

When the disc ended, he picked another randomly off the desk, popped it in.

And frowned.

Nothing. He fast forwarded through several minutes of black screen. When light finally bloomed, he slowed down to normal speed and watched, expecting more enticing sex-images but instead . . .

Gross, he thought of what he saw. *I am NOT into this S&M stuff.*

A naked woman lay spread-legged on a table. He

couldn't see her face but she didn't appear to be one of Hildreth's typical porn models. No implants, no stunning tan. She appeared young.

Somebody else was performing a genital piercing of the most extreme sort. A half-inch at a time, the folds of her vagina were being closed by chrome rings. Each ring being crimped caused the woman to flinch. When the procedure was complete, it looked as if her sex had been closed by silver stitches.

This is no porn tape. What is this shit?

On screen, for just a moment, the woman leaned up and showed her face. Shaken, red around the eyes.

It was that young woman Westmore was so concerned with, the girl in the period-piece painting. *What was her name?*

Oh, yeah. Debbie Rodenbaugh.

Had Westmore seen this? *Maybe not. Maybe I better go tell him.* It could be his last act in the mansion before he walked out of it forever.

"It's a chastity belt," a voice rose up behind him. "They're symbolizing her virginity. Belarius likes symbols of homage."

Willis spun at the voice.

Stared.

It was Vanni, the locksmith woman.

She looked worse now than the first time he'd seen her revenant. Thinner, grayer, her gut sucked in, like a corpse in a death camp.

"I wasn't afraid of you last time, and I'm not afraid of you this time. You're a vision. You're a dead image."

By now her once-full breasts sat deflated in their emaciation, nipples so gray they were almost black.

"A revenant? A discorporation?"

"Yes."

She stepped forward, bony-hipped, legs like gray sticks. "Are you sure?"

"Positive," Willis said.

"But you only see revenants through the things you touch, right?"

"Yes."

A black smile. "Your gloves are still on."

Willis' eyes went wide. He looked at his hands.

She was right.

Fingers like hooks snapped up and grabbed his throat. Willis tried to shout but couldn't—the pressure choked off his voice. He was dragged to the floor in a blur of frenetic, dead-gray motion. Fingertips dug deeper, as if to twist his Adam's apple out of his throat like a cork.

"The house is releasing some of its stored energy," the thing that used to be Vanni said. "It's almost time. Hildreth is going to open the Rive again."

Willis flailed helplessly, gagging. The nippled flaps of breasts swayed before his dimming eyes. Drool fell into his mouth.

"There'll be so much for you to touch in Hell . . ."

His belt was whisked out of the loops on his pants and expertly wrapped around his neck. It was tightened inch by inch until his face turned beet-red and he died, convulsing on the floor.

III

"Isn't *now* the time to call the police?" Cathleen asked. She sat despondent on the same lounge chair that had occupied Adrianne's body before she'd jumped—or been thrown— off the roof.

"I don't know, I don't know," Westmore fairly babbled. "It's the legal thing to do, but I think by now we all know that something else is going to happen soon."

"It's a mistake to call the police just yet," Nyvysk asserted. Moonlight paled his face. "And I don't think we should tell Vivica yet, either. It's not logical, I know. But Westmore's right. We can't bring Adrianne back. And something is going to happen here; our job is to find out what it is. The police will seal the house if we call them now."

Mack was looking over the side. "We can't just leave her body there."

"No, we can't. We'll bring it in. We'll put it in one of the walk-in refrigerators in the kitchen. I don't know."

They're more concerned about what Hildreth has planned than they are about legal protocol. But then he stopped and thought. *And . . . so am I.*

"I knew Adrianne well," Nyvysk went on. "She's a fairly dedicated Christian; she's not concerned about proper burial and such things. She, like myself, believes that her spirit will live forever. I'm content that she's in heaven. She would *want* us to keep investigating the state of the mansion."

"Yeah, and what if you're wrong?" Karen sniped. "How do you know *what* she'd want? She's dead."

"She's only dead physically. If it were me, I'd want the rest of the group to go on with our mission," Nyvysk finished.

"I don't know why I agree but I do," Westmore offered. "But we should bring the body in. Mack and I can do that." He glanced at Nyvysk, Karen, and Cathleen. "Why don't you three go look for Willis?"

"Good idea," Nyvysk agreed.

"Yeah, and what if Willis is the one who killed Adrianne?" Mack suggested with an edge to his voice.

"I'm optimistic that he's not," Nyvysk said. "We'll find him, then I'll spend the rest of the evening graphing the gauss readings. They've been steadily increasing in certain areas throughout the day."

Cathleen appeared concerned. "Why didn't you tell us that earlier?"

"I didn't want to alarm anyone . . ."

Karen seemed testy—or afraid. "You mean those ion things? Why would that alarm anyone?"

"It may mean that the revenant charge in the house is changing, getting stronger," Cathleen answered her.

Nyvysk nodded. "For the next step in whatever exactly Hildreth planned."

"Fine." Westmore tried to keep his thoughts in line. "You guys go do what you're gonna do. Mack and I'll bring in Adrianne's body. Let's do it now, keep busy."

When Westmore and Mack left the roof, Nyvysk said to Karen, "I need a word with Cathleen, in private, if you don't mind."

"Great!" Karen snapped. "Somebody in the house might be a killer and you two want to keep secrets from me!"

"Relax," Cathleen said. "We'll be down in a minute."

Karen left in a huff.

"Something's bothering you?" Nyvysk said when Karen had left.

"I . . ."

"What?"

"You and Karen go look for Willis, all right? I want to do something else."

Now the moon cut Nyvysk's large frame into sharp silhouette. "I understand. And good luck."

Cathleen sighed and watched him walk away.

She wondered if she'd ever see him again.

IV

Westmore felt choked up when they'd gone outside and wrapped Adrianne's naked body in a blanket. At least the bugs hadn't gotten to it yet. Mack turned the alarm back on when they came back in, then helped Westmore stow the body in the walk-in.

"You don't trust me at all, do you?" Mack asked.

Westmore closed the walk-in door. "No."

"You think I killed her?"

"No—er, I don't think so. I'm not trusting anybody now," Westmore said and lit a cigarette.

"All right, here. See this—"

Westmore went rigid when Mack produced a small pistol from his pocket. It was smaller than the one he'd seen upstairs in the office drawer.

How long had he been carrying it?

He handed it over to Westmore, grip-first. "Now you can protect everybody from big bad *me*."

"It was nothing personal." Westmore took the gun. It was an interesting gesture, at least. "I don't expect you to trust me anymore than I trust you—or pretty much anybody."

"Somebody you might want to keep an eye on is Karen," Mack said next.

"Why's that?"

"Just take my word for it."

"I don't believe for a minute that Karen threw Adrianne off the roof, Mack."

"Why not? She's psycho. She's stone-cold crazy, and Willis is an eight-ball, too. Don't you understand the deal with all these people? They're all half-insane. You don't know *what* they're capable of."

Westmore just shook his head. "You want to know who I'm most suspicious of?"

"You mean it's not me?"

Westmore saw little harm in telling him what he'd seen. He was curious about Mack's reaction. "Vivica told me she's never been in the house before."

"Yeah?"

"Yeah. But I just saw her on a porn disc getting boned dog-style on the foyer stairs." Westmore kept his gaze open on Mack's eyes. "By you."

"So what? She's a nymphomaniac, and so was every chick in the place," Mack said. "More people have probably gotten it on in this house than any house in fuckin' history. Hildreth let her do whatever she wanted."

"And what she wanted to do was *you*. Mack the stud."

"Hey, I'm not gonna apologize because women tend to have a thing for me. Sounds like you're jealous."

Oh, Jesus. "Why would she tell me she's never been in the house?"

"I got no idea, man."

Westmore wasn't sure what he'd been getting at, not that it really mattered. Mack's reaction had seemed normal. "And speaking of Vivica . . ." He slipped out his cell phone, to see it she'd returned his call during the commotion on the roof. *Still nothing from her* . . . But there *was* a message.

Westmore played back the voicemail . . .

"It's me again," Tom said. "I ran those numbers you gave me . . ."

Westmore took out the same numbers that he'd copied off the file in his computer.

INPUT REQUEST: FEED
STRAT APOGEE

RESPONSE: 06000430
ASSIGNMENT POINT: 00000403

"Strat apogee means straticulated—it's a type of orbital apogee. The assignment point is a time and date; it's how astronomers log them, all in a line like that. The first four zeros is a time—midnight—and the zero-four, zero-three is April third."

April third. Midnight, the thought immediately clicked. *The night of the slaughter* . . .

"That's the assignment point—or the starting point," Tom went on in the message. "It looks like Hildreth was running a math problem and this was the question. The response is the answer, and that's a time and date, too. Zero-six-zero-zero is a time—six a.m. Zero-four, three-zero the date: April 30th. Look on your calendar, paisan. That's tomorrow morning. And what exactly happens tomorrow morning at six is this: There's a star called M39 that will be at its *apogee* for the first time in recorded history. To an astronomer it's a big deal. This star hasn't been this close to the earth since we were apes."

Tomorrow morning, the thought churned in Westmore's head. *Whatever it is that Hildreth planned is happening then—* and just then the clock tolled midnight. *In six hours* . . .

"One other thing," Tom's message continued. "This guy Hildreth, you mentioned he was into occult stuff? Well, to somebody like that, April 30 is important. It's an occult festival day called the Eve of Beltane—the day before May Day. Pagans thousands of years ago would perform rituals on the Eve of Beltane, as a gesture of worship to the gods of the underworld—demons, what have you. They believed that these demons would bless them on that day because on Beltane Eve, the borders between hell and earth are the thinnest, or some shit like that."

There was a long pause on the line, pages flipping as Tom had obviously been checking notes. "So there you have it, my friend. I'll send you my bill. Have a good one—or, I should say . . ." Tom chuckled on the recording. "Have a happy Eve of Beltane."

The message ended.

Westmore's mental gears were spinning. Here, at least, was most of the puzzle Vivica had hired him to solve. "It's in six hours," he muttered.

"What?" Mack asked.

"On April 3rd, Hildreth butchered everyone in this house as the first part of a rite. The last part of that rite begins in six hours . . ."

V

Cathleen glittered again. She lay naked on the same lounge chair that Adrianne had used when she'd gone into the last OBE of her life. Her resolve outweighed her fear—or she hoped it did. Whoever had killed Adrianne could easily do the same thing to her, from the same exact place.

But it truly was time. It was time to find out.

The moonlight on her bare skin made the pontica dust seem to effervesce along with her sweat. Mentally, she lowered her heart-rate, respiration, and blood-pressure—just as she could move objects with her mind, she could do the same with her own metabolism, a trait not uncommon among skilled mentalists. The calmness of the night began to caress her, tracing her skin, hardening her nipples. The stone dust felt radiant and hot, and soon so did the rest of her.

She urged herself down, down . . .

Yes, it was time to end all of this madness at the house, but she knew she couldn't do that without answers.

And she wondered who would find her first once she'd entered theta-sleep . . .

Adrianne? Or Hildreth?

VI

Westmore and Mack branched off in an effort to search for Willis. *Do I really think he killed Adrianne?* he asked himself. He supposed he didn't—she'd probably jumped. *She was unstable to begin with—then the mansion became too much for her.* These were fragile people.

But still . . .

He thought of a worst-case scenario, regarding Willis. If somebody'd killed him . . . *Where's the best place to hide the body?*

The passages?

He'd have to travel those passages in two hours anyway, to let Clements in. He found the curtain and entered, suddenly very glad he had Mack's pistol in his pocket. He cruised the entire network of narrow corridors, impressed that he wasn't terribly scared. The tulip-shaped wall light lit the way, however dimly. What if he turned a corner and found someone standing there, staring at him?

Shut up, he told himself.

When he got to the small library at the end, he'd found nothing suspicious—or at least nothing suspicious as far as secret passages went. It was dusty back here, ill-used. The only footprints in the sheen of dust on the floor were clearly his own.

I better get back to the others, he surmised. *This is a waste of time.*

He turned to leave but stopped.

Something on the floor.

Westmore stared down.

Another track of footprints could clearly be seen now. Had they been there before?

They were bare footprints, smaller, and—

Obviously a woman's, Westmore realized.

His eyes followed the prints, down the final short corridor, to the hidden exit door.

When Westmore came back into the mansion's proper area, his suspicions were pinwheeling. *Who knows about the hidden exit door?*

Probably none of the group, but Mack and Karen? They were a good bet.

Were those *Karen's* footprints?

There was no way to tell, but he knew something else a moment later—

A scream ripped down the stairs with the tenor of a referee's whistle.

And it most *assuredly* was Karen's.

He sprinted up the steps—two flights, he sensed—then another scream ripped down the dark hall.

The office, he knew, and then ran there.

The others—minus Cathleen—stood behind the desk, Nyvysk standing behind Karen. She looked fractured, the others pale by what they gazed down at.

"What?" Westmore asked.

"Karen found Willis," someone said.

The tactionist's body had been stuffed in the leg-well of the desk.

"Christ. What happened to him?"

"Strangled, it appears," Nyvysk said. "See the ligature mark around his neck?"

The image glaring up at Westmore seemed alien. Willis' face was blue marbled with pink, eyes bugged.

"We don't know for sure about Adrianne, but I don't think anyone'll argue that *this* is murder. Jesus."

"Murder," Nyvysk added, "or a cursory sacrifice."

"So that means the 'charge' of the house is strengthened?" Westmore asked. "Am I getting that right?"

"You're getting it quite right."

"Shit on all that," Mack said. "Who was the last person to see Willis alive?"

Nobody answered.

After an indeterminate silence, Nyvysk posed, "Wasn't the safe *open* yesterday?"

They all looked to the wall. *I think it was,* Westmore thought. *I left it open when I found the slip of paper . . .*

Now it was closed again.

Westmore tested the latch-handle.

Locked.

He dialed in the 9-digit acrostic, turned the latch, and opened the safe.

The safe contained a single, rather unremarkable object: Patrick Willis' belt.

VII

The hairs on the back of Nyvysk's neck stood up stiff as bared wire-threads when he lugged the gauss-meters and their carrying cases into the South Atrium, then began to plug them into the wall socket to charge them back up. For formality, he aimed them outward at different angles and plugged them into the processor connected to the television. *Can't hurt to take some readings down here, too.*

But he couldn't really focus.

His neck was tingling.

It was that sensation they'd all been getting over the past day: the charge of the house gradually stepping up. There could be no mistake. Adrianne's death only contributed to it, as had Willis', not to mention the girl from the lock company who was clearly dead too, wherever her body might be.

Accumulating revenant momentum . . . He looked at the gauss meters and realized the metaphor. *The mansion is charging its OWN batteries, for a massive discharge that Hildreth planned a long time ago—perhaps YEARS ago. Whatever the event is, he lit the fuse on April 3rd. And that fuse burns down to the powder keg in*—he glanced at the clock: 1:15 a.m.—

In less than five hours.

He'd brought the gauss-meters down from the Scarlet Room to recharge their portable power-packs. *Where should I try them next?* he wondered. The Scarlet Room should be generating the best revenant images . . . yet it hadn't so far. After all those murders, the place should be teeming. But the readings he'd gotten thus far had been no more intense than other, more typical perimeters of the mansion. *They'll accelerate, more than likely,* he thought as he finished plugging in the packs. *As the mansion gets closer to whatever it's gaining toward.*

It was gaining toward something—that was for sure. Now the hairs on his arms were standing up too. Even the fillings in his teeth, somehow, buzzed.

"Nyvysk," he heard the voice.

An excited whisper.

He'd barely heard it, to the extent that he thought it must just be in his head. Then:

"My love . . ."

Now the voice filled the room, and he knew who it was. *Saeed* . . .

It did seem to be emanating from the intercom, but when he walked over, it came from another direction.

"We can be together as life never permitted . . ."

Nyvysk turned around again.

He didn't have time to see much, but he heard one more thing.

"Come to me in this beautiful death . . ."

VIII

It's time, Westmore thought.

Ten minutes before two.

He retraced his steps through the passageways and when he got to the small library, he noticed the footprints were still there. Bare, female footprints leading out but not back in. *Not my imagination,* he thought.

But the footprints could've been old, couldn't they? They could've been left by one of the starlets back before the murders. *I didn't think of that . . .*

But he wasn't necessarily convinced, either.

When he opened the hidden door, his heart lurched. A figure was facing him.

"Hope I didn't make ya shit your pants." It was Clements, with a sly smile on his face, and a small backpack on. He looked at his watch. "You're right on time."

Damn him. Westmore relaxed. "What's in the backpack?"

"Flashlights, tools, guns."

No thermos of coffee? "Where's Connie?"

"Outside, with the car." Clements checked the magazine

in an inordinately large pistol, then stuck it back under his shirt. "She's got one of my other cell phones—I'll call her up when we find Debbie, then she'll bring the car up and take you both back to my house."

Westmore scratched his head. "Where will you be?"

"Here. Looking for Hildreth—if we don't find him first. One way or another, he goes down tonight."

Westmore didn't argue. Clements followed him back through the bowels of the mansion. "Where is everybody? I don't want to be seen unless there's no way around it."

"Everybody's downstairs except Cathleen," Westmore explained. Then he gulped. "But Adrianne Saundland and Patrick Willis are dead."

"How'd that happen?"

"We don't know for sure. But it's clear Willis was murdered, and Adrianne may have been too."

Clements shook his head. "Probably Hildreth. Still think nothing's going on here?"

"Oh, I *know* something's going on here," and then Westmore explained the apogee that would occur at 6 a.m.

"What a fuckin' psycho satanic freakshow," Clements said with a chuckle.

"What are you going to do if you run into Cathleen?"

"I'll take her out to the car."

"What if she doesn't want to go?"

"Then I'll take her out to the car at *gunpoint* and lock her in the trunk. I ain't fuckin' around."

"Yeah, I guess you're not." They'd taken the channel of stairs back to the third floor. The curtain hung before them. "Here we are. What's the game plan?"

"You go do your thing, act normal," Clements said. "I'm going to start upstairs, room to room, and work my way down."

"I already did that—"

"Great, and I'm gonna do it again. Debbie's here, I *know* it. Put your cell on vibrate. If I find her, or any shit goes down, I'll call. You do the same. Here—" He pulled up his shirt to get one of his pistols. "Take this."

Westmore showed him the gun Mack had given him. "I already got one."

"Smart man. I'm gonna go find Debbie now. See ya later." Clements opened the curtain.

"Be careful," Westmore said as an afterthought.

"I don't need to be careful. *Hildreth* is the one who needs to do that," and then he was past the curtain and gone.

Westmore felt prickly as he went downstairs. It made him wonder about what the others had mentioned so many times: the *charge* of the house, and the likelihood that it was increasing. What exactly did that mean? And how would the nature of this charge affect the house by 6 a.m.?

But these ponderings ceased when he stepped into the South Atrium. Karen and Mack were there. Westmore's cigarette fell out of his mouth when he looked down.

"He's dead," Karen said, a crack in her voice.

Mack was on his knees, before Nyvysk, who lay sprawled in the corner.

"What happened!"

"I don't know, we just walked in and he was lying there," Mack answered.

"There aren't any wounds," Karen added. "And no blood."

"His heart's not beating, I can tell you that."

Westmore knelt, and felt for a pulse himself. Nothing. The body was still warm. "This had to have happened within the hour." When he looked around the long room, he noticed the gauss scanners pointing at them. "Are those things on?"

"I don't even know what those thing *are*," Mack said.

"They measure ion-fluctuations in the air," Westmore said absently.

"Those things we saw on the screen the other day?" Karen inquired.

"This was one of them. It looks like he was charging their batteries and doing some readings at the same time." Westmore walked toward the processor on the conference table.

"I don't get it," Mack said.

"One of the scanners is pointing right into the corner . . ."

Westmore flicked some switches on the processor. He was fudging it but eventually he got the machine to rewind. Then he played it back.

On the large television before the couch they watched. The frame showed the corner of the room—empty at this point—in normal light. Suddenly, Nyvysk backed up into it, eyes wide and grim. In a moment, he was backed up into the corner, as if retreating from something.

"It looks like he's afraid," Karen said, a hand to her face.

"Afraid of what?" Mack said.

"Maybe this'll show us." Westmore hit another switch, which overlayed the ion-scan. The screen turned black, except—

The area in which Nyvysk stood glittered with luminous, dandelion-yellow dots. The dots were arranged to a vaguely human shape.

"Those sparkles are Nyvysk?" Karen asked.

"Yeah, or I should say they're a recording of the ions in the air that are changing their electrical charges by his physical body being there—"

"And what's *that?*" Mack asked next, with some alarm.

Another arrangement of lit dots entered the frame, also human-shaped.

The shape slowly approached Nyvysk, then seemed to embrace him.

And the shape that was Nyvysk collapsed.

Westmore hit the normal-light button again. They saw Nyvysk lying dead in the corner, but they also saw—

"What the hell is that?" Mack asked.

A churning shape. It was black like a shadow yet it seemed to have some barely formed substance in it.

Karen trembled. "It looks like one of the things that raped me. A discorporate, Cathleen called it. But that one on the screen is darker; it looks more solid, more shape to it."

"Then Nyvysk was right about what's happening in the house," Westmore said. "The charge. It's getting steadily stronger, and I guess it'll be at its peak at 6 a.m."

"The apogee," Mack said.

"Yeah."

All three of them looked at the clock. It was past 3 a.m. now.

"That thing that killed Nyvysk," Mack asked. "Was that Hildreth?"

"I don't think so. Hildreth was taller, wasn't he? I think whatever killed Nyvysk was something from his past—that's *here* now."

Mack seemed more ill-at-ease than ever. "I'm not in it for this. Me and Karen—we just work for Vivica now. We're not signed up for shit like this. If the things in this house—ghosts or whatever—can kill people that easily . . ."

"It could happen to us," Karen finished with a fret.

"Maybe, but I don't think so," Westmore said. He eyed the ornate liquor cabinet across the room. *Shit, I could use a drink now.* "The mansion seems to be targeting the people it's in tune with—*psychic* people."

"Adrianne and Willis," Mack said.

"But Nyvysk wasn't psychic," Karen said.

"No, but he was a priest who used to perform exorcisms," Westmore said. "Or maybe I'm totally wrong and we're all screwed. But I'm sticking around till 6 a.m. You two want to leave, go ahead. I wouldn't blame you."

"Let's stay, stick together," Mack suggested.

Karen seemed less enthusiastic but willing. "At least let's find Cathleen."

But when the doors clicked open, and they all turned, they saw that Cathleen had found them.

She walked silently into the room, her dress clinging by profuse sweat to her body's contours. Her mouth was open, her eyes wide as she looked back at them.

"Cathleen," Westmore began. "What—"

"I'm not Cathleen . . ."

"It's one of those trances again," Mack said.

"She's possessed," Karen whispered.

Not possessed, Westmore remembered. "She's a medium. Someone else is speaking through her."

"Hildreth," someone said.

Cathleen moved closer. "No. He can't touch me now." As she moved, she seemed unstable, exhausted yet determined to do something. "At 6 a.m. Hildreth reopens the Rive."

"The what?" Mack asked.

"The doors of the Chirice Flaesc will open. But they won't open in Hell. They'll open *here.*"

"What happens then?" Westmore asked shakily.

"Then what went in on April 3rd will come back out, six-hundred and sixty-six hours after she entered on the night of the slaughter."

"You mean Deborah Rodenbaugh, don't you?"

Cathleen nodded tranquilly. "The virgin, yes. The ultimate homage, the perfect innocence defiled. It's all a symbol, since time immemorial. Belarius will be done with her, and unless you stop him, he will have succeeded."

Westmore stepped closer. "Succeeded at what?"

"When the Rive opens, all becomes here as it is there. All becomes flesh. Hildreth was Belarius' disciple. He arranged everything, has been planning this for years. But the tether of my spirit is pulling me now. I can't stay—"

"Don't go yet!" Westmore shouted. "We need to know more!"

Were the lights in the room wavering?

"The house is getting stronger," Adrianne said through Cathleen's mouth. "Which means the things *in* the house are getting stronger."

They stared back at her.

"Hildreth is getting stronger . . ."

There was the faintest crackling sound. Then Cathleen's long bright-blonde hair lifted up as if by massive static.

She toppled to the floor.

"My God," Karen said.

When Westmore and Mack went to pick Cathleen up, she shrieked, flailed her arms at them. "Get away, get away!" and with the outburst Westmore and Mack were thrown back. The chairs around the conference table fell over, the gauss-sensors blew ten feet across the floor, and several paintings dropped off the wall to the floor.

"Cathleen!" Westmore shouted at her. "It's us! Relax! You're okay!"

When Cathleen's eyes snapped open the screen on the television imploded.

"Jesus!" Mack exclaimed. "What's that all about?"

"She was coming back from the trance, and she was confused." Westmore helped Cathleen to the couch. "I guess she lost control of her telekinetic abilities."

"Like in the office, when Hildreth was talking through her," Karen ventured.

"Yeah."

Cathleen's eyes were fluttering open; she brought a hand to her forehead when she looked around the room. "Oh, God. I didn't hurt anybody, did I?"

"No, we're all fine. Are you?"

Cathleen laxed back, staring. "Adrianne found me . . ."

"Yes. Do you remember what she said?"

A pause, and then Cathleen said, "Yes," and then she looked fearfully to the clock. "Two and a half hours."

"Did Adrianne say anything else to you, before she began communicating to us?"

"I . . . think so." Cathleen frowned. "Damn it, I can't remember."

Westmore sat down and lit a cigarette. Mack and Karen both poured themselves strong drinks.

"What do we do now?" Karen asked.

"Wait," Cathleen said. "For the Rive to open."

"It'll happen in the Scarlet Room. So that's where we're going," Westmore made the decision. "Right now."

IX

Clements had slipped into the office during his search. He shook his head when he saw Willis' body behind the desk. *Poor stupid sap . . .* But true nausea swept over him when he errantly glanced at a lit computer monitor and saw—

Holy mother of God, those sick, sick pieces of shit!

It was Debbie, leaning groggily up on a table after having her vagina closed by tiny chrome rings.

I can't wait to kill Hildreth, my God, I just CAN'T FUCKIN' WAIT!

Staying in the office would be fruitless, and so would examining more DVD's for evidence of Debbie. He'd seen all he needed to. *At least it wasn't a snuff film, those sick fuckers . . .*

Clements spun, drew one of his guns.

Was that a chuckle he heard?

Clements smiled. "If that's you, Hildreth—come and get me." He left the office, without a trace of fear, and began to check the rest of the house.

X

Connie was stringing, but it wasn't too bad now. She'd gone a week without crack—the longest since she'd first put the pipe to her lips. She was edgy, nervous, "crackbugs" crawling on her skin. But Clements had been right: a lot of the physical addiction was going away, leaving her only to deal with the psychological. She knew she'd be able to do it if he didn't abandon her.

She'd never known a man like him. *He doesn't want anything, not like the johns, not like every other asshole out there with a big line of bullshit . . .*

Connie knew she shouldn't take her blessings for granted. This was her last chance.

The nightsounds irritated her—crickets and spring peepers. It seemed too loud. And in spite of the night's humid heat, the moonlight on her face felt cold.

She cast her eyes to the mansion; her gut twisted.

Please be careful in there, she thought.

She kept patting her pocket, to make sure the cell phone was still there. Clements and the others probably wouldn't be out for several hours. She wandered off the road a bit, then began walking around the woodline without really thinking about it. Before she knew it, she was a third of the way around the outer grounds and found herself entering a path that descended into the trees.

Where the— Oh, shit . . .

She'd wandered back to the cemetery without even realizing it. *What is wrong with you, Connie? A week without crack has made you scatterbrained . . .*

The last place she wanted to be was the cemetery. She remembered what they'd found last night. The bum's dead body in the coffin had been bad enough, but in the other hole? *Those rotten . . . THINGS.* Connie didn't care what anyone said. They sure as shit didn't look human to her.

So what was she doing?

Instead of walking out of the graveyard, she walked around the gate, to the hole with the things. Could a dead human really look like that? *Like big plastic bags full of butter,* she thought, queasy. She didn't know what morbid curiosity caused her to do this but she did it just the same.

She turned on her flashlight and shined it down into the hole.

And stared.

The hole was empty.

And she would've doubted that anyone heard her scream as she turned around and found a naked woman standing right in front of her. The woman looked like she could've crawled out of a grave herself: gray skin sucked down tight over veins, ribs showing, belly sucked in. Her pubic bone jutted like someone with anorexia, and her eyes were so dark and sunken they could've been pits.

"You should've gotten in that car and driven away," the woman said but by now decomposition had degraded her voice to a liquefied rasp. The woods sucked up Connie's next shriek and then the corpse standing before her—in life a locksmith named Vanni but in death a marionette of the abyss—shoved Connie into the empty hole.

The corpse looked down, a bony silhouette before the moonlight, and then another figure was standing next to it, tall, erect, poised.

Connie screamed once more when she realized it was Reginald Hildreth, and she screamed even harder when the four Adiposians began to climb down into the hole, faceless in their glee, lard-colored genitals inflamed.

XI

By 4:30, Clements had searched a good deal of the mansion's upper floors. He encountered no one, nor any trace of Debbie or Hildreth. If anything, the house seemed drab, incapable of whatever event it was that Westmore expected. At one point, he ducked into one of the parlors, at the sound of voices. Peeking through the door's gap, he spied Westmore and the others moving up the stairs at the end of the hall, probably on their way to this Scarlet Room where Hildreth had butchered most of the victims on April 3rd.

He stood still, watched them disappear, and continued. Clements still didn't want to be seen, not yet, and not unless it was absolutely necessary.

He'd already checked the Scarlet Room, one of the first places he'd searched. A red room—that was all. Nothing of interest, nor suspicion. *Just some insane rich guy's obsession,* Clements thought. *What the fuck does that psychopath expect?*

It didn't matter, though. Clements knew deep down that Hildreth was in this house somewhere . . .

When he was done checking all the rooms on the third floor, he ducked back into the office and withdrew his cell phone. *Better check up on Connie . . .* He dialed, waited, waited some more.

Christ. Why isn't she answering?

He could go back outside but he didn't want to chance that. *Might not be able to get back in.* Maybe the house frame was obstructing the cell's line of reception.

That's what the problem is, he made the mistake of thinking.

Clements made one more mistake before leaving the office—not a mistake as much as an oversight.

He didn't notice that Willis' body was no longer behind the desk.

XII

Westmore parted the drapes and peered out the high, gun-slit window for no real reason. The night stared back at him, tinged by moonlight that seemed brighter than it should be. *Damn, I'm tired,* he thought. He turned back around to see that Karen and Mack had already fallen asleep on two red-velvet couches. Cathleen sat at the red-veneered table in the room's rear. She could barely keep her head up.

"What time is it?"

"Quarter of five," Westmore said, looking at his watch. The Scarlet Room stood around them in its church-like appointment. But the room felt dead.

"Why is it," Westmore began, "that the one room in the house that should feel the creepiest—and looks the most satanic—doesn't feel that way at all?"

"Wait till 6 a.m.," Cathleen said. "Charges can change drastically."

"Do you believe all this stuff about the apogee?"

"I don't know." She rubbed sleep out of her eyes. "I guess we should, though. We've seen too much already."

You can say that again, Westmore thought. "What should we do if—" but the rest of his sentence trailed off. Cathleen had fallen asleep.

Westmore didn't *want* to fall asleep himself, in spite of his exhaustion. Was he too afraid of what he might wake up to? *I just don't want to miss the stroke of 6 a.m.,* he assured himself.

The others were all sound asleep now. Coffee would be a good idea, so he left the Scarlet Room, closed the doors quietly behind him. There was a coffee machine in the office, so he trudged down to the third floor. Only then did he wonder about Clements. If he'd found anything, he would've called. *I wonder where he is by now?*

In the office he walked around the desk to turn on the coffee machine but stalled.

Willis' body was gone.

Westmore was uncomprehending. *Who the hell would . . .* He was sure Willis was dead. None of the group could've moved the body because he'd been with them. Had Clements moved it?

Why would he?

Why would anyone?

Impulse took him quickly down the stairs, into the South Atrium—

Nyvysk's body was gone.

He dashed to the kitchen and flung open the walk-in refrigerator.

Adrianne's body was gone.

This is supremely fucked up.

Next he ran back to the foyer, ran up the steps to the second floor, turned at the landing to proceed to the third.

And all the lights went out in the house.

He stood now in total dark. The house ticked around him, and he felt a prickly static on his arms. Then—

smack!

Something cracked him on the head from behind. Westmore collapsed on the landing.

Unconsciousness dragged his eyes closed. Before he passed out altogether, though, he saw the faintest light at the top of the stairs—light that was somehow dark—and in that light stood the image of Reginald Hildreth.

He was smiling.

XIII

Clements dialed Connie again, waited and waited. There was no answer. *DAMN IT! Where is she?*

When the lights went out, he was shrouded by confusion more than fear. Was it a simple power outage, or had someone turned the power off deliberately? Suddenly Clements felt inept and lost.

He didn't know the layout of the house at all. His flashlight beam took him down another strange hall, with grim statues and strange faces in portraits scowling after him. He knew he should go find Connie, but—

It was getting close to six o'clock.

He followed another long hall. Two double doors. When he entered . . .

The room's murk was so dense it seemed to reduce the brightness of the flashlight by half. *Where am I?* Clements thought, stupefied. *What is this?*

Nude, wax-white bodies had been suspended upside-down in the center of the room. They'd all been beheaded.

Barely able to think, Clements came forward. A numb instinct caused him to draw his gun, a large semi-automatic pistol. A round nearly went off when he stumbled, and when he looked down to see what he'd stumbled on—

He moaned, sick to his stomach.

It was Connie's head that he'd stumbled on, and when his eyes dragged up to the first hanging body, there could be no mistake. It was Connie's thin and very pale corpse which hung there.

A sweep of the flashlight showed him more heads on the floor: Nyvysk, Willis, Adrianne Saundland, and their own stripped bodies hanging in vicinity. *Madness,* Clements thought. *Hildreth is still alive. He did this.*

At least there was one relief. None of the bodies was Debbie's.

The farthest wall back seemed to shimmer scarlet. Buckets sat on the floor; it was clear what had been done.

He drained all their blood . . . into those buckets. Then threw the blood on the wall.

Next came a *click!* and an ear-splitting *BANG!*

Clements fell to the floor. Pain shot across his head: the bullet had grazed his temple.

But he wasn't afraid.

He was *elated.*

"Okay, Hildreth!" he shouted. "Let's go!"

And then he opened fire.

XIV

Westmore's consciousness surfaced through a throbbing black fog. A steady pain beat in his skull—with a sound.

A bell.

No, a chime.

He leaned up on the stairs when it occurred to him what the chimes were.

The clock!

The pendulum clock in the foyer. It was sounding 6 a.m.

He struggled up, against a strange gravity, then ran up the stairs, crossing one landing to the next. His shoes felt like bricks when he stomped down the hall and threw open the doors to the Scarlet Room.

He hesitated a second, then plunged in.

Only moonlight through the windows lit the room. The room stood empty, normal.

And there was nobody in it.

Karen, Mack, and Cathleen were gone. They'd been sleeping here an hour ago.

And absolutely *nothing* was happening in the Scarlet Room.

He turned at a start.

The clock could no longer be heard; 6 a.m. had come and gone, but next he was sure he heard a series of very distant sounds from somewhere deep within the house.

Gunshots. Downstairs somewhere.

And where were the others?

I don't think I'm up for a shoot-out, he knew, yet more shots resounded. It must be Clements. He had one gun—the one Mack had given him—and though he knew little of firearms, he managed to extract the clip to check the ammunition.

That asshole!

The clip was empty.

Now he was starting to see. He ran downstairs, more shots thudding. He stopped in the office because he remembered the pistol in the desk that he'd seen the first day. And when he pulled open the drawer—

DAMN it!

The other pistol was gone.

What am I gonna do now? Spit?

But Clements had guns, and it was certain he was the one shooting somewhere downstairs. But a flickering caught his eye; he turned to look, saw that last DVD he'd checked out was still playing, on auto-replay mode.

It was Debbie Rodenbaugh. Earlier, he hadn't seen all of this segment: the beautiful young woman receiving a most extreme sort of genital piercing. But now he saw the rest of the segment, and the girl's face as she leaned up when the procedure was complete.

Deborah . . .

The face of the piercer was never shown, but it was definitely a man. Westmore could easily tell by the arms and size of the hands.

Jesus Christ. What did they do to her? And why?

Sick thrills, in a house that *thrived* on sick thrills . . .

Gunshots still rang downstairs somewhere. He made to leave but nearly shouted aloud when his cell phone rang.

He answered instantly, expecting Clements.

But it was not Clements who spoke.

"Have you figured it out yet?" a low, female voice asked.

"Who is this? Vivica?"

"It's happening now. The Rive is opening. Can you see it? In the Scarlet Room?"

"I just came from there!" he bellowed. "And *jack-shit* is happening! All this stuff about Hildreth opening a Rive— it's BULLSHIT! And who are YOU?"

"They fooled you. They made you think the Scarlet Room is on the fifth floor. It's not. It's downstairs. The parlor on the fifth floor used to be green. They just put in red carpet and wallpaper."

"What!"

"The Scarlet Room is downstairs, and the doors to the Chirice Flaesc are opening now. You should be there . . ."

"WHERE? Where downstairs!" Westmore shouted further.

"The South Atrium is the real Scarlet Room."

A breath locked in Westmore's chest.

"Hildreth turned it into a dolmen—with sex and blood and evil," the caller went on. "It's the only thing you didn't figure out. But you figured out the time, from the paper in the safe. You figured out the combination. It's the only thing that they didn't know."

"Who's they?" Then another question clicked in his head. "And how did you get my cell phone number?"

"Get down there," the soft voice urged. "When the temple comes to our world . . . there's nothing more spectacular."

Westmore shouted so loud his throat went ragged. "Who ARE you?"

"Faye Mullins."

The survivor . . . The girl in the psych ward . . .

"Tell me everything you know!" Westmore pleaded. "I need to know NOW!"

The line went dead.

XV

Clements only had muzzle flashes to use for target acquisition. Someone was popping some serious caps at him. But it was too dark—and he was too keyed up on defending himself—to notice that parts of the room were changing.

When he emptied the clips of his .44 automatic—a series

of heavy, concussive BOOMS—his unseen attacker stopped firing. Clements unshouldered his backpack and pulled out the sawed-off Remington pump. He drew a bead as best he could, watched over the sites, and waited.

"Don't shoot," a voice cracked out. "Listen."

"I'm listening, Hildreth."

"I'm not Hildreth. He's in there."

In where? Clements thought.

"You can't handle what's happening here. Just leave. Get out of the house and leave. You're not worthy to go in. I am."

"Go in *where?* Stop bullshitting me, or I'm gonna come and get you."

"I'll tell you more if you swear you won't shoot."

Clements smirked, cheek pressed to the shotgun stock. "All right."

Footsteps clattered. Clements didn't want to give his position away by turning on the flashlight. But the moon was sufficient.

It was Mack who stepped forward.

You sleazy, lyin' motherfucker . . .

"You're in way over your head, but I've been part of this since Hildreth began to put the plan together. It all started on April 3rd, and it's ending now. Can't you see what this room is becoming?"

For a moment, Clements was tempted to look around the room to see what Mack was talking about, but then he warned himself, *Don't fall for it. Don't take your eye off the site.*

"Keep talking, buddy."

"This shit happening here isn't for you," Mack said. His pistol was stuck in his pants. "I'm the one who should go into the Rive. You wouldn't know what you're doing. Just leave. You'd never make it back out alive."

"What the fuck are you talking about, asshole?"

"Just leave."

Mack stepped into a brighter slant of moonlight, and that's when Clements saw . . .

Mack's arms were slick to the elbows with blood.

He's the motherfucker who killed Connie . . .

Clements liked to think of himself as a man who kept his word, but right now that ethic wasn't making it.

"I promised I wouldn't shoot," he called out. "But fuck it," and then he squeezed off one 12-gauge round. The shotgun jumped in Clements' hands.

Mack's left arm blew off. He spun around, sending a plume of blood round in an arc, and then Clements fired the next round at Mack's head.

Mack collapsed.

Kiss my ass, you piece of shit. But what had he been talking about? Hildreth was *in there?* Where was *there? And what the fuck was he talking about—the ROOM changing?*

Clements reached for the flashlight but by now there was no need. The room seemed edged now in firelight, the greatest of which appeared more like a *pillar* of light at the end of the room.

And the rest of the room . . .

Good God.

The room was, somehow, *flesh,* webs of what appeared to be skin branching out from the back wall that minutes ago was just an adorned *wall.* But now the wall throbbed as if alive, and at its center glowed a seam.

Clements stared a few moments more before he could comprehend even one-percent of what he was actually looking at.

There's doors, he realized. The lit seam was a gap between two high, rectangular doors composed of the same skin-like substance that was slowly crawling over the rest of the room. Sweat glistened from pores; fat blue veins beat heartily beneath the skin. As Clements strained his eyes, it occurred to him what the rear of the room was becoming.

It's a fuckin' temple . . .

Columns of flesh could now be seen. And that hot, glowing gap between the doors was growing wider.

The doors are opening.

A tall figure stood within the furnace-like glow.

Hildreth, Clements knew.

The voice reverberated. Clements wasn't sure if the echoic words rang in his ears or in his head.

"What you seek is here. Come in . . . and take it."

Clements stood dumbstruck. Within the door, on a floor of beating skin, lay a naked woman: Deborah Rodenbaugh.

"Only a precious few in history have ever had this honor. Rise to that honor now, and step into our domain. Take Debbie out, back into the world from whence she came—the world that awaits."

The idea of opening fire with the shotgun never struck Clements. He left the gun on the floor and began to step forward.

With each step forward, Hildreth seemed to step back, though his feet didn't appear to be moving, until eventually he faded away into the infernal light.

And something deeper in the temple gained form. A face, a visage so abominable, description in any human language was not possible.

And Clements entered the Temple of Flesh, the throne of the Sexus Cyning and the lord of all lust—Belarius.

XVI

Westmore entered the South Atrium only with enough time to see the doors of the Chirice Flaesc close completely. Beheaded bodies hung from the rafters like the most macabre decor. In some areas the atrium's green-velour wallpaper had peeled away, revealing the room's genuine blood painted walls that had been covered up to disguise the room.

This was the real Scarlet Room, and Westmore knew that the Rive had opened and closed in his absence.

Mack lay sprawled and still in the corner by the kitchen door, an arm gone, his clothes drenched by the vast pool of blood he lay in. Westmore made out the severed heads of Nyvysk, Willis, Adrianne, and Connie, all clearly the final sacrifices which triggered the Rive's opening, their blood drained and slopped on the walls in order to peak the charge of the mansion.

On the floor lay a naked woman, unconscious.

Debbie Rodenbaugh . . .

She seemed intact, and Westmore could see her breasts rise and fall. *She's still alive,* he realized.

But Clements hadn't remained quite as intact after physically carrying Debbie across the threshold of two worlds.

He'd been cut in half, sternum-level, as the doors had closed on him. Deader than dead.

But he got her out.

Westmore flung Clements' backpack on, stuck the shotgun in it, then picked Debbie Rodenbaugh up in his arms.

Though the Rive was closed now, and the incarnation of the Chirice Flaesc come and gone, the mansion still retained some of its charge. Westmore could feel hairs on his arms and neck still sticking up. He stalked right out of the house, to the front court where the cars had been parked. *Thank God I still got Karen's keys,* he thought.

But then he stalled as he carefully trod down the front stone steps.

Where IS Karen?

He didn't think any of the bodies in the Scarlet Room were hers.

I can't just leave her here . . .

But then he noticed something else.

Oh shit!

All of the cars in the front court, including Karen's black Cadillac convertible, were—

Trashed . . .

The tires were punctured, the hoods propped open to reveal missing sparkplug wires.

I'm gonna have to walk out of here.

Not much of a prospect. Carrying a hundred-and-twenty-pound girl three or four miles to the main road?

But when Westmore looked down more closely, he thought, *No, no, no . . .*

He lay Debbie down across the car's closed trunk, because *inside* the car, in the back seat, lay Karen.

Please don't be dead . . .

He opened the door, put a hand on her shoulder and lifted her up. Her head lolled.

No. Please.

Then relief swept through him when she roused. Karen hugged him when recognition came.

"My God. It was all true. The house . . . was changing."

"Yes," Westmore said.

Karen stifled sobs. "I was so scared, I came out here to get away but someone wrecked all the cars."

"Mack, I think. He's dead, and so are the others. I think Mack used them for some sort of final sacrificial rite. But I found Debbie Rodenbaugh. We have to get out of here."

He helped her out, and she looked astonished at Debbie's unconscious body. Westmore grabbed a light jacket from one of the other cars and wrapped it around Debbie.

"We'll have to walk out," Karen realized. "And she's out cold. Come on, I'll help."

"You're right, it was all true," Westmore explained as they each shouldered one of Debbie's arms and began to hustle away from the house. "And the Rive that Nyvysk was talking about—it opened. And Debbie came out."

"You mean, she's been . . . in there . . . since April 3rd?"

"Yeah."

They trudged farther away. Westmore knew that the Rive was closed now, but there was still *something* emanating from the mansion. The house was like a battery not quite dead; there were still a few dregs of energy playing out.

"I saw things in there," Karen said. "I saw more revenants. I think I even saw Hildreth's ghost."

"So did I. On the stairs. Then somebody knocked me out from behind. Mack, I'm sure." But as they approached the darkness of the woodline, he remembered . . .

"What a minute! Clements' car!" he almost rejoiced.

"Who?"

"Never mind. There's an access road right over here—"

"Are you sure?" Karen asked.

"Positive. And there's a car there. If the keys are in it, we can drive out of here."

"Let's go!"

They were jogging now, carrying Debbie along. When they plunged into the narrow opening in the trees,

Clements' dented Olds 98 sat silent in moonlight. Westmore passed Karen a flashlight from the backpack. *Please, God, please, God . . .* "Check to see—"

Karen shined the light inside. She nearly squealed in delight. "The keys are in it!"

I guess I never really believed in God before. But I sure as shit do now, Westmore thought. Debbie was still unconscious; they lay her in the back seat, then Westmore jumped behind the wheel. Karen stayed in back, hauled the door closed.

"What . . . ," Karen began, "happened to her? Between her legs?"

"They did some sick S&M job on her—Hildreth and his people," Westmore said. "Put chrome rings in her—"

"There's no rings . . ."

Westmore turned around. Karen had the flashlight on, flashed it down on Debbie's pubis. The chrome rings that Westmore had seen closing her vaginal lips on the DVD were no longer there. They'd been removed, leaving each hole torn. Westmore gulped back some nausea. "Torn out," he choked. "It must've happened when—"

"When she was on the other side of the Rive . . ."

Don't think about it, he ordered himself.

"Look, she's still breathing, her pulse is strong, and she's not bleeding. Let's just get out of here," Karen said.

"Yeah." Westmore touched the ignition. "You know, with our luck, the car won't start."

Karen didn't say anything.

Westmore turned the key, and the motor started on the first try. It was probably the most refreshing sound he'd ever heard. "The only thing left to do is go home."

"Yeah, but . . . why is something telling me that this is too easy?"

Westmore put the car in drive. "Because it probably is," and then the Oldsmobile's rear tires spat dirt and gravel, and they lurched off.

Home, Westmore thought, wending through the narrow passage of trees. Clumps of Spanish moss dangled from low branches. Green lizards darted up tree trunks as the big car roared by. But around the next turn—

"Damn it!"

"Oh, fuck!"

Westmore slammed on the brakes.

A tree had been felled across the road.

"You were right," Westmore said. "It *was* too easy."

"Drive over it."

Westmore looked at the tree. It was about a foot thick but with sprawling branches. "I could try. But I might not get over it; then we'd be stuck. The car might bottom out, or we could lose the oil pan."

"Fuck," Karen said again. "I say try driving over it. Take the chance."

It seemed the best idea. But just as Westmore looked to back up, Karen screamed.

In the headlight beams, something had stepped into the road just behind the tree. Westmore's vision froze on it.

It wasn't human, yet it was something he'd seen before.

"It's one of those things," he murmured.

An Adiposian.

It stood tall, lank but globose in the hell-rendered fat that made up its atrocious physique. It had no face yet it looked right at them. The rimmed seam for a mouth gaped, showing a great fat flap of tongue. Between its legs hung large, abominable genitals.

"One of the buried Adiposians!" Karen shrieked. "It was resurrected when the Rive opened, and it'll remain alive until the charge of the house is totally dead!"

It's one of those things Clements and I dug up last night, Westmore realized.

"Do something!" Karen screamed.

Westmore slammed the car in reverse, floored it, and turned around, then slammed the brakes again.

"Shit!"

They both looked out the rear window. In the back-up lights, they could see that another tree had been knocked down.

"We're trapped on the road!" Karen shouted. "And—"

Another Adiposian was behind them, slowly approaching.

Only one thing left to try, he thought and grabbed the shotgun. He jumped out of the car, trotted out several steps and stopped. The faceless thing continued stepping forward, and it was then that Westmore noted that is was a *female* of the species. Breasts like bulbs of fat, with snot-colored nipples that stood erect in some abyssal excitement. The tongue licked drooling lips, and the thing's splayed hand stroked the fat cleft of its sex.

That thing has plans for me, Westmore realized. He didn't know from guns, so he shouldered the shotgun, aimed, and simply pulled the trigger.

"Hurry up and shoot!" Karen's voice exploded.

Nothing happened when he pulled the trigger. Perhaps God was not looking out for him after all. An instinct caused him to grip the shotgun. He jacked the slide back, then forward, like they did on TV, and then he aimed again and squeezed the trigger.

BOOM!

"Jesus!"

The 12-gauge magnum load took the Adiposian's pale head clean off, splattering hot fat in a gust across the road.

When it fell still, it seemed to deflate, the slop filling its skin emptying. The report slammed the shotgun butt into Westmore's shoulder; he barked in pain and was sent back against the Oldsmobile's trunk.

"The other one!" Karen warned next.

The first Adiposian had traversed up most of the road by now. Westmore was more confident than afraid when he strode around the car, jacked another round, and—

BOOM!

—squeezed off another round into the featureless meat that was the thing's face. The Adisposian collapsed in a splatter. The most repugnant stench of Westmore's life filled the humid air.

He got back in the car. "That was almost fun," he admitted.

"What now? We're still blocked from both sides."

Karen was right. The trees had barricaded them. "I guess we'll have to walk out. But—"

"There's more than two of those things out there," Karen pointed out.

There'd been three or four in the makeshift grave. "I know, I—" Then Westmore got the worst feeling in his belly. He turned around, faced Karen.

"It was just me and Clements who dug those things up. We didn't tell anyone."

"What?"

His eyes leveled on her in the dashlight. "How did you know there were more than two of those things?"

"Shit," Karen whispered under her breath.

Westmore reached for the shotgun beside him but Karen had a pistol to his head first.

"Don't even try," Karen said. "I swear to God I'll kill you. Nothing can interfere. I'll take Debbie to Vivica's myself if I have to."

She reached over the seat and took the shotgun.

"You bitch," he said.

"Sorry. You don't understand. I didn't even think any of it was real," she began. "Until the day after the first rite. I was just going along with it 'cos I had to."

"Why? Why did you *have* to?"

"Hildreth and Vivica paid me more money than I've ever been paid. And I had to protect my daughter. Shit, at first I just thought I was accommodating the shits and giggles of a nutty old man and his wife. But it didn't take me long to see that they were for real. They killed or ruined anybody who jeopardized Hildreth's plan for tonight, Beltane Eve, during the apogee that celebrates Lucifer's fall. They killed Debbie's parents, they killed that bum to pass for Hildreth's body. They paid people off, falsified court records, paid graft to cops and newspapers. And they wrecked Clements' career. They fucked up a lot of other people, too, without thinking twice. They didn't have to say it to my face, Westmore—it was clearly implied. My ass was in the ringer, too, and if I didn't go along with the program I'd wind up in the ground myself. I had to protect my daughter."

"Your daughter? The one at Princeton? What's she got to do with this?"

"She's not at Princeton—I lied," Karen admitted. "She's at Oxford, registered under a phony name."

"Debbie Rodenbaugh," Westmore figured.

"Um-hmm. And I know damn well if I ever even *thought* about blowing the whistle on the Hildreths, or if I stopped helping them—my daughter would be dead in two minutes."

"So it was you and Mack, Vivica's people on the inside."

"That's right. And it was me and Mack who buried the four Adiposians on the night of April 4th. They came through when the Rive opened, and they stayed alive for several hours after the first rite, until the mansion's charge was totally dead."

"So you and Mack killed the lock-girl, too, I guess. And Willis and Adrianne and Nyvysk and—"

"Mack may have, I didn't kill anyone," Karen asserted.

"You just turned the other way."

She didn't respond.

"And what about Cathleen?" it just occurred to him. He hadn't seen her body in the Scarlet Room. "She must be dead too."

"She's with us," Karen said.

"What's that mean?"

"It doesn't matter, Westmore. She has uses that Vivica's interested in. Forget it. Just drive me to Vivica's with the girl. Then you can go. Vivica's not afraid of you—she actually kind of likes you—"

"Great."

"And if you start any trouble or tell anyone what happened here tonight, she'll simply have you killed. Just let it be. The only thing she didn't know was the exact time and date." Karen chuckled dryly. "But you solved that puzzle. Mack told Vivica once you got all the information about the piece of paper in the safe. In a weird way, you helped fulfill Hildreth's plan more than anyone."

The observation didn't set well with Westmore. "What's the rest of the plan? What was the purpose?"

"Her," she said, pointing to Debbie's still-unconscious body. "Hildreth cultivated her. He'd already made his pact. His instructions were clear. Debbie Rodenbaugh was exactly what they needed. A naive, innocent virgin. The first rite on April 3rd opened the Rive to the temple of Belarius, and then Debbie was *put in* to the Rive. She's been there since then. And six hundred and sixty-six hours after that first rite was tonight. The Rive opened again, and—"

"And Debbie came out," Westmore realized. Finally he understood the purpose of the chrome rings, which were gone now. *Belarius tore them out . . .* "And now she's pregnant."

"Yeah. So just forget it. Take me to Vivica's, then leave. There's nothing you can do." She nudged the pistol against the back of his head. "Or else I'll have to kill you, and I don't want to do that, 'cos I always liked you, too."

Westmore saw now that the gun she wielded was the same gun he'd seen in the office drawer. If she was sitting up front, he could take a chance on grabbing for it, but in the back seat?

I'd be dead in a second.

"So just drive. Step on it and drive over that first tree." She smiled brightly. "You'll make it. You're good luck."

Westmore saw no options, but a moment later, one was unfolded for him.

The window in the back door shattered inward. Karen screamed through a rain of glass and several deafening shots were fired upward. Gunsmoke filled the interior, and when Westmore looked around into the smoky madness, he saw that the other two Adiposians were indeed afoot.

They smashed the window and were pawing at Karen.

Her pistol thunked to the floor. "Help me!" came her crazed shriek. "Westmore, help me!"

One of them had two fistfuls of her hair, and the other had her throat.

"Help me!" she pleaded one last time.

"Not tonight," he said and floored the gas pedal.

As the car pulled off, Karen was pulled out. He didn't care to look in the rearview to see what was commencing.

The big car rocked down the road, barreled over the fallen tree with a trounce. Westmore's head smacked the roof, but the car cleared the tree without serious damage.

And then he drove away, with Deborah Rodenbaugh still unconscious but still alive in the back seat.

Epilogue

Seattle, nine months later

I

Westmore's first hangover in almost four years was undoubtedly the worst of his life. *Why do people drink?* he wondered. When he looked up from the bed, Debbie sat on the decrepit couch, eating Pop Tarts and watching television. She wore a robe, her gravid belly like a great satchel in her lap. He dragged on his own robe and grabbed his cigarettes. "Good morning—er, good afternoon."

"Try good evening," she corrected, eyes rapt on the TV.

She's got to be kidding. He opened the door and stepped out. Beyond the shabby room's narrow portico, rain poured in all of Seattle's glory. A glance down each side of the motel showed him no other lights on in any of the other rooms, as though he and Debbie were the only guests. It was nighttime now.

Jesus, I've been in bed twenty-four hours? That's what I call sleeping off a drunk.

He felt irresponsible and useless; he was supposed to be taking care of her. All the way through to—

He watched cars soar by in rain, the highway only twenty yards from the front of the motel. The fast, gritty hiss of tires helped blank his mind but it wasn't much solace. *There's no more time to keep my head in the sand,* he thought. *She's probably going to give birth by tomorrow.*

What then?

But Westmore already knew the answer to that.

Horns blared on the highway just ahead, a near crash. When a bus roared by—at probably sixty miles per hour— its tires plowed into standing water and threw a great black wave up from the street. Westmore stepped back inside and closed the door.

A shower revitalized him to an extent. Bloodshot eyes looked back at him in the mirror. *Shit . . .* He thought about shaving but discarded the idea when he noticed how badly his hands were shaking.

Dark, moody piano music drifted from a small clock radio on the windowsill. It somehow made him feel less of a failure. But he hadn't really failed, had he? He'd come all this way and protected her, and his only foul up had been one fall off the wagon. *It could be worse,* he supposed.

He knew he'd only fail if he lost his nerve after she had the baby.

He'd brought his clothes in with him—he'd feel awkward dressing in front of her. Hungover like this, it took some effort pulling his pants back on; he almost fell over in the bathroom's close confines. His pants hadn't fully dried yet; he could feel his gun still stuck in the wet pocket. Eventually he combed his hair, brushed his teeth and gargled. The next glance in the mirror was more inspiring. *At least I don't look dead anymore.*

When the piano piece ended, Westmore walked out of the bathroom only to find a gun in his face.

"Sit down."

Westmore obeyed. Mack had a sizeable pistol in his right hand. He didn't have anything in his left hand because . . . he didn't *have* a left hand, nor arm. Scars streaked one side of his face from 12-gauge pellets.

"Clements didn't miss by much," Westmore said.

"Belarius protects those who bow down to him." Mack grinned. "Tonight's a very special night."

Debbie sat wide-eyed on the bed, with someone else beside her.

"Don't think about trying to get away, sweetheart," Vivica Hildreth said. "We won't hurt you, but the same doesn't go for your friend, Mr. Westmore."

Diamonds glittered around the rich woman's neck, in the V of her Burberry raincoat. She also wore the funky gem-studded flipflops she'd been wearing the day he'd met her in her penthouse. "It's good to see you, Mr. Westmore. You've done a fine job protecting our prize."

"Debbie?" Then Westmore said the most stupid thing. "You're gonna have to kill me to take her."

Mack and Vivica laughed.

"It all worked out perfectly." Vivica's eyes glittered with the diamonds. "And in your own way, you helped quite a bit."

"We owe you one," Mack said, still grinning.

"And so does our Lord . . ."

Westmore sighed. "How did you find me? I spent cash, I never used a credit card, and I've only stayed at fleabags where you don't have to show ID to check in. There's no money trail; we've been moving all over the country like this for nine months."

"How did we find you?" Vivica repeated the question. Her smile shot to Mack. "Show him."

Mack opened the front door and said, "Come in" to someone. A frail figure in a dark rain jacket entered. At first Westmore didn't even know who it was.

"*Cathleen?*"

Hollow eyes looked back at him. She looked skeletal now, the once bright-blonde hair lank and dulled by streaks of gray.

"What happened to you, for God's sake?"

"Oh, we signed her up with Uncle Smack," Mack answered. He dragged one of her coat sleeves up, revealing ugly clusters of needlemarks. "We control the bitch now."

Cathleen glanced up at the comment, disdain in her lusterless eyes.

"In fact," Mack continued. "It's almost time for her to take another bang. You can watch, Westmore."

"She's quite an addictive personality," Vivica offered. "Addiction suits her. It's heroin in place of sex now. She's proven quite useful since she's been under our thumb."

"My God, Cathleen," Westmore almost moaned. "How could you let them do this to you?"

"I'm sorry," Cathleen whispered, her head bowed in shame.

"She tipped over quick," Mack said. "It was a cinch. And she's a great piece of ass, too. You should've snagged some when you were at the mansion."

Another hate-filled glance upward from Cathleen.

"But you still haven't answered my question," Westmore reminded. "How did you find Debbie and me?"

"Cathleen's famous for her spoon-bending tricks, but to us her other talents were far more applicable," Vivica said.

Westmore smirked. "I don't get it."

"She's not just a medium, Mr. Westmore. You know that. And she's not just a telekinetic and a crystal-gazer, either."

"She's a diviner, you asshole," Mack clarified. "She can find things with her mind."

Vivica daintily crossed her legs, adding, "The heroin's killed what remained of her telekinetic and medium powers. But Cathleen can still see the future. We simply made her tell us where you'd be today." The woman stroked Debbie's hair in a way that was almost maternal. "And tonight we take our precious Debbie back, for the miracle that she and Belarius will bestow upon us." The elegant face leveled on Westmore. "It's too bad that you won't be alive to witness the birth of our Lord's son. But you'll go down in history, Mr. Westmore, as the chaperon of Hell's first mother, an acolyte of Belarius and the steward of the first child to ever be conceived in the abyss."

Westmore only stared.

"We knew you were here several days ago," Vivica continued. "Didn't you think it was odd that no one else is occupying this motel?"

"I didn't really notice."

"We booked every room here, except yours."

"Why?"

"Nobody to hear the shots when I blow your ass away, genius," Mack chuckled.

Westmore slumped. *What am I gonna do now?* The only thing he could think of was stalling. "Can I at least have a cigarette?"

"The final request of the condemned man," Vivica quipped. "Of course."

"But no cigarettes," Mack began, "until *after* I snag your piece," and then he reached into Westmore's pocket and removed the small revolver. He placed it on the tacky dresser. "There. No funny stuff."

Shit. He lit a cigarette, then, and sighed smoke.

But Cathleen was looking right at him.

What? he wondered.

She made the tiniest gesture with her eyes.

Westmore's anticipation ticked like a clock in his gut. What did Cathleen mean? When he lowered his cigarette to tap an ash in the glass ashtray—

Holy shit!

—the ashtray flew across the room as if catapulted. Before Mack could comprehend what had happened, the ashtray sailed hard into his face, one rounded glass corner hitting him square in the eye.

Mack's pistol fell from his hand. Westmore lunged.

"You bitch!" Mack roared. Blood poured down his face from one eye.

Vivica had leapt up. "Traitorous whore!"

"Debbie!" Westmore yelled as he dived to the floor for Mack's gun. "Get out of here now!"

Debbie jumped from the bed. Vivica shrieked, was about to grab her, but in the same instant, Cathleen looked up at the wall where a large mirror hung over the dresser.

Then the mirror came *off* the wall and shattered over Vivica's head. Vivica fell to the floor.

When Westmore grabbed the gun on the carpet—

"OOOW!"

—Mack stomped on his hand, then kicked it away. Then they both leapt for it at the same time.

And Mack got there first.

He was on his belly, had his hand on the gun.

"Cathleen!" Westmore pointed to the other gun on the dresser.

The gun flew off. *Oh, so her telekinesis is dead, huh?* Westmore thought. He felt glorious when he caught the gun in mid-air and fired one shot into Mack's back with an ear-splitting bang.

Mack collapsed again. "Piece of shhhhit," he managed to voice. "You don't shoot a man in the back."

Westmore shot him in the back again—

BANG!

—and again.

BANG!

A final shot blew out the back of Mack's skull.

Then Westmore thought: *Debbie . . .*

He gave the gun to Cathleen. "Watch Vivica! I'm gonna go get Debbie."

The whites of her eyes were blood-red now from her telekinetic outburst. She feebly grabbed Westmore's wrist. "You . . . won't make it . . ."

Westmore tore himself away and ran out of the motel.

Rain pelted him. *Where is she?* The roar of highway traffic on the wet road deafened him. And that's when he saw her, drenched.

Standing right at the edge of the highway.

"Debbie! Don't!"

She turned to look back at him. Her eyes were afraid now, this close to the event.

"Please! Don't!" Westmore shouted again through the rain.

She stood limp, unconsciously bringing a hand to her belly. "I have to. Either way, I could never live with myself."

"Have it! Then I'll kill it!"

The rain turned her hair into a black mop. She shook her head. "I couldn't live with that, either."

The words exploded from Westmore's throat. "IT'S NOT A BABY!"

Debbie smiled meekly, turned, and stepped into the road, whereupon an eighteen-wheeler full of brand-new cars plowed into her at once. There was no time for the driver to even hit his horn.

Westmore turned away after a glimpse of Deborah Rodenbaugh's body being fed through the massive rear tires.

I guess that's what she really wanted all along, he thought, coming back inside. Cathleen didn't have to ask. She gave him the gun back, Vivica still collapsed in the corner.

"It's over," he said.

Cathleen hesitated. "Did you . . . see it?"

"No."

Westmore picked up the bloody ashtray, then lit another cigarette. "Let's go home," he said, exhausted.

Cathleen had tears in her eyes. "I'm all fucked up, Westmore. I don't think I can make it."

"Bullshit. If you can throw ashtrays across the room with your mind, you can quit drugs. I'll take care of you."

Cathleen offered a ghost of a smile.

"But what do we do with her?" he said.

Vivica was just coming to in the corner. Her eyes burned, but the rest of her face remained composed. "You think you've won but you haven't."

"I'd really like to kill you," Westmore said. "You're an evil person. You're a murderer and a cold, calculating bitch."

"I, like my husband, am an unwavering servant of Belarius, Mr. Westmore. And you haven't won this battle. Mack and Karen weren't my only attendants. I have many."

Westmore was so tired. "What are you talking about?"— but then he caught himself—"no, wait a minute. I don't even *care* what you're talking about," and then he raised the pistol and put a bullet into Vivica's belly.

Westmore and Cathleen both jumped at the shot.

Vivica doubled over a moment but then managed to look up, an inexplicable smile on her face. She just shook her head, grinning at him. "I will live forever in the temple of my Lord," she choked out.

"No. You're gonna *die,* in a shitty little Seattle motel—" Westmore fired another bullet into her belly. "Oh my gosh! I sure hope the neighbors don't call the police!"

Even now, though, she somehow maintained her smile, bloody as it was. "Belarius . . . take me home . . ."

"One last thing," Westmore complained. He glared at Vivica's feet. "Those flipflops look asinine . . . but I'll bet the diamonds are worth a bundle to a jeweler."

A final shot put a hole in Vivica's forehead.

Westmore removed the flipflops, then pried the gems off their straps. He took Vivica's necklace, rings, and purse, and Mack's wallet.

Cathleen looked shocked. "I didn't think you had it in you."

"I don't. I'm just really tired of all this, and I want to go home." He helped her up. "Come on, let's go to the Greyhound station."

Leaving the bodies wouldn't be a problem. He hadn't had to show ID checking in. There was plenty of cash in Vivica's purse, plus credit cards, plus more cash in Vivica's rental car outside.

Minutes later, he and Cathleen were driving off in the rain.

The wipers thumped rhythmically across the windshield. Cathleen leaned her head against Westmore's shoulder as he drove.

"She was right about one thing," Cathleen murmured.

"What's that?"

"We didn't really win. And she does have other people in her circle. The rich always do. They're all at the mansion right now."

Westmore gave her a confused stare in the dashlight. "What do you mean?"

She let out a long, frustrated breath. "Debbie Rodenbaugh was their ideal choice, the one Hildreth groomed for the rite. But they also had a sort of contingency plan . . ."

All the lights had been shut off; instead the mansion glowed darkly in candlelight.

And Debbie Rodenbaugh wasn't the only virgin who'd entered the Rive nine months ago on April 3rd.

The midwives and other attendants gathered closely round the great four-poster bed that had been brought down into the Scarlet Room. Before them, Faye Mullins began to convulse in the initial throes of childbirth—

If one could even call what was about to come out of her a child.

MESSENGER
EDWARD LEE

Have you ever wanted to be someone else? Well, someone else is about to become *you*. He will share your soul and your mind. He will feel what you feel, your pleasure, your pain. And then he will make you kill. He will drive you to perform horrific ritual murder and unimaginable occult rites. You are about to be possessed, but not by a ghost. It's something far worse.

The devil has a messenger, and that messenger is here, now, in your town. He has something for you—a very special delivery indeed. It's an invitation you can't refuse, an invitation to orgies of blood and mayhem. Don't answer the door. There's a little bit of Hell waiting for you on the other side.
